# C.J. CHERRYH

# HEAVY TIME

D0092372

WARNER BOOKS

A Time Warner Company

WARNER BOOKS EDITION

Questar® is a registered trademark of Warner Books, Inc.

*Book design by H. Roberts*

Warner Books, Inc.
666 Fifth Avenue
New York, N.Y. 10103

 A Time Warner Company

Printed in the United States of America

This book was originally published in hardcover by Warner Books.

First Printed in Paperback: March, 1992

10 9 8 7 6 5 4 3 2 1

FROM THE HUGO AWARD-WINNING AUTHOR OF
*DOWNBELOW STATION, MERCHANTERS LUCK,*
AND *CYTEEN*: A hard-edged, riveting thriller, as
human turmoil, corporate conspiracy,
overwhelming ambition and unbearable grief
explode in the isolation between worlds . . .

# HEAVY TIME

## SENSATIONAL PRAISE FOR C.J. CHERRYH AND *HEAVY TIME*

* * *

"CHERRYH REMAINS NEAR THE TOP OF THE FIELD IN
BOTH WORLD-BUILDING AND CHARACTERIZATION. . . . In
her gifted hands, Merchanter is becoming one of the best-
built and most lived-in futures in science fiction."
—*Chicago Sun-Times*

* * *

"SMOOTHLY WRITTEN . . . THE CHARACTERS ARE
INTRIGUING . . . THE PLOT COMPLEX. . . . Cherryh's short,
reverberant sentences have the feel of the best tough-guy
detective fiction, and she is marvelously skillful in establishing
her characters' motivations." —*Cleveland Plain Dealer*

* * *

"TAUT, GRIPPING, REALISTIC WORK." —*Kirkus Reviews*

* * *

"C.J. TIGHTENS THE SCREWS . . . AN INTENSELY
ABSORBING BOOK."
—**Lois McMaster Bujold, Nebula Award winner**

* * *

*more . . .*

"The universe Cherryh creates is gritty, tough and incredibly detailed. . . . The characters are well-drawn."
—*SFRA Newsletter*

\* \* \*

"C.J. Cherryh writes intelligent, realistic science fiction."
—*Columbus Dispatch*

\* \* \*

"Cherryh is especially strong in her in-depth portraits of three very different space survivors with threats to their security and minds." —*The Bookwatch*

\* \* \*

"*Heavy Time* is another tense, convincing C.J. Cherryh novel . . . offer[ing] gritty adventure, strong characterization, and Machiavellian dealings aplenty. It's vintage Cherryh."—*Locus*

\* \* \*

"Highly recommended. . . . [Cherryh's] singular ability to create a believable vision of a spacefaring future is exceeded only by her talent for populating that vision with 'real' people." —*Library Journal*

\* \* \*

"The pace is rapid . . . like most Cherryh novels, is well worth reading." —*Analog Science Fiction/Science Fact*

\* \* \*

IT was a lonely place, this remote deep of the Belt, a place where, if things went wrong, they went seriously wrong. And the loneliest sound of all was that thin, slow beep that meant a ship in distress.

It showed up sometimes, sometimes missed its beat. "She's rolling," Ben said when he first heard it, but Morrie Bird thought: Tumbling; and when Ben had plugged in the likely config of the object and asked the computer, that was what it said. It said it in numbers. Bird saw it in his mind. You spent thirty years tagging rocks and listening to the thin numerical voices of tags and beacons and faint, far ships, and you knew things like that. You could just about figure the pattern before the computer built it.

"Got to be dead," Ben Pollard said. Ben's face had that sharp, eager look it got when Ben was calculating something he especially wanted.

Nervous man, Ben Pollard. Twenty-four and hungry, a Belter kid only two years out of ASTEX Institute when he'd come to Bird with a 20 k check in hand—no easy trick, give or take his mother's insurance must have paid his keep and his schooling. Ben had bought in on *Trinidad*'s outfitting and signed on as his numbers man; and in a day when a lot of the new help had a bad case of the Attitudes and expected something for nothing, damned if Ben didn't wear an old man out with his One More Try and his: Bird, I Got an Angle—

Regarding this distress signal it wasn't hard at all to figure Ben's personal numbers. Ben was asking himself the same questions an old man was asking at the bottom of his mortgaged soul: How far is it? Who's in trouble out there? Are they alive? And . . . What's the law on salvage?

So they called Base and told Mama they had a Mayday, had she heard?

Base hadn't heard it. That was moderately odd. Geosyncs over the Well hadn't heard it and ECSAA insystem hadn't picked it out of all the beeps and echoes of tags and ships in the Belt. Base took a while to think, approved a course and dumped them new sector charts, with which Mama was exceedingly stingy: Mama said Cleared for radio use, and: Proceed With Caution. Good luck, Two Twenty-nine Tango.

Spooky, that Base hadn't heard that signal—that she claimed that was a vacant sector. So somebody was way off course. You lay awake and thought of all the names you knew, people who could be out here right now—good friends among them; and you asked yourself what could have happened and when. Rocks could echo a signal. Lost ships could get very lost. That transmitter should be the standard 5 watts, but a dying one could trick you—and, committed, boosted up to a truly scary $v$, about which you could also have second thoughts, you had a lot of things on your mind.

The rule was that Base kept track of everything that moved out here. If your radio died you Maydayed on your emergency beeper and you waited til Mama gave you clear instructions how she was going to get you out of it—you didn't expect anybody to come in after you. Nowadays nobody went any damn where out of his assigned sector without Mama confirming course and nobody used a radio for long-distance chatter with friends. You get lost in the dark, spacer-kids, you go strictly by the regulations and you yell for Mama's attention.

That ghosty signal was doing that, all right, but Mama hadn't heard... and by all rights she should have. Mama said it could be a real weak signal—they were running calculations on the dopplering to try to figure it... Mama claimed she didn't hear it except with their relay, and that argued for close.

Or, Mama said, her reception could have a technical problem, which at a wild guess meant some glitch in the software on the big dishes, but Mama didn't talk about things like that with miners.

Mama didn't talk about a lot else with poor sod miners.

"You remember those 'jackers?" Ben asked, waking up in the middle of Bird's watch.

"Yep," Bird said, working maintenance on a servo motor; he tightened a screw and added, then: "I *knew* Karl Nouri."

"You're kidding."

"Only twenty years back. Hell, I drank with him. Nice guy. Him and his partner."

That got Ben, for sure. Ben slid back into his *g-1* spinner and started it up again. But after a while Ben stopped, got out, hauled on his stimsuit and his coveralls and had breakfast, unshaven and shadow-eyed.

A man felt ashamed of himself, disturbing the young fellow's rest.

But the remembrance of Nouri went on to upset Bird's sleep too.

No one was currently hijacking in the Belt—the company had wiped out Nouri and his partners, blown two of them to the hell they'd deserved, luring help in with a fake distress signal, killing crews, stripping logs for valuable finds and ships for usable parts—

Nouri's operation had worked, for a while—until people got suspicious and started asking how Nouri and his friends were so lucky, always coming in with a find, their equipment never breaking down, their ships real light on the fuel use.

Careful maintenance, Nouri had insisted. They did their own. They were good at their work.

But a suspicious company cop had checked part numbers on Nouri's ship and found a condenser, Bird recollected, a damn 50-dollar condenser, with a serial number that traced it to poor Wally Leavitt's ship.

They'd shipped Nouri and five of his alleged partners back to trial on Earth, was what they said, company rules, though there'd been a good many would have seen Nouri himself take a walk above the Well.

But worse than the fear in the deep Belt in those days, was the way everybody had looked at everybody else back at Base, thinking: Are you one of Them? or. . . Do you think *I* could be?

One thing Belters still argued about was whether Jidda Pratt and Dave Marks had been guilty with the rest.

But the company had said they were. The company claimed they had solid evidence, and wrote down personable young Pratt and Marks in the same book as Nouri.

After that, hell, freerunning miners and tenders hadn't any rights. The company had never liked dealing with the independents in the first place: the company had made things increasingly difficult for independent operators once it had gotten its use from them, and the Nouri affair had been the turning point. No more wildcatting. Nowadays you documented every sneeze, you told Big Mama exactly what you'd found with your assay, they metal-scanned you when you went through customs, and you kept meticulous log records in case you got accused of Misconduct, let alone, God help you, Illicit Operations or Illicit Trading. If you helped out a buddy, if you traded a battery or a tag or a transponder back at Base, you logged the date and the time and you filled out the forms, damn right you did: you asked your buddy to sign for a 50-cent clip, if it had a serial number on it, and the running unfunny joke was that the company was trying to think up a special form for exchange of toilet paper.

Nowadays it was illegal to keep your sector charts once you'd docked: Mama's agents came aboard and wiped your mag storage, customs could strip-search you for contraband datacards if it took the notion, and you didn't get any choice about the sector you drew when you went out again, either—'drivers moved, by the nature of what they were, you had mandated heavy time, no exceptions, and Mama didn't send you to anything near the same area. It was illegal to hail a neighbor on a run. You spent three months breathing each other's sweat, two guys in a crew space five meters long and three meters at the widest, so tight and so lonely you could hear each other's thoughts echo off the walls, but if one freerunner tried to call another a sector away from him, he and his partner went up on Illegal Trading charges faster than he could think about it, it being illegal now to trade tips even with no money or equipment changing hands: the company reserved the right to that information, claiming miners had sold it that data and it had a proprietary right to assign it to interests of its own—meaning the company-owned miners: to no one's great surprise the courts had sided with the company. So it was also, by the company's interpretation of that ruling, illegal to hail another ship and share a bottle or trade foodstuffs or any of the other friendly deals the Nouri crackdown had put a stop to.

So when they'd advised Base they wanted to move out of their assigned sector on a possible ship in distress, Mama had taken a nervous long time about giving them that permission. BM—Belt Management—was a sullen bitch at best, and you *never* tried to tell Mama you were doing something purely Al-truistic. Mama didn't, in principle, believe that, no'm. Mama was suspicious and Mama took time to check the records of one Morris Bird and Benjamin Pollard and the miner ship *Trinidad* to find out if *Trinidad* or either of her present crew had demonstrated any odd behaviors or made any odd investments in the recent past.

They could use their radio meanwhile to talk to the beep. Mama would permit that.

And evidently Mama finally believed what they heard—a 'driver ship fire-path crossed the charts she sent, which might well explain an accident out there, and *that* could make a body a little less anxious to go chasing that signal, but it seemed a little late now to beg off: they had the charts, they'd seen the situation, they couldn't back down with lives at stake, and Mama had set all the machinery in motion to have them check It out.

Right.

Mama couldn't do a thing for them if it did turn out to be some kind of trouble. Mama had indicated she had no information to give them on anybody overdue or off course, and that was damned odd. The natural next thought was the military—they asked Mama about that, but Mama just said Negative from Fleet Command.

Meanwhile that beep went on.

So Mama redirected a beam off the R2-8 relay, boosted them up along what Mama's charts assured them was a good safe course, and they chased the signal with the new charts Mama fed them, using the 'scope on all sides for rocks or non-rocks along the way—there was a good reward if you could prove a flaw in Mama's charts; if you had the charts legally, then you could work on them: that was the Rule.

At this speed you just prayed God the flaw didn't turn up directly in your path.

But as sectors went it was the Big Empty out here, nothing but a couple of company tags and one freerunner's for a long, long trip. Mama's charts were stultifyingly accurate . . . except the source of the beep, which seemed to be a weak signal. That was Mama's considered current opinion.

Meaning it was close.

Fourteen nervous days of this, all the while knowing you could make a big, bright fireball with depressingly little warning.

Naturally in the middle of supper/breakfast and shift change, the radar finally went blip! on something not on its chart, and Bird scalded himself with coffee.

The blip, when they saw it on the scope, did match the signal source.

"Advise Mama?" Ben said.

Bird bit his lip, thinking about lives, Mama's notoriously slow decisions, and mulling over the regulations that might apply. "Let's just get the optics fined down. No, we got no real news yet. We're doing what Mama told us to do. Looks like we can brake without her help. No great differential. And I seriously *don't* want Mama's advice while we're working that mother. That's going to be a bitch as is."

"You got it," Ben said with a nervous little exhalation. Ben set his fingers on the keys and started figuring.

"Looks like it caught a rock," Bird said, pointing out that deep shadow in the middle of what ought to be the number one external tank.

"Looks." Ben had been cheerful ever since optics had confirmed the shape as a miner craft. "Sure doesn't look healthy."

"It sure doesn't look good. Let's try for another still, see if we can process up a serial number on that poor sod."

"You got it," Ben said.

They crept up on it. They put a steady hail on ship-to-ship—having that permission—and kept getting nothing but that tumble-modulated beep.

It was no pretty picture when they finally had it lit up in their spots.

"One hell of an impact," Ben muttered. "Maybe a high-$v$ rock."

"Could be. God, both tanks are blown, right there, see? That one's got it right along the side."

"Those guys had *no* luck."

"Sudden. Bad angle. Lot of $g$'s."

"Bash on one side. Explosion on the other. Maybe it threw them into a rock."

"Dunno. Either one alone—God help 'em—maybe 10 real sudden $g$'s."

"Real sudden acquaintance with the bulkhead. Rearrange your face real good."

"Wouldn't know what hit 'em."

"Suppose that 'driver did bump a pebble out?"

"Could be. Cosmic bad luck, in all this empty. Talk about having your name on it. What do they say the odds are?"

"Hundred percent for these guys."

Another image capture. White glared across the cameras, a blur of reflected light, painted serial designation.

"Shit, that's a One'er number! One'er Eighty-four Zebra..."

Not from their Base. Outside their zone. Strangers from across the line.

The tumble carried the lock access toward their lights. Bird said, "Hatch looks all right."

"You got no notion to be going *in* there."

"Yep."

"Bird, love of God, there's no answer."

"Maybe their receiver's out. Maybe they lost their radio altogether. Maybe they're too banged up to answer."

"Maybe they're dead. You don't need to go in there!"

"Yep. But I'm going to."

"I'm not."

"Salvage rights, Ben-me-lad. I thought we were partners."

"Shit."


It was a routine operation for a miner to stop a spin: and most rocks did tumble—but the tumble of a spindle-shaped object their own size and, except the ruptured tanks, their own mass, was one real touchy bitch.

It was out with the arm and the brusher, and just keep contacting the thing til you got one and the other motion off it, while the gyros handled the yaw and the pitch—bleeding money with every burst of the jets. But you did this uncounted times for thirty-odd years, and you learned a certain touch. A trailing cable whacked them and scared Ben to hell, and it was a long sweaty time later before they had the motion off the thing, a longer time yet til they had the white bullseye beside the stranger's hatch centered in their docking sight.

But after all the difficulty before, it was a gentle touch. Grapples clicked and banged.

"That's it," Bird said. "That's got it."

A long breath. Ben said reverently: "She's ours."

"We don't know that."

"Hell, she's salvage!"

"Right behind the bank."

"Uh-uh. Even if it's pure company we got a 50/50 split."

"Unless somebody's still in control over there."

"Well, hell, somebody sure doesn't look it."

"Won't know til we check it out, will we?"

"Come on, Bird, —shit, we *don't* have to go in there, do we? This is damn stupid."

"Yep. And yep." Bird unbelted, shoved himself gently out of his station, touched a toe on the turn-pad and sailed back to the locker. "Coming?"

Ben sullenly unclipped and drifted over, while Bird hauled the suits out and started dressing.

Ben kept bitching under his breath. Bird concentrated on his equipment. Bird always concentrated on his equipment, not where he was going, not the unpleasant thing he was likely to find the other side of that airlock.

And most of all he didn't let himself think what the salvage would bring on the market.

"Five on ten she's a dead ship," Ben said. "Bets?"

"Could've knocked their transmission out. Could be a whole lot of things, Ben, just put a small hold on that enthusiasm. Don't go spending any money before it's ours."

"It's going to be a damn mess in there. God knows how old it is. It could even be one of the Nouri wrecks."

"The transmitter's still going."

"Transmitters can go that long."

"Not if the lifesupport's drawing. Six months tops. Besides, power cells and fuel were what Nouri stripped for sure."

Ben's helmet drifted between them. Ben snagged it. "I'm taking the pry-bar. We're going to need it getting in. Lay you bets?"

Bird picked his helmet out of the air beside him and put it on: smell of old plastics and disinfectant. Smell of a lot of hours and a lot of nasty cold moments.

This might be the start of one, the two of them squeezing into the wider than deep airlock, which was claustrophobic enough for the one occupant it was designed for.

It truly didn't make sense, maybe, insisting both of them get rigged up. It might even be dangerous, putting shut locks between them both and operable systems; but you chased a ghost signal through the Belt for days on end, you had nightmares about some poor lost sods you'd no idea who, and you remembered all your own close calls—well, then, you had to see it with your own eyes to exorcise your ghosts. If you were going to be telling it to your friends back at Base (and you would), then you wanted the feel of it and you wanted your partner able to swear to it.

Most of all, maybe you got a little nervous when your partner started getting that excited about money and insisting they owned that ship.

Most especially since Nouri and the crackdown, and since the company had gotten so nitpicking touchy—you wanted witnesses able to swear in court what you'd touched and what you'd done aboard somebody else's ship.

Bird shut the inside hatch and pushed the buttons that started the lock cycling. The red light came on, saying DEPRESSURIZATION, and the readout started spieling down toward zero.

"Sal-vage," Ben said, tinny-sounding over the suit-com. "Maybe she'll still pitch, do you think? If those tanks are the most of the damage, hell, they're cans, is all. Can't be that expensive. We could put a mortgage on her, fix her up—the bank'll take a fixable ship for collateral, what do you think?"

"I think we better pay attention to where we are. We got one accident here, let's not make it two."

The readout said PRESSURE EQUALIZED. Ben was doing this anxious little bounce with his foot braced, back and forth between the two walls of the lock. But you never rushed opening. Oxygen cost. Water cost. Out here, even with all the working machinery aboard, heat cost. You treated those pumps and those seals like they were made of gold, and while the safety interlocks might take almost-zero for an answer and let you open on override, it was money flowing out when you did. You remembered it when you saw your bills at next servicing, damn right, you did.

The readout ticked down past 5 mb toward hard vacuum, close as the compressor could send it. Ben pushed the OUTER HATCH OPEN button, the lock unsealed and retracted the doors and showed them the scarred, dust-darkened face of the opposing lock. The derelict's inside pressure gauge was dusted over. Bird cleared it with his glove. "760 mb. She's up full. At least it didn't hole her."

Ben banged soundlessly on the hatch with the steel bar and put his helmet up against the door.

"Nada," Ben said. "Dead in there, Bird, I'm telling you."

"We'll see." Bird borrowed the bar and pried up the safety cover on the External Access handle.

No action. No power in the ship's auxiliary systems.

"No luck for them," Ben said cheerfully. "Pure dead."

Bird jimmied the derelict's external leech panel open. "Get ours, will you?"

"Oh, shit, Bird."

"Nerves?"

Ben didn't answer. Ben shoved off to their own lock wall to haul the leech cord out of its housing. It snaked in the light as he drifted back. Bird caught the collared plug and pushed it into the derelict's leech socket. The hull bumped and vibrated under his glove. "She's working," he said.

"Sal-vage," Ben said, on hissed breaths.

"Don't spend it yet."

Rhythmic hiss of breath over suit-coms, while the metal vibrated with the pump inside. "Hey, Bird. What's a whole ship worth?"

A man tried to be sane and sensible. A man tried to think about the poor sods inside, an honest man broke off his prospecting and ran long, expensive risky days for a will-of-the-wisp signal, and tried to concentrate on saving lives, not on how much metal was in this ship or whether she was sound, or how a second ship would set him and Ben up for life. The waiting list for leases at Refinery Two meant no ship sat idle longer than its servicing required.

"130 mb. 70. 30. 10." The pressure gauge ticked down. The vibration under his hand changed. The valves parted.

Ice crystals spun and twinkled in front of them, against

the sullen glow of borrowed power. Ice formed and glistened on the inner lock surfaces—moisture where it didn't belong.

"Doesn't look prosperous," Ben said.

Bird pushed with his toe, caught a handhold next to the inner valves. His glove skidded on ice. Ben arrived beside him, said, "Clear," and Bird hit the HATCH CLOSE toggle.

"Going to be slow." He looked high in the faceplate for the 360° view, watching the derelict's outer doors labor shut at their backs.

"You sure about that battery?" Ben asked.

Bird hit CYCLE 2. The pumps vibrated. "Hell of a time to ask."

"Are you sure?"

"Thirty years at this, damn right I checked. —Whoa, there."

The HUD in the faceplate suddenly showed a yellow flasher and a dataflow glowing green. The one on the airlock wall glowed a sullen red.

"CONTAMINANTS." Ben let go a shaky hiss of pent breath. "It's not going to be pretty in there. —Bird, do we have to go through with this? There's nothing alive inside."

"We're already there. Can you sleep without knowing?"

"Damn right I'll sleep, I'll sleep just fine. —I don't want to see this, Bird. Why in hell do I got to see this?"

"Hey, we all end up the same. Carbon and nitrogen, a lot of $H_2O$ . . ."

"Cut it out, Bird!"

"Earth to earth. Dust to dust." The indicators said 740/741 mb. and PRESSURE EQUALIZED. "Lousy compressor," Bird said, pushed the INNER HATCH OPEN button. Air whistled, rushing past the pressure differential and an uneven seal. The doors ground slowly back. External audio heard it. 10° C, his HUD said about the ambient. Not quite balmy. "Heater's going down. Heater's always next to last. —You do know what's last, don't you, Ben-me-lad?"

"The damn beeper." Ben's teeth were chattering—nothing wrong with Ben's suit heater, Bird was sure. Ben's breath hissed raggedly over the suit-com. "So Mama can find the salvage. Only this time we got it, Bird, come on, I don't like this. What if that leech pulls out?"

"Plug won't pull out."

"Hell, Bird!"

Inner doors labored to halfway open. Bird caught the door edge and shoved himself and his backpack through into the faintly lit inside.

A helmetless hardsuit, trailing cables and hose, drifted slowly in front of them, spinning in a loose cocoon of its attachments. A cable went from its battery pack to the panel, last sad resort: the occupants had had time to know they were in trouble, time to drain the main batteries and the leech unit, and finally resort to this one.

Bits and pieces of gear drifted in the dimmed light, sparked bright in their suit-spots, cords, clips—everything a tumble could knock free. Fluids made small moons and planets.

"Mess," Ben's voice said. "Isn't it?"

Bird caught the hose, tugged gently to pull the suit out of his way, and checked the suit locker. "One suit's missing."

"I'm cutting that damn beeper," Ben said. "All right?"

"Fine by me."

Stuff everywhere. Cables. A small meteor swarm of utility clips flashed in the light. Globules of fluid shone both oily-dark and amber. A sweater and a single slipper danced and turned in unison like a ghost.

"Lifesupport's flat gone," Ben said. A locker banged in the external audio, while Bird was checking the spinner cylinders for occupants. Empty. Likewise the shower.

A power cell floated past. Dead spare, one from the lock, one guessed.

A globule of fluid impacted Bird's visor, leaving a chain of dark red beads.

"Come on, Bird. Let's seal up. Let's get out of here. They're gone. Dead ship, that's all. Don't ask what this slop is that's floating. The 'cyclers are shot."

Drifting hose. More clips. A lump of blankets under the number two workstation, spotted in Bird's chest-light. "Looks like here's one of them," Bird said.

"God! Let it be! Bird!"

"Carbon and water. Just carbon and water." Bird held the counter edge and snagged the blanket.

The body drifted past the chair, rolled free as the blanket floated on to dance with the sweater.

Young man in filthy coveralls. Straight dark hair and loose limbs drifted in the slow spin the turnout gave him.

Not much beard.

Bird caught a sleeve, stopped the spin, saw a dirty face, shut eyes, open mouth. Dehydration shrank the skin, cracked the lips.

"Don't touch him!" Ben objected. "God, don't touch him!"

"Beard's been shaved, maybe three days."

"God knows how long ago—he's dead, Bird. That's a dead body."

Bird nudged the chin-lever over to sensor array, said, "Left. Hand."

The HUD showed far warmer than the 10° ambient.

Pliable flesh.

"Isn't a body, Ben. This guy's alive."

"Shit," Ben said. Then: "But he's not in control of this ship. Is he?"

Long, long door closing, with an unconscious man crowding them three to the lock, and the underpowered motors going slow and threatening breakdown. Then they could Mode 2 Override their own airlock, mixing air supplies and keeping pressure up for their passenger's sake. "Go ahead and seal it behind us," Bird said. "Keep it just the way it was, in case Mama asks questions."

"God, we got a CONTAMINANTS flashing in *our* lock now. Why the hell don't we have a transfer bag? God, this guy's all over crud."

"We'll think of that next time. Come on, come on. Do it."

Ben swore, made the numbingly slow seal of the wreck's doors, then pulled their leech free and hit HATCH CLOSE on their own panel, sending One'er Eighty-four Zebra toward an electronic sleep, still docked with them, her last battery on the edge of failure.

"Man was a total fool," Ben muttered. "He should've hooked the ship in to feed that suit, not the other way around. Should have let her go all the way down."

"Would've made sense," Bird said.

"So where's the partner?"

"God only. Push CYCLE. I can't reach it."

Ben got an arm past him and the rescuee and hit the requisite button. Their own compressor started, solid and fast, a healthy vibration under the decking.

Then the whole chamber went red and a blinking white light on the panel said INTERNAL CONTAMINANT ALERT.

"Shit," Ben groaned.

"You got that right."

"Bad joke, Bird. That stuff got past the filters!"

"Just override. Tell it we're sorry, we can't help it."

Ben was already punching at the button. Ben said, "We don't need any damn corpse fouling up our air, howsoever long he takes to get that way. —God, Bird, we *own* that ship!"

"Just let's not worry about it here." Bird felt the slight movement in his arms. Hugged the man tight, thinking, Poor sod. Hold on. Hold on awhile. We got you. You're all right. He said to Ben, "He's moving."

Ben drew an audible breath. "You know, we could put him back in there. Who's to know?"

"Bad joke, Ben." The PRESSURE EQUALIZED lit up. "Hatch button. Come on, give me a hand, huh? I can't turn around."

"We can't damn well afford this!" Ben said. "We're into the bank as far as—"

"Ben, for God's sake, just punch the damn button!"

Ben punched it. The hatch opened, relieved the pressure at Bird's back, gave him room to turn and haul their rescuee inside. He carefully let the man go and let him drift while he sailed back into the lock and secured the leech into its housing. Then he drifted back through and shut the inside hatch.

Ben was lifting his helmet off—Ben was making a disgusted face and swearing. Their air quality alarm had the warning siren going and the overhead lights flashing—it was that bad. Ben grabbed their guest by the collar and started peeling him out of his clothes.

Bird got his own helmet off and let it float, stripped off his gloves and helped Ben peel the unconscious man to the skin, trying not to breathe, bunching the coveralls and stimsuit continually as they peeled them off, trying not to let them touch the air. He hesitated whether to go for a containment bag or shove them in the washer and maybe foul the cleaning fluid for the rest of the trip. The washer was closer. He crammed them in, slippers and all, levered the small door shut and pushed the button. The stench clung to his bare hands. His suit was splotched with yellow and red stains.

He heard a faint voice not Ben's, protesting incoherently, turned and saw Ben pulling the shower door open, the young man trying to resist Ben's pulling him around. Ben pushed the man inside and pulled the door to—a knee was in the way and Ben shoved it, while their uninvited passenger, drifting behind clear plastic, slammed a weak fist against the clear plex door.

"Be a little damn careful, Ben."

Ben pulled the outside seal lever down, flung up the service panel beside the door, pushed the Test Cycle button, holding the shower door shut the while. The shower started. Their guest slammed the door with his fist again, drifted back against the wall as the water hit him.

"What's the water temp?"

"Whatever you left it."

"I don't remember what I left it. —Cut it, Ben, he's passed out."

"He's all right, dammit! We've spent enough on this fool, I'm not living with that stink! It's my money too, Bird, in case you forget! It's my money right along with yours we spent running after this guy, it's my money pays for those filters, and that smell makes me sick to my stomach, Bird!"

"All right, all right. Take it easy."

"It's all over us!"

"Ben, —shut up. Just shut up. Hear me?"

The air quality siren was still going. It was enough to drive a man crazy. They were having a zero run, hardly anything in the sling. They'd spent nerve-wracking hours getting the ship linked and now Ben had gotten so close to money he could taste it. Ben got a little breath, looked as if control was still coming hard for him, as if he was somewhere between breaking down and breaking something.

Bird shoved over to the lifesupport control panel and cut the siren. The silence after was deafening. Just the shower going and their own hard breathing.

Ben was a hard worker, sometimes too hard. Bird told himself that, told himself Ben was a damned fine partner, and the Belt was lonely and tempers got raw. Two men jammed into a five by three can for months on end had to give each other room—had to, that was all.

Ben said, thin-lipped, but sanely, "Bird, we got to wipe down these suits. We have to get this stink off. It's going to break down our filters, dammit."

"It won't break down our filters," Bird assured him quietly, but he went and got the case of towel wipes out of the locker. The shower entered its drying cycle. The guy was floating there, eyes shut, maybe resting, maybe unconscious. Bird reached for the door.

Ben held the latch down and pushed the Test Cycle a second time.

"Ben," Bird protested, "Ben, for God's sake, the guy's had enough. Are you trying to drown him?"

"I won't live with that stink!"

The man—kid, really, he looked younger than Ben was—had drifted against the shower wall and hung there. He was moving again, however feebly—and maybe it was cowardly not to insist Ben listen to reason, but a small ship was nowhere to have a fight start, over what was likely doing the kid no harm, and maybe some good. You could breathe the mist, you could drink the detergent straight and not suffer from it. Dehydrated as he was, he could do with a little clean water; and cold as he'd been, maybe it was a fast way to warm him through.

So he said, "All right, all right, Ben," and opened the box of disinfectant towels, wiped his hands and chest and arms and worked down.

"I can still smell it," Ben said in a shaky voice, wiping his own suit off. "Even after you scrub it I can still smell it."

"That's just the disinfectant."

"Hell if it is."

Ben was not doing well, Bird thought. He had insisted Ben go over there with him and maybe that had been a mistake: Ben wasn't far into his twenties himself; and Ben might never have been in a truly lonely, scary situation in his whole stationbound life. Ben had spooked himself about this business for days, with all this talk about hijackers.

On the other hand maybe an old dirtsider from Earth and a Belter brat four years out of school weren't ever going to understand each other on all levels.

They shed the suits. They'd used up three quarters of their supply of wipes. "Just as well our guy stays in the shower," Bird said, now that he thought calmly about it, "until we have something to put him in. His clothes'll be dry in a bit." He cycled the shower again himself, stowed his suit and floated over to the dryer as it finished its cycle. The clothes were a little damp about the seams, and smelled of disinfectant: the dryer's humidity sensor needed replacing, among a dozen other things at the bottom of his roundtoit list. He read the stenciled tag on the coveralls. "Our guy's got a name. Tag says Dekker. P."

"That's fine. So he's got a name. What happened to his partner, that's what I want to know."

Maybe that was after all what was bothering Ben—too many stories about Nouri and the hijackers.

"He wasn't doing so well himself, was he?" Dekker, P. was drifting in the shower compartment, occasionally moving, not much. Bird opened the door, without interference from Ben this time, and said, quietly, before he took the man's arm: "Dekker, my name's Bird, Morrie Bird. My partner's Ben. You're all right. We're going to get you dressed now. Don't want you to chill."

Dekker half opened his eyes, maybe at the cold air, maybe at the voice. He jerked his arm when Bird pulled him toward the outside. "Cory?" he asked. And in panic, bracing a knee and a hand against the shower door rim: "Cory?"

"Watch him!" Ben cried; but it was Ben who caught a loose backhand in the face. Dekker jabbed with his elbow on the recoil, made a move to shove past them, but he had nothing left, neither leverage nor strength. Bird blocked his escape and threw an arm around him, after which Dekker seemed to gray out, all but limp, saying, "Cory, . . ."

"Must be the partner," Bird said.

"God only. I want a shower, Bird." Ben snatched the half-dry coveralls from him and grabbed Dekker's arm. "Hell with the stimsuit, let's just wrap this guy up before he bashes a panel or something."

"Just hold on to him," Bird said. Bird caught the stimsuit that was drifting nearby, shook the elastic out, got the legs and sleeves untangled and got hold of Dekker's arm. "Left leg, come on, son. Clean clothes. Come on, give us some help here. Left leg."

Dekker tried to help, then, much as a man could who kept passing out on them. His skin had been heated from the shower. It was rapidly cooling in the cabin air and Ben was right: it was hard enough to get a stimsuit on oneself, nearly impossible to put one on a fainting man. He was chilling too fast. They gave that up. By the time they got him into the coveralls and zipped him up he was moving only feebly, half-conscious.

"Not doing real well, is he?" Ben said. "Damn waste of effort. The guy's going to sign off—"

"He's all right," Bird said, "God, Ben, mind your mouth."

"I just want my bath. Let's just get this guy to bed, all right? We get a shower, we call Mama and tell her we got ourselves a ship!"

"Shut up about the ship, Ben."

A long, careful breath. "Look, I'm tired, you're tired, let's just forget it til we get squared away, all right?"

"All right." Bird shoved off in a temper of his own, drifted toward the spinner cylinders overhead, taking Dekker with him—carefully turned and caught a hold, pulling Dekker toward the open end. "Come on, son, we're putting you to bed, easy does it."

Dekker said, "Cory, —"

"Cory's your partner?"

Dekker's eyes opened, hazed and vague. Dekker grabbed the spinner rim, shaking his head, refusing to be put inside.

"Dekker? What happened to you, son?"

"Cory, —" Dekker said, and shoved. "I don't want to. No!"

Ben sailed up, grabbed Dekker's collar on the way and carried him half into the cylinder, Dekker fighting and kicking. Bird rolled and pushed off, got Dekker by a leg, Dekker screaming for Cory all the while and fighting them.

"Hold on to him!" Ben said, and Bird did that, holding Dekker from behind until Ben could unhook a safety tether from the bulkhead, held on while Ben sailed back to grab Dekker's arm and tie it to a pipe.

"Damn crazy," Ben said, panting. "Just keep him there. I'll get another line."

"That's rough, Ben."

"Rougher on all of us if this fool hits the panels. Just hold him, dammit!"

Ben somersaulted off to the supply lockers, while Bird caught his breath and kept Dekker's free arm pinned, patting his shoulder, saying, "It's all right, son, it's all right, we're trying to get you home. My name's Bird. That's Ben. What do you go by?"

Several shallow breaths. Struggles turned to shivers. "Dek."

"That's good." He patted Dekker's shoulder. Dekker's eyes were open but Bird was far from sure Dekker knew where he was or what had happened to him. "Just hold on, son." A locker door banged, forward. Ben came sailing up with a roll of tape.

"I'm not sure we need that," Bird said. "Guy's just a little spooked."

Ben ignored him, grabbed Dekker's other arm and began wrapping it to the pipe. "Guy's totally off his head." Dekker tried to kick him, Dekker kept saying, "My partner— where's my partner?"

"Afraid there was an accident," Bird said, holding Dekker's shoulder. "Suit's gone. We looked. There wasn't anybody else on that ship."

"No!"

"You remember what happened?"

Dekker shook his head, teeth chattering. "Cory."

"Was Cory your partner?"

*"Cory!"*

"Shit," Ben said, and shook Dekker, slapped his face gently. "Your partner's dead, man. The suit was gone. You got picked up, my partner and I picked you up. Hear?"

It did no good. Dekker kept mumbling about Cory, and Ben said, "I'm going down after a shower. Or you can."

"I'm scared we left somebody in that ship."

"You didn't leave anybody in that ship, dammit, Bird, we're not opening that lock again!"

"I'm not that sure."

"You looked, Bird, you *looked*. If there was a Cory he's gone, that's all. Suit and all. We've done all we can for this guy. We've spent days on this guy. We've spent our fuel on this guy, we've risked our necks for this guy—"

"His name's Dekker."

"His name's Dekker or Cory or Buddha for all I care. He's out of his head, we got nowhere safe to put him, we don't know what happened to his partner, we don't know why Mama doesn't know him, and that worries me, Bird, it seriously does!"

It made sense. Everything Ben was saying made sense. The other suit was gone. They had searched the lockers and the spinners. There were no hiding places left. But nothing about this affair was making sense.

"Hear me?" Ben asked.

"All right, all right," Bird said, "just go get your shower

and let's get our numbers comped. We have to call in. Have to. Regulations. We got to do this all by the book."

"Don't you feel sorry for him. You hear me, Bird? Don't you even think about going back into that ship."

"I won't. I don't. It's all right."

Ben looked at him distressedly, then rolled and kicked off for the shower.

Bird floated down to the galley beside it, opened the fridge and got a packet of Citrisal, lime, lemon, what the hell, it was all ghastly awful, but it had the trace elements and salts and simple sugars.

It was the best he knew to do for the man. He drifted over to Dekker, extracted the tube and held it to Dekker's lips.

"Come on. Drink up. It's the green stuff."

Dekker took a sip, made a face, ducked his head aside.

"Come on. Another."

Dekker shook his head.

Couldn't blame him for that, Bird thought. And you damn sure didn't want anybody sick at his stomach in null-g. He tested whether the cord and the tape were too tight, decided Dekker was all right for a while. "We'll let you loose when your head clears. You're all right. Hear me? We're going to get you back to Base. Get you to the meds. Hear me?"

Dekker nodded slightly, eyes shut.

Exhausted, Bird decided. He gave the man a gentle pat on the shoulder and said, "Get some sleep. Ship's stable now."

Dekker muttered something. Agreement, Bird thought. He hoped so. He was shaky, exhausted, and he wished they were a hell of a lot closer to Base than they were.

The guy needed a hospital in the worst way. And that was a month away at least. Bad trip. And there was the investment of time and money this run was going to cost them. Half a year's income, counting mandatory layouts.

Maybe Ben was right and they did have a legal claim on this wreck—Ben was a college boy, Ben knew the ins and outs of company law and all the loopholes—and maybe legally those were the rules, but Bird didn't like thinking that way and he didn't like the situation this run had put them in. If it was a company ship they had in tow and if it was the company itself they were going to be collecting their bills from—that was one thing; but the rig with its cheap equipment wasn't spiff enough for a company ship. That meant it was a freerunner, and that meant it was some poor sod's whole life, Dekker's or somebody's. Get their expenses back, yes, much as they could, but not rob some poor guy of everything he owned. That wasn't something Bird wanted to think about.

But Ben could. And Ben scared him of a sudden. You worked with a guy two years in a little can like this and eventually you did think you knew him reasonably well, but God knew and experience had proved it more than once—it was lonely out here, it was a long way from civilization, and you could never realize what all a guy's kinks were until something pushed the significant button.

# CHAPTER

# 2

THE old man went away. Dekker heard him or his partner moving about. He heard the shower going, over the fan and the pump noises in the pipes beside his head. The ship was stable. That was a feeling he had thought he would never have again. He had dimmed the lights, cut off everything he could and nursed it as far as he could til the 'cyclers went and the water fouled.

And here he was free of the stimsuit, light as a breeze and vulnerable to the chill and the lack of *g*. He was off his head, he knew that: he scared the people who had rescued him, he knew that too, and he tried not to do it, but they scared him. They talked about owning his ship. They might kill him, might just let him die and tell the company sorry, they hadn't been able to help that.

Maybe they couldn't. Maybe he shouldn't care any longer. He was tired, he hurt, body and soul, and living took more work than he was sure he wanted to spend again on anything. He had no idea how long and how far a run was still in front of him getting home. He didn't think he could stand being treated like this all the way. Everything smelled of disinfectant, and sometimes it was his ship and sometimes it was theirs.

But Cory never answered him wherever he was, and at times he knew she wouldn't.

The old man drifted up into his sight again, put a straw in his mouth and told him to drink. He did. It tasted of copper. The old man asked him what had happened to his partner. Then he remembered—how could he have forgotten?—that she was out there and that ship was, he could see it coming—

"No!" he cried, and winced when it hit, he knew it was going to hit, the collision alert was screaming. He yelled into the mike, "My partner's out there!" because it was the last thing he could think of to tell them.

"Your partner's dead!" somebody yelled at him, and another voice, angry, yelled, "Shut up, dammit, Ben! You got no damn feelings, give the guy a chance. God!"

He was still alive and he did not understand how he had survived. He hauled himself to the radio, he held on against the spin as long as he had strength. "Cory," he called on the suit-com frequency, over and over again, while the ship tumbled. Maybe she answered. His ears rang so he couldn't hear the fans or the pumps. But he kept calling her name, so she would know he was alive and looking for her, that he'd get help to her somehow...

As soon as he could get the damned engines to fire.

Or as soon as he could get hold of Base and make that ship out there answer him....

Ben said, "We're *due* salvage rights, whether he's company or a freerunner, *no* legal difference. It's right in the company rules, I'll show you—"

Bird said, carefully, because he wanted Ben to understand him: "We'll get compensated."

"Maritime law since—"

"There's the law and there's what's right, Ben."

"*Right* is, we own that ship, Bird. He wasn't in control of it, that's what *right* says."

Ben was short of breath. He was yelling. Bird said,

calmly, sanely, "I'm trying to tell you, there's a lot of complications here. Let's just calm down. We've got weeks yet back to Base, plenty of time to figure this out, and we'll talk about it. But we're not getting any damn where if we don't get our figures in and tell Mama to get us the hell home. Fast."

"So how much are you going to spend on this guy? A month's worth of food? Medical supplies? We're going to bust our ass and risk our rigging for this guy?"

Bird had no answer. He couldn't think of one to cut this off.

"This is my money too, Bird. It's my money you're spending. Maybe you own this ship, maybe I'm just a part-share partner, but I have some say here." Ben flung a gesture toward Dekker, aft. "That guy's going to live or he's going to die. In either case he's going to do it before the month is up. Much as I want to be rid of him, there's no need busting our tails—we have double mass to move, Bird, and hell if I'm dumping the sling—"

"All right, we're not dumping the sling. Not ours, not his either, if we can avoid it."

"And we're not putting any hard push on the rigging. There's no point in risking our necks. Or putting wear on the pins and the lines. We don't call this a life-and-death. We can't cut that much time off. And hell if I want to meet a rock the way this guy did."

It made better sense than a lot else Ben had been saying. Bird took that for hopeful and nodded. "I'll go with you on that. A hard push could do more harm than good for him, too."

"Guy's going to die anyway."

"He's not going to die," Bird said. "For God's sake, just shut up, he can hear you."

"So if he doesn't? A month gets him well, and we pull into station and he looks healthy and he says sure he was managing that ship just fine—"

"Just let it alone, Ben!"

"I'm going to get pictures."

"Get your pictures." Bird shook his head, wishing he

could say no, wishing he had some way to reason with Ben, but if getting a vid record would make Ben happier, God, let him have the pictures. "We have the condition of that ship out there, we have the log records over there—"

"Charts—" Ben exclaimed, as if that was a new idea.

"We're not touching that log. No way. That part of the law *I* know."

"I'm not talking about that. Look—look, I got an idea."

An idea was welcome. Bird watched doubtfully as Ben punched up the zone schema, pointed on the screen to the 'driver ship and its fire-path to the Well, the same thing that scared them even to contemplate. "*That's* got a medic. That's got a friggin' company captain in charge. We just ask Mama to boost us over there just across the line and *they* can take official possession."

"Damn right they would. The company doesn't run a charity."

"It's an R1 ship! They're obligated to take him. They have no choice. The law says a 'driver is a Base: they can log us right there for a find if we bring it in, and this is a find, isn't it? Same as a rock. We can turn it in, money in the bank, and we can apply to do some clean-up along with its tenders for the rest of our run—that's damn good money. Sure money. And we got the best excuse going."

"Ben, that's a 'driver captain you're talking about. They don't *have* to do anything. You want him to tell us we've still got to turn around and take this guy in to Base, maybe clean to R1, if he takes it in his head—he can do that. You want him to tell us he'll hold Eighty-four Zebra for us—and then contest his fees in court when he shows up three years from now with one hell of a haulage charge? We got this run to pay for, we got serious questions to answer, because there's a whole lot that's not right about this, and I'm not taking my chances with any Court of Inquiry back at Base with all the evidence stuck out on a 'driver that for all we know isn't coming in for three or four more years. If you want to talk law, now, let's be practical!"

Ben's mouth shut.

"A 'driver does any damn thing it wants to. Three years'

dockage charges, supposing they're on the start of their run. Three years' haulage. You want to try to pry a claim away from the company then? Not mentioning the cost of getting it there. We're short as is. You want to hear them say ferry it back ourselves anyway? Twice the distance? Or get us drafted into its tender crew on a *permanent* basis? You know what they charge a freerunner for fuel?"

Ben looked very sober during all of this. Ben bit his lip. "So that's out. You know, we could just sort of knock that fellow on the head. Solve everybody's problem."

Ben, who was scared to death of looking at a body.

"Yeah, sure," Bird said.

And from aft: "What time is it? What's the time?"

Ben glanced up. "Now what does he want?"

Bird checked his watch. "2310," he shouted back.

"I want my watch."

"God," Ben muttered, shaking his head. "We have four weeks of this guy?"

"*I want my watch!*"

Ben yelled: "Shut up, dammit, you're not keeping any appointments anyway!"

"Patience," Bird said, but Ben shoved off in Dekker's direction. Bird sailed after, arrived as Dekker said quietly,

"I need my watch."

Ben said: "You don't need your watch, you're not going anywhere. It's 23 damn 10 in my sleep, mister, you're using our air and our fuel and our time already, so shut up."

"Ben, just take it easy."

"I'll shut him up with a wrench."

"Ben."

"All right, all right, all right." Ben took off again.

Dekker said, "I can't see my watch."

Bird floated over where he could read the time on Dekker's watch. "2014. You're about three hours slow."

"No."

"That's what it says."

"What day is it?"

"May 20."

"You're lying to me!"

"Bird," Ben said ominously, and came drifting up again to reach for Dekker, but Bird grabbed him.

"I can't take four weeks of that, Bird, I swear to you, this guy's already on credit with me already."

"Give *me* a little slack, will you? Shut it down. Shut it up. Hear me?"

"I've dealt with crazies," Ben muttered. "I've seen enough of them."

"Fine. Fine. We get this guy out of a tumble, he's been whacked about the head, he's a little shook, Ben, d'you think you wouldn't be, if you'd been through what he has?"

Ben stared at him, jaw clamped, grievous offense in every line of his face.

Ben was in the middle of his night. That was so. Ben was tired and Ben had been spooked, and Ben didn't understand weakness in anybody else.

Serious personality flaw, Bird thought. Dangerous personality flaw.

He watched Ben go back to his work without a word.

Good partner in some ways. Damned efficient. Good with rocks.

But different. Belter-born, for one thing, never talked about his relatives. Brought up by the corporation, for the corporation.

Talk to Ben about Shakespeare, Ben'd say, What shift does he work?

Say, I come from Colorado—Ben'd say, Is that a city?

But Ben didn't really know what a city was. You couldn't figure how Ben read that word.

Say, I went up to Denver for the weekend, and Ben'd look at you funny, because weekend was another thing that didn't translate. Ben wouldn't ask, either, because Ben didn't really want to know: he couldn't spend it and he wasn't going there and never would and that was the limit of Ben's interest.

Ask Ben about spectral analysis or the assay and provenance of a given chunk of rock and he'd do a thirty-minute monologue.

Damn weird values in Belt kids' mindsets. Sometimes Bird wondered. Right now he didn't want to know.

Right now he was thinking he might not want Ben with him next trip. Ben was a fine geologist, a reliable hold-her-steady kind of pilot, and honest in his own way.

But he had some scary dark spots too.

Maybe years could teach Ben what a city was. But God only knew if you could teach Ben how to live in one.

Bird was seriously pissed. Ben had that much figured, and that made him mad and it made him nervous. He approved of Bird, generally. Bird knew his business, Bird had spent thirty years in the Belt, doing things the hard way, and Ben had had it figured from the time he was 14 that you never got anywhere working for the company if you weren't in the executive track or if you weren't a senior pilot: he had never had the connections for the one and he hadn't the reflexes for the other, so freerunning was the choice, . . . where he was working only for himself and where what you knew made the difference.

He had come out of the Institute with a basic pilot's license and the damn-all latest theory, had the numbers and the knowledge and everything it took. The company hadn't been happy to see an Institute lad go off freerunning, instead of slaving in its offices or working numbers for some company miner, and most Institute brats wouldn't have had the nerve to do what he'd done: skimp and save and live in the debtor barracks, and then bet every last dollar on a freerunner's outfitting; most kids who went through the Institute didn't have the discipline, didn't refrain from the extra food and the entertainment and the posh quarters you could opt for. They didn't even get out of the Institute undebted, thank *God* for mama's insurance; and even granted they did all that, most wouldn't have had the practical sense to know, if they did decide to go mining and not take a job key-pushing in some office, that the game was not to sign up with some shiny-new company pilot in corp-rab, who had perks out to here. Hell, no, the smart thing was to hunt the records for the old independent who had made ends meet for thirty years, lean times and otherwise.

Namely Morris Bird.

Freerunning was the only wide gamble left in the Belt—and freerunners, being from what they were, didn't have the advantage of expert, up-to-date knowledge from the Institute—plus the Assay Office. But with Morrie Bird's thirty years of running the Belt, his *old* charted pieces were bigger than you got nowadays, distributed all along the orbital track, and he got chart fees on those every month, the company didn't argue with his requests to tag, and those old charted pieces kept coming round again, in the way of rocks that looped the sun fast and slow. Sometimes those twenty-four- and twelve-year-old pieces might have been perturbed, and if somebody tried to argue about the claim, your numbers had to be solid after all those years—besides which, to find the good chaff that might remain to be found, you had to have more than guesswork. That was the pitch he had to offer along with 20 k interest-free to finance some equipment Bird badly needed; that was why Bird should take a greenie for a numbers man in a time when experienced miners went begging: company training, the science and the math and the complete Belt charts that Assay got to see—and they had done damned well as a team—*damned* well, til they'd got one of those absolutely miserable draws Mama sometimes handed you—a sector where there just wasn't much left to find but a handful of company-directed tags on some company-owned rocks.

So right now they were in a financial slump, Bird was under a strain, and Bird had odd touchy spots Ben never had been able to figure—all of which this Dekker had evidently hit on with his crazy behavior and his pretty-boy looks. Dekker was up there in their sleeping nook mumbling about losing his partner (damned careless of him!) and now Bird was mad at *him*, acting as if it was *his* fault the guy was alive and the find that might have been their big break turned out complicated.

Maybe, he thought, Bird did want that ship as much as he did, maybe Bird was equally upset that this fellow was alive, Bird having this ethic about helping people—Bird might well be confused about what he was feeling.

Dangerous attitude to spread around, Ben thought, this charity business—and unfair, when Bird even thought about forgoing that ship for somebody who owed him and not the other way around, at his own partner's expense. It was a way for Bird to get had, and a man as free-handed as Bird was needed help from a partner with a lasting reason to keep him in one piece.

"Bird?" he called out from the workstation. "I got your prelim calc. No complications but that 'driver and our mass."

Bird came over to him, Bird said he'd finish it up and call Mama. Bird touched him on the shoulder in a confusingly friendly way and said, "Get some sleep."

Ben said, because he thought it might make Bird happier, "You. I'm wired." At the bottom of his motives was the thought that a little time next to Dekker's constant mumbling about Cory and his watch might make Bird a little less charitable to strangers.

But Bird said, "You. You're the one needs it most."

"What's *that* supposed to mean?"

"It means what it means. You're tired. You've worked your ass off. Get some rest."

"I don't think I'll sleep right off. That guy makes me nervous. This whole situation makes me nervous."

"Bad day. Hard day."

He decided Bird was being sane again. He was relieved. "You know," he said, "we might just ought to get a statement out of this guy. You know. Besides pictures. I'm going to get a tape of this whole damn What-time-is-it? routine, show what we got to cope with. Might just prove our case."

Bird shook his head.

"Bird, for God's sake."

"Ben," he said firmly.

Ben did not understand. He flatly did not understand.

"Just go easy on him," Bird said.

"So what's he to us?"

"A human being."

"That's no damn recommendation," Ben muttered. But it was definitely a mistake to argue with Bird in his present mood: Bird owned the ship. Ben shook his head. "I'll just get the pictures."

"You don't understand, do you?"

"Understand what?"

"What if it was you out there?"

"I wouldn't be in that damn mess, Bird! You wouldn't be."

"You're that sure."

"I'm sure."

"Ben, you mind my asking—what ever happened to your folks?"

"What's that to do with it?"

"Did *they* ever make a mistake?"

"My mama wasn't the pilot. —That ship's not going to be book mass, with that tank rupture. Center of mass is going to be off, too. Need to do a test burn in a little while, all right? I don't want to leave anything to guesswork."

"Yeah. Fine. Nothing rough. Remember we have a passenger."

Ben frowned at him, and kept his mouth shut.

Bird said, pulling closer, "I got to tell you, Ben, right up front, we're not robbing this poor sod. He's got enough troubles. Hear me? Don't you even be thinking about it."

"It's not robbing. It's perfectly legal. It's your rights, Bird, same as he has his. The same as he'd take his, if things were the other way around. That's the way the system is set up to work."

"There's rights, and there's what *is* right."

"He's not your friend! He's not even anybody's friend you know. Bird, for God's sake, you got a major break here. Breaks like this don't just fall into your lap, and they're nothing if you don't make them work for you. That's why there's laws—to even it up so you can work with people the way they are, Bird, not the way you want them to be."

"You still have to look in mirrors."

"What's mirrors to do with anything?"

"If we're due anything, we're due the expenses."

"Expenses, hell! We're due haulage, medical stuff, chemkit, and a fat salvage fee at minim, we're due that whole damn *ship*, is what we're due, Bird."

"It won't work."

"Hell if it won't work, Bird! I'll show it to you in the code. You want me to show it to you in the code?"

Bird looked put out with him. Bird said, with a sigh, "I know the rules."

Bird had him completely puzzled. He took a chance, asked: "Bird, —have I done something wrong?"

"No. Just give me warning on that burn. I'm going to shoot some antibiotics into our passenger, get him a little more comfortable."

Ben said, vexed, figuring to argue it later, "Better keep a running tab on the stuff, if that's the way you're playing it."

"There isn't any damn tab, Ben! Quit thinking like a computer. The guy can have kidney and liver damage, he can have fractures, he can be concussed. You can calc a nice gentle burn while you're at it. We're not doing any sudden moves with him."

"All right. Fine. Slow and easy." Ben tapped the stylus at the keys, with temper boiling up in him as Bird left— downright hurt, when it came to it. He tapped it several times on the side of the board, shoved away from the toehold and caught up with Bird's retreat. "Bird, dammit, what in hell have I done?"

Bird looked at him as if he were adding things in his head.

Maybe, Ben thought, maybe Bird just didn't like to be argued with. Or maybe it was that pretty-boy face of Dekker's. Dekker was a type he thoroughly detested, because for some people there didn't need to be any sane reason to do them favors, didn't matter they were dumb as shit or that they'd cut your throat for their advantage, people believed them because they looked good and they talked smooth. It suddenly dawned on him that Bird was acting soft-headed about this guy with no good reason; and he decided maybe Bird taking care of Dekker himself wasn't a good idea at all. He said, quickly, quietly, "It's the bank I'm worried about. And this guy's intentions. He's not in his right zone. He's a long way from it. We don't know him. Maybe he was thrown here, maybe he wasn't. We don't know what he is. He could be some drop-off from the rebels—"

"There aren't any 'jackers, Ben. And he isn't any rebel. What's he going to spy on? A ship you can see from deep out with any decent optics? You've heard too many stories."

"All right, all right, he's one of the good guys. You want him tucked in safe and sound, you want a dose of broad-spectrum stuff and maybe some vitamins in him, I'll take care of it. *You* set up the burn."

"You're already running on it."

"I said I'll take care of him!"

Ben kited off toward the med cabinet, and Bird's first thought was, So maybe I talked some human sense into him. And then, cynically: Maybe at least he figures he's precarious with me right now, and covering his ass is all he's doing. You don't change a man that fast.

Then he saw Ben fill a hypo and thought, God, he wouldn't!

Bird kicked off from the touch strip and sailed up beside Ben. "I'll do it."

"I'll take care of it."

Bird snatched at the bottle. It floated free. It turned label-side toward him as he caught it and it *was* antibiotic Ben had been loading.

Ben scowled at him. "You're acting crazy, Bird. You're acting seriously crazy, you know that?"

"I'll handle it," Bird said. "Just wait on that burn a few minutes."

Ben scowled at him, shoved off from the cabinet and sailed backward toward the workstation. Offended, Bird thought, with a twinge of irritation and of conscience at once—not sure what Ben really had intended. Ben had no patience or sympathy for Dekker or anyone else—so he'd thought.

Or was it just plain jealousy Ben was showing?

Ben belted back in at his keyboard. Ben was not looking at him, pointedly not looking at him.

Bird kicked off to the side, drifted up to Dekker—Dekker looked to be asleep, Bird hoped that was all. At least he'd given up asking what time it was. Bird popped him on the arm with the back of one hand.

Dekker waked with a start and an outcry.

"Polybact," Bird said, showing him the needle. "You got any allergies?"

Dekker shook his head muzzily. Bird gave him the shot, snagged the Citrisal pack out of the pipes where air currents had sent it, uncapped the stem and put it in Dekker's mouth.

Dekker took a sip or two. Turned his head. "That's all."

"We're going to do a test burn. After that we'll be doing a 140, going to catch a beam home. Has to be our Base, understand, unless we get other instructions. We're out of R2."

Dekker looked at him hazily. "No. No hospital. 79, 709, 12. That's where we were. We had a find—big find. *Big* find. I'll sign it to you. Just go there. Pick my partner up."

"Your partner was outside when the accident happened?"

Dekker nodded.

"What happened? Catch a rock?" It happened. Usually to new crews.

Another nod. Dekker's eyes were having trouble tracking. "Kilometer wide. Iron content."

Freerunning miners didn't *find* nickel-iron rocks that big. Rocks that big had been mapped by optics: those rocks all had long-standing numbers, they belonged to the company, and if they were rich, they got 'drivers assigned to them, they got chewed in pieces, and they streamed to the recovery zone at the Well by bucketloads. But Bird didn't argue that point: Dekker didn't seem highly reasonable at the moment, and he only said, "A whole k wide. You're sure of that."

"It's the truth," Dekker said. "We got a tag on it. Uncharted rock. You can have it, if you'll go back there and find her."

"Cory's a her."

"Cory. Yes." He was going out again. "God, go back. Go back there, listen to me, anything you want . . ."

"You want another sip?" Bird asked, but Dekker was out again, gone. Bird shoved off and arrowed down to grab a handhold by Ben's workstation, but Ben said:

"I'm already ahead of you. Man said 79, 709, 12? No signal in that direction but the 'driver."

Nothing but the 'driver, Bird thought. God. "Hear any tag?"

Ben shook his head.

Bird bit his lip, wondering—

Wondering, dammit, how long that particular 'driver had been there. A while, damned sure. But Mama only told you what you needed. You could work out the rest from what you could gather with your own ears and your radar, but who wanted to?

Who, in a question about a company tag and a private claim, —wanted to?

Ben said in a low voice, "Do you suppose that fool tried to skim the company on a rock that size?"

Bird thought, I want out of here.

But what he argued to Ben was: "We just don't ask. We don't know anything and we sure as hell aren't getting in their way. Whatever claim's out there already has a 'driver attached."

"Makes other claims kind of moot, doesn't it?"

"Don't even ask."

Company prerogatives, secret company codes and direct accesses—company ships could talk back and forth at will; bet your life they could.

And count that that 'driver ship was armed—if you counted a kilometer-long mass driver as a lethal weapon, and Bird personally did. You didn't want to argue right of way or ownership with a 'driver captain. They were ASTEX to the core and they were a breed—next to God.

Ben said, "Told you we should have left this guy on the other side of the lock. It's still not too late."

"Cut the jokes. It wasn't funny the first time."

"Bird, there's a hell of a lot more than he's telling. Big find, hell. They were skimming a company claim."

"We don't know that."

"Well, that's all I want to know. Suddenly I'm damn glad we haven't been talking to that 'driver. I don't like this, damn, I don't."

"I don't know anything. You don't know anything. We didn't look at that log. Thank God. Let's just get us out of here."

"We could offer to give evidence."

"We don't know what we're swearing to. We don't *know* what happened."

"We *could* look in that log."

"Sure, a skimmer's going to log his moves. What's he going to write? '1025 and we just blew a chip off a 1 k rock'? If we touch that panel over there we'll leave a record of that access, and maybe that's not a good idea. Do I spell it out? Don't be a fool."

"I can fix that log. I think I can bypass that access record if you really want to know."

"Don't depend on it. 'Think' isn't good enough. No. We don't run that risk. Best claim we've got is that we haven't seen those records and we don't know a thing. We don't have a problem if we just keep clean. No shady stuff. Nothing. Clean, Ben."

"Knock that guy in the head," Ben muttered. "Be sure there's no questions. Then there's no problem."

God, he thought. Is that what they teach this generation?

The ship jolted.

Dekker yelled aloud, struggling to get free. Someone—a familiar voice now—shouted at him to shut up.

Another, gentler, said, "That was just getting in position, Dekker. Take it easy."

He had another blank spot then, woke up with the nightmare feeling of increasing g, not knowing where it was going to stop, or what had started it. Something pressed into his back and he thought, God, we're spinning—

"Cory!" he yelled.

"Shut up, dammit!"

"Dekker." This came gently then, with a touch at his shoulder. A smell of something cooked. Freefall. He blinked and looked at the gray-haired man, who let a foil packet of something drift near his face.

"We've done our position," the man said to him, he couldn't remember the name, and then did. Bird. Bird was the good one. Bird was the one who didn't want to kill him. "We're going to catch our beam tomorrow and we're going home. Seems Mama thinks we're in no hurry or something, damn her. I'll let you loose if you can keep awake." Another pat on the shoulder. "You know you've been off your head a little."

"What time is it?"

"Shush," Bird said, "don't go asking that."

"I want to know—"

Bird put a hand on his mouth. "Don't do that," Bird said, looking him in the eyes. "Don't do that, son. You don't need to know. You really don't need to know. Your partner's just lost, that's all. A long time ago. There's nothing anybody can do for her."

He didn't want to believe that. He didn't want to wake up again, but Bird caught the packet drifting in front of his face and held the tube to his mouth, insisting.

He took a little. It was warm, it was soup, it was salty as hell. He turned his head away, and Bird let it go, leaving a tiny planetesimal of soup cooling in the air, drifting away with the current. Bird brushed at it, caught it in his hand, wiped it on his sleeve.

Blood everywhere, shining dark drops. . . .

Everything was stable. Clean and quiet. Nothing had ever gone wrong here. Nothing had ever *been* wrong. He kept his eyes open for fear of the dark behind them and tried another sip of what Bird was offering him, while the first was hitting his stomach with an effect he was not yet sure of.

Why am I here? he asked himself. What is this place? This isn't my ship. What am I doing here?

Maybe he asked out loud. He didn't keep track of things. "To Refinery Two," Bird told him.

He shook his head. He got a breath and thought, Cory's still in the ship, they've left Cory back in the ship—

He reminded himself, he could do it now with only a cold, strange calm: No, Cory's dead— Not that he could remember. He kept telling himself that over and over, but he could not remember. She was still there. She was wondering what had happened to him. She was trusting him to do the right thing, the smart thing. She was waiting for him to pick her up . . .

The dark-headed one, the young one, Ben, rose into his vision, carrying a length of thin cable and a davies clip. Ben hung in front of his face and reached behind his neck with the cable.

"Hell!" he yelled, and used a knee, but Ben grabbed a handful of his coveralls and it missed its target.

Oh, shit, he thought then, looking Ben in the face. He thought Ben would kill him.

Bird said, from the other side, "Easy, son. It's temporary. Hold still."

He had thought Bird was all right. But Bird held him still and Ben got the cable around his neck. The clip clicked.

"There," Ben said. "You can reach the necessaries . . . reach anything in this ship but the buttons. And you don't really want those, do you?"

He stared eye to eye at Ben and wondered if Ben was waiting to kill him while Bird was asleep. He remembered hearing them talk. He wondered whether Ben was going to hit him right now.

"You understand me?" Ben asked.

He nodded, scared, and likewise clear-headed in a tight-focused, adrenaline-edged way. He stayed very still while Ben started untaping his left wrist from the pipe. He didn't think either ahead or backward. It was just himself and Ben, and the old man saying, holding tightly to his shoulder, "I apologize. I sincerely apologize about this, son. But we can't have you wandering around off your head. Ben's not a bad guy. He really isn't."

He remembered what he'd overheard. He had thought

Bird wanted to keep him alive, and now he wasn't sure either one of them was sane.

Ben freed his left arm. Bird untied the right. Moving both at once hurt his chest, hurt his back, hurt everything so much his eyes teared.

Ben went away forward. Bird stayed behind, put a hand on his shoulder. "No difference between our config and yours, the standard rig, by what I saw. Anything you can reach, you can use. Wouldn't use the spinner with that cable attached, understand, but you got g while you were tumbling, God knows probably more than enough. Your stimsuit's clean, but you'd as glad be free of it a day or so, wouldn't you? You're probably sore as hell. —Right? Just don't try to use the shower, cable won't let it seal, we'll have water everywhere. Anything else you got free run of. Copy that?"

"Yeah."

Bird gathered up the trailing cable, put it in his hand, closed his fist on it. "When you're moving about the cabin, do kind of keep a grip on that. We don't want you hurt. Hear? Don't want that cable to pull you up short. We're not going to do a burn without we warn you, but all the same, you keep a hand to that. Hold on to it."

Just too many things had happened to him. He could not figure what his situation was or what they wanted. He shoved off, drifted away from the bulkhead to get the packet of soup that had come adrift. Braking with his arm against a pipe was almost more than he could do. He let go the cable, confused, and banged his head.

Someone caught his foot and pulled, gently. It turned him as he came down and he saw Bird with a packet of soup in his own hands.

"There's solid food," Bird said, "when you can handle it. Use anything from the galley you need. You got pretty dehydrated."

He hated all this past tense, implying a major piece of time he didn't remember. From moment to moment he told himself Cory was gone, and every time he did that he felt a sense of panic. He brushed a touchpad with his foot, stopped, drank a sip and watched Bird sip from his own packet. He kept thinking, They're lying to me, they're not taking me home. . . .

Finally he asked Bird, "What 'driver is it out there?"

"What about a 'driver?"

"You were talking about a 'driver. What 'driver were you talking about?"

Ben yelled up from below, "Don't tell him a damn thing, Bird. He hasn't earned it."

He looked from Ben down at the workstation up to Bird, resting by the bulkhead.

"Ben's excitable," Bird said. "Just have your breakfast. Or supper, as may be."

But Ben was drifting up to them. Ben braked with the shove of a hand against the conduits. "I'd like to know," Ben said, "what you've got to pay for this trip. Eat our food, breathe our air, take up our time and our fuel. We're aborting a run for you. We just got effin' *started* and we're headed back to Base, damn near *zeroed* on your account, mister. You got any assets to pay for this? Or just debts?"

"We have money," he said, and then knew he shouldn't have said that to these people. He said, desperately catching up the thread of his thought—he hoped he hadn't lost anything between: "So what 'driver is it?"

Ben said, "How much money?"

"Ben," Bird said.

"I want," he said carefully, "I want you to call that 'driver and ask about my partner."

"Ask what about your partner?" Ben asked.

"Ask if they—" He stuttered on the thought. He never stuttered, and still he could not get it out. "—if they p-picked her up."

"So why should they? What were you doing here, poaching in another Refinery's zone?"

"We w-weren't." Dammit. "*It* was."

"What do you mean, 'it was'?"

"Ben," Bird said, and then, looking at him: "Forget he asked."

He didn't understand. He was so weak he couldn't track what they were saying from moment to moment, and hostile questions, zero g and unaccustomed food were all one confusion of balance and orientation. There was a constant buzz in his head that rose and fell like the fan-sounds. From moment to moment he knew Cory was alive, and from moment to moment he thought about the time and wanted to check his watch to be sure.

But that was crazy. He began to know it was. The only hope Cory had now was that 'driver ship. Maybe it had picked her up. Maybe it had.

"He's not telling the story he started with," Ben said. "Man's lying somewhere. A collision with a rock, he said. An explosion took one whole damn tank out. The other one's got a bash you could park a skimmer in. You want to see the videotape, man? I can show you the tape."

"Didn't hit a rock," he said, shaking his head. He had no idea where this was going. He had no idea what they were accusing him of, whether this was going on record or what they wanted from him.

"Why would it explode?"

"The 'driver clipped us."

"Facing *away* from the Well? Whose Zone were you in?"

"R1."

"'Driver, hell. You ran it into a rock, didn't you? Just plain ran it onto a rock."

"No."

"Ben," Bird said, "take it easy. The guy's confused."

"'Take it easy.' —Some people with trouble deserve it, you know."

"We don't know anything," Bird said. "His memory isn't going to be all that good, with what he's been through."

"Looks healthy enough. Looks damned well healthy enough on our air and our food. Looks like he's making real good progress."

Ben talked about claiming the ship, he recollected that—they were after the ship and they claimed they were taking him to R2, not home; now they were talking about other debts—

They talked as if they wanted to put him to work for

them. He had heard about Nouri. It had happened before in the Belt. Guys with all sorts of kinks went out in ships . . . and when they were ready to come in to Base, they might not want to take the evidence with them.

God, he thought, and looked off toward nowhere. The only thing in the vicinity was that 'driver ship. If they had never reported finding Cory—

The instruments . . . something coming at him over the horizon—

Explosion like a fist hit them. *G*-force. He reached after the fire controls.

No power. Nothing . . .

Ben left him. Bird left him. He saw Bird talking with Ben, holding on to Ben's arm, he couldn't make out what they were saying.

Then Ben shouted, "We own that ship!" and Bird: "Just shut it down, Ben, shut it down, for God's *sake*, Ben!"

They started arguing again, yelling at each other about money, about what they were spending on him, and Bird took his part, saying, over and over again, "It's not your damn decision, Ben!"

He watched, turning so he could see, phasing in and out of clear awareness, the fan-sound going in his ears, the soup he had drunk lying queasy on his stomach. He was afraid at one point Ben was going to hit the old man, and that Ben was going to end up in control of the ship.

The argument broke up. He grayed out a while. He came to with something near him and looked into a cyclopic glass lens, a camera pointed at his face, Ben's face behind it. That scared him. He stared back, wondering whether Ben had a real kink or whether Ben was just a hobbyist. He was afraid to object. He just stared back and tried not to throw up.

Then Ben cut the camera off and said,

"Got you, you son of a bitch," and drifted off.

He thought, This guy's crazy, he's absolutely crazy . . . Ben wanted his ship. Ben wanted him dead. He had this cable around his neck, that Ben had put there. He was afraid to sleep after that, afraid Ben was going to do something stranger still, and adrenaline kept him focused for a while. But things started going away from him again, he was back in the dark with the tumbling and the pressure building in his head, and then he was back again with that lens in his face and Ben going crazier and crazier. . .

He had no idea how long those times were or whether he had dreamed the business with the camera. When he looked, Bird was sleeping in a makeshift net rigged down toward the bow, and Ben was back at the workstation keyboard as if he had never moved, never had done anything in the least odd. He watched Ben for a while, wondering if he had hallucinated, wondering if it was safe to move with Bird asleep, because he was beginning to feel an acute need of going down to the head, and he was scared to do anything that Ben might conceivably object to.

Finally he shoved off very slowly and drifted down feet first toward the shower/toilet.

Ben looked around at him. He touched the other wall and caught the shower door, and Ben seemed not to care.

Don't use the shower, he remembered that—he kept the cable in his left hand the way Bird had said, but for a space he lost track of where he was again: then he was inside the shower where the toilet was, finishing his business. He thought for a panicked moment. They're lying, this is our ship all along. It was even the same ribbed pattern on the green shower wall. He could feel it when he touched it, real as anything he knew. He thought: Cory can't be dead, she isn't dead, there isn't any other ship—

But there was the cable snaking out the door, there was the clip that wouldn't come off—he tried to brace himself with his feet and his shoulders while he worked, he pulled the clip cover back to squeeze the jaws with his bare fingers, but he could get no leverage on it and all the while Cory was out there with no way to get back—

He looked at his watch. It said 0638. It said, March 12. He thought, The damn watch is wrong, it can't be March 12. I'm back where I started. Cory's going to die. Oh, God—

The clip cover slipped and he pinched his finger, bit his

lip against the pain and thought, I've got to get rid of this, got to get hold of the ship, get the radio—

He looked around him for leverage, anything that could double for a pliers and put a pinch on the jaws with the clip cover retracted. He tried the soap dispenser, pried the small panel up, worked himself around upside down with his foot braced against the wall, pulled the spring cover back from the jaws with the fingers of his left hand, and held the pressure point under the metal edge of the panel with the leverage of his right hand, pushing the panel edge down on the clip, hard as he could, trying not to let it slip—

# CHAPTER

## 3

CAME a thump from the shower, and Ben thought to himself: He's been in there a long time.

He slipped his seatbelt off, shoved off in that direction and snatched a handhold at the shower corner, catching a hazy image of Dekker upside down and crosswise in the stall.

What in hell? he wondered. He flung the door back—could make no sense at first of what Dekker was doing. Then he saw the bloody fingerprints on the locker door, the whole angle of Dekker's neck and arm forcing the soap dispenser panel shut on the clip. Dekker let it go of a sudden, the panel banged, and Dekker came off the wall at him, grappling for a hold, trying, he realized in panic, to get the cable looped around his throat.

He yelled, flailed out and caught the cable, their tumble winding them both into the cable Dekker was trying to get around his neck, and in sheer panic he hit him, hauled up on the cable and kept hitting him, hard as he could.

"Ben!" Bird yelled. He half-heard it: he just kept pounding away, his fist gone numb, his breath so choked he had no idea whether he was snagged in the cable or not. Bird grabbed his arm, yelling, "You're going to kill him! —Ben, dammit, stop!"

He realized then that Dekker was no longer fighting. Bird pried him out of his grip, Dekker floating loose and limp. Bird shook at him again, said, "God, have you lost your mind?"

Sympathy for a damned lunatic—no thanks for stopping Dekker from killing them. He was shaking from the scare Dekker had given him, he hurt from Dekker's hitting him, and Bird took Dekker's part.

"That sonuvabitch tried to pry the clip loose!" he said, and shook free of Bird's grip, grabbed Dekker, hauled him up again where the pipes and conduits were, and fumbled the roll of tape out of his hip pocket. Dekker was still limp as he started wrapping his wrist to a cold-water pipe, but he hurried, afraid he would come to.

"Stop it!" Bird cried, and came up and shoved him away.

His hand hurt. Bird was taking the lunatic's part. So he went down and got into stores and dispensed himself a beer: he didn't speak to Bird, he didn't trust himself to say anything at the moment. His jaw was sore. A tooth felt loose. His lip was cut. He had never had a fight in school and it had not been his idea to have one this late in his life, except a guy wanted to kill him. He yelled up at Bird, "Don't you let that sonuvabitch loose! Don't you do it, Bird!"

He took a gulp of beer, still shaking, his legs and arms jerking spasmodically, his breath so erratic he had trouble drinking. Not scared, mad, that was all. Damned mad. The guy tried to kill him and Bird shoved him off and started making sympathetic noises at the guy that had meant to do them both in. Bird owned the ship. Bird gave the orders. And Bird thought they could trust this sonuvabitch. . . .

"Toss me up a cold pack," Bird yelled down.

He did that: he opened up medical and sent it up to Bird and Bird didn't even look at him.

Bird cut the penlight. At least Dekker's pupils were the

same size and they both reacted, which was about all he knew to look for. Dekker was bleeding from the nose in little droplets. He mopped the air with his handkerchief, to keep it out of the filters, wiped Dekker's chin, then caught the cold pack and applied it to Dekker's face and the back of his neck.

Dekker began to show signs of life, confused, struggling with the tape for a moment before he reached over with his free hand and started tearing at it. Bird grabbed that hand, restrained it, saying, so only Dekker could hear, "Easy, easy, just stay quiet, it's all right. Just take it easy—you're not doing any good that way. Cut it out, hear?"

Dekker was breathing hard, staring at him or through him, he had no idea. Dekker wanted loose, couldn't fault him for that—couldn't be sure he was sane, either; and God only knew what was going on with Ben. Dekker gave a jerk at the wrist he was holding.

"Uh-uh," he said. "Just stay still. You leave that tape alone for a while. Hear? Just let it be."

Dekker said, "Liar."

"Yeah, right." You went to sleep and things were half-way under control and you woke up with two guys trying to kill each other and it wasn't highly likely to make sense. "You're bleeding into our filters. Just stay still—damn!" as Dekker choked and sneezed beads of blood. He snagged them with the handkerchief, one-handed, pressed it against Dekker's face. "I don't know what you did, son. Did you do something to piss Ben off?"

Dekker only shook his head, denial, refusal, he had no idea. Dekker blew blood into the handkerchief, gasped a bubbly breath and mumbled, "Cory. Call Cory."

"Not likely she's answering." He shoved Dekker's hand at his face. "Hold that." He snagged the ice-pack that was coming back after its impact with the wall, and gave Dekker that too. "Just keep the cold on it. If you're going to bleed, bleed into the handkerchief, all right? Don't blow at it. Just let it be."

Dekker looked at him past the bloody handkerchief and

the cold pack. Sane for a moment, maybe. Or just too miserable and too short of breath to be crazy for a while.

He collected himself and his headache and the remnant of his patience, shoved off and drifted down to Ben. Ben intended to keep his back to him, it seemed—so he turned, touched a cabinet and changed course. You got used to reading faces upside down or sideways. Ben's was sour, upset, and Ben was trying not to notice being stared at— only drinking his beer and trying to be somewhere else.

"I got a problem," he said. "Ben?"

"We both got a problem," Ben said shortly, as if he was not going to say much else. But Ben said then: "The guy was trying to kill us. He damn near had that clip undone, with a panel edge for a pliers. What was he going to do then, huh, Bird? You reckon that?"

"God only. Just go easy. We got a long way back."

"Go easy," Ben scowled. "Listen, I saved and did without all my life to get that 20 k, you understand? Nobody ever handed me a break, nobody ever gave me a damn thing, and here we have the best break anybody could look for—"

"It doesn't say we own that ship. It doesn't."

"God, Bird, —"

"We'll be all right." He could understand Ben's panic, on that level: the 20 k was hard come by, all right, so was everything. "We won't go under."

"Go under! You're old enough to know better, Bird. I put my whole life savings into this operation!"

"So have I," he said shortly, and hauled himself down and turned so he could see Ben's face rightwise up. "Thirty plus years' worth. And listen to me: you don't go hitting the guy again. He's had enough knocks to the head."

"So who is he? Who is he that you owe him a damn thing, Bird? Is there something about this guy I don't know? Somewhere you've met this guy before?"

He looked at Ben with this feeling they were not communicating again: he listened to Ben's single-minded craziness with the uncomfortable feeling he might yet have to take a wrench to his partner.

But just about the time he thought Ben might really blow, Ben gave this little wave of his hand and a shake of his head. "All right, all right, we're going in, abort our run— forget it, forget I said anything."

"What day is it?" Dekker asked from across the cabin. "Cory? *Cory?*"

"The 21st," he told him. "May 21st."

Ben raked his hand through his hair, rolled an anguished glance toward Bird. "I want rid of him. God only knows what happened to his partner. Or if there ever was a partner."

"*Cory?*"

"Shut up!" Ben screamed at Dekker. "Just shut it up!"

Bird bit his lip and just kept it to himself. There were times you talked things over and there were times you didn't, and Ben certainly didn't act in any way to discuss things at the moment.

"Just get our confirm out of Base," Bird said, and ventured a pat on Ben's shoulder. "It's all right, Ben. Hear?"

"Shut him up," Ben begged him. "Just shut him up for a while."

Dekker worked at the tape on his wrist, such as he could—his fingers were swollen, his ribs hurt, and he could not understand how he had gotten this way or whether he had done something to deserve being beaten and tied up like this—he flatly could not remember except the shower, the green ribbed shower, the watch—it was that day, something was going to happen to Cory—if it was that day... but Bird said May, not March.

January has thirty days. No, 31. February 28. March...

Thirty days hath September...April, March, and November...

"April, *May,* and November. Shut *up!*"

March 12. Thirty-one days. 21 less 12.

No, start in January. That's 30, no, 31, and 28—or 29 if it's leap year -is it leap year?

"It's not a leap year!"

28 and 12—no, start again. Thirty days in January—

"It's May effin' 21st, Dekker!"

Reckoning backward—twenty-one days in May—

Couldn't happen. Couldn't be then—

"You reset my watch, damn you! You're trying to drive me crazy!"

Bird came drifting up to him, put his hand on his shoulder, caught the cold pack that was drifting there and made him take it again. Bird said, quietly, on what previous subject he had no idea at all, "Time doesn't matter now, son. Just take it easy. We're about ready to catch our beam. You'll hear the sail deploy in a bit."

"Refinery Two," he said. He remembered. He hoped he did. He hoped it wasn't all to happen again.

"That's right." Another pat on his arm. Bird might be crazy as Ben, but he thought there was something decent in Bird. He let Bird tilt his head over and take a look at his eye, the right one, that was swelling and sore.

"Bird, do me a favor."

"You're short on favors right now, son. What?"

"Call my partner."

"We're doing all we can."

He didn't believe that. He especially didn't believe it when Bird pulled another cable loop out of his pocket and grabbed his other wrist. He resisted that. He tried to shove Bird off, but when he exerted himself he kept graying out and losing his breath. "Let me go," he asked Bird, quietly, so Ben wouldn't hear. God, his ribs hurt. "Let me loose."

"Can't do that, son. Not today. Maybe not for a while. Ben says you've been bashing things." The cable bit into his wrist and one clip snapped.

"Ben's a liar!" No. He hadn't meant to take that tack. He tried to amend it. A second clip snapped—woven steel cable looped around a pipe or something. He tried not to panic. He tried to be perfectly reasonable. "He's right. I was off my head awhile. But I'm all right now. Tell him I'm sorry. I won't do it again."

"I'll do that." Bird squeezed his shoulder in a kindly way. "Nobody's going to hurt you, son. Nobody means you any harm. We just got three people in a little ship and you're a little confused. Try to keep it a little quiet. You'll be all right."

The oxygen felt short. He tried not to panic. He didn't want them to tell him he was confused. "Bird," he said, before Bird could get away. "There's a 'driver right where I came from. Isn't there?"

"I wouldn't know that, son. I don't know for sure where you came from."

"79, 709, 12."

Bird nodded slowly. "All right. Yes. There is a 'driver near there."

He found his breath shorter and shorter. He said, calmly, sanely, because he finally found one solid thing they both agreed on. "All right. I want you to call it. Ask about my partner."

"You sure you *had* a partner, son?"

Reality kept getting away from him. Time and space and what had happened did. He fixed on Bird's gray-stubbled face as the only reference he had. "Just call the 'driver. Just ask them if they picked up my partner. That's all I ask."

"Son, . . . I honestly don't know what you might have been doing out there in a 'driver's assigned territory. You understand me?"

He didn't. He shook his head.

"How long have you been in the Belt, son?"

"Couple years." He wasn't sure of that number any longer either. He was sure of nothing in regard to time. He thought again—look at my watch—got to know—which direction to reckon.

"Freerunner?"

"Yeah."

"You ever make any money at mining?"

Ben asked those kinds of questions. "Maybe."

"Haven't ever done any skimming, have you?"

His heart jumped. He shook his head emphatically, wanting Bird to believe him. "No." He couldn't remember what conversation they were in, what they had just said, why Bird was asking him a thing like that.

Bird said, "We're just damn close to that 'driver's

fire-path, understand, and if we got one accident, we sure don't need another, you read me?"

Things were dark awhile. Bird gave him more of the soup, told him it was breakfast and they were all right. He wanted to think so, but he didn't believe it any longer. He heard voices near him. He thought he remembered Bird asking him questions after that. He wasn't sure. He dreamed he answered, and that Bird let him loose awhile to get to the toilet. But maybe that was the other time.

From time to time he remembered the collision. His muscles jumped, and then he would realize that was long past and he was still alive. "What time is it?" he asked, and Bird caught him by the side of the jaw, made him focus eye to eye.

"Son, *don't* cross Ben again. Don't ask him the time. Don't ask me. Your friend's dead. She's *dead*, you understand me?"

Bird's grip hurt. Bird was angry and he didn't know why.

"We got the confirm from Base," Ben shouted up.

"Yeah," Bird called back, and patted Dekker's face. "Got a draft coming from that vent. I'll get you a blanket, tuck you in—we're about to catch the beam."

"Yeah," he said. He was confused again. He thought that Bird had said that would be some time yet. But he'd given up knowing where they were. He hung there, nowhere for a while, listening to Bird move around. He heard hydraulics working, heard that series of sounds that meant a sail deploying. He thought, So we're going in. He didn't really believe it. It wasn't going to happen. It wasn't possible any longer. He couldn't come back from this. He just kept seeing the shower wall, the watch on his arm, perpetual loop, maybe because he *was* dead . . .

Bird came back with an armful of blankets and jammed one between his head and the pipes, one at the small of his back. "Don't lose that," Bird said, and took a bit of webbing and tied it around him and the blankets and the conduits, telling him he had to, it was for his safety, but he had stopped believing Bird. He thought about Sol Station. Mama coming home from work. Cory meeting him at Refinery One dock. Hi, there, she'd say. I'm Cory. And a person who'd been a lot of letters and a lot of postage would be flesh and blood...

If he could get to dockside, if they brought him that far, she'd be there... if he could get to the 12th he could get there again...

He'd run out on his mother, Cory had run away from hers. His mother just let him go. Cory'd sent those letters that would always be stacked up in her mail-file and waiting for her... He'd say, Don't read them, but Cory would. Then she'd be down with a guilt attack for days, and go off by herself and spend hours at a rented comp writing some damn letter home—but he wouldn't. There was a lot he should have said when he'd had the chance. But it was Cory that didn't get any more chances, and that wasn't fair.

"Stand by," Bird yelled up at him. "Dekker? Hear me? We're about to catch the beam. You all right up there?"

He thought he answered. He was thinking: We're not going home. We're not ever going home again. There's going to be all these letters stacked up and waiting for Cory, and Cory won't ever read them. They'll just tell her mother... and she'll kill me...

"Dekker! Dammit, pay attention!" Ben's voice. "Answer!"

"Yeah," he said.

*"Dekker!"*

He said it louder. The acceleration pressed his body against the blankets Bird had tucked between him and the pipes. The tape cut off circulation and his fingers on that hand went numb. He began to be dizzy: the ship was going unstable—all of it came back, the explosion and the ship tumbling, things flying loose—

"Cory!" he yelled; or maybe that was then. He had no more idea. Someone told him to shut up and he remembered that he had been rescued, but he had no idea where they were going or whether he was going to live.

Finally the pressure let up and he hung there with his head throbbing and the feeling slowly returning to his hands. Pressure in his sinuses and behind his eyes built to a blinding headache when he tried to wonder what was happening or where he was.

"What time is it?" he asked, but no one paid attention to him. He asked again, his voice cracking: "What time is it?" and Ben sailed up into his vision, grabbed him by the knee, grabbed him by his collar and hit him across the face.

"Shut up!" Ben yelled at him. He tried to use his knee and turn his face to protect himself. Ben hit him again and again, until Bird came in from below and pulled Ben off him, yelling at Ben to stop it. Bird said, "Go back to sleep, Ben." And Ben yelled back: "How can I sleep with What time is it? What time is it, God, I'm going to strangle him before the hour's out—I'm going to fuckin' kill him!"

"Ben," Bird said quietly, taking Ben by the shoulder. "Ben. Easy. All right. —Dekker, . . . *shut the hell up!*"

After that, it could have been next day, next week, a few hours, he wasn't sure. Ben came floating up to him, carefully took him by the collar and gathered it tight, and calmly said, right in his face, "It's my watch now, hear me? We're all alone. Do you hear me, Dekker?"

He nodded. He looked Ben in his close-set eyes and said yes again, in case Ben hadn't understood him.

"You want to know what time it is, Dekker?"

He shook his head. He remembered that made Ben crazy. Ben wound his grip tighter, cutting off the blood to his head.

"If you ask the time just one damn more time I'm going to break your neck. You understand me, Dekker?"

He nodded. The edges of his vision were going. Ben went on looking at him with murder in his eyes.

He remembered—he was not sure—Ben taking pictures of him while he was unconscious. He thought, while Ben was shutting the blood away from his brain, This man is crazy. He's crazy and I'm not that sure about Bird. . . .

"Hear me?" Ben said.

He tried to say yes. Things got grayer. The ship was spinning. Ben let him go and went away. Then he gulped several lungfuls of air and started shivering. He wished Bird would wake up, he wished he knew where he was going now, and whether Cory would be waiting on the dock. They said Refinery Two, but that was like saying Mars or the Moon: places were different, and you didn't know where you were going even if you knew the name.

The Belt was like that. It was always like that. The rules changed, the company tried to screw you, but Cory always did the figuring, Cory had had college, Cory knew the numbers, and he didn't.

He wished they had never taken him off that ship. He wished they had never found him. Or maybe he was dreaming. He had no idea now what was real.

Dekker was off his head again, mumbling to himself, just under the noise of the pumps and the fans. Ben put a hand over that ear and tried to concentrate on the charts, feeding in info that was going to come in handy, because Big Mama didn't like to tell freerunners anything except what she had to—but with a spare and illicit storage, an enterprising and close-mouthed freerunner could vastly improve on Mama's charts, look at the sector she offered you, and *tell* which runs to take at any cost and which to lease out if you had any choice.

So you paid close attention while you were running, you listened to the sectors you were passing through blind and used your radar for what it was worth, on all the sectors around you while you ran on Belt Management's set, (they swore) safe course out and home; and you filed every piece of information you could get your hands on, listening for the older tags, making charts of the new, figuring where good rocks might cluster, assembling the whole moving mass of particles around you, because when Jupiter swept the Belt on his twelve-year course, slowing rocks down, speeding rocks up, and now and again changing certain orbits by a million or so k or flinging certain rocks clear out of the Belt, those all-important numbers did change. It was Sol's set of dice, but Jupiter did make the game interesting, and the freerunners with the best numbers and the best records were the freerunners that survived. Rocks hit each other now and again, 'driver-tenders got careless, and now and again you might find an uncharted big bit of some old rock long since ground to bits and used, a chunk still running the old orbit path, give or take what rocks did to each other and what Jupiter did and what the occasional 'driver did when it went firing loads through the Belt to the Well: not much to hit out here, but now and again, generally thanks to some 'driver, they did, with shattering results. Sometimes, again, strange rocks just wandered through, old bits of comets, Oort Cloud detritus, God only: every rock had its path, they all danced with Sol, but some were distant partners—and with the mass they were hauling now, you just hoped to hell Mama liked you, and gave you solid numbers.

"We're not real easy to stop," he had said to Bird, among other things.

"We could brake," Bird had said.

And he: "Yeah, yeah, and we're carrying more mass than those cables are rated for."

"Won't happen," Bird said.

Thinking like that infuriated him. The thought of the rigging failing, the thought of, at best, a walk outside for repairs, at worst, the whole sail failing beyond repair—*Trinidad* taking, at this heading, the long, long fall into the Well— made him crazy. He was already holding on to his temper with his fingernails and Bird came out with *It won't happen*.

He had fantasies of killing Dekker.

Maybe Bird.

But that was as crazy as Dekker was.

He kept feeding in the information. He kept building and refining his portable record. He ignored Dekker as much as possible. Thing about null-*g*, you couldn't get your finger to stay in your ear. Not easily. He thought about his earplugs, over in the cabinet, but those worked *too* well for his peace of mind.

He cast a glance askance at Bird sleeping so quiet in his net, where they had strung it between the galley and the number one workstation, Dekker being just too close to the spin cylinders. Dekker might have been crazy long before this—and Bird just might be soft enough to let the guy loose on his watch. That was all it took, let Dekker near a wrench or, God forbid, get his hands on something sharp.

All that blood in the ship, all those little red splatters on the suits—did a cut on the forehead bleed like that?

He had to have it agreed with Bird. They had to keep that guy confined—somehow, someway. They couldn't sleep in nets for a month, they needed the spinners: and the idea of being blind and tucked in a spinner for six hours wondering what Dekker was doing on Bird's watch already upset his stomach.

And, damn, he intended to keep every move logged, everything they did, everything this Dekker did, every spate of What time is it?

Dekker would get the time, all right. Logged on and logged off.

He'd get the expenses written down, too, exactly the way he knew how to do it in a record Management would accept—because Benjamin J. Pollard wasn't letting an old man's softheadedness rob them of a break like this. Hell. No.

# CHAPTER 4

REFINERY Two was only slightly prettier than a rock, but it did come welcome—that k-plus wide sooty ring that you only caught sight of on camera—and most to Bird's knowledge were eager to see it, and did turn the optics on, long before it was regulation that you had to get visual contact. There she hung, magnified in the long lens, spinning with a manic vengeance, with her masts stuck up like spindles and her stationary mast surfaces bristling with knobby bits that were pushers and tenders, and shuttles from the Shepherds and such. A few, hardly more than ten or so at any one time, counting company rigs waiting crew change, were ships a lot like *Trinidad*, a whole lot like *Trinidad*, if you took plan B on your outfitting, and opted for green in the shower.

A lot of the fitting inside Refinery Two was a lot like *Trinidad*, too, except, one supposed, if you got down to corporate residence levels, and there was about the same chance of freerunners seeing that in person as getting a guided tour of the company bunker on Mimas.

Belters lived and Belters died and Refinery Two just

rolled on, this big factory-hearted ring which was the only close to g-1 place miners and tenders in R2 zone ever got back to. She swallowed down what the Shepherds gathered in, she hiccuped methane and she shat ingots and beams and sheet and foam steel. She used her own plastics and textiles or she spat them at Mars, in this year when Jupiter was as convenient to that world as Sol Station was. But nobody knew what went to Mimas. Some said what was down there repaired itself and had more heart than any company exec—but that was rumor and you didn't want to know. Some said it wasn't really the ops center it was reputed to be, in case of something major going wrong at the Well: some said it was the ultimate bunker for the execs—but you didn't say *war* in polite society either and you didn't think too much about the big frame that sat out there aswarm with tenders and construction craft, a metal-spined monster that took rough shape here at the source of steel and plastics before it moved on to final rigging at Sol. You called what was going on out in the Beyond a job action or you called it a tax strike or you called it damned stupid, but if you were smart you didn't discuss it or that ship out there and you didn't even think about it where Mama might hear.

A-men.

"Well," he sighed, "she's still here. Kept the porch light on and the door open."

Ben didn't say, What's a porch light? You never could get a rise out of him like that.

"Used to sit outside at night," Bird said, "look up at the stars—you know what a shooting star is, Ben, lad?"

"No." Ben's tone said he was not at the moment interested to know. He was working approach, as close as his second-class license would let him. "I'm about ready to hand off. You got it?"

"Yeah."

"Dockmaster advises they copy on the request for meds. They're on their way."

"Good on that." He saw Ben furiously ticking away at the comp. "—I got your handoff. Take it easy."

"Take it easy. We got meds and customs swarming in here, we have to have the records straight."

"Everything's in order. I checked it. You checked it. —You're sure they copy on that mass."

"Yeah. I made 'em say-again." Ben was going through readout. No papers. Everything was dataflow. BM wanted forms, and it was all dataflow, not at all like the old days when if you fouled up some damn company form you got a chance to read it over slow and easy and say it right. Now in this paperless society the datalink grabbed stuff and shoved new blanks at you so fast you didn't have time to be sure all your answers made sense.

"You got all that stuff," Bird said. "And welcome to it. Damn, I hate forms."

"No worry."

Ben had a sure instinct for right answers. Ben swore it was a way of thinking. Ben input something and said, "Shit! Shut him up!"

He only then realized Dekker was talking, mumbling something in that low, constant drone of his. "I can't half hear him, he's all right."

"I can hear him! I can damn well hear him— Where are we? Where are we? What time is it? I tell you—"

"Easy."

"I've *been* easy. I'm going to kill him before we make dock, I swear I am."

"No, you're not. He's being quiet. Just let him alone."

"You're losing your hearing. You can't hear that?"

"Not that loud."

"The guy's crazy. Completely out of it. Only good thing in this business."

"Ben, . . . just—drop it, Ben. End-of-run-nerves, that's all. Just drop it, you mind?"

There was a cold silence after that, except the click of buttons. And Dekker's voice, that *was* loud enough to hear now and again once you thought about it.

Long silence, except for ops, and approach control talking back and forth with them, walking them through special procedures.

"I'm sorry," Ben said stiffly.

Maybe because they were closer to civilization now. And sanity.

"Where are we?" Dekker asked.

"God!" Ben cried, and leaned far back in his seat. He yelled up at Dekker: "It's June 26th and we're coming into Mars Base, don't you remember? The president of the company's going to be at the party!"

"Don't do that," Bird said. "Just leave the poor guy alone."

"He's alone, all right, he's damn well alone. Another week and we'd be as schitz as he is."

Another call from Base: *"Two Twenty-nine Tango* Trinidad, *this is ASTEX Approach Control: tugs are on intercept. Stand by the secondary decel."*

"Approach Control, this is Two Twenty-nine Tango. We copy that decel. We're go." He shut down his mike, yelled: "Dekker! Stand by the decel, hear me?"

"Break his damn neck," Ben muttered.

There was no time for debate. They had a beam taking aim. Approach Control advised them and fired; pressure hit the sail and bodies hit the restraints—they weren't in optimum attitude thanks to that ship coupled to them, and it was a hard shove. Dekker yelled aloud—hurt, maybe: they had him padded in and tied down with everything soft they could find, but it was no substitute.

It went on and on. Eventually Dekker got quiet. Hope to hell that persistent nosebleed didn't break loose again.

*"Two Twenty-nine Tango* Trinidad, *this is ASTEX Approach Control: do a simple uncouple with that tow."*

"Approach Control, this is Two Twenty-nine Tango. We copy that uncouple. Fix at 29240 k to final at 1015 mps closing. O-mega."

Bird uncapped the button, pushed it, the clamps released with a shock through the frame, and One'er Eighty-four Zebra went free—still right up against them, 29240 k to their rendezvous with the oncoming Refinery and they were going to ride with the tow awhile, until the outlying tugs could move in and pick it off their tail.

Ben muttered. "I got everything customs can ask on that ship. Got all the charges figured, too."

"Just leave it, Ben."

"I want that ship, Bird. I want that ship. God, we got the proof—I got all the proof they need—"

"Ben, —"

"Look, they do their official investigation. But this guy's *incompetent*, he was *incompetent* when we boarded. What's he going to do, ask 'em the time? The law's on our side." Ben was cheerful again. "We got it, Bird, we got it."

"Let the guy alone," he said. "Forget about that ship, dammit!"

"I'm not forgetting it. Hell if I'll forget it. We're filing on it. Or I am. You can take your pick, partner."

"There's such a thing as wanting things too much. You can't ever afford to want things that much. It's not healthy."

"Healthy, hell. *I'll* take care of us. All you have to do is sit back and watch me go, partner, I know the law."

"There's things other than law, Ben. —Just stow the charts, hear me?"

"I'm not stowing the charts."

"We're going to get searched, dammit, just put the damn things in the hole or friggin' dump 'em, we can't get 'em off this time—"

"Guys run 'em in all the time, customs doesn't give a damn—just say they're vidgames. They don't even boot to check."

"Ben, dammit!"

"I haven't spent all this work to give up those charts. They're going to go over us with a microscope, Bird, —"

"Thirty years nobody's found that hideyhole, not customs and not the lease crews. Just drop 'em in. You think they're going to go at us plate by plate over a rescue?"

*"Two Twenty-nine Tango* Trinidad, *this is ASTEX Approach Control: tugs are 20 minutes 14 seconds, mark."*

"Approach Control, this is Two Twenty-nine Tango. We copy: 20 minutes 14 seconds. No problem, tow is clear. Proceeding on that instruction."

Ben said, "You got an Attitude this trip. I don't understand it, Bird, I swear I don't understand it."

"You know Shakespeare, Ben?"

"Haven't met him."

They were still speaking as they made dock. Barely.

"We got 'er," Ben said.

Several significant breaths later Ben said, "I'm sorry, Bird."

"Shakespeare's a writer," Bird said.

"One of those," Ben said.

"Yeah."

"You got him on tape?"

"There's a tape. Hard going, though."

"Physics?" Ben asked.

"*Two Twenty-nine Tango* Trinidad, *this is ASTEX Dock Authority, check your pressure. Will you need a line?*"

"We copy 800 mb, B dock. No line, we're 796."

"*Trinidad, we copy 796. Medical units standing by on dockside. Stand by life systems sample.*"

"Shit," Ben groaned, "they're going to stall us on a medical. They damn well better not find some bug aboard, I'll skin him."

"Won't find any bug. Get our data up, will you?"

They were nose to the docking mast. *Trinidad* shuddered and resounded as the cradle locked. She hissed a little of her air at the sampler.

ASTEX said: "*Welcome in*, Trinidad. *Good job. Stand by results on that sample.*"

The dockside air went straight to the back of the throat and stung the sinuses, icy cold and smelling of volatiles. It tasted like ice water and oil and it cut through coats and gloves the way the clean and the cold finally cut through the stink Bird smelled in his sleep and imagined in the taste of his food. Time and again you got in from a run and the chronic sight of just one other human face, and when you looked at all the space around you and saw real live people and faces that weren't that face—you got the sudden disconnected notion you were watching it all on vid, drifting there with only a tether and a hand-jet between you and a dizzy perspective down the mast—worse than EVAs in the deep belt, a lot dizzier. Dock monkeys kited about at all angles, checking readouts, taking samples, talking to empty air. Bird's earpiece kept him informed about the meds inside the ship, the receipt of the manifest and customs forms at the appropriate offices—

"Morris Bird," the earpiece said, thin voice riding over the banging and hammering of sound in the core. "This is officer Wills, Security. Understand you found a drifter."

He hated being sneaked up on, hated the office-sitters that would blindside a man and made him look around to see where they were—or whether they were there and not a phonecall. He turned and saw three of them in ASTEX Security green, sailing his way down the hand-line.

"Yessir," he said, before they got there. "Details have already gone to BM. Any problem?"

"Just a few questions," Wills said. Before he got there.

# CHAPTER 5

"YOU have any theories to explain what happened?"
Wills asked. The cops hung face to face with him, all of
them maintaining position with holds on the safety-lines,
and you about needed the earpiece to hear at the moment
over the thundering racket from a series of loads going down
the spinning core. Bird, mindful of the Optex Wills was
wearing, shrugged, shook his head and said, mostly honestly:
"Could've caught a rock. Helluva bash on one side. On the
other hand, the bash could've been secondary. Maybe he
was working real close in and just didn't see another one
coming, dunno, really, dunno if it's going to be easy to tell.
We didn't go outside, just got a look on vid. We did make
a tape."

"We'll want that. Also your log. Did you remove anything from the wreck?"

"We took out the rescuee and the clothes he was
wearing. Nothing else. We washed 'em and he's still wearing
'em. He had his watch, and nothing in his pockets. He's still
wearing the watch. Anything else we left aboard, even his

clothes and his Personals. You wouldn't want to open up without a decon squad. It's a real mess in that ship."

"Any idea where the partner is?"

"Evidently she was outside when the accident happened. He kept trying to call her, kept trying when he was off his head, I guess he tried til he couldn't think of anything else. They're from R1. Her name was Cory. That's all we ever figured out. His life systems were near gone, ship was tumbling pretty bad. He'd taken a lot of knocks." He hoped to hell that would cover Ben's ass about the bruises. He felt dirty doing it, but he would have felt dirtier not to. "Kid was pretty sick from breathing that stuff, kept hallucinating about having to call his partner—evidently did everything he could to find her, sick as he was." He tried to put Dekker in the best light he could, too, fair being fair. "When we got to him, I guess he just finally realized she was gone. Fever set in—he's been off his head a lot, just keeps asking over and over for his partner, that's all."

"What would he say?"

"Just her name. Sometimes he'd yell Look out, like he was warning someone. Kid's exhausted. Like when you give up and then the adrenaline runs out."

"Yeah," Wills said. "Didn't happen to say why they were out of their zone?"

"He didn't know they were out of their zone."

"So he did say something else."

"We had to explain we were taking him to R2. It upset him. He was lost, disoriented. The accident must've happened the other side of the line."

Cops never told you a thing. Wills grunted, monkeyed along the lines toward the hatch as if he was going inside. The other officers followed. But one of the blue-suited meds was outbound, towing a stretcher with Dekker aboard, and the other meds were close behind. The cops stopped them at the lines just outside the hatch, delayed to look Dekker over, talk to the meds, evidently asked Dekker something: there was a lot of machinery noise on the dock—they must be loading or offloading—and he couldn't hear what they said or what Dekker answered. They only let the meds take him away, and that course came past him.

They had wrapped Dekker up in blankets, had him strapped into the stretcher, and Dekker looked wasted and sick as hell. But his eyes were open, looking around. The meds brought the stretcher to a drifting stop and said, "You want to say goodbye?"

It was one of those faces that could haunt a man, Dekker's lost, distracted expression—but Dekker seemed to track on him then.

"Bird," he said faintly through the noise and the banging overhead. "Where're they taking me?"

Dekker looked scared. Bird wanted it over with, wanted to forget Dekker and Dekker's nightmares and the stink and the cold of that ship, not even caring right now if they got anything for their trouble but their refit paid. He sure didn't want an ongoing attachment; but that question latched on to him and he found himself reaching out and putting a hand against Dekker's shoulder. "Hospital. That's all, son. You're on R2 dock. You'll be all right."

Bird looked at the meds, then gave a shrug, wanting them to go, now, before Dekker got himself worked up to a scene. They started away.

"Bird?" Dekker said as they went. And called out louder, a voice that cut right to the nerves, even over the racket: *"Bird?"*

He exhaled a shaky breath and shook his head, wanting a go at the bar real bad right now.

Ben came out of the hatch with their Personals kits. The police stopped him and insisted on taking the kits one by one and turning them this way and that. They were asking Ben questions when he drifted up, and Ben was saying, in answer to those questions, "The guy was off his head. Didn't know what he'd do next. Screaming out all the time. Thinking it was his ship he was on. We had to worry he'd go after controls or something."

He scowled a warning at Ben, but not a plain one: there was the Optex Wills was making of every twitch they made. Ben was looking only at the officers. He said, to explain the scowl, "You'd be off your head too if you'd been banged around like that."

"In the accident," Wills said, fishing.

"Ship tumbling like that," he said. "The wonder is he lived through it. *Couldn't* have helped his partner. All he looked to have left was his emergency beeper, and when that tank blew, it didn't go straight—you got this center of mass here, see, and you get this tank back here—"

You got too technical and the docksiders wanted another topic in a hurry.

Wills said, interrupting him, "Go into that with the Court of Inquiry. We'll want to log those kits. Leave them with us and we'll send them on to your residence. What's your ID?"

"On the tag there." Ben indicated his kit. "1347-283-689 is mine. Bird here's 688-687-257. Ship's open. Look all you like."

"You can go now."

You never got thanks out of a company cop either. Bird scowled, looked at Ben, and the two of them handed their way up lines toward the hand-line. A beep meant a boom was moving. Red light stained the walls. But the alarm was from the other end of the big conduit- and chute-centered tunnel that was the cargo mast. You could get dizzy if you looked at the core itself, if you let yourself just for a moment think about up and down or where you were. Bird focused on the inbound gripper-handle coming toward him, ignored the moving surface in the backfield of his vision—caught it and felt the first all-over stretch he'd had in months as it hauled him along. Ben had caught the one immediately behind him—he looked back to see.

"Customs," he remarked to Ben, in a lull in the racket from the chutes. "I hope they've talked to the cops."

"No trouble. We haven't even got our Personals. Cops've got 'em. Cops have got everything. They gave me this receipt, see?" He used his free hand to tap his pocket. "Hell, we're just little guys. What are we going to have? We'll get a wave-through. You watch."

"They'll give us hell."

"So don't tell 'em it was out-zone. We reported it where the rules say. We got rights. Meanwhile we're gone into a public contact area and there's no use for them to check us, is there?"

"Rights," he muttered. "We got whatever rights Mama decides to give us, is what we got. —What did you tell that cop about Dekker? Did you tell them he was crazy?"

"Hey, they don't need my help to figure that. The meds belted him in good and tight when they took him away."

"What did you tell them?"

"I said he wasn't too clear where he was. They asked about the bruises, and I said he got loose, all right? I said he was after the controls and he's crazy, besides which he fought us when we had to get him back and forth to the head."

"That's a couple of times, Ben, for God's sake..."

"Hey. We got this guy tied to the plumbing, bruises all over him, all ages, what are we going to say, it was a month-long party out there?"

"Yeah," he said, and shut up, because the chute was sucking another load down, and down here you could hear the hydraulics. His stomach was upset. It had been upset for the last week, when it had been clearer and clearer Dekker was not going to be able to support a thing they said, that Dekker was liable to say anything or claim they'd met eetees and seen God. This is it, Ben had said when Dekker had tried to get at the engine fire controls. They'd put Dekker to bed taped hand and foot: Dekker had screamed for an hour afterward, and Ben had gotten that on tape too.

He had wanted to erase that video. Dekker had enough troubles without that on permanent record with the company: Dekker could lose his license, lose his ship, lose everything he had, and he didn't want to hand BM the evidence to set it up that way—but Ben had said it: Dekker wasn't any saner than he had been. Dekker would have been dead in a few days if they hadn't found him, and as much as they'd done to patch the kid together, he didn't seem likely to need much of anything but a ticket back to the motherwell and a long, long time in rehab.

"Poor sod," he said.

Ben said: "Good riddance." And when he frowned at him: "Hell, Bird, I've seen schitzy behavior before, I've seen damn well enough of it." There was profound bitterness behind that: he had no idea why, or what Ben was talking about, but Ben didn't volunteer anything else. Ben was talking about the school, he decided, or the dorms where Ben had spent what other people called childhood. It didn't matter now. The trip was over, Dekker was with the meds, the whole business was out of their hands, and Ben knew Shakespeare wasn't a physicist. Good for him. They'd patch up their partnership and take their heavy time while somebody else leased *Trinidad* out—and paid them 15-and-20 plus repairs and refit: could do that all the time if they wanted, but you didn't get rich on 15-and-20 while you were sitting on dockside spending most of it.

Got to give up sleeping and eating, he was accustomed to joke about it.

Ben would say, intense as he always was when you talked about money, We got to get us a break, is what.

They got off the line in customs, explained they didn't have their Personals, the cops had them, no, they didn't have any ore in their pockets and they didn't have any illegal magmedia on them, all the records were on the ship, yes, they had contacted another ship out there, they'd hauled a guy in, they hadn't taken anything off it, no, sir, yes, ma'am, they'd tell Medical if they got any rashes or developed any fevers or coughs, Medical had already told them that, yes, sir.

God, no, they didn't volunteer to customs that it was an out-zone ship, yes, sir, they'd reported the contact, no, it was an instructed contact: the agents' questions were strictly routine and the stress-detectors didn't beep once.

Customs validated their datacards, logged them both as active in R2, and they went back to the hand-line for the lifts.

Ben said, conversationally, while they were each trailing by a gripper handle, Ben in front this time: "You can quit worrying about the charts. Got the card in my pocket."

His heart went thump. "Dammit, Ben, —"

"Hell, it was all right."

"I told you leave it!"

"Where the cops'd find it?"

"You could've said. God!"

"Hey. You're a lousy liar. Was I going to burden your conscience? You passed the 'detectors—so did I, right?"

Ben could. Stress detectors depended on a conscience.

"You're just too damn nervous, Bird."

"You could've left 'em under that plate, dammit. You could've done what I told you to do—"

"You want to get caught, *that's* the way to do it— conceal something on the cops. I didn't conceal it. It was right in my pocket. God, Bird, *everybody* does it. If they wanted to clamp down, why do they let us have gamecards? Or vid? Why don't they check that? I could code the whole thing onto a vidtape."

"If too many people get too cocky, just watch them. Some nosy exec gets a notion, and you can walk right into it, Ben, you can't talk your way out of everything."

"Everything so far."

"Hell," he muttered. They were coming to the end of the hand-line, where you got three easy chances to grab a bar and dismount in good order instead of (embarrassment) shooting on down to the buffer-sacks that forcibly disengaged a passenger before the line took the turn.

Ben was first on the bar, swung over and pushed 8-deck on the lift panel before he caught up. "I'll ride down with you."

"So where else are you going?"

"Where do you think?"

"Shit, Ben."

"Somebody will. Probably there's a line of creditors on the ship. But we'll at least get the 50/50. Damn right we will."

"You're bucking for back trouble, and you won't get a damn thing. There'll be a rule."

"Young bones. I won't stay long. And there's no real

choice, Bird, you have to file the day you get in. *That's* the rule."

"So file at the core office."

"Trust those bastards? No do. Corp-deck's it."

"Out of your mind," he muttered as the car arrived. They floated in, took a handhold. The car sealed, clanked and made its noisy, jerky interface with the rotating heart of the core, and started solidly off down the link. He didn't argue any more with Ben. If Ben had the fortitude to go down a level past helldeck an hour after dock and stand in some line to file to claim the poor sod's ship, he didn't know what to do with him. He only sighed and stared glumly at the doors and the red-lit bar that showed them approaching another take-hold.

"Bird, you got to take better care of yourself. What have you got for your old age?"

"I'm in it, and I don't plan to survive it." The car clanked into the spoke, and they shot into it with the illusion of climbing, until they hit that queasy couple of seconds where distance from R2's spin axis equaled out with the car's momentum as far as the inner ear was concerned. Then the ear figured out where Down was, the car's rolling floor found it a half-heartbeat later, and bones and muscles started realizing that the stimsuits you worked in, the spin cylinders you slept in and the pills you took like candy didn't entirely make up for weeks of weightlessness. Knees would feel it; backs would. The red-lit bar that showed their distance from the core was shooting toward 8-deck.

Meg and Sal were on 6; he had found that out on their way in. He'd left a message for them on the 'board, and he planned on company tonight. That and a drink and a long, long bath. Maybe with Meg, if she answered her messages.

If she wasn't otherwise engaged.

The car stopped. He got out, on legs that felt tired even under 8's low g, muscles weary of fighting the stimsuit's elastic and now with g to complicate matters. Ben got out too, and said, "Meet you at the 'Bow."

Ben didn't even slow down. He just punched the button to go on down as far as the core lift went, to 3.

Bird shook his head and headed off down 8-deck—damned if he was even going to call up his mail before he hit the bar at the Starbow. Mail would consist of a bank statement and a few notes from friends as to when they'd gone out and when they'd be back. His brother in Colorado wrote twice a year, postal rates out here being a week's groceries and Sam not being rich. It wasn't quite time for the biannual letter and outside of that there wasn't mail to get excited about. So screw that. He just wanted a chance to get the weight off, get a drink, see a couple of familiar female faces if fate was kind, and never mind Ben's wet dreams. Ships didn't come without debts, probably multiple owners, not mentioning the bank, and the company would find some technicality to chew up any proceeds they could possibly make from the ship, til it was hardly worth the price of a good rock, plus expenses. Ben was going to work himself into a heart attack someday, if ulcers didn't get him first.

The meds said, and the Institute taught you, some null-g effects got worse every time you went out: your bones resorbed, your kidneys picked up the calcium and made stones, and the body learned the response—snapped to it faster with practice, as it were, and Ben believed it. Science devised ways to trick gravity-evolved human systems, and you took your hormones, you spent your sleeptime in the spinner and you wore the damn stimsuit like a religion. Most of all you hoped you had good genes. They told gruesome tales of this old miner whose bones had all crumbled, and there was a guy down tending bar in helldeck who had so many plastic and metal parts he was always triggering the cops' weapon scans. He didn't intend to end up like that, nossir, he intended eventually to be sitting in a nice leasing office collecting 15-and-20 on *two* ships, free and clear of debt, and letting other poor sods get their parts replaced. He had no objection to Morrie Bird sitting in that office as vice president in charge of leases, for that matter: Bird had the people sense that could make it work, and Bird couldn't last at mining forever: they'd already replaced both hips.

So Bird went off to the easy adjustment of 8-deck in

blind trust that Mama would do the right thing and assay their take in the sling and record all the data they'd shot to the offices during their approach—while the one of them who'd worked for Mama for two years and knew the way Mama worked took the immediate trip down to 3-deck, and the frontage of the debtors' barracks he'd once lived in. Oddity was endemic hereabouts—you could look down the strip now and spot a guy dressed head to foot in purple, but he wasn't necessarily crazy—at least you could lay money he didn't claim the company'd done this or that or ask you the time every five minutes.

God, he hated remembering this place. But he still kept an ultra-cheap locker there, with a change of clothes—

Because you had to dress if you were going to go call in debts, nothing rad or rab, just classic. Good sweater, good pants, casual coat. Real shoes. You had to look like solid credit to get what he was after. And his legs were in good enough shape, all things considered: he'd foreseen this, and taken his pills and worked out all the way back—burning off the desire to strangle Dekker, Bird had probably thought, regarding those unusually long sessions on the cycle and the bounce-pads.

But he could walk, at least. He could peel out of the coveralls and the stimsuit, shower in the public gym, dress himself in stationer style and go down past helldeck to 1, where he weighed Earth-normal, walking like an old man, it might be, but he'd taken a painkiller while they were coming in, and it was just a matter of taking it easy—going where Mama knew damned well a spacer directly back from a run wasn't comfortable going—which was why so many tricky little company rules said you had to sign the forms in person, on the day you docked, at the core office if you wanted Mama to take her time—or in the main offices if you wanted Expedition. The inner decks being notoriously short of lawyers, a lot of spacers never even realized Expedition was possible.

You could put in a company-backed claim on salvage, for instance: go to the general office, file to have the company run procedures and wait it out; but that threw it into

ASTEX administrative procedures, which ground exceedingly slow, and put it in the hands of ASTEX Legal Affairs, which usually found some t uncrossed or i undotted. Up there you could file a claim for expenses, but you only got that after Mama had adjudicated the property claims, unless you knew to file hardship along with it; and you could file for salvage, but you had to know the right words and be sure the clerk you got used them: half the low-level help at the core couldn't spell, let alone help you with legalese.

Best of all, you could pay a call on an old classmate from the Institute, break the queue *and* get the precise by-the-book words on the application.

8-deck was transient and gray and lonely: you might see a handful of miners in from their runs, not to mention the beam-crews and the construction jocks and whoever else worked long stints in null; you saw the occasional Shepherds and 'driver crews, transiting to their own fancy facilities, and a noisy lot of refinery tenders and warehouse and factory workers and dock monkeys on rest-break (there were a lot of refinery operations on 8)—and sometimes, these days, some of the military in on leave—but you didn't get anything like the flashy shops or the service you had down on helldeck. Here you kind of bounced along between floating and walking, being careful how fast you got going, being careful of walls and such—your brittle bones and your diminished muscles and your head all needed to renew acquaintances with up and down—slowly, if you were smart.

The public part of 8 was all automats, even the sleeperies— no enterprising station freeshop types behind the counters, even for the minim shifts that Health & Rehab would let a stationer work on 8. It was robot territory, just stick your card in a slot and you got a sleepery room or a sandwich or the swill that passed here for bourbon whiskey: but that was all right for a start, everything was cheaper than helldeck and your whole sense of taste was off, anyway, for the first bit you got used to refinery air.

You found no luxury here that didn't come out of an automatic dispenser, unless you were working for the company—

in which case you saw a whole other class of accommodations, the adverts said: they said a whole lot better came out of the vending machines behind those doors—but Bird had never seen it. 'Driver crew and Shepherds didn't need the waystops that miners did—if they were up here they were slumming, on a 1-hour down from some business in the mast; but generally they went straight to helldeck, where big ship officers and tech crew had cushy little clubs and free booze, and Access with all sorts of perks on the company computers.

Adverts said you could get at least a sniff of those perks, even as a miner—if you let the company own your ship and provide your basics; but that meant the company could also decide when you were too old or you didn't fit some profile, and then you were out, goodbye and good luck, while some green fool got your ship. God help you, too, if Mama decided you weren't prime crew on that ship, and some company-assigned prime crew got shunted out to work tender-duty for three years at a 'driver site—which effectively dumped all the relief crews back at the Refinery onto the no-perks basics, to do time-share in a plastics factory. Work for the company and you could fill in your time swabbing tanks in the chemicals division til you got too old, and then they set you down on retirement-perks and let you sweep floors in some company plant to earn your extras.

Hell, no. Not this old miner.

But a lot of years he had been coming back to 8, and he'd seen changes—or maybe he had felt livelier once upon a time. 8 these days echoed to footsteps, not to music and voices. The bright posters had all gone years ago, the month the company had gone over to paperless records-keeping. The company favored gray paint or institution green, except for pipes that came wrapped with hazard yellow and black.

You used to get the unofficial bills here too, the paste-ups that would appear overnight—saying things like TOWNEY LIES and FREE PRATT & MARKS—Mama hadn't liked those in the best days, nossir, the bills that said things like EQUAL ACCESS and the take-one flyers that used to give you the news the company wouldn't. They'd all gone. No paper.

You still found the old barred circle, you still found PEACE and FREE EMIGRATION scratched in restroom plastic, right alongside the stuff you could figure Neanderthals must've carved in Stone Age bathrooms—you found MINIM and RABRAD and SCREW THE CORP, along with other helpful suggestions in the toilets . . . far more frequent here than down on helldeck, he guessed because sanding down the panels in light g made a bitch of a lot of dust, and spray paint was as bad. Or maybe it was because Security didn't come up here much and the ordinary maintenance crews were contributing to it too. So the crud and the slogans stayed in the bathrooms, not even covered by paint, while 8-deck got nastier and dirtier and showed its age like some miners he knew.

He was in a sour mood—maybe the cops, maybe Ben's stupid chance-taking with the datacard, maybe just that he was tired of the shit and tired of feeding a company that was trying to blow itself to hell; and right now specifically because the cops had their Personals, which meant he was stuck in the stimsuit and his day-old coveralls until the cops turned his kit loose: damned if he was going to buy new knee and ankle wraps at vending machine prices.

But he did buy a bottle of aspirin, a cheap men's personals pack, and a far too expensive bottle of cologne: the hips were gone, the ankles were going, the hair was gray and thinning, but the essentials still worked and he did have hopes. He walked into the bar in the front of the ambitiously named Starbow Hotel and, with his card in the slot at the desk, punched Double and Guests Permitted.

In the midst of which transaction somebody grabbed him from behind and swung him around, clean off his feet.

"Hey!" he yelled, as the turn brought him face to face with dusky-skinned Sal Aboujib, who grabbed him the same as the one behind—

That *had* to be Meg Kady.

He hugged Sal back in this bouncing unstable minim-g dance. He said, "Damn, you're both fools!"

But he'd hoped with all his heart they'd got his message.

"Old friend of Marcie Hager's," Ben said at the counter, down in Records. "Is she in?"

The clerk looked over his shoulder, looked at him, looked at the line that stretched out the door, said, uncertainly: "She might be."

"Thanks," he said warmly, smiled, and on an adrenaline rush and a dogged determination not to show the pain, walked cheerfully past the counter, through clerk territory and on back to the hallway: men in good suits didn't stand in that line. Ben Pollard didn't. He walked as far as an office that said *M. Hager, Technical Supervisor,* wiped the sweat off his face, rapped on the door, opened it and leaned in the doorway.

"Hello there, beautiful."

Marcie Hager looked up from the desk, looked non-plussed for an instant. Then: "Ben Pollard. God, I thought you'd shipped out to Mars or something."

"Mind if I sit?"

She said, after a second's consideration, "Of course not. Come on in. Coffee? —Are you all right? You're white."

"First day back. Came down from 8. —You're looking good."

"Last time I saw you, you were in Assay." Marcie got up, poured two instant coffees. "White? Sugar? —Back from where?"

"White. Plain. —Assay for a while. Then I bought into a ship."

Marcie's brows went up. Estimation of his finance clearly did. So did her interest. "Social call?"

He grinned, sat down with the coffee, said, after a deliberately slow sip, "I ran into a piece of luck. I thought you might be able to help me."

You went to the company school, you learned what bought what from whom: some were cheap and some cost more than a freerunner could possibly pay, but you always kept track of your old classmates and, on call, you did favors such as Marcie Hager was about to—because favors got you favors, and that, for one thing, meant he didn't have to stand in that line.

"Yeah?" Marcie said, and sat down and sipped her own coffee. "Sounds interesting."

Meaning Marcie thought somebody with a ship equity four years out of school just might be going somewhere even a Technical Super in Records might find useful—even if freerunning was as high-risk an investment as there was, it was disposable cash and high-interest returns in the short term; and it was capital that a Technical Super in Records, with all her Access perks, couldn't lay hands on—

But not as if Marcie was going to ask cold cash for favors. In Marcie's position, subject to company scrutiny, you never left a datatrail.

"Just a little expediting. A claim for salvage. I don't want to be at the bottom of the list of creditors. This guy owes us, big."

Marcie's left eyebrow titled. "Like in—major salvage."

"Ship salvage." He leaned back, eased a very sore set of muscles in his back, took another slow sip of coffee. "Number's One'er Eighty-four Zebra."

"Mmmn. Not from this zone, Benjie. That's a *long* procedures delay. Where in *hell* have you been?"

"Yeah, well, —but—" He turned on his nicest smile. Rule One: you didn't deal in plain words. Rule Two: you were careful about cash. Rule Three: you didn't ask favors of prigs—but Marcie certainly wasn't that.

Marcie said, "Just so you know," and turned on her terminal. Marcie's kind might not trade in cash, but Marcie said, while she was idly tapping her way through a chain of accesses, "What ever happened to Angie Windham, you know?"

"Don't know. But you know Theo Pangoulis went bust? He bet everything he had on that shop—could have told him nothing succeeds in that location."

Marcie scowled. That wasn't the kind of offering you gave: they were seriously negotiating now, and her fingers stopped moving.

He said, "On the other hand, I do hear from Harmon Phillips."

"Do you?"

"You know he's on Aby Torrey's staff. Up in Personnel."

"That's interesting," Marcie said. "—Have you got your numbers ready?"

It was swill, but there was g enough to keep it in the glass and you in your seat if you sat easy, and there was sure as hell good company—the two prettiest sights in the belt, Bird swore: Soheila Aboujib, a grin gleaming on her dark face, her ears and fingers aglitter with her reserve bank account, laughed, elbowed Meg in the ribs and said, "He's been out there too long."

"Let me tell you," he said—and did, in the light traffic of the Starbow's autobar: they were in a crowd of dockers and tender- and pusher-jocks. The piped music adjusted itself up, affording a little privacy to people at the back corner table.

"Yow," Meg said, when she had the essentials. "So Ben's down in Admin, is he?"

"If he didn't break a leg," he said. "I tell you, I'm worried about him. He's been acting like a crazy man from the time we linked on with that ship."

"I dunno." Meg was what the young folk called rab, and the hairdo this time was what his generation called amazing, shaved bare up the sides, red as fire atop, a mass of curls trailing down her neck and all these bangles on her ears. With Meg you'd never know what you'd see—sometimes it was braids and sometimes that hair turned colors. Meg Kady, she was, Hungarian on one side, Sol Station Irish on the other, Meg said—but sometimes it was Scots; and once, overheard in a bar, she'd said it was Portuguese Martian. God only knew about Sal Aboujib, who had a coffee complexion and coffee-black eyes: with Sal it was braids today, a hundred of them, with metal clips, but you never knew—sometimes that hair changed styles and colors too.

Either one of them was too pretty for a gray-haired, brittle-boned old wreck—had to be his brains they were after picking, he was sure: get him drunk and ask him questions, buy a dinner and try to get specific coordinates out of glum, close-to-the-chest Ben—neither one of which had ever been too successful. But you never figured what made friends: you just took up with people, found out who you could trust, and if you found a good one you kept those contacts polished, that was all—never could remember how they'd taken up with him—well before Ben, back when he'd been working with various hire-ons, something to do with a mixed-up drink order (he'd been far gone and so had they) and a game of pitch-the-penny in quarter g with a crowd of equally soused tender-jocks.

Never could remember who'd finally gotten the bill.

"From over the line?" Meg asked, regarding the strayed ship, and he said, "One'er number. Clean-talking kid, real young, maybe twenty, twenty-two. Partner's dead out there. Tank blew. His partner was outside."

"Brut bad luck," Sal said with a shake of her braids. A little grimace. Then: "You seriously got rights on that ship?"

"Ben thinks so. Thinks so enough to risk his knees. He's been working out for weeks. I figured he was going to pull this, but I did think he'd at least check in first."

Meg said: "Want us to track him? We've been scuzzing along on 6, in no hurry, figuring on a friend showing up—could've done 3 two days ago. We can go down . . ."

"He'll get back. If he doesn't I'll call the hospital."

"You two feuding?"

"Ben gets a little over-anxious."

"Yeah, well. That's Ben. —But if it worked, if you did get salvage—can you just take the ship?"

"It's not going to work. Company'll find an angle. You watch."

"Que sab?" Meg said. "But if it did—"

"Meg, he's been damn crazy. Ever since we found that ship. I tell you, I was afraid—" He'd been too long away from a drink. He hadn't dared indulge, on the return trip, and this one hit him like a hammer. He almost said: Afraid of him, —but that word could get back to Ben, and he didn't want that. He said, instead, "Ben works real hard. But sometimes he gets to looking most at where he's going, not what he's doing."

Meg reached out and laid a hand on his arm. "Yeah, well, cher, you want us to talk to him?"

"No, no, it's between him and me. Let him get this bug out of his works. He's going to find nothing but a string of bills to that ship's account. It's probably in hock for its last fuel bill. If we get expenses I'll be happy."

"Can't blame him for trying," Sal said. "Hell, I'd brut kill for a chance like that."

You never knew on some things whether Sal was kidding.

"Look," Meg said, squeezing his wrist. "What say you screw the med-regs, cancel here and come down to 6 with us?"

"Meg, my old knees—"

"Old, hell. We got a nice berth there at the Liberty Bell. You just stay here and collect Ben when he comes in. We'll party tonight. Get the spooks out. We knew we were waiting for somebody."

"Yeah," said Sal. "Just give us a little time to clean up the room."

"Clean up, for God's sake—what are we? Strangers?"

Meg elbowed his arm, getting up. "Hey, we just got to get a few things out of it. Female vanity."

He gave a shake of his head and sipped his bourbon. A few things out of the room. The things might well be male. But he charitably didn't suggest that.

And it was (charitably) true Meg and Sal might do some feminine fussing-up in the place; and it was no real surprise that Meg and Sal might bounce a casual acquaintance or two in favor of him and Ben—they were simpatico, for some reason God only knew; they were also on *Trinidad*'s lease-list, though they were just in themselves, and in no position to take a ship out for another month or three.

"See you below," they said, and went.

Pretty woman like that could've talked him down to helldeck tonight if she'd insisted: pretty woman like that—

Who lied like a company lawyer.

Meg was an ex-shuttle pilot, native to Sol Station (or

Mars)—accused at Sol Station of political agitation (or arrested for smuggling, depending on how many Meg'd had). Either one in fact could've gotten her deported down to the motherwell if they'd gotten the evidence she'd evidently managed to dump. In either case, the company had (she said) invited her to leave places conveniently close to sources of luxuries. Meg had taken up with Sal when she got here—Sal herself had gotten bounced out of Institute pilot training, Sal never had said why, but it didn't matter: there were a number of things Sal *would* have done, and you could take your pick. Sal was smart, she'd had at least her class 3 license, and by his reckoning, she had what the good numbers men had: she went past the numbers to *see* the Belt in her head. It was formal schooling and experience Sal lacked—and the way Sal had been getting it, in the School of Last Resort, you just hoped to live long enough.

He was sure the pair skimmed, occasionally—just clipped a little off another freerunner's tag if they didn't know him personally.

But not from their friends. Or if they had—he figured they'd pay it back when they had it to pay and never tell you they stole it. That was the kind they were, even Sal, who was real loose about a lot of things, and he counted that honest. Everybody got desperate enough sometime. He'd done it himself once or twice or three. And paid it back to the guys he'd done it to, without ever telling them he'd done it. He understood that kind of morality.

So he'd lease *Trinidad* to Meg and Sal now and again—a classier ship than they could generally get, with equipment other rigs didn't have. They were learning. They took advice. He'd lease to them this time, if they'd been ready to go—he *liked* them, that was reason enough.

But all of a sudden there was this other ship: he'd seen that idea light up in their eyes—that if by some stroke of cosmic luck they did get a second ship, then *somebody* had to be leasing it, didn't they, maybe on a primary basis? Surely he wasn't going to sell it to the company. God only how far their imaginations took those two.

Damn, he asked himself, what was the jinx on that ship,

that it made Ben crazy and now it had Meg and Sal thinking about something they just weren't damn-all good enough yet to ask for?

While nobody gave two thoughts to the poor sod in hospital who was screwed out of everything he had, not to mention the owners and the lease crews over at R1 who might be screwed.

Sometimes he thought he was too old and too far from his beginnings. Sometimes he dreamed about pine trees and sagebrush and sunsets.

But he dreamed very realistically about poverty too—recalled what it was to scrape and save to get up to space for schooling; then by desperation and some fast talking to make it out to Asteroid Exploration, Inc., to a program that let you lease-purchase: they'd been that desperate for miner pilots then, desperately looking, in the start-up of the current push.

Most of them that had come out then were probably dead now: he knew about the ones on R2, and he was the last of that lot. The plain station labor that had gone into refinery jobs and processing—God only: maybe a lot of them were dead too. He remembered young faces; he remembered the talk about what they were going to find, how they were all going to get rich on company wages.

Yeah. And now that the mapping was mostly done and the company had its 'drivers working real smoothly, the company didn't want the freerunners anymore. E-co-nomics, they said. Freerunners didn't fit the system the way it had grown to be, all company-run, and ASTEX stacked the deck any way it liked. You couldn't complain and you couldn't get clear—because that took money you didn't have; or if you did sell your ship back to the company you got to Sol Station with, after passage, 50, 60 k in pocket, back at your starting place aged 50 plus with your bones all brittle and that 60 k all you had for your retirement and your medical bills.

But he read his brother's letters and he knew beyond a doubt that thirty years was too long an absence for anyone: Earth had changed, attitudes had changed—people worried about things that didn't worry him and they didn't worry where he knew they should. Earth was at war with its colonies, shooting hell out of human beings, while Earth-folk argued whether the eetees at Pell had souls, and blamed the government for the market crash when company merchant ships went on strike about the damn visas. You had the rabs walking around in shave-jobs and glitter and scrawling slogans because society was going to hell and the human race with it; you had the Isolationists who wanted to shut down the far star-stations and not speak to anybody but Earth and Mars and the Belt; and you had the Federationists and the Separationists and the pacifists and the neo-nationalists and the New Evangelicals all of whom thought they knew how to reform the human race; you had the Euconomists and the anti-geneticists and the ones that claimed there was a youth drug from space that the governments had embargoed, but the rich could still get it; and you had various defense departments in the United Nations and United Internationals building those bloody huge warships to enforce the embargoes against the rebels in far space, while the Free Trade Party that had won the election in the PanAsian Union wanted to get rid of all the embargoes, cancel the visas and let people go where they wanted to go—but out there in deep space things changed, things changed constantly, faster than anybody could keep up with. He had not quite been born when somebody out at Cyteen had discovered Faster Than Light and rewritten the book, and hell if he understood FTL physics *or* its politics, but the company built its ships out of the metal he'd found. They'd armed the traders of the Great Circle before he was born, and right now they were building those new translight carriers to Teach the Colonies a Lesson. All this had been going on near a hundred years, but it was breeding at FTL rates now— they'd shot the rab reformers at the company doors back in the '15, they'd established the visas, they'd shunted Earth Company operations out into half a hundred subsidiaries like ASTEX that only tangled the company's books beyond the capacity of any single Earth-based government to audit, and nobody was responsible for a damned thing. They'd had draft riots at Sol Station a year ago, four kids killed, they'd had two officials up for falsifying military supply records, so the rumor had been, —while out here in the Belt there were construction workers and those great steel skeletons you weren't supposed to talk about, that eventually, after a handful of years, powered up and pushed themselves on toward Sol Station for finishing. All this went on. But if you looked at the vid on the wall and wondered what else might be going on you didn't know about, the company News & Entertainment division was running a program on hydroponic gardening.

Damn crazy life. Sometimes you sat out there in the Belt with one other guy in a little ship and wondered what would happen to you both if humanity did go crazy and blow itself to hell. Lately you kept an anxious ear to the news Mama doled out daily and tried to figure out who was actually running things in the motherwell, because damned if the company was going to tell you about it in so many words: ASTEX, Asteriod Explorations, was part of the Earth Company, which had the whole damn United Defense Command on its leash; the whole thing was a damn alphabet riot—ASTEX, EC, SS, UI, MEX, and FN, for starters, and everybody was sleeping in more than one bed, governmentally speaking—

Which he preferred not to. Maybe the kids in the colored hair and the glowpaint and the nose-rings were right. Maybe humankind would blow itself up. Maybe Belters would survive out here and breed themselves a whole new human race—

One that thought Shakespeare was a physicist.

He got up and carded himself a drink—canceled the rez for himself and Ben at the Starbow, while he was at it, since he hadn't used the key that had dropped from the slot; and seriously wondered if his back was going to take it on 6—in various considerations.

"Bird?"

Well, so Ben had survived. Ben was back with excitement bubbling in his voice. He turned around as Ben stopped and caught his balance against the vending machine.

"Bird, we got a chance. We got a real chance." A gasp

for breath. "Broke my neck getting up here." Another breath. "Ship's got a double registry—over on Refinery One. Paul Dekker and Corazon Salazar. *She's* Cory, *she's* the partner—and his title's completely clear."

"You're kidding. He's no more than a kid."

"Dunno what she was, but they owned that ship. They owned her clear—no liens, no debt, nothing, Bird, we got it! We got the only claim against it! We're first in line!"

He picked up his drink out of the dispenser and just held it in a shaking hand. You didn't think about things like that, you didn't ever start wanting something that just couldn't happen. But knowing they had bills to meet and the company paying claims so slow nowadays—

God forgive, he started thinking then—if Dekker was crazy—if they really were *due* that ship . . .

"Your name's Dekker," they asked. Meds. He remembered them. But how he had gotten here he couldn't remember. He didn't know how long he had been here. He didn't know how long he had been out just now. He asked questions back, but he never got much help from their answers.

Sometimes he thought he was on a ship like his own ship; sometimes he thought he had been hallucinating all of it. "Bird?" he asked sometimes. Sometimes he was afraid Ben was going to come floating up and hit him.

Sometimes he thought Bird and Ben had been something he'd dreamed in this place, and he simply couldn't figure how he had gotten here, unless Cory had somehow gotten the ship straightened out and brought him in. He felt tranked. He thought, This is a hospital. This is Base. We're home. We're safe. . . .

"Where's your partner?" someone asked him.

He slitted his eyes open, lifted his head so far as he had strength to do. He saw a white coat, a man writing on a slate.

"Where's your partner?" the med asked him. "Do you remember?"

Black. An alarm screaming. The ship jolted and spun—

he struggled against the weight of his own arm to reach the controls, wondering whether the autopilot could possibly straighten them out or if it had engaged already. He didn't know. He hit the switch. Something jolted the ship, threw him against the workstation—

"Mr. Dekker. Do you recall what happened?"

Green-walled shower. The watch showed March 12.

"What day is it?" he asked. But they didn't answer him. He tried to see his watch, but he couldn't move his arms. "Bird, what time is it? For God's sake, *what time?*"

The man in white wrote on his slate and said, "What time do you think it is?"

"Give me my watch. Where's my watch?" It wasn't on his wrist. It had lied to him. Or it was his only way back. "Where's my watch, dammit! —I want my watch!"

The man left. Others came in and shot something into his arm. After that he could hear his heart beating heavier and heavier, and he was slipping into dark.

"Bird?" he asked, thinking Ben must have something to do with this. "Bird, wake up—Bird, help me—*Bird, wake up and help me!*"

# CHAPTER 6

GLASS touched glass, in the Liberty Bell, on 6. "Here's to friends," Sal said, and Bird, telling himself it was far too soon to plan on anything, had made up his mind not to tell Meg and Sal a thing.

But that had gone by the side the minute they'd seen Ben's smugly cheerful face.

"You got it!" Meg said, before they even got their drink orders in.

"We're at least tracking," Ben said. "We're gaining on it. They're going to expedite the claim."

For the life of him, Bird couldn't figure how Ben managed to get around people in offices. But he did.

So here they were, on their way to feeling no pain at all, .7 g be damned.

It wasn't as if Meg and Sal would leave them cold tomorrow if the deal fell through. They weren't that kind. But they sure as hell enjoyed the party tonight.

They enjoyed it afterward too, piled into two adjacent rooms in the Bell—actually the party traveled and they had to throw this one pair of tender-jocks out twice, who complained they'd been invited.

"No, you weren't!" Sal Aboujib said. And shut the door and slid down it, laughing. Meg was laughing too much to help her, so they hauled her up and picked her up, Sal yelling that they were going to drop her on her head.

So they fell on the bed—which at low g meant a slow bouncing, all of them, while up and down went sort of alcoholically crazed for a moment.

"God," Bird said, falling back on what he thought was mattress. "I'm zee'd."

Meg fell on him with a vaporous kiss and he stopped caring which way was up.

Turned out when they waked it was Ben and Sal's bunk they were in, but that was no matter, Ben and Sal had just gone off next door. But they had last night's sins to pay for—a hangover in low g, with your sinuses and your ears playing tricks, was hell's own reward.


"Cory?" Dekker asked. "Cory?" But he was not in the ship, he was inside white walls with white-coated medics who asked him over and over "What happened to Cory?" and he couldn't altogether remember what their truth was, or what they wanted him to say. He asked for Bird, and they asked him who that was, but someone said in his hearing that that was the man who'd brought him in.

From where? He tried to remember where he had left Bird, or what had happened, but it always went back to that shower stall, the watch showing him the time . . . March 12. And it was his choice what would happen that day . . .

He slept again. He was more comfortable when he waked. His hands were free and they let him sit up and gave him fruit drink. A man came and sat down by his bed with a slate and started asking him questions—How old are you? Have you any relatives? all rapid-fire. It was the sort of thing they asked if you'd had an accident, something about next of kin. It scared him. The shower in this room wasn't the shower he remembered, he could see the white walls through the door. He'd jumped ahead. Cory wasn't with him, and he was in a hospital having to go through these questions like some actor in a vid. It couldn't be real. God, he didn't want his mother to hear he was lying in a hospital somewhere she couldn't help, he'd screwed up enough: he just said he was from Sol Station and shut up.

"What was your relationship with Corazon Salazar?" they asked him then, cold and impersonal. He said, going through the ritual, "She's my partner."

But if he went on answering, they'd write it down as true and he'd be here, he couldn't go back to the shower, he'd be out of the loop and he'd have no chance to fix it: Cory would be dead then. No way back.

The man asked, "Did you have relations with her?"

That made him mad. "That's not your business."

The man asked: "Did you ever quarrel?"

"No."

The man made a mark on his slate. "What did you invest in that ship?"

He didn't understand that question. He shook his head.

"Did you put any money into it?"

He shook his head again. "That wasn't the way it worked. Cory was the money." Cory was the brains too, but he didn't admit that to a stranger. Cory was the one who had no question what she wanted. But the man didn't ask that. The man said, "What happened out there?"

He couldn't go back to the shower now. No green walls. White. He thought, What should I tell them? And the man said, "Does that upset you? You said Ms. Salazar was working outside the ship. Why?"

He said, not sure what he might have changed, "We were working a tag."

"Did Ms. Salazar regularly do the outside work?"

"I'm the pilot." Two answers right. He felt surer now.

"I see. So she hired you. And gave you half interest in her ship. For nothing."

He nodded.

"Where did you meet?"

"We wrote letters back and forth. We'd been writing a long time. Since we were kids."

Another note on the slate. "Then it was more than a business relationship."

"Friends."

"You didn't have a falling-out, did you?"

He looked at his watch. But it wasn't there. They'd taken it.

The man said, "Did you quarrel?"

"We never quarreled."

"She always did what you wanted? Or didn't she, this time?"

He didn't understand. He shook his head. He thought about the shower, but it wasn't vivid this time. Even the green seemed faded.

The man asked: "Why did you cross the line? To cover what you'd done?"

He didn't understand what they were getting at. He shook his head again, looked furtively at his wrist, remembered he mustn't do that. It upset people. Like Ben. It upset Ben a lot. . . .

"Tell me the truth," the man said. "What were you doing out there?"

"We had a tag," he said. "We were working it."

He lost the room of a sudden. It was dark and there were the boards lighting and blinking. He tried to find the safe white wall again.

"Did you leave her there?" the man said. He couldn't remember what he'd just said, he could only see the boards, and someone was holding him down. He got an arm free. People were yelling. There were flashes of the white room, there were faces over him and they were all holding him. He yelled: "Let me go!" and felt a sharp explosion against his shoulder, but they kept holding him, telling him to calm down.

He said, out of breath, "I'll be calm. I'll be calm, I don't want any more sedatives—"

Because when they drugged him he had no idea where he was or how long he was out or where he went in that dark . . .

He opened his eyes again with a terrible leaden feeling,

as if he weighed too much and he couldn't wake up—but he knew where he was, he was in the hospital. Two very strong men were holding him down and asking him how he felt now.

He was out of the dark. He said, when he had gotten a whole breath, "I'm fine. I'm fine. Just don't give me any more shots, all right?"

"Will you talk to us? Will you behave?"

"Yes," he said.

The man in white leaned over him then, took hold of his wrist and asked him, "Are you still worried about your watch?"

His heart gave a little thump, making him dizzy. But he knew it was a test. He wasn't supposed to ask the time. They beat him when he did that. Or gave him shots. He shook his head, wanting to stay awake now.

The doctor said, "We're going to take some readings while we talk. Is that all right?"

Another test. He made up his mind then: it didn't matter what the truth was. If he didn't say exactly the right thing they'd give him shots. He'd been in trouble in his life—but this was serious. This was a hospital and they thought he was crazy.

The doctor asked him, "Are you still worried about your watch?"

Black. The siren going. He heard something beeping wildly. A timer was going off and he didn't remember setting it. He could see the doctor frowning at him—he tried to track on the doctor: he knew how important it was. And when he did that, the beeping slowed down.

"That's better," the doctor said. "Are you all right? Do you want to tell me what just happened?"

He got a breath. He said, calmly, trying to pay no attention to the beeps, "Cory was outside. We were working this tag—"

"On which side of the line?"

"On this side." Stupid question. The beeps went crazy a moment, when his heart did. He got it calm again. "We were working this tag. A big claim. Big. Kilometer wide . . ."

"Are you sure, Mr. Dekker?"

"It was that big. And we were out there. We'd shot our tag, but it wasn't a good take. Cory said—" The beep sped up again and he slowed it down, staring at the wall, remembering Cory saying, We're not letting those sons of bitches— "—We had to fix it. And she was going to go in—"

"You couldn't handle a rock that size."

"It was stable. Not that bad." Again the beep. He said, before it could get away from him. "But this damn 'driver— he wasn't on the charts—he wasn't slowing down. I said—I said, 'Cory, get in here, Cory, he's still not answering me, Cory, get inside—'"

"Get the trank," the doctor said. The beep became a steady scream. Like the collision alert. Lights were flashing.

"I said, I kept saying, 'You sonuvabitch, my partner's out there, my partner's outside, I can't pull off—'"

They hit him with the trank. Two of them were holding him. But he kept screaming, "'I can't pull off, you sonuvabitch!'"

"It's not working," somebody said.

The doctor pushed his eyelid up, leaning close, said, looking elsewhere, "Get the chief," while breath came short and the monitor was beeping a steady panic:

"They didn't list it," he said. "It wasn't broadcasting—"

The doctor said, "Make up another dose. 50 ccs."

"It wasn't on the damn charts—"

"Easy," the doctor said. "We understand you. —Cut that racket."

The beeper stopped. He took an easier breath.

"Good. Good." Another dark space then.

Somebody had had an accident, an R1 ship turned up in R2 zone, probable 'driver accident—which should be BM's job, but it was in William Payne's day-file, straight from Crayton's office, in General Administration.

The memo said: Handle this. We need minimal publicity.

Payne paged through the file. A freerunner pilot in hospital—making wild charges about a 'driver captain violating regulations . . .

God. The Shepherd Association was hardnosing it in contract talks, the company trying to avert a strike—Payne shook his head. Not quite his job, but it was very clearly an information-control situation, and that *was* his department, as executive director of Public Information. One could even, if one were paranoid, suspect a set-up by the Independents— but it seemed the pilot's physical condition was no fake, and a miner was dead.

Bad timing—damned bad timing for this to come in.

The question was how far the rumors had already gotten. Freerunners had done the rescue. That was one problem. News & Entertainment could run another safety news item, give the odds against a high-*v* rock, remind everyone it was a remote possibility—or maybe best not to raise the question. The Shepherd Association wanted an issue. It was begging for a forum. Meanwhile the police were going over the wreck, poking about—*that* was a department Public Information couldn't entirely handle. Best keep them away from the issues in the case.

A release from the pilot was the all-around best fix. Evidently BM had a crack team going over that ship—that was good: if there was a mechanical fault, settle the problem there, no problem. Get a statement from the pilot, fix culpability if there was any—

Not with a company captain, damned sure, and not in a lawsuit that could bring the Shepherd Association in as friends of the court. That certainly wasn't what Crayton meant by "settlement."

A hand touched Dekker's face. It gave him the willies. He couldn't do anything about it. Couldn't even open his eyes yet.

"Mr. Dekker, would you answer a question for me? There's something I don't understand."

He got a breath. Two breaths. Did get his eyes open, marginally. "What?"

"Why the watch?"

"Kept the time."

"Mr. Dekker."

Clearer and clearer. It was the doctor again. He made a try at sitting up, inched higher on the pillows.

"How are we feeling, Mr. Dekker?"

"Like shit."

"You were talking about the watch."

Beep.

"*Explain* to me about the watch, Mr. Dekker. Why does it upset you?"

He wished he knew the answers to that one. The doctor stood there a long time. Finally he thought, Maybe this one's going to listen. He said, tentatively, "We had some stuff linked to the main board. *Way Out* was old. The arm didn't work off the main board. It was supposed to be a three-man, you know, the way some of the ships used to be..."

"Go on, Mr. Dekker. The watch."

"You couldn't work the arm and see the log chrono. Real easy to lose track of time when you're working and we didn't trust her suit indicators. So we used my watch." His voice shook. He was scared the doctor was going to interrupt him and order him sedated if he lost it. And he wasn't sure if he was making sense to the man. "It only timed an hour, you know, the alarm was a bitch to set—so we'd set it to January 1. —What day is it?"

"July 15th, Mr. Dekker."

He despised crying. He didn't. He wouldn't. The doctor was getting impatient. He took deep breaths to help him. "Don't give me any shots. I need to figure—how far is it..."

"Don't distress yourself, Mr. Dekker."

January has thirty-one days. February is 28. March, 12. 71.

Out there in space. Seventy-one days. She'd have been out of air in 4 hours. Oh, God, ...

"Mr. Dekker."

"March has thirty days. Or 31?"

"31."

12 from 31 is 19. Nineteen days in March. April is—

Thirty days hath September. . . April, *June*, and November. . .

The doctor patted his shoulder. One of the orderlies came back.

"No!" he yelled. "I've almost got it, dammit!"

They shot him with it anyway. "Be still," they said. "Be still. Don't try to talk now."

49. They found me on the 21st. 49 and 21. Do you count the 12th twice?

I'm losing it . . . start again.

Or can I trust my memory?

It was still 6-deck and still a waiting game. Every day Ben went down and checked the lists. Every day it turned up nothing but PENDING. *Trinidad* herself was still hung up in the investigation—there was no way they could lease her, no matter that there were a dozen teams applying; there was no way they could even start her charge-up, and every day she sat at dock she was costing money instead of earning it. Bird haunted the supply shops, pricing the few small parts she needed; but they couldn't even get access to her, the way Bird put it, to fix the damned clothes dryer.

"You can't hurry the police," Ben said, trying to put a reasonable face on things. "It can't be much longer."

And Sal, between sit-ups—they were working out in the gym: "I thought you could fix anything."

"Not in my range of contacts," he said, frustrated himself. Nudging Security was asking for more investigation.

"Hell," Bird said, mopping his face, leaning on the frame of a weight machine. "I sincerely hope they just get something decided. My heart can't stand much more of this prosperity."

Meg didn't say anything but, "Easy, Bird."

Payne said: "No, dammit, just don't answer. Tell Salvatore—no, *don't* tell Salvatore. I'll talk to him. . . ."

Hell of a day. A Shepherd crew and a tender crew mixed into it in a bar and a bystander was in hospital; and *this—*

Some clerk in R1 had return-sent the Salazar kid's mail as Deceased, Return to Sender, and the sender in question, Salazar's mother, had hit the phone asking for information on her daughter. The operator in ASCOM, knowing nothing about it, had sent the call to Personnel, the confused clerk that took the call in R1 Personnel there couldn't find Salazar's file and insisted to the bereaved mother there was no such person, while *her* supervisor had tried to stall for a policy clarification out of R1's Administrative levels, then realized she was out of her depth and tried to send it through to a higher level, after which it had bounced confusedly from department to department until a secretary in Legal Affairs put the call on hold and the woman hung up.

Salazar's mother was on the MarsCorp *board*, for God's sake. Nobody had told him. Nobody had told Towney. Nobody had flagged the dead miner as a problem—

Alyce Salazar's next phone call had hit the president's desk. Not Towney's, in ASTEX. *Hansford*, in the Earth Company's Sol Station headquarters. Hansford had called Towney, Towney had had to release the file, and Hansford's office had released the details to MarsCorp.

Alyce Salazar had found out Dekker had survived, and immediately claimed it was no accident, he was a scoundrel who'd seduced her daughter, kidnapped her to the Belt, and killed her for her money.

Which turned out to have been a fair amount, before expenses. There was a binding surviving-partner clause—

But Alyce Salazar was an *angry* woman, one *damned* angry woman . . . and lawyers were talking to lawyers at very expensive phone rates.

"Mr. Crayton is on the line," Payne's secretary said.

God, . . .

"Mr. Crayton, sir, . . ."

Crayton said, "Have you got the letter?"

"Yes. I have it up now."

"One went to Security."

Oh, my God, . . . "I'm sorry, sir. I certainly didn't—"

"Not from your office. From Ms. Salazar. She wants that boy's head. You understand the implications? We *need* this mess cleared up. We don't want him in court. I want you to patch this up. Get the facts straight. We've got to have an answer for this one."

Still no police clearance. And on a certain afternoon in the Bell, when Ben was in the bar doing some technical reading, Meg slipped into the chair across the table, leaned both arms on the table and said, "Benjie, cher, let's go do talk."

He'd thought at first Meg was just bored, Bird being out of sorts for the last couple of days; and he wasn't totally surprised, back in her room, to end up in bed in mid-shift, —not the first time for him and Meg, but it was all the same unusual, even if he was entirely sure—and he was—that Bird wouldn't take exception. The side-shaving was a turn-on. The mop on top and down the back was several shades brighter than elsewhere, but it was beyond a doubt Meg's right color; and she had some kind of creature tattooed around one leg—snake, Meg had told him once, early on in their acquaintance. Bird had told him what kind it was and said if it bit you, you were dead in three minutes. He thought that might well fit Meg, if you got on her bad side.

But he wasn't on her bad side. He had it figured by then that Meg had ulterior motives, though Meg wasn't the sort to hold a man off while his brains scrambled—he swore he couldn't do anything until she'd told him what was going on, but she proved that wrong: she had him truly gone before she started asking him about the ship, about Dekker, about the way Bird was stewing and fretting—

"Bird's severely upset," Meg said. "You think there's a chance on that ship? —Because if there isn't, you got to talk to him."

"Dekker's brain's gone. No question. Yeah, there's a solid chance on that ship, there's a good chance."

"Bird says if you get anything it'll have to be in court. Bird's saying you won't win. That it's all just a waste. But he doesn't act it. —Is there anything the company can turn up? I mean, you didn't seriously transgress any regs out there..."

So that was what was bothering Meg. Meg and Sal had

to be looking for a lease for their next run, if that ship wasn't going to come through—or if they were only going to sell it to the company. Meg and Sal hadn't been betting elsewhere: that was what he suddenly figured, and they were down to decisions. "There isn't going to be any court. I promise you. You know what Bird's problem is? He's scared he's going to make money. Every time you get to talking about it—he just looks off the other way. If I hadn't filed on that ship, you think he'd ever have done it? Hell, no. He'd have waited till he got his legs. Then he'd have said, well, it's too late, there'd be other creditors—you tell me what goes through his head, Meg. I swear I don't know."

"Dirtsider."

"So?" One of Meg's stories had her born on Earth, too. But that didn't seem to be the version Meg was using today. "Are they all like that? Is it something in the water?"

"Bird grew up poor."

"So I grew up an orphan. So what's that got to do with anything?"

"It's habit with him: when he gets enough—that's all. That's all he wants from life. He doesn't want to be rich. He just wants enough."

It didn't make any sense—not at least the why of it. He held the thought a moment, turned it over, looked at its underside, and decided he wasn't going to understand. "Well, it's not enough for me. Damn well not enough for me."

Meg sighed. "Haven't ever seen enough to know what enough is."

"Damned short rations," he said. "That's what Bird's 'enough' comes to. And it doesn't keep you fed when your legs and your back give out. Doesn't get you insurance."

"Insurance," Meg chuckled. "God, jeune fils. . . ."

"That's a necessity, dammit! Ask me where I'd have been if my mama hadn't had it."

"Yeah, well. —She was a company pilot, wasn't she?"

"Tech." He rolled over. He didn't like to talk about things that were done with or people that didn't come back. They didn't matter. But the example did. "You don't get any damn where halfass protected. Insurance—my company schooling—Bird's knowing who to lease to—"

"Like us?"

Oh, then, *here* was the approach. Meg was looking at him, chin on hands, putting it to him dead-on, with no Bird for a back-up. He didn't want to alienate Meg and Sal— especially Sal. They weren't the best miners in the Belt, but they had other benefits—not all of them in bed. And he kept asking himself if he was using good sense, but the answer kept coming up that there might be miners better at their job, but if you wanted a couple of stick-to-a-deal, canny partners, present company and Sal weren't damn bad.

Some of Bird's friends, now—had his affliction. And they were going broke or had gone.

Meg said, "You suppose you could put in a word with Bird, explain how we'd be reasonable. We'd work shares."

Not every day somebody as tough and canny as Meg needed something from him—seriously needed something. He toted it up, what the debts might be, what the collection might be. If one looked to have a long career leasing ships—one needed a couple of reliable partners who knew the numbers. And Sal in particular had possibilities—if Sal could get a grip on her temper and shake out that who-gives-a-damn attitude. Sal also had useful contacts. While Meg—

He said, he hoped after not too long a pause: "I could talk to him. What are friends for?"

"Wake up." Someone shook at Dekker's shoulder. "Come on, Dekker. Come on. Come out of it."

He didn't want to come back this time. It was more white coats. He could see that with his eyes half shut. But there was dark green, too, and the gleam of silver. That didn't match.

A light slap at his face. "Come on, Dekker. That's fine. —Do you want an orange juice?"

It never was. It was a cousin of that damned Citrisal. But his mouth was dry and he sipped it when they put a straw between his lips and elevated his bed. G felt heavier here. He thought: This isn't the same place. We're deeper in.

"How are you feeling?" his doctor asked him.

But he was looking suddenly at the company police, realizing what that uniform was.

"Paul Dekker?" the head cop said. "We want to ask you a few questions."

He heard that beep again. That was him. That was the cops listening to his heartbeat, and it was scared and rapid.

"Have you found her?" he asked. Cops always came with bad news. He didn't want to hear what they might have to say to him.

But one of them sat down on the side of his bed. That man said, "What did you do with the body?"

"Whose body?" For a moment he honestly didn't know what they were talking about, and the monitor stayed relatively quiet. Then his pulse picked up. "Whose body?"

"Your partner's."

The beeps became hysterical. He hauled the rate back down again, saying calmly, "I couldn't find her. They hit us. I couldn't find her afterward."

"Mr. Dekker, don't play us for fools. We'll level with you. Don't you think it's time you leveled with us?"

"This ship ran us down—"

"—and it wasn't on the charts. Come now, Mr. Dekker, you know and I know you had a motive. College girl comes out here with her whole life savings, and here you are—not a steady job in your life, no schooling, not a cent to your name. How'd you get here? How'd you get passage?"

"Cory and I were friends. From way back."

"So she puts up the equity, she just insists the ship go down as joint ownership, with a death provision in there—"

"No."

"Or was that your idea?"

"I don't even know what you're talking about."

"You signed it. We've got your signature right at the bottom."

"I didn't read it. Cory said sign, I just signed it!"

The officer had reached for a slate the other cop had.

He pressed buttons. "We have here a deposition from your port of origin, from one Natalie R. Frye, to the effect that you and Ms. Salazar quarreled over finances the week you left. . . ."

"Hell if we did!"

"Quote: 'Cory was mad about a bill for a jacket or something—'"

"I bought a jacket. She thought I paid too much. Cory'd wear a thing til it fell apart. . . ."

"So you quarreled over money."

"Over a jacket. A damn 38-dollar jacket. We fought, all right, we fought, doesn't everybody?"

"Ms. Frye continues: 'Cory had been sleeping around. Dek didn't like that.'"

"Screw Natalie! She wasn't a friend of ours. Cory wouldn't spit on her."

"*Did* Ms. Salazar 'sleep around'?"

"She slept where she wanted to. So did I, what the hell?"

"Well, that wouldn't matter to anyone, Mr. Dekker, except that she never got back."

The beeps accelerated, not from shock: a fool could see where this was going. He was shaking, he was so mad, and if he went for the bastard's throat they'd trank him and write *that* down, too.

"Cory's lost out there," he said doggedly. "A ship ran us down—"

"Mr. Dekker, there was no other ship in that sector."

"That's a lie. That's a damn lie." He reached frantically for things they couldn't deny. "Bird knew it was there. Ben knew. We talked about it. It was a 'driver, was what it was—it wasn't on my charts—"

The officer said, dead calm: "Bird and Ben?"

"The guys that picked me up!" He was scared they were going to tell him *that* never happened either. But *someone* had brought him in. "I called that sonuvabitch, I told it we were there, I told it my partner was outside—"

"Are you sure the rock didn't block the signal?"

"No! —Yes, I'm sure! I had it on radar. Why in hell didn't it see me?"

"We don't know, Mr. Dekker. We're just asking. So you did see it coming. And did you advise your partner?"

They made him crazy, changing the rules on him. One moment they accused him. Then they believed him. Sometimes he seemed to lose things.

"Didn't you say you'd hit a rock? Wasn't that your story at one point?"

He was lost and sick and the drugs still had him hazed. The beeps increased in tempo. He wasn't sure whether it was his heart or something on com.

"So where did you manufacture this ship, Mr. Dekker?"

"It was out there."

"Of course it was out there," the officer said. "You had it on your charts. Your log showed that. How could we doubt that?"

He was totally confused. He put his hands over his ears, he tried to see if the alarm going was his heart or something in his head. "Call the 'driver, for God's sake. See if they picked Cory up."

"Didn't you call?" the cop asked.

"Yes, dammit, I called, I called and it didn't answer. Maybe my antenna got hit. I don't know. I called for help. Did anybody hear it?"

"A ship heard you. A ship picked you up."

"Different." He was tired. He didn't want to explain com systems and emergency locaters to company cops. "Just call the 'driver out there."

"If there is a 'driver out there," the cop said, "we'll ask. But if they had picked up your partner, wouldn't they have notified their Base? Don't you think they'd have called that in?"

He thought about that answer. He thought about the way that ship had ignored warnings. He thought about it not answering his hails. He thought—It's not hours, is it? It's months, it's been months out there.

The alarm sounded again. He wanted it calm, because when he didn't do that within a certain time they sedated him, and he was trying to be sane for the police. "I don't know they heard me. Just call them."

"We're going to be calling a lot of people, Mr. Dekker." The cop got up from his bed. "We're going to be asking around."

They walked to the door. The doctor went with them. He lay there just trying to keep the monitor steady and quiet, on the edge of hysteria but a good deal saner than he wanted to be right now. He remembered Bird, he remembered Ben. He was relatively sure he had come here on their ship. But sometimes he even feared Cory might not have existed. That he had always been in this place. That he was irrevocably crazy.

# CHAPTER
# 7

IF 8 was gray and automated, 6 was green paint and a few
live-service restaurants and shops, but the time still dragged:
you worked out in gyms, you hit the shops til you had the
stuff on the counters memorized, you skipped down to
3-deck for a while and maybe clear to 2 for an hour til your
knees ached and your heart objected. The first few weeks
after a run were idle time, mostly: you didn't feel like doing
much for long stints. You'd think you had the energy and
then you'd decide you didn't; you sat around, you talked,
you filled your time with vid and card games and when you
found your legs, an occasional grudge match in the ball court
or sitting through one of the company team games in the big
gym on 3-deck was about it. But mostly you worked out til
you were about to drop, if you had to wrap your knees in
bandages and pop pills like there was no tomorrow—and
that was what Bird did, because the younger set was chafing
to get down to heavy time that counted, down in the neon
lights and fast life of helldeck—down in the .9 g on 2 that
was as heavy as spacers lived—specifically to The Black
Hole, that was the accommodation they favored, and the

hour Mike Arezzo called and said he had two rooms clear, adjacent, no less, they threw their stuff in the bags and they were gone.

Checking in at The Hole felt like coming home—old acquaintances, a steady traffic of familiar faces. Mike, who owned the place and ran the bar out front, kept the noise level reasonable and didn't hold with fights, pocket knives, or illegal substances. Quiet place, all told. Helldeck might have shrunk from its glory days: worker barracks and company facilities had gnawed it down to a strip about a k and a half long, give or take the fashionable tail-end the corporates used: that was another ten or fifteen establishments—but you wouldn't find any corporate decor in The Hole; no clericals having supper, not even factory labor looking for a beer. The Hole was freefaller territory: dock monkeys and loaders, tenders, pushers, freerunners, construction crew from the shipyard and the occasional Shepherd—not that other types didn't stray in, but they didn't stay: the ambient went just a bit cooler, heads turned and the noise level fell.

It went the other way when lost sheep turned up.

"Hey, Bird!" Alvarez called out, and heads turned when they walked in. Guys made rude remarks and whistles as Meg sauntered up to the bar and said, "Hello, Mike."

Mike said, accurately, "Vodka, bourbon, vodka and lime, gin and bubbly. . ." and had them on the bar just about that fast.

Home again for sure. Close as it came.

"How's it going?" Mike asked. "Persky says you got a distress call out there. Pulled some guy in."

"Yeah. Young kid. Partner dead. Real shame."

Alvarez said, "What's this with *Trinidad* hanging off the list? The *cops* impounding her?"

God, the other thing helldeck was good for was gossip.

"Nothing we did," Ben said, fast. "But Mama's got her procedures. You contact a ship from across the line—"

"Across the *line*—"

Some parts of a story you saved for effect. They were worth drinks, maybe supper. "Wait, wait," Alvarez said,

"Mamud and Lal are over at The Pacific, I'll phone 'em. Wait on that."

—You got one grounded bird here, Bird had used to joke, when it came to getting about in .9 g: hard as null-g was on the body, you got so frustrated with walking on helldeck—it took so *long* to get anywhere, and the Trans was always packed. Food and drink didn't have to be chased— that was the plus. But when you first got in you always felt as if you'd forgotten your clothes: you got so used to the stimsuit moving with you and fighting every stretch, you kept checking to make sure you were dressed. Air moved over your skin when you walked. And how did you spot a spacer in a fancy restaurant? Easy. He was the fool who kept shaking the liquid in his spoon just to watch it stay put—or who set something in midair and looked stupid when it didn't stay there.

He was also the poor sod always in line at the bank, checking his balance to see if Assay or Mining Operations had dropped anything into his account—or, in this case, down at the Security office to see if, please God, the technicalities had been cleared up and some damned deskpilot might just kindly sign the orders to get his ship out of port.

No.

And no.

The 28th of *July*, for God's sake, and the cops hadn't finished their search.

And when he decided to stop by the bank and check the balance, to see if the last of the 6-deck bills had come in, dammit, the bank account showed a large deduct.

So . . . the aforesaid spacer hiked the slow long way to the Claims Office, and stood in line in this scrubby-poor office to find out the state of affairs with *Trinidad*'s claims- pending and its tags. Ben had gotten into his nice office- worker suit and gone clear around the rim to say hello to friends in Assay who just might hurry up the analysis—and you'd sincerely hope it wouldn't run in reverse.

"Two Twenty-nine Tango," he told the clerk, who said, "*Trinidad*, yeah, Bird and Pollard, right?"

"Right."

The clerk keyed up and shook his head. "I hate to tell you this—"

"Don't tell me we got a LOS. You don't want to tell me that."

"Yeah. —You got a pen? I'll give you the number."

"I got my list," he said, and fished his card out of his pocket and stuck it in the reader on the counter.

"That's number T-29890."

"Shit!" he said, and bit his lip. On principle he didn't cuss with friendly clerks. But it was the second best tag they had, a big rock for these days. Iron. And he had been careful with it. He raked his hand through his hair and said, "Sorry. But that one hurts, on principle."

"Maybe better news tomorrow. They do turn up again."

"Yeah," he said, "thanks."

So they'd lost a tag. It happened. You sampled a rock, you took a sample in and ran your on-site tests, and if you liked it and thought Mama would, you called and told her you had potential 'driver work here. You got your big bounty when your second, official Assay report confirmed your work; and you got a certain monthly fee just for having it on the charts; but you didn't get paid percentage on the mineral content until some 'driver finally got around to chucking it back in bucket-loads, until the Shepherds got it in, and the refinery reported what it *really* had. Which happened on the company's priorities, not yours.

And if you had a Loss of Signal that meant Mama had to do the bookkeeping on it, and Mama had to re-tag it, pick it up on a priority, or let it go until another pass—all that was shitwork Mama didn't like to do, when a nice neat tag that stayed on was what you got that bonus for, and back it came unless you personally could firm up those numbers and keep track of it. If it got perturbed out, as did happen, you could lose it altogether, or have to fight it in Claims Court.

So, well, this one was too good to let slip or leave to chance. Maybe a little computer work could find it. There was a remote chance it could just be occulted for a while, something in the way that wasn't on the charts—a LOS could sometimes put Recoveries onto another find, in which case you got that credit; it had happened in the long ago; but generally a rock just, in the well-known perversity of rocks, got to turning wrong, and managed to turn in some way that the strip transmitter was aimed to the 3% of the immediate universe Mama's ears didn't cover—or the transmitter could have died: they didn't live forever, especially the junk they got nowadays.

So it was hike over to Recoveries and pay a couple more c's out of the account for the technicians to pull up a file and figure probable position and talk to it and listen with a little more care, first off, in the hope of getting contact, before they went to the other procedures. Meanwhile the bank didn't pay interest on what Mama had taken out, that was why they did immediate withdrawals these days: every damn penny they could gouge.

"Odd-shaped rock," he typed on the form, and invoked the data up out of Mama's storage. Photos. And mass reckoning. And the assay report on the pieces they'd knocked off it.

The Recoveries clerk took the dump, looked at it, and lifted an eyebrow. "Thorough. Makes our job a lot easier. We might have a real chance of waking this baby. Or getting a 'driver on it before it gets out of reach. Real nice piece, that."

That made him feel better at least. You kept the people in Recoveries happy and they maybe paid a little more attention to getting you found or a little more urgency to getting you picked up—unlike the guys who took only one sample and that from the only good spot on the rock.

A lot of novice miners had gone bust that way—talk Mama into a whole lot of expensive tags on junk, just collect the bounties and puff up the bank account and buy fancier analysis gear—and a few took the real risk and outright falsified the samples. It paid off in a few instances—but the sloppy work that usually went along with that kind of operation sooner or later started showing up in reprimands and fines, and a crew got back to Base some trip to find out their bank account had been holed while they were gone—

Mama didn't ask you to write a check these days: under the New Rules, she just took it, and you could sue if you thought you'd been screwed—if you could afford to hire the company's own lawyers.

And you'd never say that 'drivers ever, ever cheated in reckoning the mass they'd thrown; and you'd never *ever* say that a refinery would short their receipts. 'Driver captains and refinery bosses never, ever did things like that.

But you did do real well to get a reputation for being meticulous, taking multiple samples, being clean with your records, making it so 'drivers and tenders *knew* your tags were worth going after. Knowing your mass. Photographing all the sides, including after the tag was on. Most of all knowing the content—rocks being their individual selves and damned near able to testify in court who their parents were.

No skimmer liked to mess with his claims, no, sir— because Morris Bird was real friendly, he was on hailing terms with most of helldeck; and when he got a few under his belt he told everybody far and wide how he kept accidents from befalling his claims and how suspicious it was if it came in short.

There had only been one or two uncharitable enough over the years to remark that sleeping with the two most likely to do the skimming couldn't hurt. But he had stood up for Meg and Sal, and so had no few others.

It made him happier just thinking about it—

Made him outright laugh, thinking how that had probably done more to reform Meg Kady than all the Evangelicals and the Islamic Reformeds who handed out their little cards on helldeck.

Sal, now, he thought—reforming Sal was a whole different proposition.

You got all kinds on helldeck—except you didn't walk it in any business suit, not if you didn't want to get laughed out of The Hole. So Ben shed it at the locker he kept on 3-deck, put on his casuals and his boots, after which it was safe to go home.

Change of clothes, change of style—Ben Pollard went most anywhere he cared to go on R2 and nobody would find him out of place.

But fact was, helldeck was where he most liked being— down in the hammering noise and the neon lights. He'd been scared as any company clerk when he'd first laid eyes on it, at 14, even if his mama had belonged here—but even at that age he'd known sure as sure that Ben Pollard was never going to have the pull to get out of the company's lower tiers. He'd learned how it really was: the ideal the company preached might be classblind; but funny thing— kids without money ended up like Marcie Hager, in the middle tiers, where you had certain cheap perks, but you'd never get a dime of cash and you'd never get further—and aptitudes and Institute grades had damned little to do with it. President Towney's son, for an example, was about as stupid an ass as had ever graduated from the Institute—and they put him in a vice-presidency up in the methane recovery plant . . . while Ben Pollard, a Shepherd's kid, got a stint at pilot training (at which he was indifferent) and geology, at which he was good; and a major in math, thank God. But he couldn't get into business administration, not, at least, tracked for the plum jobs. They went to relatives of company managers. They went to company career types, who had paid their dues or whose parents had, or who tested high in, so he had heard, Company Conformity.

Shit with that. He took a little jig step on his way back from the Assay office, and on helldeck nobody took exception to a little exuberance—if a guy was happy, that guy must have reason: in a society that lived on luck you wanted to brush close to whoever looked to have it, because that guy might lead you to it.

What he had was a card in his pocket that said they had a couple of nice pieces, and that money was going into the bank, dead certain. You tagged things and you didn't know how long it was going to be til the 'driver got there, but what you had in your sling was money—and in this case, a good chunk of it.

Yeah!

"Meg or Sal in?" he asked Mike at the bar when he got to The Hole—he knew where Bird probably was, where Bird had been this time of day for the last week.

Mike said, "They aren't, but the cops were."

He looked at Mike a moment. It was hard to change feet that fast. "Cops."

"They weren't in uniform. But they had badges. Anything I should know?"

He sighed, said, because, hell, you needed the local witness on your side if it came to trouble: "All right, Mike. The guy we rescued—out in the Belt. We got a claim in on the ship. He owned it. Sole survivor. The guy's crazy. God only knows what he's said. Police are probably checking us out to be sure we're on the straight."

Mike looked a shade friendlier at that. And interested. "Claim on the ship, is it?"

He tapped his key on the bar. "More of a long, long story. But that part's blackholed. You, we trust. Let me go check this out."

He went back through and down the hall where the sleeping rooms were, opened the room he had (at least on the books) with Bird.

"Shit!" was his first reaction.

Not as if they had much to disarrange, but thieves could have hit and been neater. Four days to get their Personals out of police hands and here was everything they owned strewn over the sink, the lockers open, their laundry scattered on the bed—and a big bright red sticker on the mirror that said: *This area was accessed in search of contraband by ASTEX Security acting with a warrant. Please check to be sure all your personal items are present and report any broken or missing articles or unsecured doors immediately by calling your ASTEX Security Public Relations Department at . . .*

He pulled the sticker off the mirror. Paper thicker than tissue was worth its weight in gold. Literally. You could fold the thing and write important secret notes on the edges if you could find a pencil, which was equally frigging scarce.

Shit. shit. *shit!*

He opened the side door that led into Meg and Sal's room—it was technically a quad. Same mess, only more so. Meg and Sal had more clothes.

Meg and Sal were going to kill them. That was one thought going through his head. The other was outrage—a sense of violation that left him short of breath and wanting to break something.

What in hell were they looking for?

Something off that ship?

Datacard?

He had a sudden cold thought about the charts. But he had that datacard in his pocket, where he always carried it. He felt of his pocket to be sure.

Damn!

He headed out, locked the door, walked down the hall and tried to collect himself for Mike, who asked, "Anything wrong?"

"Not that I know. Be back in a bit." He kept going, to the nearest Trans to get him up to 3-deck.

He had this terrible cold feeling, all the ride up, all the walk down to the gym and the lockers. His hands were shaking when he used his personal card to open the locker. He suddenly thought: Everywhere I use this card they can trace it. Same as in the Institute. There's nothing they can't get at. . . .

He got the door open, he felt of his suit pocket—

The card with the charts was there. He'd been so excited about the Assay report he'd forgotten to switch it back.

But, God, where's it safe now?

In the room they've already searched?

Maybe they'd expect him to do that. And they might be looking for one kind of trouble—but if they found something illegal—

Damn!

Dekker opened his eyes tentatively, hearing someone in the room—realized it was his doctor leaning over him. The drugs had retreated to a distant haze.

"About damn time," he said.

The doctor moved his eyelid, used a light, frowning over him. "Mmm," the doctor said. Pranh was his name. Dekker read it on the ID card he wore.

"Dr. Pranh. I don't want any more sedation. I want out of here. —What did the police find out?"

Pranh stood back, put his penlight in his pocket. "I don't know. I suppose they're still investigating."

"How long?"

"How long what?"

"How long have they been investigating?"

"Time. Does that still bother you?"

It still touched nerves. But he was able to shake his head and say—disloyal as it felt to say—"I know Cory's probably dead. Right now I want to know why."

Pranh's face went strangely blank. Pranh looked at the floor, never quite at him, and started entering something on his slate.

"You haven't heard from the police," Dekker said. It was hard to talk. There was still enough of the drug in him he could very easily shut his eyes and go under again, but he kept pushing to stay awake. Pranh didn't answer him, and he persisted: "How long has it been?"

"Your partner *is* dead. There's no probably. Denial is a normal phase of grieving. But the sooner you get beyond that—"

"I don't know she's dead. You don't know. For all I know that ship picked her up. I want to talk to the police. I want a phone—"

"Calm down."

"*I want a phone, dammit!*"

"It's on the record. A rock hit you, a tank blew."

"There wasn't any rock—"

"You said there was. Are you changing your story?"

"I'm not changing anything! There was a 'driver out there. It didn't answer our hails, it ran right over us—"

"Denial," Pranh said quietly. "Anger. Transference. I've talked to the investigators. There's no 'driver. There never was a 'driver near you. One was working. It's possible there was a high-$v$ rock. A pebble."

"Pebble, hell! I want to talk to the police. I want to know what that 'driver captain says! I want a phone!"

The doctor went to the door, leaned out and spoke to someone outside. And left.

"I want to talk to somebody from Management!" he yelled at the empty doorway. "Dammit, I want to talk to somebody who knows what's going on out there!"

But all that came through the doorway was a pair of orderlies with a hypo to give him.

He swore when they laid hands on him and when they gave him the shot; and he swore all the while he was sliding back down again. He felt tears running on his face, and his throat was raw from screaming. He thought of Cory, Cory shaking her head and looking the way she did when something couldn't be fixed.

Can't do it, Dek.

And he said to himself and to Cory, Hell if not.

Two pieces of news Ben had for Bird when he walked into the *Hole*, and good as one was, the bad won. Hands down.

"We got an LOS on a big one," Bird muttered as he sat down on his bed. He threw that out flat, because it was completely swallowed up in this. "Sure it was cops?"

"They left a note. A sticker." Ben showed it to him, folded, from his pocket. "It was worse than this. I straightened up some—folded Sal and Meg's stuff."

"Got them too."

"Got them too."

"Damn." He shook his head. It was all he could think to say.

"Maybe," Ben said, "maybe they're just checking us out. I mean, legally, they can search anything they want—and we have this claim in—"

"Legally I'm not sure they can," he said, tight-jawed. "But the complaints desk is hell and away from R2." Then he thought about bugs, signed Ben to hush, got up and took him out and down the hall to a table in the bar. By that time he figured Ben knew why. Ben looked worried as he sat down.

"Two beers," he said to Mike Arezzo. And brought them back and sat down. He said to Ben: "They could have bugged the place. But if we ask to move, they'll be asking why and they'll get interested."

"I don't know why they're on us in the first place," Ben said. "It's that damn Dekker, I know it is. No telling what story he's telling them."

"We don't know that."

"Well, it would be damn useful to know. I can talk to somebody in—"

He laid a hand on Ben's arm. "Don't try to fix this one. I don't care who you know. It's too dangerous."

"Dangerous, hell! We haven't *done* anything but save that guy's neck!"

Ben really believed in some things. Like The System and The Rules he regularly flouted. "You remember you asked me about Nouri and his lot. And I said that wasn't that long ago. Police can do any damn thing they want to. They did then. They still can. Your company education tell you that?"

"There are regulations they have to follow—"

"That's fine. There's regulations they sometimes don't follow. Remember Nouri? Wasn't anything they didn't search on these docks; and you didn't say, I got my rights. The company has its easy times and it has its crackdowns, and both of us can remember when toilet paper didn't have stuff in it to break it down so you can't make press-paper anymore, you got to use those damn cards you stick into these damn readers that we don't know where the hell they connect to; *I* can remember when ships could kind of work in and out of the sectors and you could link up and share a bottle: now they'll slap a fine on you you'll never see the top of. I can remember when they didn't care about this stupid war with people clear the hell and gone away from here, that they say now can just come in here and blow us to hell, and once upon a time we didn't have the company bank taking

LOSes out of your account if you paid for a search, not until Recovery turned up an absolute no-can-do. I've seen a hell of a lot change, friend. I've heard about how the company has to do this and the company has to do that, and if we organize and everybody stands together the company's going to give in. Hell! We're not the Shepherds, the company doesn't have to give in. The company can replace us, the company's *aching* to replace us, and if it wasn't for the charter that says they have to deal with independents on a 'fair and equitable basis' they'd have screwed us all right out of existence. They teach you that in company school?"

"There are still rules. They're still accountable to higher management."

"Yeah, they're accountable. The only accounting that matters is the balance sheet. We shouldn't have filed on that ship, Ben. We shouldn't have done it."

"You're not making sense. It's the company's rules. They set up the salvage rules. You're saying they're not going to follow them?"

"Ben, the rules aren't supposed to cost the company money. *That's* the Rule behind the rules. I've had a bad feeling about this whole business from the beginning. You don't win big. You never win big."

"If you don't take the breaks you have you damn sure don't win anything!"

"You're all shiny new and bright polished. I was that a long time ago." He took a mouthful of the beer and swallowed. "I remember when they started making this stuff, too. You don't want to see the vats this came from."

"Yeah, well, maybe everything you remember was better. Maybe everything now is shit. Or maybe it was always like this."

"We didn't always have the company on our necks. We didn't always have them gouging every penny they can get their hands on, we didn't always have a friggin' military shipyard next door making us a target—we haven't always had all this damn happy stuff on the vid all the time, when we know nothing *happy* is going on back home, Ben!" It was too much to say, even out in the bar, where bugs weren't likely. It was too much even to think about. Ben looked confused.

"Here's home, Bird. This is home."

"Yeah," he said. "It's mine, too. But sometimes I'd like to kick its ass."

Meg and Sal came in the door. They had to explain to them how it was.

Sal said, "Sons of bitches," meaning, he hoped, the cops. But Meg and Sal were smarter than Ben in some ways. They shut right up, and said a dinner would patch things—

Funny, he thought then, that they had never even once thought that the cops could have been searching after something Meg and Sal had done, and them almost certainly skimmers, and just back from a run. But the company never minded skimming much, the way it never minded how Sal took money from guys—Sal just didn't do favors for free, unless she was your partner. And truth be known she got a bit out of Ben, the way they'd just gotten their dinner paid for. Company brats understood each other.

The gals didn't even look much upset, just kind of shrugged it off and shook their heads as if two guys who got into somebody else's trouble could expect police. Or maybe they were just trying to keep everybody level-headed, you never knew with women. They might be madder than hell and thinking how they'd like to break certain guys' necks, but they'd think about it awhile and figure they were *owed* for this, more than a couple of beers.

So they said they'd go straighten up, and they left. Ben lingered a minute finishing his beer and then said he'd go check the bank and make sure the money got logged right, which was an excuse: God only knew where Ben was really going.

Bird said, "Don't you try anything."

Ben said yeah and left.

Maybe he should have warned the gals about bugs. Probably they were chewing up him and Ben right now. But maybe it was better they did talk in the room, make whoever might be bugging the place think that they didn't suspect a thing. They knew about the ship, all right. But they didn't know what else there was to worry about.

Like that 'driver sitting out there where that ship had come from.

'Driver chewing away at what miners found—extracting and sorting and sending bucketloads to old Jupiter, who slowed it down again so the Shepherds could bring it in to be sheet and foam and such. Mama always assigned sectors according to the 'drivers' work patterns, so you knew there was one somewhere by, but *between* you and the Well, with its business end pointed the other way. Anytime you thought about going near a 'driver's actual fire-path, you had to think about how big it was and how small you were and how what it threw came so fast you'd never know what hit you. 'Driver paths were the one item of information Mama gave out for five or so sectors away, not even regarding the line that divided R1 work zone from R2. Every firing of the 'drivers had to be logged and reported to Mama as to exact time. You couldn't move a 'driver without Mama's permission. You sure couldn't hide one.

So Mama just forgot to put a 'driver on Dekker's charts? It had been on the ones Mama dumped to *Trinidad*—right where Dekker had given them the coordinates for the accident.

Damn, you didn't want to have thoughts like that.

Lot of pressure on Mama lately—a lot of crazy behaviors out of ASTEX's upper echelons—like mandatory overtime in the factories, like trying to revise the contract with the Shepherds, to let them install a few company-trained crew members on Shepherd ships—a fool could see where that was heading. None of the Big Shakeups had ever made sense, but damn-all anybody could do if the Earth Company got behind it. *They* could change the rules, they could change the *laws* if there was one in their way. The EC had so many senators in its pocket and the EC was so many people's meal ticket in one way or another, especially with this ship construction boom; and there were so many blueskyers bone ignorant about space and politics—

Living down at the bottom of the motherwell like his

own brother did, writing him once a year about the wife and the kids and two pages at Earth to Belt mail rates about how he was putting in green beans this spring. God. Did people still think about things like that?

"Just sign this," they said, and shoved a slate under Dekker's hand—they had raised the bed up, propped him with pillows, but the trank was still thick and he could hardly focus. It was heavy g this time. It felt hard to breathe.

"What is this?" he asked, because he hadn't gotten cooperation out of anybody in this place and he didn't trust any of them. It might be a consent for them to go cutting on him, or giving him God knew what drug, and damned if he was going to sign it unread, in this place heavy as 1-deck.

They said—the *they* who came and went sometimes, cops, doctors, orderlies, he wasn't clear enough to figure that at the moment—"It's just so you can get out of here. You want to get out of here, don't you?"

"Go away," he mumbled, sick at his stomach.

"Don't you want to leave?" He had dropped the stylus. They put it back in his fingers.

He tried to get a look at it, then. It took a lot of work to make out the letters out of the general haze. But it said: AFFIDAVIT. Legal stuff. He worked some more at it. Finally he saw it was an accident report.

Accident. Hell.

He threw the thing. Maybe he broke it. It hit the wall and fell with a clatter like broken plastic. He thought, It wouldn't do that upstairs.

He said, "I'm not signing anything without a lawyer."

Hell of a mess they'd left. Meg was maddest about the jewelry. She sat there untangling earrings and swearing. "Ought to say we're missing something. Serve the cops right."

And Sal, sorting through the stubs of makeup pencils: "Blunted every damn point. Corp-rat pigs."

"*We* haven't done anything." It took some thinking, but

that was the case. Meg unwound tiny chains and felt an upset at the pit of her stomach. "Sons of *bitches* why the hell'd they toss everything together. . . ."

Sal came over and leaned on her fist on the bed. Signed, fast and sharp, Careful. Which didn't help the feeling in Meg's stomach at all. If they were bugged, and the way things were going she'd believe it, they could make those bugs vid as well as audio.

They didn't need this trouble. They *wanted* a chance at that ship, but they sure didn't need this trouble, and trouble for the guys was what it smelled like.

They could move out. There were sleeperies besides the *Hole*. They could kiss Ben and Bird off and go find another lease after all; but if that second ship did come Bird's way—

Then they'd want to cut their throats, was what. Bird and Ben were the best operation they had a chance with: no chance for her in the company. Not much for Sal either: with a police record you could work as a freerunner, but you didn't get any favors and you didn't fly for the company, and if anything went wrong on the deck you were on, you were first on the cops' list.

Just about time something went right for a change. There'd been enough bad breaks.

Like the sector they'd just drawn, which got them a nice lot of ice and rock, in which Mama wasn't keenly interested, no, thank you. That was the kind of allotments lease crews got lately: there were thin spots in the Belt, they were passing through one, and the ship owners took the good ones if they had to break health and safety regs to get out again.

Well, hell, you hung on. You stuck it. You skimmed when you had to and you did your damnedest. Meg Kady swore one thing: she wasn't going to die broke and she wasn't going to be spooked by any company cop throwing her stuff around.

Her hands got real steady with the little chains. She felt her mouth take on this little smile. Fa-mil-iar territory. Amen. "Cops on Sol are higher class," she said to Sal, right cheerfully. "These shiz don't take any courses in neat, do they?"

"Sloppy," Sal said. "Severely sloppy."

Salvatore sank into his chair, shoved a stack of somebody's problems aside, and took his inhaler from the desk drawer and breathed deeply of the vapors—enough to set himself at some distance. He took a deeper breath. The drug hit his lungs and his bloodstream with an expanding rush, reached his nerves and told him to take it easy. He hated scenes. Hated them. Hated young fools handing Security more problems and doctors who invoked privilege.

Most of all he hated finding out that there was more to a case than Administration had been telling him.

The phone beeped. He took another deep breath, let it go: his secretary would get it; and he hoped to hell—

"Mr. Salvatore," his secretary said via the intercom. "Mr. Payne."

Third call from PI that day. This was not one Salvatore wanted, and he knew what Payne had heard. God, he wasn't ready for this.

He punched in, said, "Mr. Payne, sir."

"I'm told we have a problem," the young voice on his phone said: Salvatore's office didn't have vidphones—he was glad not to have. Payne was junior, a bright young man in the executive, V.P. in charge of Public Information and PR, directly under Crayton, who was directly under Towney himself, and there was absolutely no doubt somebody else had been chewing on his tail—recently, Salvatore decided. So Payne passed the grief down *his* chain of command, to Security. "That damned fool is going to keep on til we have a corporate liability. This isn't going to help anyone, Salvatore."

"I understand that."

"Look, this is coming from upper levels, you understand *that?*"

"I do understand that, yes. . . ."

"This is getting to be a damn mess, is what it's getting to be. The girl's mother is after that kid and the whole company's on its ear. We've got contracts to meet. We've got schedules. We need that release. We need this case settled."

"I'm advising him to sign it, Mr. Payne." Salvatore took a deep breath—of unadulterated office air, this time. God, who was Payne talking to? "We're working on it. There's a possibility, the way I see it—" He took another head-clearing breath and took a chance with Payne. "There's an indication the kids might not have been where their log said they were. It could have been a mistake, it could have been deliberate. I think they may have been skimming."

There was a long silence on the other end. God, he hoped he'd not made a major mistake in saying that.

"What we have," Payne's voice said finally, quietly, "is a minor incident taking far too much company time."

"Yes, sir."

"I can't be more plain than that. We *don't* need an independent involved in the courts, especially a kid with camera appeal. I've got the data on my desk, I'll send it over to you. There *was* no 'driver. We have the log. There was no such entry. I'll tell you what happened out there, captain, these two kids were up to no good, very likely skimming, probably scared as hell and taking chances with a rock way too large for their kind of equipment. Dekker either screwed up and had an accident that killed his partner, or there was a mechanical failure—take your pick of the safety violations on that ship. Maybe we should be prosecuting on negligence and probably on skimming, but I can give you the official word from Legal Affairs, we're not prosecuting. The kid's been through enough hell, there's no likelihood that he's going to be competent to testify, or that he won't complicate things by raising extraneous issues in a trial, and we're not going to have this drag on and on in a lawsuit, Salazar's or his. There's people on this station would love that, you understand me, captain?"

"I do, sir."

"So get this damn mess cleared up. You hear me? I want that release. I'm sending you the accident report. You understand me? We have elements here perfectly willing to use somebody like Dekker. I don't want this blown out of proportion. I want it stopped."

He thought about the recorder on his desk. His finger hesitated over the button. He thought better of that move. But he wanted to make Payne say it. "Stop the investigation?"

"Put out the fire, Mr. Salvatore. We have a damage control situation here. I want this resolved. I want this problem neutralized. Hear me?"

"Yes, sir," Salvatore said—which was pointless, because Payne had hung up. He punched in a number, the outer office. He said to his aide: "Get me Wills on the phone. *Now!*"

Dammit, if the kids were skimming—charge them. You skim from the company, you get busted. Period. But the girl's mother insisted not. The girl's mother insisted *her* daughter wouldn't involve herself in a shady operation. Beyond a doubt Dekker had murdered her daughter for the bank account.

Good point, except it was one doggedly determined killer, who'd wrecked his ship and sent himself off the mental edge for an alibi. He'd seen miners do crazy things, he'd investigated one case that still gave him nightmares, but nobody had held Corazon Salazar here at gunpoint and nobody had any indication Dekker was after money. By what his investigation had turned up, the girl had quit college, taken money from a trust fund, paid *Dekker's* way out here and laid down everything she had for an outdated ship and an outfitting—

A mortal wonder they'd gotten back alive the first time—and if anybody'd been kidnapped out here, it sounded more like Dekker... who was just damned lucky to have been found: physics had been in charge of that ship, the second those tanks ruptured: damned sure the kid hadn't— and God and the computers knew why it had stayed in the ecliptic, but it didn't sound like good planning to him.

*Hell, Dek didn't handle money,* one of the interviewees had said, in the investigation on R1. *He just flew the ship. Always tinkering around with it. . . .*

*Social? Yeah, he'd be with Cory, but he'd be doing vid*

*games or something—he used to win bar tabs that way. Real easy-going. Sometimes you'd get a little rise out of him, you know, showing off, that sort of thing, but he always struck me as downright shy. The games were his outlet. He'd be off in the corner in the middle of a crowd, Cory'd be at the table talking physics and rocks, yeah, they were a real odd pair, different, but it was like Cory did the headwork and Dek was all realtime—*

*Yeah, Dek had a temper. But so did Cory. You never pushed her.*

*Yeah, they slept together—but they weren't exclusive. Minded their own business—didn't get real close to anybody. People tried to take advantage of them, them being kids, they'd stand their ground . . . Cory more than Dek, actually. She'd draw the line and he'd back her up . . . not a big guy, older guys used to try to hit on him—he'd stand for about so much, that was all, they'd find it out.*

*Honest? I don't know, they weren't in anything crooked I ever heard . . .*

There *was* a 'driver out there. He had the up to date charts. Company records had it arriving March 24 and the accident as March 12. But the ships' logs were tied up in BM regulations and the mag storage had been dumped. A panel by panel search of the two ships hadn't turned up any illicit storage, and Wills hadn't found any datacards in the miners' rooms.

Which didn't mean no datacards had gotten off the ship. *Hell* of a case for customs to wave past. Administration could come blazing in demanding answers on that.

But no one had told him early on there was any question about the charts; and he consequently hadn't told Wills. And now the evidence was God knew where. Or if it still existed. You tried to do some justice in this job. There was a kid in hospital in more trouble than he was able to understand, up against a woman with enough money to see him hauled back to Sol—and into courts where Money, the military, dissatisfied contractors, and various labor and anti-war organizations were going to blow it up into an issue with a capital I.

Salvatore understood what they were asking him to do. Found himself thinking how they didn't demote you down, just sideways, into some limbo like an advisory board no one listened to, out of the corporate track altogether.

He had a wife. A daughter in school, in Administrative Science—a daughter who looked to her father for the contacts that would make all the difference. Jilly was bright. She was so damned bright. And how did he tell her—or Mariko—this nowhere kid in hospital was worth Jilly's chances?

He took another deep breath from the inhaler, thought: Hell, Dekker's been no angel. He's got a police record on Sol, juvenile stuff. Mother bailed him out. Nothing he's done that we can prove . . .

But kids don't know what they're doing. If the kid can't use good sense, use it for him.

He felt the slight giddiness the inhaler caused: don't overdo it, his doctor said, and rationed the inhalers: his doctor didn't have William Payne on his back. Or a wife and daughter whose lives a recalcitrant kid could ruin.

If Dekker had used his head he wouldn't be where he was. Salvatore knew kids: kids never made mistakes, kids were too smart to make mistakes—but this kid *had* made a mistake, he was in far over his head. His partner was dead, a lot of survivor-guilt was wound around that—give the kid an out, that was the answer. No kid was going to understand politics and labor unions and defense budgets. Dekker had nothing to win that way and nothing but grief if he tried. Give him an excuse, offer him a way not to be accountable for his mistakes.

Before his mouth put him in real trouble.

*The Department of Statistics says that the rise in birth rates this year reflects the rising number of females in the population, which will only continue to rise. Commenting on this, a spokesman for James R. Reynolds Hospital said today that the company should place contraceptives on the general benefits list. The average number of hours worked has fallen 10% during the last five years while the standard of living has continued to rise . . .*

"Screw that," Meg said.

"That's what they don't want you to do," Sal said.

*... population increase of 15% during the last decade....*

"Then why in hell are they doing overtime?"

*... President Towney declares that R2 is facing a population crisis, and urges all women to consider carefully their personal economic situation. Statistics prove that women who postpone childbearing until after age 30 will on average enjoy a 25% higher standard of living. President Towney reminds all workers whether male or female that those who desire to advance in the company should Be Careful....*

"Think they'll advance us if we're careful?" Meg snorted.

"Maybe we should go tell them we're waiting," Sal said.

You got the vid blasting away in the gym. You couldn't escape it. They were sitting there sweating, waiting the breath to do the next round with the machines, and Towney was blithering again.

On the other hand...

Meg looked at her nails. It was a hobby, growing nails in heavy time. They all got clipped when you went to serious work. Or they broke off, eventually, in the dry cold.

Mostly she didn't want to look up, because there was this chelovek just come in that she sincerely didn't want the notice of. *This* gym, Sal wanted. And she'd said to Sal she'd as soon do something a little less exclusive.

"Sal."

"Yeah, I see 'im."

Meg looked from under her brows, tried to look like furniture, heart thumping.

Tall guy, hair shaved up, Nordic or something: his name was Mitch, he was a Shepherd tech chief, and he was a friend of Sal's. Not of hers—most definitely not of hers. Mitch had seen them and done this little take, just a half a heartbeat, and gone on over to the weights.

"I think I'd better evaporate," she said to Sal.

"No. Sit."

It was fairly well Shepherd territory they were in, this little gym near the end of helldeck. It was a gym Sal had always had rights in. She didn't. And this Mitch—Mitch never had approved of their partnership . . . mildly put.

Sal got up and went and talked with him. Meg tried not to be so forward as to read lips, but she could read Sal, and it wasn't thoroughly happy.

Then Sal put her arm around Mitch and steered back toward her.

"Meg," Mitch said.

It was her cussed nature that she wouldn't stand up. She strangled a towel, tilted her head to get a look at him against the lights and gave him a cool smile. "B'jour, Mitch, que pasa?"

He did rab the way Shepherds did, fash. He meant the same in his way. He didn't speak the speech, damned sure. Didn't do the deeds. He said, "Kady. How are you doing?"

"Oh, fair."

"That's good. That's good, Kady. No noise, no fusses. You're friend of a friend of a friend, you understand. That's gotten you this far. I must say I've been impressed."

"You're a sonuvabitch, Mitchell. Nice not seeing you lately."

Mitch smiled. Good-looking sonuvabitch. And having the authority to toss her out of here, and out of Sal's life.

"Don't screw up, Kady. You're on tolerance. You've run the line damned well so far. I've told Sal, there's a real chance on you."

"Take it and screw with it. I'm *not* on your tolerance."

Mitch's brows went up. Then he got this down-his-nose look, shrugged and walked away.

Meg rubbed the bridge of her nose, not wanting to look at Sal. She didn't know why she'd done that. Honestly didn't know why. It wasn't outstanding good sense.

"Sorry, Aboujib."

"Yeah, well." Sal dropped down to her heels, arms on knees. "He asked, he got, he knew he was pushing. He's all right."

"Yeah. I know how all right he is. Sumbitch. Little-g god. Shit-all he's done for you."

Silence from Sal a moment. She'd gone too far with that

one. Finally Sal said, "They've heard about the upset in our room. Mitch wants us out. Says lease and go, get out. They're worried."

"Hell if!" Meg said. "We're *close*, dammit. What's he bloody care?"

Sal's dark face was all frown. "We do got a warning.".

"Yeah, well, Aboujib."

"Severe warning."

"Wants me out of here, too, let's be honest. *You* get a lease, *I'll* stay here and hold us a spot on the ship."

"Didn't say that."

"I'm not saying split, dammit, I'm saying I stay here and hold us a spot and you keep your friends happy."

"He's advising both of us."

She took a tag end of the towel, mopped her forehead, an excuse to gather her composure. "We're that close. Dammit, Sal, you don't get that many breaks. There won't be another."

Sal didn't say anything for a moment. Meg sat there thinking, Sal's break's with them: her real break is with them, if she toes the line. Damn sons of bitches. Couldn't help her. Couldn't take her in. Toss a kid out like that . . . make her turn spirals til she's proved herself—hell if, Mitchell.

Sal said, finally, "Come on. Out of here."

On the walk, out in the noise and the traffic of the 'deck: "I don't think there's a bug there—Mitch wouldn't talk, else. But there's a word out, Meg: I got to confess, I maybe said too much."

"About what?"

"Ben got data off that they got when they were after that ship. He's been working with it and he doesn't give a damn what it is to anybody else, it's his charts and he's not going to see it dumped. He said that."

Meg took a long, long breath. "Merde. That's what you told Mitch?"

"Mitch came to me. They wanted a copy."

"Ben'd kill you."

Sal kept her voice low, beneath the noise and the

echoes. "Yeah. I know it. But they won't make the same use of it—just the information, just those chart numbers. You got to fund me, Kady. Mitch's got my card right now. Access to our locker for the next while."

"Shit, Aboujib!"

"On the other hand—"

"This thing's got too many hands as is!"

"On the other hand, Shepherds have got their eyes on us after this. Dunno what they can do with those charts— but they're thinking there's something just damn ni-kulturny about Bird's ship being tied up, about this kid getting killed out there, about the cops looking through the stuff—"

"You told him this. You went to him."

Sal ducked her head. "I was worried. Worried about whether we shouldn't cast off and get clear of this, if you want the truth. You ask yourself why the cops would turn our rooms upside down, ask yourself if there's any damn thing we've been involved in out of the ordinary except we got two friends trying to file on a ship."

"Aboujib, —"

"Yeah, I know. I was just asking a question. I said I thought it could be data they're looking for—"

"Aboujib, do you seriously mind telling me in the hereafter when you're going to pull a lift like this?"

"Yeah, well, I figured you'd worry."

"I'd have killed you. —Ben know?"

"No."

"So how long before he finds out? God, Aboujib, that jeune fils is no fool. He could've bugged the damn card."

Sal pursed her lips. "Did."

"Then he does know?"

"Neg. Of course not. He and I both came through the Institute."

# CHAPTER

# 8

IT was tests: put the washer on the stick, fit the pegs in the stupid holes. Add chains of figures. Dekker knew what they were up to when they gave him the kid toys.

"Screw that," he said, and shoved the whole box onto the floor—wishing it was lighter g. But it made a satisfying racket. He looked up at the disconcerted psychologist and said, "Screw all of you. I'm not taking your tests until I see a lawyer."

He stood up and the orderlies looked ready to jump, the petite psychologist frozen, slate held like a shield.

He coin-flipped the washer he had in his hand. Caught it before it fell, then tossed it toward the corner, looking at the orderlies.

"You want to come along?" Tommy said. He was the one who talked.

"Yeah," he said, shrugged, and walked over to the door where Tommy and Alvie could take hold of him. They had worked it out: he walked and they didn't break his arms.

If he was quiet they kept the restraints light and he

could keep his hands free. It was hell when you couldn't scratch.

"Vid," he said when they were putting him to bed. There was vid in this room. Tommy turned it on for him. He didn't even want to ponder where he'd been, what they were doing, it was just one more try, no different than the rest.

But it scared him.

Another doctor walked in, turned off the vid. He'd never seen this man before. But it was a doctor. He had the inevitable slate, the pocketful of pens and lights and probes. And a name-badge that said Driscoll.

Driscoll walked over, sat down on the edge of the bed.

"Don't get friendly," Dekker said. "I'm not in the mood."

He enjoyed seeing the bastard sit back and take on an offended surliness. He was down to small pleasures lately. Driscoll consulted his slate mysteriously. Or Driscoll was the one who had the memory problems.

"I understand your impatience," Driscoll said.

"I'll talk to a lawyer."

"We have your test results."

"You didn't run any test."

Driscoll looked at his slate again: "Impaired motor function, memory lapses. . . ."

"That's bullshit."

"Mild concussion, prolonged isolation, oxygen deprivation, exposure to toxic materials—a possibility of some permanent dysfunction—"

"Bullshit!"

"Inappropriate behavior. Hostility."

"Get the hell out of my room. Where's Pranh?"

"Dr. Pranh is on leave. I'm taking his cases." Driscoll made a note on the slate. "I take it you'd like to get out of here."

"Damn right."

"I'll order the forms."

"I'm not signing any forms."

Driscoll got up, reached the door and hesitated. "Try to

control those outbursts, Mr. Dekker. Staff understands your problem. But it would be all around easier if you'd make an effort. For your own sake. —Are the hallucinations continuing?"

Dekker stared at him. "Of course not," he said. He thought, That's a damn lie.

But it scared him. It pushed his pulse rate up. They'd turned off the beep, but that didn't mean they weren't listening, or that it wasn't going into storage somewhere.

Eventually a younger man came in, with another slate— walked up to the bed and said, "How are you feeling?"

The badge on this one said Hewett. He hardly looked twenty. He had a pasty, nervous look. Maybe they'd told him he was crazy.

Dekker didn't answer him; he stared, and the young man said, "I've got your release forms." He offered the slate. "You sign at the bottom—"

"I'm not signing this thing."

"You have to sign it."

"I've asked for a lawyer. I'm not signing that thing."

Hewett looked upset. "You have to sign it, Mr. Dekker."

"No, I don't."

"You want out of here, don't you?"

"They want me out of here." He was cold. The air-conditioning seemed excessive. He thought if there was a pulse monitor going it must be going off the scale. "I'm not going to sign that thing. Tell them they can do it. They've lied about everything else."

Hewett hesitated this way and the other, said, in hushed tones, "Just sign it. That's all you have to do."

"No." He shut his eyes. Opened them again as Hewett left.

He wanted out of here. He no longer thought he was safe from anything here. But he didn't see a way.

Rush for the door? If he got to the outside, especially if he hit anybody, the cops would have him on charges, God knew what. Sign the form and then go for a lawyer? A signed form was all that mattered to these people. It was all they listened to. And what kind of legal help was he going to get here? A company lawyer? Company witnesses?

He'd had a brush with the law on Sol Station—kid stuff. He'd learned about lawyers. He'd learned about hearings. Judges went in with their minds made up.

Another white coat came in. With a slate. This one walked up, held it out, and said, "This is for your medical insurance. Sign it."

He eyed the slate, eyed the woman suspiciously.

"It just authorizes payment of your bills. You're damned lucky you have it. You're a hundred percent covered."

He took it, looked at it. It looked legitimate. It listed him and it listed Cory. He signed the thing, and he remembered fighting with Cory, an outright screaming argument about that policy, saying, We don't need insurance, Cory, God, if you have an accident out here, that's it, that's all—it's a damn waste of money...

And Cory had said, the college girl, from just a different way of life than his: I've never been without insurance. We're at least having medical. I don't care what it costs. If we need it, it'll always be there...

In the crazy way Cory did things—argue about a damn jacket and spend a thousand dollars a year on a company policy that wasn't going to do them a damn bit of good. He started crying. He didn't even know why. The medic stood there staring at him a moment, and he put his arm over his face and turned as far over as he could. She left. But he couldn't stop.

Tommy came in and said, "Do you want a shot, Mr. Dekker?"

He grabbed his pillow and buried his face in it. So Tommy went away.

"Got something for you," Marcie Hager said, in her office in Records, with that peculiar smugness that Ben remembered. He came away from the doorframe—he had come to the Records office on a cryptic Drop by—from Marcie. This after a *nice* bottle of wine that showed up with a buzz at Marcie's door some days past. You never paid Marcie's kind in funds. But you did want to be remembered.

Marcie said, a very faint whisper, "Got a little flag on

your claims case. Seems Dekker's license has just been pulled."

He pursed his lips. "Grounds?"

"Doesn't say. Just turned up on the flag."

"Mmmn," he said. He winked at Marcie, said: "Thanks," with a little lift of his brows. "Big thanks."

Marcie looked self-satisfied. "I did enjoy that." Meaning the wine, he was sure. But it didn't mean the wine paid everything. Marcie had her sights set on promotion—something to do with personnel. He didn't forget that.

So Dekker's license was being pulled.

He walked out of the Records, hands in pockets, reckoning what he knew and who he knew, and finally decided to stroll over to a certain small office in Admin—nothing much. Records.

But Fergie Tucker worked there.

Fergie was just plain bribable.

"Hello, Fergie," he said, leaning on the counter. "How about lunch?"

"The guy's got no license now," Ben said, over a sandwich in Io's flashing neon decor. You never could tell what you were eating in here—everything flashed red and orange and green and the music made the wine shake in the glasses, but Tucker liked it. "He's out on a medical. Psych, if you ask me. He was crazy, out of his head all the way back—no way in hell he was in control of that ship."

Tucker took a drink. Strobe light turned the wine black, then flashed red on Tucker's face as he set the glass down, a jerky movement synched with the bass flutter down the scale. The wine shook. The air quivered. Tucker said, more loudly than he liked, "What exactly do you want?"

"Ex-pe-dition," he said, leaning close.

"Huh?" Tucker said. Tucker's hearing had to be going.

"Expedite!" he said, over the bass line. "There's no damn way he was in control. That's the law. He has to be in control, or we own that ship."

"I know the law."

"Well?"

Tucker shrugged, and took a big bite of his sandwich. Which left him sitting there while he disposed of it. Tucker had been a pig in school and he was still a pig. But he was a high-ranking pig. And he could move data along if he wanted to.

"Everything in order?" Tucker asked finally, when the mouthful was down.

"That application's so clean it squeaks. Vid. Before, after, and during. Clean bill from the cops."

"Court of Inquiry?" This around a mouthful.

"We haven't gotten any complaints. Nothing filed on us. On him, maybe. But I know that title's clear. It's *his*. The partner's dead, died out there. Sole title's with the guy, there aren't any other liens on it. We're *it*."

Tucker's face was orange now, with moving shadows. Sitar run. Clash of cymbals. Bass in syncopation.

"So what are we talking about?"

"Just slip it ahead in the queue."

Tucker swallowed. Said, slowly, "Has to have a grounds. Give me one."

He said, carefully, "What's grounds?" and inclined his head as far across the table as he could get it. The music was on a loud stretch.

"Where is this ship? What's its status?"

"At dock. Lifesupport's a mess. Tanks are blown. Filthy as hell and the cops have it."

"Chance of ongoing damage?"

"Could be. Depends. Have we got a better one?"

"Hardship."

"On who?"

"The claimant? Have you suffered damage?"

God, it was so close he could taste it. "Financial?"

"Any kind of damage? Can you document it?"

"Yes!" He winced. The music vibrated through the table top. He held the explanation a moment, then shouted, "We spent our reserve getting that mother in. We're short at the bank, we couldn't lease our ship out when we came in because the cops had it impounded, now we don't know what to do—she's past time she should have gone, you know, here we are a good way through our heavy time, but she's sitting idle; we got crews stacking up want to lease, and we need the money, but you only get a percentage on a lease if we do let her go out."

"So? Where's the hardship?"

"We could have to be here because of legal questions on the other ship—we're trying to be in compliance with the rules, but we don't know which way to jump. We've already lost a big chunk of our capital and we're scared to leave for fear of sending the whole deal out the chute, you understand what I'm saying? We've been waiting months already. We're coming to the time we should be out of here and we can't be."

"Yeah," Tucker said. "You know, somebody else could even slip in with a bid and take that ship, if word got out she was up for claim, if you weren't around to, sort of, oil the gears."

Tucker was a real bastard. He stared at Tucker, thinking, Don't you think about it, you scum, —while the music went from green to red and his blood pressure went up and up.

"Yeah," he said, "but we *are* due a Hardship."

"Yeah, well, you know those things are hell to fill out. You have to use the right words, say exactly what the clerks around in Claims like to hear. And you have to have somebody take it over there that can put it on the right desk."

"Guaranteed?"

"Guaranteed." Tucker's pig eyes looked him up and down. "Ship owner has collateral like hell. Never has anything in pocket. How're your finances running?"

"Five hundred."

"Five thousand."

"The hell!"

Tucker shrugged, slid his eyes away, filled his mouth with sandwich. The bass fluttered up and down the scale.

"All right!" Ben yelled.

*Trinidad* was free. That had come through this morning. Thank God. Bird nursed the beer to the bottom and the last lean froth—wanted a second one, but the tab at The Hole was already too high. August friggin' 15th, and *Trinidad* was still at dock.

Meg patted his shoulder, went over to the bar. He figured what she was doing, then, and turned half around to protest, but Mike was already drawing the first one, and Sal Aboujib laid her hand on his from his other side. "Beer's cheap," Sal said. "Let her buy this one. We owe you a few."

He had a slateful of figures that wouldn't balance, Ben was still arguing about staying on, Dez Green and Alvarez and a good many of the other independents who'd been in when they arrived had all checked out on runs, and he was trying right now to decide whether old bones could run the risk of shortening their own time here, or whether they should just lease *Trinidad* out to Brower and his mate and sit at Base running up sleepery and food bills—maybe even lease her to Meg and Sal. *Promise* them the new ship if they got it. In that consideration they were short of supplies, the bank was not cooperating, and the damned LOS never had turned up again. They could try one more thing to get Recoveries to wake it up, but that computer time was expensive—and he just wasn't sure it was worth it. They'd had another minor LOS yesterday, not on one of their own, but on one they had a 15-and-20 on, on Peterson's lease; and he wished to hell he knew whether it was just bad luck, Peterson's fault, or whether there'd been any assignment in that sector when the thing went dead: the company just didn't like to hand out that kind of information. There were hotheads on helldeck that'd go for somebody if they got the wrongful or rightful notion they'd been robbed. Couldn't blame Mama on that one. Fights with chains and bottles were hell on the cops.

So they took the second LOS and they were going to have to tighten belts, that was all. And he knew why Meg and Sal were moping around with him and Ben instead of out running down a lease or even hitting on them for *Trinidad*, when that would have been the logical thing.

*Hard* at this point to tell them they weren't good enough to make enough to rate any prime lease, and they'd better go court somebody else, when Meg and Sal were courting them with all the finance they had and they were, dammit, day by day letting them do it, standing by them when anybody else would have called them fools.

You know, he'd told them more than once, at the first; I got to be honest with you: I don't think that ship of Ben's going to come through.

Did that drive them off? Hell no.

He should have said, plain and cold: Meg, I hear you're one hell of a pilot, and Sal, you're not bad at the numbers, but you just haven't got the years—haven't got the math, haven't got the sense of how things work—

Should have said, a long time ago: You two shouldn't ever have made a team: two greenies in the same ship is never going to get better fast enough for what you want.

But he knew what kind of slimespots they'd already shipped with before they'd proved on *Trinidad* that they could go it alone, and started getting leases: and Meg had courted him real hard just before Ben showed up with the cash and the schooling—he still flinched when he recalled having to tell Meg that; and Meg taking it real well, though she looked as if she'd got it in the gut. Maybe Sal even knew. And she and Sal had stayed teamed, even so.

They'd take good mechanical care of a ship, and bring her back sound and clean. Last lease he'd had with Hall and Brower, you couldn't say that. And they might do better with decent charts—and a little help from Ben.

Sal and Ben were a close pair lately. Those who knew Ben might snicker; and those who knew Sal would never in a million years win a bet on what really went on for some of those hours in the room, which was Ben talking numbers and Soheila Aboujib ticking away with her rented comp, with her lip caught in her teeth and this frown that would break glass—Sal could look madder than any individual he knew except Crazy Bob Crawford. Ben was hard to shake when he got an idea, but when it came to plain determination to make it, Aboujib and Meg Kady both were right up there with the cussedest.

We could do worse, Ben kept saying—when who to

lease to had never been Ben's department, just which draws to lease and which to work—but he couldn't say Ben was wrong, except today it came to him that they'd blown near two months here, and they only now got *Trinidad* free. He and Ben could go ahead and make a run—

Yet here they both were, with karma piling up with the pair who'd stayed by them. He couldn't figure how he'd gotten into this, or when it had gotten too late—but when the cops had raided them and thrown Meg and Sal's stuff all over, that had been a real bad time to tell them shove off and forget it—

It seemed a worse time this morning, with their account bleeding money and him into Meg for a beer. He knew he ought to say, coldly as he could: Meg, Sal, don't you buy me a damn other drink this morning, because you're not getting what you're after, and you're wasting your money on what isn't going to come through—

But Meg set the mug down in front of him, patted him on the shoulder and sank into the chair beside him. "We got an idea, Bird. You and Sal go out in *Trinidad*. Ben and I stay here to keep that application alive and take care of problems— we get us a little finance, put what Sal and I got in the pot with yours—make sense?"

"I got to say—" was as far as he got toward a desperate *I don't think this is a good idea, and I can't take your money—*

—when a familiar step came up behind him and a hand slapped a paper down in front of him.

His eyes must be going. For a moment it failed to make sense as what it was. A piece of real paper. With official print.

And Ben landing in the chair on his other side, grabbing his arm, shaking him and saying, "We got it! We got it, Bird!"

"The ship?" Of a sudden he knew it was a ship title. He'd handled *Trinidad*'s—years ago, before he put it in the bank vault. "It says Two-Two-Ten-Charlie. That's not the number. . . ."

"Same ship. Same ship with the blown tanks. They

renumbered it. Like she was new. New start. Everything. We can sell her or we can fix her. We got her, Bird!"

He felt a little dizzy. He took a drink of the beer. Meg grabbed his arm from the other side. Sal was on her feet hugging Ben, and Ben was ordering drinks.

"Wait a minute!" he said, "wait a minute! Free and clear?"

"Free and clear," Ben said. "We got a few charges to pay, but hell, we got the collateral, now!"

"What charges?"

"We got—8, 9 k to pay. . . plus the dockage."

"Nine *thousand!*"

"Administrative. It's nothing, Bird, —*nothing*, against the value of that ship. Figure it! It's ours!"

"I don't believe it."

Ben pointed on the paper, where it said: *joint ownership*, and both their names. That wasn't the terms of the split they'd always had, but, hell, he thought, Ben had hunted down the forms, Ben had done the legwork, Ben had pushed the thing when he never thought it would happen.

Mike came over, Mike heard how it was, and gave them a round of drinks on the house—The Hole never did that. But Mike did now.

They had more than was good for them.

Which was when Ben said how he'd heard Dekker was going to be in hospital a long, long time. How he'd gotten his license pulled.

Brain damage, Ben said.

"Shit," he said, suddenly sick at the stomach.

"Hey, I told you," Ben said. "Dekker's a certified mental case."

"They pull him all the way?" Sal asked.

Ben shrugged. "Close as makes no difference. *If* he gets re-certified there's no way they give him a class 1. D3, maybe, but no way he can ever be primary pilot. Ship's *ours*, on account of it was a tumbling wreck when we got it, and just because he was inside it is im-ma-terial. He was just baggage. He couldn't stop it and he was in no shape to help himself."

Poor guy, he thought.

"Fact is," Ben said, "we *still* got a stack of bills against his account. And if he's gone for a long walk, he doesn't need the money: they'll just ship him out to the motherwell. I got an attachment on his bank account."

That was too much. "Now, wait a minute, Ben, we *got* the ship."

"And the repair bills. And our fuel and our dock time—and *its* dock time, don't forget that. They'll stick us with all those bills."

Unpleasant thought. "And the clean-up inside," he said. "God, have you got any figure what that's going to cost?"

"I dunno," Ben said. "But we can get our expenses back."

He was disgusted with himself, being happy to hear that. Maybe there was a lot of disgust at the table. Meg and Sal had gotten real quiet.

But Ben pulled out his pocket slate and started running figures. "What we can do, we do the repairs ourselves, we use the reserve cash—"

"Whoa, wait a minute. That's our private insurance fund."

"You don't have to think like that now. That *ship* out there's our insurance fund. We got flexible capital now, Bird, sure we want a reserve, but we got to get that thing in running order. We risk it now, while it's in this shape; we don't lease *Trinidad* this run, we can do that work in a month if we push it, and we build back our fund. It'll work."

"Hell," he said, "I don't know. This poor guy—"

"It's not our problem," Ben said.

"Ben, . . ."

Ben gave him a bewildered look.

"We don't take anything more from that guy. That's flat. No more charges against him."

Ben didn't say anything for a moment. Ben looked as if he were worried about the objection, or confused. Finally: "Yeah, well, all right. But we're talking about a guy that may not make it out of the psych ward."

"If he does."

"Yeah, if he does, fine. So we're all right, so we collect it and if he gets out we can stand him a stake. If not, who cares?" Excitement got the better of him, he broke out in a grin and slapped Bird on the shoulder. "We got it, Bird, we got it, we got it made."

The guys went off to somewhere, talking about checking out prices on tanks, happy, mostly—they all should be. Everything had worked.

But Meg sat there with Sal turning her glass in a pointless circle and scared for a moment that didn't clearly make sense. She wasn't superstitious, as a rule. Maybe she'd gotten to distrust a winning hand: it always seemed to be the big breaks that stung you, the ones that made you lose your sense of reality and pushed you to commit to big mistakes— like the break that had had her believing that sumbitch back at Sol.

"No damn luck at all," she said. "Poor bastard's had all up and down, isn't he? Good old MamBitch. Screwed him good."

"Yeah," Sal said. "Didn't Mitch say?"

"Suppose he *is* crazy?"

"Ben swears he is."

"Brut bad luck for him."

"Company'd only get that ship. That's who we're screwing."

"That's the truth."

"Bet MamBitch passes a reg real fast says this can't happen again. Bet MamBitch never severely figured some- body'd get through the shitwork and file all those forms. They don't count on us knowing how."

"Ah, but they paid off. That proves MamBitch is honest, doesn't it? Then she'll pass her rule."

Sal gnawed her lip, tilted her head to one side, a clash of metal-clipped braids. "That gives Mama credit for brains. That's never been proved."

"That's the truth. True here, true everywhere."

Clink of glasses.

"Here's to one more poor bastard," Sal said. "Up the corp's."

"Yo," Meg said. "Here's to regulations."

"Stupidity," Sal said.

"Inefficiency."

"Venality."

"Is that a division?"

"Right under the corp-rat president."

Clink. "Here's to somebody Responsible."

"Must be on Mars."

"Sure ain't here."

A quiet snort. And a look in Sal's eyes that was dead serious.

"Screwed," Sal said.

"Yeah," Meg said, "but what's new? Maybe he'll get lucky. Maybe they'll ship him back to his zone, let him re-train."

"Lay any bets? He could have *friends* there."

"No takers," Meg said, and stirred a water-ring with her finger.

Sal said: "Worth a nudge."

Meg looked at her then, and Sal made a little shrug, gave her a lift of the brows with this smug look in her eye.

"You let it alone, you and your friends."

"No worry, Kady."

"Yeah." Cold as ice, Sal was; but sometimes you got this feeling she was thinking of something that risked her neck and she was breathing it in like an oxygen high. Sal was a Shepherd's daughter. Sal was also an orphan—in one deep dive into the Well.

That was worth remembering, too.

# CHAPTER

# 9

THEY'D asked his shoe size at breakfast. Now they turned him out of bed, gave him underwear and socks that came folded, likewise a cheap little Personals kit, a pair of brand new boots (black) and coveralls (blue) with fold-marks all over, so he looked like a mental case. They let him shave himself this time, but his hair hung around his ears and down into his collar: he didn't even remember the last time Cory had cut it. He just stood there in front of the mirror staring at a hollow-cheeked, wild-eyed stranger and didn't understand what Paul Dekker had to do with this gaunt crazy person. He didn't remember that small white scar on his temple, didn't understand how it could have healed so far without him ever knowing he'd gotten it. . . .

Tommy took him gently by the arm—he liked Tommy more than Alvie. Alvie just did his job; Tommy cared. Tommy always gave him that little moment to get his balance, that moment to figure out that he had to do what they wanted, because Tommy had his orders, but Tommy was never rough with him, and Tommy guided him now with a real concern for his comfort.

"Where are we going?" he asked.

"Just down the hall," Tommy said. "It's all right, Mr. Dekker."

"Not going to be any more tests."

"No, sir. Just down to the office."

Things kept echoing in his head. He said, "Tommy, did they give me something?"

"When they did the tests this watch, yes, sir. Still a little groggy?"

"Dizzy," he said.

"Yes, sir. We'll just take it slow, all right? Good chance you're going to be leaving this afternoon."

That scared him. He thought, Where to? Where is this place? They'd let him out and he'd be somewhere he didn't know and Tommy wouldn't be there. Just strangers.

Tommy opened a door for him and brought him into an office. He didn't want to stay here. He didn't want to be alone with any more doctors. Tommy set him down in a chair and he grabbed on to Tommy's arm. "Stay here," he said.

Tommy patted his shoulder. "It's all right." The doctor was coming in from the other door, same stamp as all the others. Tommy had said the doctor's name and he didn't care, he just wanted out of here. But Tommy stayed right there with his hand on his shoulder a moment and when the doctor ordered him, Tommy left him there.

"How are we doing?" the doctor said.

"Screw you," he said—couldn't muster any enthusiasm about it. He felt as if he was floating.

"Don't like this place, do you?"

That question wasn't even worth answering. He wanted to go back to bed. Wanted to watch vid or something. Or sleep.

"Still having the memory lapses, Mr. Dekker?"

He honestly didn't know. He shook his head.

"I'm Dr. Visconti. Outpatient Services. Dr. Driscoll says you're doing much better."

Maybe he was supposed to say something about that. He didn't. He just nodded.

Visconti said, "There's an answer here from Management, on your request for a Court of Inquiry. Do you want me to read it to you? Do you want to read it?"

"I'll read it," he said, and Visconti pulled a card from his pocket, slipped it into the slate that was lying on his desk and offered it to him. It said,

> Mary Finn, Special Judge
> Legal Affairs Technical Division
> Re inquiry: Belt Management, Div. 2,
> Mining & Recovery
> ASTEX
> MEMO TO:
> Mr. Paul F. Dekker
> c/o James R. Reynolds Hospital
> R2/ASTEX MINING

> 8/01/23

> Dear Mr. Dekker:
> We have investigated your claims regarding the fatal accident that occurred on or about March 12th of this year. We enclose the testimony of 1) Recoveries, which has attempted to trace the course of 1-84-Z and to determine the location of the accident; 2) the testimony of Mohammed Fahdi, range officer and Lyle Xavier Manning, senior captain of the ship Industry, which was the only ship of its class operating near that path; 3) the testimony of Frances E. Rodrigues, Chief of Operations of BCOM/R1, 4) the report of Gianpaulo Belloporto, chief examiner, ASTEX R2 DIV ECSAA. It is the determination of this office that a catastrophic failure of the main intake value caused an explosion of the number two primary tank of 1-84-Z, which hurled the vessel in an unanticipated acceleration toward charted asteroid 2961. . . .

"This is a damn lie. This whole thing is a lie—"

"Mr. Dekker."

"There wasn't any catastrophic failure."

"Mr. Dekker. There *was* no 'driver in your vicinity at the time. The report doesn't find you culpable. It was a very unfortunate double system failure. The pressure in that tank was building up during your maneuvering while your partner was outside. The valve had failed. The warning should have sounded. There's no evidence it did. The blowoff apparently didn't function—that part of the tank is missing and there's no way to check—"

"What are you, a psych or a mechanic?"

"It's part of our job, Mr. Dekker, to determine what did happen before we offer advice. The investigators don't find any evidence of negligence, and they don't blame you in any wise for the accident."

He shut up, just stared at the wall. Useless to argue. Absolutely useless.

"It simply wasn't your fault, you understand? It wasn't any one person's fault. There's going to be a thorough investigation at R1 maintenance—but most serious accidents, they tell me, involve a triple failure, either of human beings or of equipment. As I understand it, the pressure warning didn't sound. They're sure of that from the log recorder. The blowoff can't have functioned properly. It says here they're investigating the possibility of a primary cause in a cross-wiring of a control module in an attitude control unit—the chance that the safety interlock system actually caused a pressure increase instead of a system shutdown. If it's any comfort to you, there's going to be a design review and a mandated inspection on that particular module. Whatever the technicalities—as the experts explain it, it was bound to happen at some point during a period of frequent brief firings—the investigating board thinks when you were moving in to pick up your partner. So it's absolutely not your fault, Mr. Dekker. There's no way you could have detected the malfunction: no way you could have anticipated it, nothing you could have done when it did happen. It's not a question of blame. And you've *carried* a great deal of personal blame, haven't you, Mr. Dekker?"

"Anything you say, doctor."

"It's called transference. A terrible experience, a long

period of disorientation, periods of unconsciousness. Guilt for what you didn't do. A 'driver accident is something every miner's afraid of—something you can't defend against, a shot arriving out of nowhere, faster than anything can warn you. A loss of personal control. Just like that explosion. That fast. Cory's gone—"

"Not Cory."

"Not Cory?"

"What's the matter? Her being dead puts you on a first name basis with her? Go to hell, doctor!"

"Of course you'd have protected her. You're still protecting her. But you have to accept you're not to blame. Something blew up. There may be culpability on someone's part, but it's not with you. There was a 'driver, but it was a sector away. It wasn't firing. The events you've fantasized just didn't happen. They don't *have* to happen in order for you to be innocent. You have to turn loose of that fantasy. Your partner's gone. There's no chance she's alive now. There's no hope. There hasn't been from the first few hours after the accident. You have to give that up. You have to take care of yourself, now, Mr. Dekker."

"It's a damned lie," he said. "You haven't been here all the while, have you? They used to say there wasn't a 'driver at all. Now it's a different story."

"It's a different story, Mr. Dekker, because records are kept by zones and by sectors. You were almost correct, but you were remembering a recent position. The mind will do that to you. There wasn't a 'driver in the vicinity. The BMO at R1 and here at R2 have compared records. They know your course now. They didn't, at the start. Now they're sure the 'driver wasn't anywhere near the accident."

He couldn't answer that. His hold on what had happened had become too precarious. He decided to keep his mouth shut, before they argued him out of another piece of his memory.

The doctor took the slate, put in another card. "Are you ready to get out of here, Mr. Dekker?"

"Damn right I am."

"You'll be in outpatient for a while." The doctor passed

him the slate. "You'll have a prescription to help you sleep—I understand you still have trouble with nightmares. That's only normal. You have to work these memories out. You have to remember and deal with this tragedy. I think you understand that. But you will have the prescription, if you need it." He reached forward and offered a stylus. "Sign the bottom of the document and date it."

Dekker pushed the button, scrolled back. It said, ... *agree to the findings hereabove stated* ...

"No," he said, and shoved the slate at the doctor. "I don't agree."

"You don't feel you're ready to be released."

The doctor didn't take the slate. It stayed in Dekker's hand and his hand shook. He thought, If I sign this lie nobody will ever pay for what they did. They'll have killed Cory, and I'll have run out on her, finally even I'll have run out on her. . . .

But if I stay in here they'll make me crazy. They can tell any damn lie they want.

What's justice? What's justice, when there's nobody can call them liars?

He set it in his lap, shaking so badly he could hardly write his name, but he signed it. His eyes blurred. He handed it over.

"Can you say, right now," the doctor said, "at least *maybe* it was an explosion? *Maybe* it was an accident? Can you get that far, Mr. Dekker? Can you admit that now?"

He nodded.

"Mr. Dekker?"

"Yes," he said.

"Good," Visconti said, and took the datacard from the slate and put it in his pocket. He got up from the edge of the desk. "Come with me, Mr. Dekker. I'll take you to Dismissals."

He got up. He hurt in every joint. They went out the side door and into a corridor he hadn't known was there. He only wished Tommy had been there. He would have liked to have Tommy with him.

"Don't mind a little stiffness," Visconti said while they were walking. "I want you to walk. I want you to do low-impact exercises—you don't need any broken bones to complicate matters. No jumping. No jogging. If there's any pain in the back, stop. The card we're going to give you has all your prescriptions, with dosages and cautions. I don't have to warn you about calcium depletion, kidney stones, that sort of thing. The calcitonin regulators you're surely familiar with. What I've given you shouldn't have any interactions, but take any symptoms seriously, follow the exercise routines I've laid out exactly, precise number of repetitions. If you get any undue amount of sleep disturbance, see me, if you get blood in the urine, if you get sharp headaches, blurred vision, hallucinations or pain in the chest, put that card in the nearest reader, punch 888, and don't leave that reader. An emergency crew will find you."

"888."

"That's right. I'm your doctor of record. Don't hesitate to call me." They reached a counter in a hallway that stretched on toward the light. "This is patient Dekker, Paul F. Would you find his file and his belongings?" Visconti put out his hand. "Good luck, Mr. Dekker."

Maybe it would have been braver to have told Visconti go to hell. But it might have landed him back in the other hall again, with more stuff being shot into him and the doctors saying, Are you still having those memory lapses?

He shook Visconti's hand and waited at the counter alone when Visconti went away. His legs were shaking. His ears were buzzing. He was afraid he was going to fall and they were going to put him back to bed, so he sat down on a molded bench that made his back hurt and waited until someone at the window called his name.

They gave him his datacard and wanted him to sign another release, that he'd received his Personals and his card and his prescriptions. They handed him a bag of prescription bottles and another sack that had his watch and his old coveralls and stimsuit, he signed, and they wanted his card in the slot on the counter.

He punched Validate. He punched Read, to know what it would show him, and the reader screen showed two things valid: the ASBANK account number and his insurance. It said it was August 15. It said: ALL ACTIVE ACCOUNTS ARE IN PROCESS OF TRANSFER TO ASBANK R2 DIV.

And below that: PILOT CREDENTIALS: INVALIDATED.

He couldn't move for a moment. The clerk said, "Mr. Dekker?" and asked if he was all right.

He couldn't think. There was just a door to a lobby, a way out, and he took his card back, shoved away from the counter and walked for the light.

He had no idea where he was when he left the hospital, he only walked for a while down wide beige hallways with no clear thought in his head except that he was out of the hospital and nobody had stopped him.

But a cop did. The cop blocked his path and asked for his ID card, and he stood there scared they were going to take him back, while people in business suits walked past ignoring the situation.

The cop inserted the card in his pocket slate, with that expression that said he had to be a thief at best and that if there was anything wrong on this whole deck he had to be a prime suspect. Then the cop, still with that dead expression, stared off down the way and said to no one he could see, "Yeah. Yeah. Copy that. Thanks." Then the cop gave the card back with marginally less chill and pocketed his slate. "Just out of hospital, is it?"

"Yessir."

"You need any help, Mr. Dekker?"

"No, sir. I'm all right."

"Where will you be staying?"

"Don't know. Helldeck."

"Trans is down the way, about a hundred meters. You'll want the last car. About your fourth, fifth stop."

"Thank you," he said, and walked on in the direction the cop had pointed. ASTEX didn't want a spacer walking on their clean deck, fingerprinting their beige paneled walls. He understood the rules. He didn't even spit on the floor. He made it to the Transstation, leaned on the wall and waited til the Trans showed up and the doors opened.

People in suits got off, he stepped aboard, into an empty car, and sat down. One woman got on, sat down opposite, didn't look at him, even if there was nothing else to look at. The Trans started up, whipped along to its next stop on the rim. Somebody else got in. Eventually all the business types got off and spacer and worker types got on: the screen said NEXT STOP 2 as the Trans started off in the other direction and climbed.

If would help if he could ask his way. But people didn't do that. People kept their mouths shut in the Trans, the same here as at R1. Ads lit the info screen, advertising upcoming facilities; music blared. The first stop listed mostly BM service offices. The second was commercial. The third listed sleeperies, gyms, and bars, and that was where he got off, into the echoing noise of helldeck.

He wobbled a bit when he walked, but that wasn't unusual here, for one reason or another. He looked like a lunatic and carried plastic sacks full of everything he owned, and that wasn't unusual here either—ordinary helldeck traffic. Some religious type jostled him, a religious type who yelled something about God and judgment and aliens and wanted him to come and hear a tape. But he didn't, he just wanted to be let alone, and the guy told him he was going to hell.

For a while he was just lost—he could believe there had never been a hospital, there had never been a wreck: everything around him sounded and felt like home Base for the last two years—but the names were all different—

Cory had never existed here. His eyes and his ears kept telling him he had finally come home; but people around him were busy with their own lives, in shops with different names.

He walked, going through the motions people who belonged here went through. He didn't know what he wanted. His knees and his feet and his shoulders began to ache with the unaccustomed exercise, and he recalled, out of the long nightmare of the ship, that he had wanted a beer very badly then. So, in the process of picking up his life, he walked into a comfortable-looking bar—The Pacific, it said, with plastic colored fish and plastic coral reefs and blue lights over the bar. The customers—there were ten or so—were tenders and dock monkeys, mostly. The shapes and shadows of creatures he'd never seen reminded him vividly of Sol Station, where he had a mother who honestly might care if she saw the mess he was in.

She'd say, Paul, didn't I tell you so? Didn't I say you were being a damned fool?

She'd say, teary-eyed and exasperated beyond endurance: Paul, now, how in hell am I going to get you out of this one? You cost me everything I ever got in my life. You've done every damn thing you could to screw up. What am I supposed to do for you now?

But he'd have been drafted if he'd stayed on the station. No essential job, 18, no medical reason not, they'd have taken him; and she hadn't wanted that either, they'd agreed on that. She'd kissed him goodbye and he'd been embarrassed and ducked away, the last time he'd ever seen her—humiliated because his mother had kissed him in public. He understood now how he'd been a pain in the ass, and after all the grief she hadn't deserved, the last thing Ingrid Dekker needed was her grown son calling up, saying he was coming home— to get sucked up by the military after all, if they wanted a certified schitz—

So what the hell good could they do each other? He wouldn't take any more of her money. Or her peace of mind, whatever it was now. And she couldn't help him.

He ordered a beer and handed the bar his card, hoping the hospital hadn't cut off alcohol—not good for a man on trank, but he didn't care. The bartender looked at him and stuck the card into the reader, where he could find out as much as a bartender needed to know, namely could he pay for what he'd just ordered, and had he any active police record?

A Medical showed up. He could see the screen from where he was supporting himself on the bar. But the guy didn't argue about the beer, just drew one and gave it to him; and he found himself a vacant booth and fell into it, sipped his beer, shut his eyes and sat there a while in relative null before his brain started to conjure pictures he didn't want to recall. So he looked at the stuff the hospital had given him—took his watch out of the bag and put it on.

It said, 06/06/23: 15:48:10. 15:48:11: he watched the seconds tick along, thought, No, that date's not right. It's August. August 15.

Cory's somewhere out there. All that black. All that nothing around her.

She'd have seen the explosion, seen the ship—it could have run right over her—

Dammit, no! she wouldn't have, because that wasn't what had happened, that was the doctor's story. There wasn't any bad valve, there'd been a 'driver . . . he'd argued with it: This is our claim, hear us?

Instruments went crazy, collision alert sounding—he yelled over and over again, A-20, *Mayday, Mayday, my partner's out there*—

*You damned ass! What do you think you're doing?*

He ground the heels of his hands into his eyes, thinking how the log would show those instrument readings. The doctors kept saying something different, but maybe the cops hadn't even gotten into the ship—the doctors wouldn't know shit about the technicalities and they didn't care, they just made up stuff they thought was going to shut him up—it was their job, and they didn't want him complicating it. The way the company worked, the cops probably hadn't even looked, either, just some judge took all these reports from a 'driver that didn't want any record of what it had done and operators in BM who didn't want to admit—

—admit a 'driver had jumped a claim.

His head ached with a vengeance. He shied away from the company's reasons. He thought about the pills and sorted through the lot, reading labels.

But beyond that . . .

He looked at the time again. August 15th. The accident— (No accident, dammit.) That was the 12th of March.

March 12 to March 31 is twenty days. 20 plus 30 in April is 50. 50 plus 21 in May is 71.

January 1 to March 12. Thirty-one days in January, 28 in February, they said it wasn't a leap year, 12 in March. 31 and

28 and 12 makes seventy-one days. Seventy-one days til they found me. Seventy-one days from January 1st to the accident. No. From the accident—that was why the watch read out the 12th. The numbers are a match—that's all. And between then and now—is it coincidence? Or do months always do that? What do 30's and 31's have to do with anything sane?

He couldn't think. His mind slid off any long track it tried to take. It made his head ache. He took his datacard and used its edge to reset his watch. August. The 15th. That was it. It said August 15 and Cory was out there somewhere, while he was sitting in an R2 bar. Half a year was gone, part of it lost in the dark, part of it on the ship, part of it in hospital. The 15th of August. And his card was active here, on R2, and they hadn't said a word about sending him home: he supposed they didn't want the expense.

Or they didn't want him talking.

Screw that—if he knew anyone to tell anything to on helldeck—

If they'd gotten his ship in, if—he had anything to live on—

He remembered the license suspension—the doctors said it was oxygen deprivation and nerve damage because he dumped a stupid box on the floor and pissed off some doctor with an Attitude, that was what had gotten written down on his records. Or they'd pulled it because of the accident—but they'd cleared him of that. He could fix the license part of his problems, get the shakes out, get some sleep and do a few days in the gym—

All he had to do was sign up and pass the operationals again. No problem with that.

Except the hours requirement. . . .

The company was going to be reasonable? The thought upset his stomach.

Retake the medical exam, maybe, *put* the damned washers on the stick, this time. He could prove it never should have been pulled. Getting the ship in order might take everything he had—tanks blown, all that crud when the lifesupport went down—but he could do a lot of the cleanup himself—but the dock charges . . . they'd come in, when? July 26th? *June* 26th?

God, he didn't want to think about time any longer, didn't want to add numbers or sweat finance right now or figure out how much he'd lost. But now that he'd started thinking about it he couldn't let it go. He couldn't keep any figures straight in the state he was in, and he had no idea what the tanks were going to cost. Twenty, thirty thousand apiece, maybe, counting the valves and controllers and hookups: some value for the salvage on the old ones, but it was going to take bank finance, and they had his account tied up—it might be smarter to sell it, buy in on some other ship—

The bar had a public reader. He got up with his beer and his bag of pills and his belongings, and went and put his card in, keyed past the surface information for detail this time.

APPLICATION MADE FOR FUNDS TRANSFER: 47,289.08 in ASBANK R1 branch to ASBANK R2. ACCESSIBLE AFTER 60 DAYS. PUBLIC NOTICE POSTED 08/15/23. CURRENT AVAILABLE BALANCE: 494.50.

Sixty days. God. What could take 60 days? He wanted to know where his ship was, what berth, what those charges were so far. He typed: 1-84-Z: STATUS.

R2's computer answered: UNAVAILABLE.

Screwups. There wasn't a thing in his life that some damned agency hadn't messed up.

He took his card, went back to the bar, said, "Can I use the phone?"

The bartender held out his hand, he surrendered his card for the charges and the guy waved him to the phone on the wall at the end of the bar.

He punched up INFORMATION, asked it: DOCK OFFICE, pushed CALL, waited through the Dock Authority recording, punched Option 2, and patiently sipped his beer while his call advanced in queue. A live human voice finally acknowledged and he said, "I'm Paul Dekker, owner of One'er Eighty-four Zebra. Should be at dock. I'm getting an UNAVAILABLE on the comp, can you tell me what—"

"Confirm, One'er?"

"Yes. Towed in. Might be in refit."

"Just a minute. You say the name is Dekker?"

"Paul Dekker."

"Just a minute, Mr. Dekker."

He took another sip of the beer, and leaned heavily on the counter, his breath gone short. He'd had enough of incompetence, dammit, he'd had enough of doctors arguing with him what he had and hadn't seen and he wasn't ready to start a round with the Dock Authority. A ship *Way Out*'s size was a damned difficult object to misplace.

"Mr. Dekker, that ship was here. I'm not finding any record of it. Just a minute."

A long wait while he sipped his beer and his heart pounded.

"Mr. Dekker?"

"Yes."

"Are you sure that ship hasn't gone out?"

He was on the edge of crazy now. He said, "I'm an owner-operator. No, it hasn't gone out. It *shouldn't* have gone out. Try Refit."

"I'll check." The operator sounded concerned. Finally.

The barman was looking at him. A bunch of military drifted in and took his attention. He hadn't seen them on R1. But they were customers. He was glad of the distraction. He was in no mood for a bartender's questions.

The bartender served the other drinks. The hold continued. The soldiers settled in at a table. The barman signaled him: Refill?

He slid the empty mug down the bar, still waiting, still listening to inane music.

"Mr. Dekker?" the phone said.

"Yes."

"I'm going to put my supervisor on. Please hold."

He had a bad feeling, a very bad feeling. The beer came sailing back to him, and he stopped it and sipped at it without half paying attention.

"Mr. Dekker?" A different voice. Older.

"Yes."

"Mr. Dekker, that ship's number was changed. I'm

looking at the record right now. You're Mr. Paul F. Dekker. Would you confirm with your personal ID, please."

"12-9078-79."

"Yes, sir. That title was transferred by court order. It was claimed as salvage."

He couldn't breathe for a moment. He took a drink of the beer to get his throat working downward again.

"Mr. Dekker?"

"Did the guy who claimed it—happen to be named Bird? Or Benjamin-something?"

"I'm not supposed to give out that information, Mr. Dekker. I can give you the case number and the judge's name. If you have a question, I'd suggest you go to the legal office. We don't make the decisions. We just log what they tell us. I'm very sorry."

"Yeah." He was having trouble with his breathing. He didn't have his card to take the note the Dock Office was putting in. He didn't want to involve the barman to get it. It went wherever it went when you didn't key a Capture. "Thanks."

"Good luck, Mr. Dekker."

The Dock Authority hung up. He pushed the flasher, keyed up Information and keyed into Registry. Took the 1 choice this time and asked the robot for M. Bird.

Bird, Morris L.: 2-29-T berth 29 and 2-210-C in Refit.

He signed Registry off and keyed up information on Morrie Bird. It gave a can-be-reached-at phone number.

He called it. The voice that answered said: *"Black Hole?"*

"Is this a sleepery?"

"Sleepery and bar. Help you?"

He hung up. He drank a big gulp of beer and picked up his sacks off the bar. He asked the barman: "Where's The Black Hole?"

"About three doors down. Something the matter, mister?"

"Yeah," he said.

And left.

# CHAPTER

# 10

**H**EAVY time was, for a very major thing, a desperate chance at all the vids you'd missed, at food that Supply Services hadn't blessed, at faces you wouldn't see day after day for three months, and at the news you didn't get out there where Mama's newscast was the only gossip you got, telling you crap like, Gas production in R2 is up .3%; or: There was a minor emergency in core section 12 today when a hose coupling came loose, releasing 10,000 liters of water—

The mind conjured intriguing images—but they were thin fare to live on. Heavy time was real life: the reviews Mama radioed you out in the deep Belt of vids in the top ten only let you know what was a must-see when you got back. A stale rehash of handball scores was no substitute for seeing the interdivisional games, and electronic checkers with your shipmate was damn sure no substitute for sex.

Heavy time was anything you could afford besides your hours in the public gyms and your socializing in the sleeperies and bars and your browsing in junk shops—precious little you could buy except consumables and basics, because a miner ship had no place to store unusefuls, and mass cost fuel: but experience didn't mass much except around the waistline—so those were the kind of establishments you tended to get on helldeck, those that catered to the culturally, sexually, and culinarily deprived.

And if a couple of your partners turned up absent since quitting time into supper, with a sudden lot of credit in the bank, you knew it was probably one of the above.

*Even* if it left you doing the supply shopping and handling the guys wanting a lease, you couldn't blame him too much, and Bird didn't: Ben had never been inclined to do it, Ben had worked hard on the legal stuff and the filings, and Ben had finagled a deal with a company repair crew to get the tanks installed.

But leaving him with the phone calls...

The regular lease crews wanting a piece of *Trinidad* or *Way Out*—those you could explain to. They weren't overjoyed, but they understood. It was the horde of part-time unpartnered would-be's, most of whom you wouldn't trust to find their way up the mast and back, who called up every time a ship went on the list; and who, finding out that *Trinidad*, newly on the list, wasn't to lease, argued with you; and, worse, that a brand new ship, *Way Out*, was already first-let to one Kady and Aboujib, of less seniority and a certain reputation—

Well, it told you that you sure didn't want to lease to those hotheads anyhow. He said to the latest such to call, "Screw you, too, mister. Hell if you ever get any ship I'm handling," and hung up.

After which he walked past the looks from the other tables, back to the table by the door and the figures he was working with Meg—bills and bills, this week, pieces and parts of *Way Out*, mostly. He sat down and shook his head.

"Another fool," he said, and punched up the Restore on the slate beside his plate, trying to recall his previous train of thought, and wishing to hell they still gave you paper bills, instead of damn windows on a slate that caught the glare from the ceiling lights. "Wayland Fleming. I never let to that son of a bitch and right now I'm damn glad. —Where in hell's Ben and Sal off to, anyway?"

"Vid, I think."

"Spending money." He shook his head. "I don't know what's got into Ben."

Meg looked up with raised eyebrows and said, "Now, Bird, you *know* what's got into Ben."

No, he honestly hadn't had it figured until Meg said that—and it somewhat upset his stomach. Ben and Sal? Cold, cool Ben?

With Sal Aboujib?

"You *didn't* have it figured?" Meg said. "Come on, Bird."

That they were sleeping together, hell, yes—going at it non-stop, absolutely, but that was youthful hormones. What Meg implied was something else. A guy like Ben, who'd saved every penny all his life, out spending it on a woman?

Ben, his best-ever numbers man—being courted by Kady's? And advising him who to lease to, against his better judgment?

Meg had toted up the expense figures while he was at the phone: she had a better head for bank balances than he did, she was damned pretty, and sometimes, looking at her, even if an old blue-skyer's eyes had to get used to fire-red hair shaved up the sides and bangles up the ears, it was the likes of Meg that could keep a man interested in living.

But what was he doing suddenly sleeping steady with Meg Kady, when there were whole stints ashore he'd spent without a woman so much as looking at him? And what was Ben doing spending his money on Sal?

He was afraid he did have the answer to that, and maybe he ought by rights to be mad. Maybe he ought to throw Meg Kady out on her scheming ear and rescue Ben from Sal's finagling.

The problem with that scenario was—

A hand landed on his shoulder, jerked him around and out of his chair.

A fist sent him back over the table. He had his foot up to stop another attack, but he *knew* the wild-eyed lunatic that was standing there wobbling on his feet. Everybody in the room was out of their chairs, Meg had hers in her hands,

Mike was probably calling the cops, and Dekker was standing there looking as if standing at all was an effort.

"Where's my ship?" Dekker yelled at him.

Bird got a cautioning hand up before Meg could bash him. "Ease off," he said, and yelled at Mike Arezzo, behind the bar: "'S a' right, Mike, I know this crazy man."

"You're damn right you know me!" Dekker said. "I get out of hospital, I call the dock to get my bills, and what have I got?"

The jaw wasn't broken, but teeth could be loose. He rolled off the table and staggered to his feet with Meg's hand under his arm.

"Is this Dekker?" Meg asked.

"This is Dekker," he said. "—Sit down, son, you look like hell."

"I've *been* there." Dekker caught a chair back to lean on, getting his breath. "You damned thief."

"Easy. Just take it easy."

"*Easy!* You went and stole my ship, you lying hypocrite!"

It wasn't a kind of thing a man wanted to discuss in front of neighbors. Mike Arezzo asked, from over at the bar: "Want me to call the cops, Bird?" At tables all over the room a lot of people were listening. "I'm not having my place busted up."

"Why don't you?" Dekker gasped. "Prove I'm crazy, this time, so you don't have me to deal with. They can do the rest of the job on me—that's what you wanted, isn't it? That's what you set up for me. You took everything else. Why don't you just finish the job?"

"Mike, I'm buying this guy a drink. I want to talk to him. He's all right."

"*I don't want to talk to a damn thief!*"

"Beer, Mike, that's what he's been drinking. —Sit down, Dekker. Sit!"

Dekker breathed, still leaning on the chair, "I need those log records. Just give me the log records, that's what I want—"

"I don't have 'em," he said. And when Dekker just stood there looking at him: "She was cleaned out when they turned her over. God's truth, son. They're not going to give somebody else's log over to anybody else—I don't know if they got it stored somewhere, but her whole tape record was clean when she came to us. Zero. Nada. Everything's out of there."

Dekker was absolutely white. "The damn company killed my partner, they're saying there never was a 'driver near us—they *erased* my log—"

"Kid, shut up and sit down."

"You know that 'driver was out there! You know what the truth was before they changed it—"

Meg pulled at his arm. "Bird, —"

"Ease off, Meg. —Just sit *down*, son." People were headed for the door. People were clearing the place.

Dekker slumped against the chair-back, bowed his head, shaking it no, and Abe Persky said, brushing up close on his way out, "Not bright, kid. Understand?"

Abe left. Mike was pissed about his customers, *and* the noise—he brought the drink over and said, "Shut this guy up. We don't need this kind of trouble in here."

"We got him," Meg said, got Dekker by the shoulder and steered him for the chair. "You just calm down, hear? Bird's not a thief."

"The company's the thief—you just—"

Meg said, "Shut it down, just shut it down, jeune fils. We hear you. Listen to me. Sit fuckin' *down*."

Dekker fell into the chair, caught his head against his hands, in an ambient quiet even The Hole's music couldn't drown.

"Dunno if he ought to have this," Mike said. "I give you guys a break and you give me a crazy?"

Dekker said, looking up: "I'm not crazy!"

"Them's the ones to watch," Mike said, and set the beer down.

Dekker was honestly sorry he'd hit Bird. It was Ben he wished he'd found, before the cops came and got him. He might have killed Ben. And that might have satisfied him. But Bird had told the bartender not to call the cops, for what good that would do, the red-haired woman had made him sit down at their table and they gave him a beer he didn't need—

God, his head was pounding. His eyes ached.

The two of them—Bird and this woman with the red hair, who might be a Shepherd—sat at the table with him and told him how the company would have taken everything he owned anyway, how he had to be smart and keep his mouth shut, because he was only making trouble for people who didn't have any choice . . .

"So what have *I* got?" he asked.

"Hush." Bird grabbed his wrist, squeezed hard, the way Bird had done on the ship, telling him shut up, to keep Ben from killing him, and his nerves reacted to that: he *believed* in Bird's danger, he *believed* in Bird's advice the same helpless, stupid way he'd found himself from one moment to the next believing what the doctors told him, and he knew then he was lost. He said, pleading with Bird for help: "They're lying to me."

Bird whispered, "Hush. Hush, boy. So they're lying. Don't make trouble, if you have any hope of getting that license back."

He didn't remember he'd told Bird about his license. He couldn't even remember how long he'd been sitting here, except his hand stung, which told him how long ago he'd hit Bird. Holes in his memory, the doctors said. Brain damage . . .

"Whatever's happened," Bird said quietly, still holding his arm, leaning close, "—whatever's happened, son, we're not against you. We want to help you. All right?"

He was alone in this place, he didn't know anybody on R2 but Bird and Ben, a handful of doctors and Tommy. He sat there with Bird holding his wrist and keeping him anchored in reality, or he might go floating off right now. Bird said he wanted to help. Nobody else would, here; Belters didn't; and he couldn't get back to R1—couldn't go back home without Cory even if they'd send him. Their friends would say, Why did you let her die? Why didn't you do something? And all those letters waiting from her mother . . .

"Guy's gone," the woman's voice said.

"He's on something." Bird shook his arm. "Dekker, you on drugs?"

"Hospital," he said. He was staring at something. He could see a haze. He had no idea why he was staring, or how he was going to come unlocked and move again, except if Bird would realize he was in trouble and bring him back. . . .

Bird said, "Dekker?"

"Yeah?"

"Look, where are you staying?"

That question required some thinking. It brought the room a little clearer. "I don't know," he said, asking himself if it mattered at all. But Bird shook at his arm, saying,

"Listen. You're pretty fuzzed. How are you set? You got any funds?"

He tried to think about that, too. Recalled the 60-day delay—when he'd been on R2 longer than that, dammit, and he didn't know why the bank had waited til he got out of hospital to start transferring his account. He had no idea how he'd even bought the beers a while back. He had no idea how 500-odd dollars had arrived in his account—whether it was his, or whether he just didn't remember . . .

Bird said, "We could put you up a few days—not that we owe you, understand? Let's be clear on that. But I don't really blame you for coming in here mad, either. Maybe we can work something out, put the arm on a few guys that might help, you understand what I'm saying?"

It sounded better than Pranh or the rest of them had offered, better than the cops had given him. Bird had always seemed decent—Bird was the one who'd told him about the 'driver.

"Out there," he whispered, trying to turn his head and look Bird in the eyes to gauge his reaction, but he couldn't manage the movement: "Out there—you saw. You remember what happened. . . ."

Bird closed down harder on his wrist, numbing his fingers, hurting his arm, reminding him Bird had another face. "Better you concentrate on where you're going, son, and not think about anything else. You can't help your partner now. She's gone. Best you can do is get yourself clear. You think about it. Your Cory would want you to use your head, wouldn't she? She'd want you to be all right. Isn't that what she'd say?"

That made him mad. Nobody had a right to put words in Cory's mouth. She'd hate it like hell. But he couldn't get back from where he was. He said, staring off into nowhere, "Screw you, Bird."

"Yeah, well," Bird said. "Try to help a guy—"

Another hand landed on his arm, pulled him around until he was looking at brown eyes, shaved head, dark red crest—rab, radrab, Shepherd or whatever she was, he didn't know. He was fascinated—wary, too. He'd been rab once. But Cory hadn't approved—Cory was too frugal, too Martian to waste money, she'd say, or to waste effort on the system, even screwing it.

That senator—Broden—saying, when they'd opened fire on the emigration riots—"No deals with the lawless rabble—"

Newsflashes, when he'd been—what? Ten? Twelve? First real political consciousness he'd ever had, seeing people shot down, blood smeared on glass doors . . .

Rab style and rabfad was one thing. Shepherds wore it modified, he guessed because it annoyed the exec, and they would. But this one, extreme as she was, with marks of age around her eyes—"You're from Sol Station," the woman said. "Right?"

"Yeah."

She stared at him a long time. It felt like a long time. She might be thinking of trouble. Finally she said, her hand having replaced Bird's on his wrist without his realizing. "Severely young, severely stupid, cher juene fils. Company'll chew you up. Bird's all right. If Bird's telling you, you *do*. Or are you looking for MamBitch to save you? That's *fool*. That's sincerely *prime* fool, petty cher."

Rabspeak, from years ago. From before Cory. From a whole different life. Rabfad had turned into respectable fast-fad, except if you didn't get it out of the trend shops, except if you were truly one of the troublemakers—

Dress like that on helldeck was a statement—a code he

couldn't cipher anymore, not what the colors were, what the earrings said, what the shave-job tied you to . . . like this woman, who looked him in the eyes and talked to him—as if she saw what he had been before Cory—a damned fool wearing colors and politics he hadn't then known the meaning of—

A stupid kid, skuzzing around the station, no aims, nothing but mad and trouble on his mind—screw the system, make trouble, get high on the outside chance of getting caught—

He'd been so smart then, he'd known everything, known so much he'd gotten himself arrested, tracked into the System as a juvie Out of Parental Control—himself and his mother tagged for deportation to the well, til his mother paid everything she'd saved to get them both bailed out.

(God, Paul, you've been nothing but a disaster to me, you've done nothing but cost me from the time I knew I was carrying you—)

They'd put him in a youth program, special studies, writing letters to kids on Mars—

*My name is Cory. I live at Mars Base. . . .*

"Hear me, jeune rab? Do you read?"

He said, "Yeah. I hear you."

"Good," Meg said, patted his face and looked away, at someone else. "Kid's gone out. Beer's not a good idea."

Someone else came up close beside him. He could hear the footsteps. "Not doing real well, is he?"

He didn't know that voice.

"Kid's a little buzzed." That was Bird. Something hit his face. Jolted him. "Dek-me-lad, pay attention. This here's Mike Arezzo, owns The Hole. —Kid's had a bad break. Just out of hospital."

"This is the guy, huh?"

He could see this Mike when Mike moved back past Meg's shoulder. But he couldn't recognize him. He was only sure of Bird.

Then there was another voice he knew. "What in hell's going on here?"

His heart turned over. He couldn't move. He couldn't

think. Ben was on him, saying, "Call the cops, get this guy out of here. . . ." and Bird said, "Calm down, Ben, just calm down."

Ben was going to kill him. He still couldn't move.

Another voice said, clear and female, "Dekker, huh?"

Dark-skinned face. Hand holding his jaw, turning his head, making him look her in the eyes.

"Skuzzed out," the dark woman said. She had a thousand braids, clipped with metal. She was right. He was entirely skuzzed out. He said, dim last try at sanity, "Trank Hospital. Beer."

She said: "Fool."

Jack Malinski had grabbed Ben's arm, him and Sal out shopping the 'deck, just walking home; Malinski had said "Ben, some guy just pasted your partner down at The Hole talking wild about that ship you got—"

He'd run. He'd outright run, getting here, Sal racing along with him—gotten here out of breath. He'd thought it was some guy mad about the lease-list. But they got to the door of The Hole and it was Dekker, no question—Dekker sitting in a chair at their regular table, and Bird getting up to grab his arm and pull him aside before he hit the bastard. "I got to talk to you," Bird said, and when he said it that way, Ben had this sinking feeling he knew exactly what Bird was going to say in private, Bird with his damned stupid guilt about that ship.

Bird said, "Dekker's a little upset. They turned him out of the hospital."

"Fine, let's call the cops."

"He's all right. The guy's just at the end of his tether."

"Tether's *snapped*, Bird, for God's sake, a long time ago, nothing we can do—nothing we're *qualified* to do."

"Give him a chance, Ben. Guy's just mad. Mad and upset."

"Homicidal is what he is!"

"No. No. He's not. Come on, Ben."

"Come on, hell! Your mouth's a mess."

Bird blotted his lip with the back of his hand, looked for

traces. "Can't say I blame him. Guy's lost his partner, lost his ship, lost his license—"

"It's not our fault!"

"Ben, I got to look at myself in mirrors. You understand? It's not our fault, but it's not like we didn't get something from him, either."

"That's life!"

"Ben, . . ." Bird looked utterly exasperated with him, with *him*, as if it was his fault, Bird just closed off from him again, he had no idea why, and it upset him. He knew he wasn't likable: there weren't a lot of people who had ever liked him—while other people got what they wanted just by the way they looked. Dekker was one of those people, the sort that scared him when they got anywhere near somebody he liked—dammit, he had everything he owned and everything he wanted tied up in Bird. And in Sal. And he was willing to fight for it, if he could figure out how to do that.

Go along with it? Or pull strings in Admin, use whatever points he had to get the guy back in hospital—

Bird had his shoulder to him, looking mad, watching the table where Meg and Sal were both making over Prettyboy. You could figure. Women would—though he'd remotely hoped Sal had better sense. He gritted his teeth and said, "Bird, what do you want to do?"

"Just—" Bird was still upset. But Bird did look at him. "We got a chance to help the guy. Doesn't cost us much— give him a chance to get his bearings and get his records in shape. You can pull those strings. You know how."

It hit too close to what he was already thinking—in a completely opposite direction. "Look at him!" he cried. "The guy's gone! He's off the scope! You're thinking about financing *him?* My God, Bird!"

"Not finance. Just get him introduced around, get him a start, maybe get him partnered up with somebody decent . . ."

"We don't know what happened to the last one! Nobody damn well knows, Bird!"

Bird caught his arm and leaned close, saying, half under his breath: "Cut it. We know it wasn't his fault—"

He said, under his: "We know what he said. But he hasn't made a whole lot of sense. That's the trouble, isn't it?"

"For God's sake, Ben, give the kid a chance—you said yourself, if we got the finance, give the guy a stake—"

"I don't know why you want to hand this guy the keys to everything we own and say help yourself! What about me? What about the guy that's tossed all his funds into this well, huh? This guy could be a slash-killer for all we know, and you're wanting to use our credit on him?"

"Shut up, Ben."

He shut up. Bird turned him loose and went over to talk to Mike at the bar. Mike stood there scowling. Dekker was still sitting there with his mind bent, staring off into deep space.

Meg was in the next chair talking to him. *Sal* was leaning over him, showing cleavage. He walked over to Dekker, laid a hand on his shoulder, ready to jump if Dekker wanted to throw a punch. He squeezed Dekker's shoulder, said, casually, "Hello there, Dek. Remember me? Ben Pollard. How are you doing?"

He flinched, and he *could* move: he turned his head very slowly to look up at Ben, remembering they were not in the ship, they were in a bar in a sleepery on R2, and he'd just punched Bird. He figured Ben wanted to punch him, but Ben wasn't doing it because this was a public place.

He said, "Hello, Ben." He could almost come out of the haze. Ben was far clearer to him than the women had been. He was actually glad when Ben moved a chair and sat down, leaning into his face, holding his arm.

Ben said, "Well, how've you been, Dekker?"

"Not good," he said; and, fighting to get back from where he was, he tried desperately to be civil so long as Ben was being: maybe he *had* been crazy. Maybe Ben was honestly trying to start things over. "You?"

"We're fine. We're real fine. Sorry about the ship."

He figured Ben was trying to make a point. He wasn't going to accept it. But numbness gave him a self-control he wouldn't have had otherwise. "Yeah, well," he said.

* * *

Ben squeezed his arm. "A little zee'd, are we?"

"They gave me something." Dekker held up white plastic sacks. Ben took them from him. Prescription bottle showed through the plastic. "I'm supposed to take those."

"Not all at once," Meg muttered. "He's had enough damn pills and excessively too much beer. Man needs to get up and walk, is what he needs."

He thought, All right, let's keep people happy, give this guy a chance to show out crazy as he is—the poor little pet.

So he stood up and pulled at Dekker. "Come on, Dekker, on your feet. Walk the happystuff off."

Dekker didn't argue. He stood up. Ben got an arm around him before the knees went.

"The Pacific called," Bird came over to say. "Seems he left his card there. They're holding it."

"Guy's got a card." Ben felt a little better then, hoping there was finance on it. "Has he got a room there?"

"No, I worked something out with Mike."

Ben stopped, with his arms around Dekker.

He thought: *Shit!*

DEKKER waked, eyes open on dark, g holding him steady. But it wasn't the hospital, it didn't smell like the hospital. It didn't sound like the hospital. It sounded like helldeck, before they'd left. His heart beat faster and faster, everything out of control. Nothing might be real. Nothing he remembered might be real.

"Cory?" he yelled. "Cory?" And waited for her to answer somewhere out of the dark, "Yeah? What's the matter?"

But there was no sound, except some stirring beyond the wall next to his bed.

He lay still then, one hand on the covers across his chest. He could feel the fabric. He wasn't in a stimsuit. He wasn't wearing anything except the sheets and a blanket. He lay there trying to pick up the pieces, and there were so many of them. R1. Sol. Mars. The wreck. The hospital. The Hole. His whole life was in pieces and he didn't know which one to pick up first. They had no order, no structure. He could be anywhere. Everything was still to happen, or had. He didn't know.

A door opened somewhere. Someone came down the hall. Then his opened, the ominous click of a key, and light showed two silhouettes before the overhead light flared and blinded him.

Bird's voice said, "You all right, son?"

"Yeah." His heart was still doing double-time. He put his arm up to shade his eyes. Time rolled forward and back and forward again. He began to figure out for certain it was a sleepery, and he remembered being in the bar with Bird and Ben. It was Bird and the red-haired woman in the doorway, Bird in a towel, the woman—Meg—in a sheet. Ben showed up behind them in the doorway, likewise in a sheet, looking mad. Justifiably, he told himself, and said, "I'm sorry."

"Clearer-headed?" Bird asked.

"Yeah." Things are still going around. He recalled walking up and down the hall behind the bar, up and down with Ben and Meg and a black woman, remembered eating part of a sandwich because Ben threatened to hit him if he didn't stay awake—but he didn't remember going to bed at all, or how he'd gotten out of his clothes. He had hit Bird in the mouth. Bruised knuckles reminded him of that. "Sorry. I'm all right. Just didn't know where I was for a second."

"Doing a little better," Bird said.

"Yeah." He hitched himself up on his elbows, still squinting against the overhead light. "I'm all right." He was embarrassed. And scared. The doctors said he had lapses. He didn't know how large this one might have been or how many days he had been here since he last remembered. "Thanks."

Bird walked all the way in. "You're sounding better."

"Feeling better. Honestly. I'm sorry about the fuss."

Ben edged in behind Bird, scowling at him. "Beer and pills'll do that, you know."

"Yeah," he said. He earnestly didn't want to fight with Ben. His head was starting to ache. "Thanks for the rescue."

"Good God," Ben said. "Sorry and Thank you all in one hour. *Must* be off his head."

"I've got it coming," he said. "I know." He slipped back against the pillow, wanting time to remember where he was. "Leave the light on, would you?"

Ben said, "Hell, if it keeps him quiet—"

They left then, except Bird. Bird walked closer, loomed between him and the single ceiling light, a faceless shape.

"You had a rough time," Bird said. "You got a few friends here if you play it straight with us. Watch those pills, try to keep it quiet. Owner's a real nice guy, didn't call the cops, just took our word you're on the straight. All right?"

He recalled what he'd done. He knew he had maybe a chance with Bird, maybe even with Ben, if he could keep from fighting with him. "Tell Ben—I wasn't thinking real clear. Didn't know what ship I was on."

"You got it straight now?"

"I hope I do." His head was throbbing. He wanted desperately for them to believe him. He didn't know whether he believed *them*—but no other way out offered itself. He put his arms over his eyes. "Thanks, Bird."

Bird left. The light stayed on. He didn't move. In a while more he took his arm down to fix the room in his mind. It was mostly when he shut his eyes that he got confused; it was when he slept and woke up again. He kept assuring himself he was out of the hospital, back with people who understood, the way the doctors didn't, what it was like out there.

And the two rabs, who might be Shepherds, but who didn't talk like it—he wasn't sure what they were, or what they wanted, or why they zeroed in on him. They worried him the way Ben worried him—not the dress: the mindset— the mindset that said screw authority. No future. Get high. Get off. Get everything you can while you can, because the war's coming, the war to end all wars.

Hell, yes, Cory had said, it could end Earth. But it *won't* get the human race; that's why we're going, that's why we're heading out of here . . .

People in boardrooms had started the war over things nobody understood. And the rab had just said—screw that. And rattled hell's bars when and as they could until the company shot them down. He hadn't known that when he was a kid. He hadn't understood anything, except he was mad at what they said was happening to the human race. He'd hated school, hated the have's and the corporate brats—he'd understood corruption and pull, all right; he'd

thought he was rab and scrawled slogans on walls and busted
a few lights with slingshots, gotten skuzzy-drunk a few times
and lightfingered a few trinkets in shops before he'd figured
out what the rab was and wasn't, and why those people had
died trying to get through those doors—he'd been thirteen
then, nothing could touch him and he'd be thirteen forever...

Til Cory.

And Cory—Cory wouldn't at all have understood him
sitting at the table with two women like that. Cory would
talk to him later and say, the way she'd said more than once,
Stay away from that kind, Dek, God, I don't know where
your mind is... we don't want any trouble; we don't want
anything on our record—

Meg, the older one's name was. Meg. With the red hair
and the Sol accent he'd never realized existed until he'd
gotten out here and heard Cory's Martian burr and heard
the Belter's peculiar lilt. There might be a heavy dose of Sol
in Bird's speech. But none in Ben and none in the black
woman—all of them the last types you'd ever think to be
hanging around with a plain guy like Bird—or with each other.
*Not* likely Shepherd women—who might drink with miners,
maybe—but far less likely sleep with them... when women
were scarce as diamonds out here and available, good-looking
women could take their pick clear up to the company elite if
they wanted, if they didn't have a police record. They didn't
have to live on helldeck—unless they wanted to.

Maybe Bird didn't understand the rab... wreck everything, take what you wanted, rip the company—

So much for ideals and causes. Same here as at Sol.
Same in the Movement as in the company boardrooms. No
difference.

He squeezed his eyes shut, felt tears leak out. Raw
pain. He had no idea why. He thought—

—screw all of them. Company and not.

But he didn't mean it the stupid way the kid on Sol had
meant it, 13 and stupid and tired of bumping up against
company types, scared as hell about the rumors that said his
generation wasn't going to have a chance to grow up—he'd
gotten a knot in his stomach and lain awake half the night,

the first time he'd heard how the colonies didn't have to fire a shot—how the rebels could just drop a rock out of jumpspace, a near-$c$ missile aimed right at Earth or Sol Station. Nobody could see it coming in time. *That* for Earth—that for all the history they were supposed to memorize, all the rules, all the laws. Over in five minutes. So why learn anything that was going to be blown up? Why try for anything except grabbing as much as you could before it went bang?

But nobody'd do a thing like that. Nobody'd really hit Earth, nobody'd really hit a station and kill all those people. Of course they wouldn't.

Cory would say—just get me far enough, fast enough. Cory had told him about places he'd never cared about until she made it sound like there was an honest chance of getting there—if you had the funds. If you could get the visa. If the cops didn't stop you at the last minute and say, Wait a minute, Dekker, you have a record—

The Earth Company said no more free rides, and you had to pay off your tax debt before you could get a visa. Then your own government, the only time you'd ever see anything from your government, wrote you down as belonging to the ship you'd bought a share on, and you could go.

—Where there'll be something left, Cory would say— Cory had an absolute conviction that Out There was much better than where they were—

—on a ship that had no use for an insystem pilot. He didn't know whether that was living or not. Truth be known, he had never had any idea what he was going to do then—keep balancing on one foot, he supposed, saying yes and meaning no, going with Cory because Cory was going somewhere—and he didn't trust the draft wouldn't take the miners, too, once those ships were built—haul him off to live in a warship's gut and get killed for the company, blown to hell for the company—

Step at a time, Tommy had used to tell him when he was too zee'd to walk. Step at a time, Mr. Dekker . . .

Dammit, he wanted to fly, that was all, just get that back—get his hands back on the controls again—

The last few moments he'd thought—he'd thought, clear and cold, not at all afraid, that he could still pull it out—

That he could still make that son of a bitch pay attention to his com—

Wake somebody up on that damned ship, rattle their collision alerts if that was what it took—

He looked at the ceiling-tiles. He supposed they were real. He supposed he'd gotten this far away from the wreck. But no matter how far he stretched it, time just looped back and sank into that moment like light in a black hole. One single moment when things could have worked and didn't. . . .

Those sons of bitches on that 'driver had known he was there. Had known they'd hit a ship. They must have. Even if it had never heard him—if somehow his com wasn't getting through to them—if nothing else, when the tanks blew they'd have known it wasn't a rock they'd hit.

And if *his* com wasn't reaching them—wouldn't they have listened to the E-band after they'd hit a ship? Wouldn't they have heard Cory's suit-com?

Damned right they had.

Meg leaned close to the mirror, painting a thin black line beneath her bottom lashes. Hell to keep the eyes from running right after makeup: she blotted with her finger, tried again. The next door over opened and shut. Ben and Bird were off to breakfast, everybody dressing where their wardrobe was. Sal, mirrored past her shoulder, was putting her boots on. "We got a day to do," Meg said, with a flourish at the corner of her eye. "But we can take second shift. I vote we feel out the novy chelovek."

"Severe spook."

"Decorative spook." Eyebrow pencil. Auburn. Hard to come by out here. If you were broke you used grease pencil, and *that* was expensive. "He came straight last night, after the bogies. *Seemed* to be coming in focus. . . . Bird talked to him."

"After the things he shouldn't have said in the bar, Kady, a serious lack of governance there—*everybody* was talking about it."

"He was drunk. Gone out. Everybody knows that."

"So he's got no failsafes? Shit, Kady! Ben's got severe misgivings on this."

"Tsss." She did the other eye with three even strokes, heard Sal get up and caught her reflection with a rap of the knuckle at the mirror. "Remains to see. Later's time enough. Bird says."

"Bird says. Bird says. What's Bird have in his head, here? 'Find him a partner.' Ben can't scope it. And brut put, I don't like this 'partner' talk and I sincerely don't like Bird close with this jeune fils, whose tab I don't know why we're paying, with *our* funds, while he's got a card and access, thank you."

"So do *I* understand?" But she figured she did, more than Sal would. She looked at Sal, eye to mirrored eye, then turned and leaned against the counter, taking the mandatory three thoughts before a body should commit truth—as the saying went. But Sal was seriously upset this morning—Sal had had her eye on that ship, and Sal had been talking to Ben last night, in these rooms, that was point one, and scary enough—if that was all of it, and there were enough angles with Sal on a thing like this she wasn't at all sure. "We got to talk, Sal."

Sal stared at her a couple of beats, still hot, shrugged and picked up her jacket. "Na. Rather breakfast, actually."

Meg didn't move. Sal didn't like brut talks, especially when she'd just snapped to a judgment about a thing, but Sal constitutionally didn't like mysteries. She said, to Sal's back, "Sal—do you want to know quelqu' shoze?"

She waited, *knew* Sal was going to turn around with an exasperated look and say—

"*What* should I want to know?" As if there couldn't possibly be anything worth the nuisance. Sal came at some things with her mind as tight as her fists.

She gave the room a significant glance around, then pushed buttons she knew were buttons with Sal. "Tell you later on second thought."

Sal had this look like she'd knife something; but that only meant Sal's mind was working again; and they'd been severely careful about bugs since the cops had torn the room apart. She snagged her jacket up. They walked out into the hall and through the door into The Hole proper, where the guys had a table in the shiftchange rush—Ben and Bird already into their breakfast. You went over to the hot table at the end of the bar, you told the second shift cook, Price, that you were breakfast, and he dumped whatever-it-was into a plate while you drew your own coffee.

They took their plates and their cups to Bird and Ben's table and sat down. "'Morning," Bird said. "'Morning," Meg said back, and thought how that, too, was one of those things native Belters didn't just naturally say.

Spooky kind of partnership, when you got to thinking about it.

Spookier still, just as they sat down, that Dekker showed up in the doorway. He came part of the way to their table and made a cautious little gesture like Can-I-join-you?

Bird waved his hand, swallowed his mouthful. "Grab your plate."

Dekker was clean shaven, hair wet and combed back—quiet and polite. That was a plus. Good bones, under a jumpsuit that didn't fit. A woman did notice things like that, if she was alive.

"Could do with feeding," Bird said.

Ben made a surly shrug. Meg tried to think of something cheerful, took a forkful of The Hole's best stand-in for sausage and eggs and a sip of not bad coffee, while they were all waiting for a lunatic to come and sit down with them.

"Want to bet he'll ask the time?" Ben asked.

"Don't you open your mouth," Bird said sternly.

"Did I say a thing?"

"Nice rear," Meg said.

"Doesn't impress me," Ben said.

"Quiet."

"Yeah, he'd do that for hours."

"Ben, . . ."

"All right, all right. He's doing just fine. Hasn't jumped Price or anything."

"Ben."

Dekker came back, with his breakfast and his coffee—into a sudden quiet at their table.

"How are you feeling?" Bird asked him as he sat down.

"Hung over," Dekker said, sipped the coffee with a grimace, and, from vials in various pockets, started laying out a row of pills: not unusual, for spacer-types—bone pills, mineral pills, vitamin pills; but Dekker's collection was truly impressive.

"Dekker?" Ben said. "You having eggs with your pills, or what?"

Dekker gave this defensive little glance up, the cold sort that made Meg's nerves twitch toward a knife she didn't carry now—didn't quite meet anybody's eyes. "Yeah. Thanks, whoever put the crackers by the bed. Lived on them last night. My stomach was upset."

"They give you a doctor's number?" Bird asked.

Dekker nodded, swept up a fistful of pills, chased them one after another with coffee, and didn't ever answer that. Bird shrugged. Dekker ate his eggs. They ate theirs. Finally Dekker got up and went back to his room, saying something about needing his rest.

"Yeah, well," Ben said, staring after him.

"Man's hung over," Bird said.

Ben didn't say a thing to that except, "Are we going in to the docks?"

"Yeah," Bird said. "Afraid they're not going to move if we don't push. And we can pull those panels, right now. We can do that. But four's too crowded up there."

They were close to viable now on *Way Out*. They'd gotten the tanks mated three days ago, they'd gotten the interior blown out and certified for access, they'd gotten everything well toward completed, if they could just get the refit crews to keep after it and get the value assemblies connected... but when it was a case of getting skilled help on free time, it wasn't easy. It took inducements *and* constant look-ins to make tired crews on overtime look sharp and do it right.

"We'll be back about suppertime," Bird said. "And if you two wouldn't mind to be staying here..."

"Hey!" Sal held up a hand. "Don't make us responsible for this guy!"

"Don't let him cross Price. Or Mike. All right?"

"No!"

" 'Appreciate that." As Bird and Ben got up quickly and beat a retreat.

"Well, *hell!*" Sal said.

"There's worse."

"I'd *rather* vac the cabin."

"Hey. Don't judge too soon. That's *good* bone structure."

Sal gave her a flat, disgusted stare.

Meg said, "You can go up if you want. I can hold it here. Or we can take a walk and I can tell you what I won't say in the room."

*"Yeah,"* Wills said, on the phone, *"yeah, we did find him."*

Salvatore got a breath. "Damn right you'd better have found him."

*"Yessir."*

"So where the hell is he?"

*"Sleepery, sir, just hadn't paid a bill yet. No problem."*

"There'd better not be. You listen to me. If you can't tag him any other way you keep somebody on it. You don't let that guy slip. Understand?"

*"Yessir. Report's coming to you right now."* Wills sounded upset. But he'd been on it, when a routine print had shown no card use for a sleepery. Couldn't particularly fault Wills: Dekker wasn't the only case Wills had on his lap, a couple of them felonies, while Dekker was Minimal Surveillance. But Human Services had dropped 5 whole C's onto that card for the sole purpose of making sure Dekker stayed traceable, and it was embarrassing to the department to have him slip in the first couple of hours, in a place where he had no friends, no contacts, no credit and no way to get it.

Wills asked: *"You want Browning to ask a few questions?"*

Salvatore scanned the report, how Dekker had spent

5-odd dollars in a helldeck bar, 5.50 on beer and phone calls, and nothing else—

Browning had talked to The Pacific, who'd referred Dekker down the row to The Black Hole, and sent his card there when the management at The Hole had called for it. Browning had had the sense to query Wills before any next step, and Wills had told Browning not to follow that lead too closely: Dekker was apparently still there, The Hole was a quiet place with no apparent reason to lie to The Pacific, but Dekker hadn't used the card at The Hole after he'd gotten it—which indicated Dekker must have some acquaintance there—or that he'd found some means of support—meaning hiring out for something, ditching the card for a while, not an uncommon dodge for a man evading the cops: prostitution was the ordinary way for somebody with reason to duck the System—or if not that, he had to have friends.

Wills said: *"Bird and Pollard are staying there. We checked them earlier."*

Bird and Pollard. Salvatore searched his recent memory.

*"The ones that claimed his ship,"* Wills said. *"The ones that brought him in. Ship claim went through. The company paid. But Bird and Pollard saved his life. My guess is he looked them up, with what idea I don't know, but evidently it wasn't war. He's staying there, evidently on one of their cards."*

Not necessarily looking for trouble, then—searching out the only two people he knew made perfect sense. Healthy sense, even. Salvatore sipped at a cooling cup of coffee, thought about it, and said: "All right, all right, the boy's got himself settled. Long as he's quiet, understand? Just get a list of the current residents. Run backgrounds. That sort of thin."

*"Copy that,"* Will said. *"We can do it on a tax check."*

"Do it."

They'd gotten the lawsuit dropped—the report had convinced the EC board, a closer call than the kid knew about. But he'd signed the accident report—he was out of hospital and if he just for God's sake got a job and settled, he was fine. Visconti said rehab might not be productive right now. There was a lot of hostility.

So let him run through the Human Services money. Let him settle and think about surviving. There wasn't any negligence, there wasn't any charge to file, and Dekker didn't go to trial, however much Alyce Salazar wanted his head. Salazar was threatening civil suit now, to tie up the bank account and the insurance, but Crayton's office said don't worry about it: the daughter was over 18, the partnership was signed and legal, with a survivor's clause, and the account was jointly acquired, anyway. Dekker was safe: there was no legal way Salazar was going to get at him.

*That* card could go in the pending settlement stack.

Strolling along the frontage spinward of The Hole, Sal had things of her own to say. And for openers, since Meg wasn't getting started: "I'll tell you this, Kady, we got to get him out of there, God, of all places for him to come!"

"Natural enough."

"Natural! He said it, they friggin' took every lovin' thing he owned—what's he going to do, forget it?"

Meg walked a few steps further. Kicked at a spot on the decking. "Dunno. Difficult to say. But what are we going to do, throw him out? That's brut sure he won't forgive."

"Forgive, hell!"

Another silence. "You know, brut frank, Sal—there's a difference in Ben and Bird."

"We're talking about Dekker. Or why are we out here?"

"We're talking about that. Calmati, calma, hey?"

"So say! Doesn't make sense so far!"

"I tell you, I never had any use for the motherwell. You less."

"Damn right."

"Watch it go, right? Screw it all, all that shiz. —But—I get out here, Sal, I dunno, thinking it over—I *know* why Bird paid for this guy a room."

"So? Why did he?"

"You know you don't say 'morning."

"Of course I say morning. And what's that to Flaherty, anyhow?"

"You say it because I say it. You didn't come saying it. Or 'evening. Brut different, Sal."

"So?"

"Different the way Bird's different from us. Never saw how the motherwell matters til I figured that."

"That's shit." Sal hated soppiness. This was getting soppy, it wasn't like Meg, and it was making her increasingly uncomfortable.

"May be shit," Meg said. "But I know why Bird paid."

"Because the motherwell makes you crazy."

"Dekker's from the motherwell. At least from Sol Station—which is close enough for 'mornings."

"Accent tells you that."

"Yeah. But we *think* in accents. That's what I'm talking about. Yours and mine. I can turn my back on the motherwell, I can take what I want and leave the rest. Bird's not rab, Bird's just norm, but I know how his mind works—I dealt with there, remember."

"Are they all fools?"

"Fools, peut et'. But not the only. You mind me saying, Sal—you're going to be a skosh bizzed at me over this—"

Puzzles and puzzles. A body could be irritated at motherwell Attitudes, too. "All right. So we got this deep secret difference. It's worth five. Go."

"Head-on, then—MamBitch is scamming her kids."

"Is that new?"

"It is when you don't see it. You know, even the vids that get out here, they're pure shit, Aboujib, they're company vids. They're slash-vids, cop-chasers, fool-funnies, salute-the-logo shit, intensely company, intensely censored—you understand me? MamBitch has been robbing you all along, little bits and pieces. Robbing me too. Those sods brut *like* what's rab. Rab's no trouble to them, hell, rab's where they're going—forget Earth. Forget what's old garbage. —Only out here the *company's* going to pick what's rab. Capish'?"

"Neg." She looked at Meg with the slight suspicion Meg was talking down a long motherwell nose at her, a long thirtyish nose at that. But Meg hadn't made sense enough yet to make her mad. "This going somewhere significant eventually?"

"It's the Institute, all over again. Understand? You didn't take the shit there. But you don't say 'morning—"

"'F' God's sake, Kady, good morning, then!"

"But Belters don't say it. Bird remarked it to me once: Belters don't and Sol Station will. Belters don't give you a second cup of coffee without you pay for it. On Sol Station you expect it. Belters don't give you re-chances. You screw up once, you're gone, done, writ off—"

"E-vo-lution. Don't let fools breed."

"*Corp*-fad, Aboujib. It's wasn't always that way."

Down a damned long motherwell nose.

"You take a look at corp-rat executives the last couple of years, Aboujib? Seen the clothes? Rab gone to suits."

"So? Poor sods still got it wrong."

"No. No. They got it *right*. I don't say on purpose—I'm not sincerely sure they have that many neurons compatible— but they *like* the rab. In their little corp-rat brains, shit, yeah, dump the past, let the company say what's fad, what's rab, and what's gone—they don't ever like some blue-sky lawyer citing charter-law at 'em, so that's gone. Don't teach anybody about the issues: all us tekkie-types and pi-luts need is slash-vids and funnies, right? Tekkies don't need to know shit-else but their job. Hell, the rab never said dump all the smarts, we said Stop thinking Earth's it, wake up and see what's really going on out there; but the stupid plastics said, *Dump the past*. We said Access for the People, and the plastics say *Grab it while you can*. Corp-fad. Plastic *is*, Aboujib, plastic *sells*, plastic doesn't ask questions, plastic's always dumber than the management, and hell, no, management didn't plot with its brain how to take us over, they just wobble along looking for the easy way, and damned if we didn't give it to them."

Corp-fad made an ugly kind of sense. The Institute was without question MomCorp's way of making little corp-rat pilots—she'd seen that happening: she wouldn't salute the logo and they'd found a way to can her, right fast.

"I'm 35," Meg said after a moment or two of walking. "I'm an old rab. Eight, nine years ago they shot us down at the doors and the politi-crats in the company's bed said that good old EC was within their rights, it was self-defense, the rab was breaking the law and endangering a strategic facility, d' you believe that? Corp-rat HQ is a strategic facility? —Time the miners *and* the Shepherds had the guts to tell the whole damn company go to hell, turn the whole operation independent. But where are they, Sal? Where are they? Freerunners are mostly gone. Brut few coming out here now: the company's training the new generation, paying their bills and giving them the good sectors til they get it all in their pocket. The Shepherds let the company handle their outfitting and now they're fighting to hang on to the perks they have. The rab got themselves shot to hell in the '15 and here we got these damn synthetics swaggering around with the company label all over. The plastics don't know what we were. They turn us into clothes. Into *corp*-fad. Damn young synths make the music without the words. The Movement's probably dead back at Sol. Old. Antique. And where do I go?"

"Brut cold," she said, and put her hands in her pockets, walking step for step with Meg, Meg seeming to have finished her say. Crazy as it sounded, she wondered if the Institute *had* censored the things it didn't want them to know, on purpose, and when she thought about it, rights damned sure had changed—

Things like abolishing crew share-systems, the way they'd used to be on Shepherd ships. Like the bank refusing to honor cash-chits, the way Shepherds had paid out bonuses, and kept money outside the bank card system.

She thought about the courses she could have sailed through if she'd kissed ass. She thought about her mama and her papa's friends, Mitch among them, who'd said . . . You're a fool, kid. Should have kept your head down til you graduated. We can't make an issue, you understand? A kid with a reckless endangerment on her record isn't it. . . .

So she was a fool and the instructors washed her out, told her the same as they'd told Ben: Insufficient Aptitude.

She was learning from Meg—she'd learned more from Meg than she ever let on with the licensing board; and when the time came Meg couldn't teach her, then she'd go to Mitch a hell of a lot better than Mitch ever thought she was . . . flight school washout, Attitude problem and all.

But meanwhile her mama's and her papa's friends were going grayer and thinner and more brittle, some dying of the lousy shields they'd had in the old days, the old officers and crew hanging on to their jobs because they were the skilled crews the company urgently needed—

But the company was training new techs fast as they could, and the new head of MamBitch was talking about substituting Institute hours for the experienced Shepherds' years, requiring re-certifications every five years after you were forty.

The Shepherds had naturally told MamBitch where they'd send the cargoes the hour they did that and the company threatened to pass those re-cert rules if the Shepherds ever did it—but the company didn't have enough pilots to plug in those slots right now that wouldn't dump more than cargo into the Well, or fry themselves and their ships by pure accident. Yet.

So Big Mama had had to assign her shiny new tech crews to tend the 'drivers for now, because Shepherd crews wouldn't fly with the corp-rat cut-rate talent straight out of 'accelerated training'—and because the military was hot on Mama's neck about schedules. But time and the Belt were taking their natural toll and the day was coming, even a dumbass Attitudinal washout could see it ahead, when there'd be just too few of the old guard left to make a ripple in the company's intentions: someday company was going to pass its New Rules, and she was the right age to be caught in it. She didn't like Meg's line of thought at all, and she couldn't figure how it had much to do with anything present—which was what Meg had promised her.

"So?" she said. "So what's this leading to? What's this to do with our problem?"

"If you want to figure Bird," Meg said, "you seriously need to understand, blue-skyers don't know what short supply *is*. They don't think by the numbers: air's free and they got nothing but heavy time, so they give it away—they give it away even if they haven't got it, because that's their pride, you see? They have to say they can, even if they *can't*, because natural folk can, and anything less they won't admit to."

"Way to starve," Sal said. "Way to end up on a company job. That's pure fool, Kady. And Bird isn't."

"Air's free on Earth. Feet can go."

"If you don't mind dirt. And they got laws that say where you can go. I heard Bird say."

"Yeah, well." Meg walked a few more steps. Sal remembered then that, old business at Sol Station notwithstanding, Meg was a whole lot closer to blue sky than she ever could be, and she worried that maybe she'd cut Meg off with that zap about dirt.

But Meg went on as if she hadn't taken offense: "That's how it is for corp-rat execs, isn't it? Air's free wherever they are. Short for them is when they run out of their Chardonnay '87—I know. Hell, I used to run that freight. I know what those sons of bitches are eating, them with their Venetian antiques and their mink bedspreads."

"Venetian?"

"Italiano. Ochin expensiv. Fragil. Minks are fuzzy live crits. You wear their skins."

Sal looked at her. Sometimes Meg scammed you when she was in a mood. Hard to be sure.

"No shit. I used to freight it. Pearls, fancy woods, stuff like that. If you skimmed that stuff, you could black market it to starships or you could sell it right back to guess where?"

Sal lifted a brow.

"I guess the corp-rat got his apartment furnished," Meg said. "Or he got a cheaper source. SolCorp didn't want me going to trial, hell no. They told me I could come here and fly for myself or I could pilot some pusher back and forth off Mars for good old EC if I sincerely didn't want to go do mining."

That was half what Meg had said and half what she'd

never said—that she had been dealing black market with some exec, and it was that guy who'd blindsided her.

Things you found out, after this many years.

She liked Meg hell and away better than she had those years ago, that was sure—understood a good deal more of her thinking; but not all of it, never all of it, and she wasn't entirely sure she wanted to know where Meg had been or what Meg had been trained to do. Dive into a planetary well or bring a ship out of one—the thought gave a Shepherd's daughter the chills.

"So, well, Bird's got a little ahead at this guy's expense, he's short—Bird's not going to say no, isn't going to make this guy ask, either. Machismo. Something like. Fact is, *I've* been where this guy is and it makes me a skosh mad, Sal. It sincerely does."

"Well, I'd agree with you I don't like to see the guy screwed, hell, I put it on Mitch, and *they're* bizzed about it—but they're going to do a real fast hands-off after what he did. I'll tell you the word I don't like, Kady, it's what I heard from Persky—the guy yelled out about Bird and Ben knowing a 'driver was out there—"

"Yeah, well, he was drunk."

"Doesn't matter if he was drunk, Kady, dammit, I got very scarce favor points with Mitch—"

"Screw Mitch."

"Yeah, the hell with Mitch—Mitch'll give me a choice, get out and away from Bird, that's what he'll tell me."

"Would you do it?"

"It's all over the damn 'deck what he said—"

"Tss. They drugged him stupid, Aboujib."

"We got a live charge here, Kady. We can't afford this. *They* can't!"

"All right, I'll tell you what Bird said to me. This is a confidence. Black-hole it."

"Go."

"'Driver's sitting out there right where the accident happened. Dekker gave 'em the coordinates. Said he and his partner had found a big rock. Class B. That's where that thing is sitting, chewing it up and spitting it at the Well, fast as it can. Few more months and it won't be there."

"Why in *hell* didn't you tell me?"

"I *am* telling you. I found it out from Bird last night. That's what you can see on those charts you lifted."

"Shit! —But that doesn't make sense. Something rolls in from Out There—yeah, rocks like that happen, but *we* don't get 'em. Those things show up on optics."

"So somebody slipped—assigned the kids to it. MamBitch can't make a payout like that to a freerunner. You want to know how many'd be kiting out here? *Buying* passage out here? If it *was* iron, the way Dekker claimed, that's a friggin' national debt!"

She let a breath go between her teeth. "God."

"You know MamBitch's help. Some lowlevel fool in BM screws up, puts this freerunner out there and then his super finds out. And does any freerunner call in til he's got his sample? Not the way you and I do it: we're not having the Bitch say no, don't pursue, and then have her hand the good stuff to her lapdogs... and give the kids credit for *some* savvy about the system. They wouldn't trust the Bitch. They'd go on and sample it—get a solid assay on that thing."

"Dangerous as *hell* for a ship their size. Maybe it *was* the rock that got 'em, maybe they were just rushed..."

"Possible. I dunno. The jeune fils isn't thinking so."

"And a rock like that—untagged—where'd it come from? Thing had to have an orbit way the hell and gone. And iron?"

"We don't know shit what it was. We do know one kid is dead and MamBitch wiped the log. But those loads are going to hit the Well any day now. Drop *that* on Mitch."

"I can drop it, for what it's worth. But with a mouth like that—"

"Severely young, severely green, Aboujib. We can pull him in line."

"Kady."

"I'm telling you. Tell you something else. We *have* to pull him in line: *they* know where he was last night."

"What are you talking about?"

"*MamBitch*, Aboujib. MamBitch. He *came* there. He checked in. He knows Bird and Ben—"

"Oh, God."

"Yeah, 'Oh, God.' I've *been* through this. They've got a line on him. Not a short one, maybe, but that depends on what he gets into. And what are we going to tell Bird? Excuse us, Bird, but you sincerely got to pitch this guy out, on account of MamBitch is looking for trouble and on account of Sal's slipped Ben's charts to the Shepherds?"

"Dammit, why didn't you say something?"

"How can I say what I didn't know? I didn't hear the word ''driver.' I didn't see those charts. I didn't hear the word 'rock' til last shift—"

"Dammit!"

"You want another thought to sleep with? We're going out of here in a couple weeks, and what's *he* going to be doing—or saying—while we're out there? Can we stop him?"

"God."

"What's Mitch going to say about that?"

"I don't know!"

"We could shut him up for about three months, say."

"What are you saying? Take him *with?*"

They walked past a noisy bar doorway. Meg said, the other side: "Well, here's what I'm thinking: the jeune fils needs his license back. Say he passes the ops. He's got to have board time. Couple hundred hours. Gets him off the 'deck. Gets him shut up."

"Yeah, and where's Ben in this figuring? Ben'll *kill* that guy."

"Who said Bird and Ben?"

"Oh, God. You're out of your head, Kady."

"Look. Bird's got this debt—and *we* can pay it for him. We make it like a favor. Then Bird's got karma for us. So does this guy—who's also from the motherwell."

"Who's also bent. And we get tagged with him!"

"Tell Mitch what we're doing. Tell him we're going to bend this guy around the right way. Do *they* want him now? I don't think so. We can solve Dekker's problem, solve Bird's problem, solve Mitch's problem. *Our* rep can't get too badly bent. That's where we're useful. We get this jeune fils' sober attention and he's no problem."

Meg rolled her eyes. *Hell* of a situation wrapped around that ship that they were so close to—

Decorative is one thing, she thought. But where's the payout? —Meg hands out this air-is-free and everybody-works-partners stuff, like the preacher folk. But what's this guy really bring us?

They walked along, looking at displays in spex windows, in the deep bass rhythm of music blasting from the speakers, bouncing off the girders overhead.

She said to Meg: "I'll tell you one thing, that chelovek better not have been skimming. *We* got rep enough. And he *damn* sure better not come into The Hole on drugs again. He really better not be that kind."

"Couldn't say that this morning," Meg said.

"Couldn't say he was on the beam, either. I hate those quiet types. No joke, Meg, if we get out there and he does go schitz—what in hell are we going to do? We don't know we *can* get him straight. That guy could get severely strange out there. Then what do we do?"

"Keep him tied to the pipes, the way the guys did? I could go for that."

She caught a breath. "Warped, Kady!"

"Well, hey, —he isn't useless, is he?"

"Hell!"

"Gives Mitch three whole months. Do you want this jeune fils loose on the 'deck the way he is, talking about Bird and Ben and 'driver ships?"

"Point."

"So we just got to figure how to sign him in with MamBitch."

"What the hell do we call him? Ballast?"

Lascivious grin. "Systems redundancy?"

"Rude, Kady."

"Yeah." Meg grinned, with a sideways glance.

"Don't con me! We got more than a small problem here. Say we get this guy straight, we *still* got him in the middle of things—we got Ben, who's seriously put out, here . . . Ben's *not* going to go easy on this, he's *not* going to go shares with this guy."

"Ben better not push Bird on this. Don't expect him to figure it, just he shouldn't push. Everybody needs some room sometime."

"Serious room, here. Major with Ben, too."

"He doesn't have to work with Ben."

"Who's going to work with him? We got guys starving on the list, and any numbers man needing a pilot wants one who doesn't see eetees, f' God's sake. That jeune fils made himself a rep yesterday that he's got to live down a *long* time before they forget that—"

"There's always Yoji Carpajias."

"God." Yoji was a great numbers man. But he didn't bathe. "We'd have to steam and vac all over."

"Yeah. But there *is* Yoji. There's others. Leave Ben on prime with *Trinidad*. Us on prime with *Way Out*. If MamBitch lets Dekker re-certify, then quiet is exactly what she wants. And Dekker with his license back—is a whole lot more credible, isn't he?"

"Yeah, and how do we keep a line on him? He's poison right now. But we don't know him. We don't know *what* way he's going to turn."

"Dekker's from Sol. He's a lot more like Bird. You got to take into account he'll do things for Bird-type reasons. He's stuck by his partner, hasn't he? He'll owe us. Major karma."

The idea got through to her then, what Meg was saying. "Karma, hell. If Bird gives that sumbitch board-time, he can charge for it. Take it out of his hide, he can. Either Dekker's got finance to pay that time or Bird's for sure got a pilot on a string. That old sonuvabitch!"

"I don't think that's why Bird's doing this."

Sal gave Meg a look, thinking that through the loop a couple of times, wondering if she was following Meg through everything she'd been saying. "Yeah, but are *we* that crazy? Bird owns *Way Out*—but *we* own our time. We log that guy's board-time, and we own him til he can pay his charges with us—that's the law, that's the only damn useful thing the

Institute ever taught me. We debt that guy to us for time, *we* get him re-certified, and the company won't friggin' get him, how's that for charitable?" She came to dead stop on the decking, hands in pockets, with a whole new idea taking shape. Mitch, and *Way Out*, and a deal higher-value cards to deal with. "Maybe that's why MamBitch left the preacher-stuff out of pilot training, you think?"

Bad business, working null, floating around for hours on end compromising everything your heavy time was supposed to mend, but, hell, the meds who made the health and safety regulations hadn't priced help these days. Zero unemployment, the company claimed, or near enough as didn't count: and you could hire some real zeroes to come up and scrub, all right, but they'd play off on you and steal what wasn't bolted on, and to Bird's way of thinking and Ben's as well, it was better to take the extra dock time, do the steam and vac themselves and see what damaged systems they could fudge past the inspectors that really could be repaired instead of replaced—turn it over to a refitter like Towney Brothers, and you'd have a one hell of a bill, not least because Towney was in the pocket of half a dozen suppliers.

A-men.

So they didn't replace the shower, they just unbolted the panels and took them to the rent-a-shop on 3-deck where they could sand down the edges—no way you could tell it from new, once you screwed it back together. They took things apart and ported it down to 3, cleaned it and reassembled it, right down to the electronics. And you steamed and you vacced, and steamed and vacced and took apart and put together. Likely Ben was learning more about a ship's works than he'd ever opted for.

That was where Ben was right now, porting a big load of work down to 3 for the gals to handle or for them to do when they got down there after lunch.

Maybe they could put Dekker on time and board, if he could keep straight and if he was physically able: a miner pilot worth anything at all had to be a fair mechanic. Meanwhile—

"Bird?" Meg said out of the ambient noise of the core. He missed his purchase on a bolt and caught his finger with the power driver. He said something he didn't ordinarily say and sucked the wounded finger, looking around at the open hatch, which they had half shut and plastic sheeted to keep the warm air in and the dock noise out.

"Sorry." Meg drifted in, held the plastic aside, pretty sight in that lacy blue sweater. She turned herself so they were looking at each other right side up. "I'm sorry, Bird. —You want some help with that?"

"Doing fine," he said. He turned around again, seated the driver and put the screw home on the board he was re-installing. He took the next off the tacky-strip. "Aren't you cold, woman? And who's watching Dekker?"

"Sal and I got this idea," Meg said.

Which said it was something halfway serious. He wasn't sure he was going to like this. He reached over and snapped the tacky-strip out of the air before air currents that blew and drew from the plastic Meg was holding sent it somewhere inconvenient.

"We got this idea," Meg began again, "a kind of a partnership deal."

He heard it out. He didn't say a word while Meg was telling it: he slept with this woman and he figured he was going to hear it all night if he didn't hear it now. It moderately upset his stomach.

Meg said, "Can't help but make money, Bird."

"Yeah, saying this guy is fit to go out this soon. Saying he *can* get his license back. Put you and Sal off in a ship with him for three months? Bad enough with Ben and me. You gals—all alone out there—"

Meg blinked and said in a considerate way: "Yeah, but we won't take advantage of him."

"Be serious, Meg."

"We're major serious."

"You're letting out the heat, Meg."

"Listen to me. We can make this contract with him, Sal

says it's perfectly legal: we charge him his board-time for training, he'll pay us in cash or he'll pay us in time—"

"Indenture."

"Huh?"

"It's called indenture. I read about it. When we friggin' *had* paper, before they made the toilet tissue fall apart. You're talking about indenture. We got the guy's ship. Ben wanted to put a lien on his bank account. Now you want *him?* That *stinks*, Meg."

Meg got quiet then. Offended, he was sure. He picked off another screw and drove it into the hole.

"So what other chance has he got?" Meg asked. "Bird? —Who but us gives a damn what happens to that guy?"

He drove it in and looked around at Meg, suspicious now—it was worth suspicion when Meg Kady started talking about her fellow man.

"What's this 'us'?"

"Earthers."

It was at least the third time he'd heard Meg change her planet of origin. He was polite and didn't say that.

Meg said: "Dekker's out of the motherwell too, isn't he? Same as us."

"Sol, the way he talks."

"So you figure it, Bird—a greenie like him, paired up with another kid—she must have been. They never, ever got it scoped out, what the rules were. Worst kind of pairing he could make, nobody to show him the way—the guy didn't set out to screw up. He just didn't have any advice."

There'd be soft music next. What there was, was the heater going and money bleeding out onto the cold dock. "You want to close that plastic, woman?"

Meg ducked back and closed it. It gave him time to think there had to be something major in it for Meg and Sal. It didn't give him time to figure what it was.

"All right," he said. "We've heard the hard sell. Now what's the deal?"

Meg hesitated, rolled her eyes in a pass around that meant, We'd better not talk here, —and said, "Bird, what're you doing for lunch?"

# CHAPTER

# 12

DEKKER drowsed in the muted music-noise of the bar outside, lay in a .9-g bed half awake, having convinced himself that there wasn't anybody going to come through the door with hypos or tests or accusations. That was all the ambition he had: he was safe in this place and maybe if he just stayed very quiet there wasn't going to be anybody interested in him for a while, including Bird and including Ben.

Please God.

He got hungry, and hungrier—breakfast hadn't been much. Finally he looked at his watch, just looked at it awhile—didn't know the right hour, Bird had told him it had been off. But it was August 16th. It stayed August 16th. He knew where he'd gone off, and how absolutely unhinged he'd come—would never have thought he was capable of going off that far, would have hoped better of himself, at least. He'd kept a sort of routine on the ship once he'd slowed the tumble with the docking jets—enough to move about a little, do necessary things—irrational things, he thought now. Some of them completely inane, because Cory would have. God, he'd near killed himself doing housekeeping routines—because Cory would have.

He wasn't sure how much he'd forgotten. There were some holes he never seemed likely to patch. Other memories—weren't in any kind of order. He was scared to try to sort them—afraid he'd find some other memory to leap up and grab him by the throat, like that damned flash on the shower wall, the watch—he couldn't even remember if he'd had a shower the day of the accident. No, he thought, there'd been too much going on—

Hole there. Deep hole. Scary one. His heart was thumping. It was just the green wall, the place aboard Bird's ship that looked exactly like his own. That was where he'd gotten lost—but there were so many other places. The bar outside, the 'deck, the people he didn't know—he was hungry and he didn't want to go out and face people and questions and strangers. So he lay still a long while and listened to the beat of the music, and finally took his pills when he figured it must be time.

Then his stomach began to be upset in earnest: he figured he should go get something to eat to cushion the pills, so he ventured out as far as the bar—no one out there that he remembered but the owner, who didn't meet him with any friendliness—

No, they didn't serve lunch. There were chips. Dollar fifty a package. Want any?

He took a package and a soft drink—wanted them on his card, but the owner said he was on Bird's, and wouldn't take no.

He didn't want a fight. He took his card back and moused back to his room, upset, he didn't know why, except he didn't know what the terms were or why he was too scared to demand the damn chips go on his card—but he was, and he was ashamed of himself. He ate the chips with a lump in his throat, sat there on the bed and thought about taking a sleeping pill and just numbing out for a few hours, because he'd been dislocated out there, nothing and no one out there was familiar. He couldn't sit here and go around and around in mental circles all day, he *hadn't* the routines that had kept him sane, he was sitting here waiting for something he didn't know what, and he couldn't keep out of mental loops.

He took out the sack of pills—looked at the size of the bottle that was sleeping pills—God, he thought. What are they doing? How many of these are there?

In which curiosity, he poured the pills out on the counter and counted them.

212 pills.

Didn't intend for me to want refills on that one for a while.

He might be a little microfocused. He tended to do that lately. Maybe it was brain damage. But his amusements had gotten very narrow in hospital—bitter, constant harassment. Move, and counter. They moved. You moved. You didn't trust them. They never made consistent sense.

He spilled pills out onto the nightstand and started counting. Vitamin pills, potassium, 30 or so each. The calcitropin stuff, enough for a month . . . Big bottle labeled: Stomach Distress: As needed. Another labeled: For Pain: 1 every 4 hours. 40 of those. Decongestant: 45 pills: 1 every 4 hours. Diuretic: 60 pills: 1 daily. Drink plenty of liquid. Anti-inflammatory: 40 pills, Take 2 before meals. Depression: 60 pills: Alcohol contraindicated.

He sat there with those piles of pills, the one of them making this towering great heap on the counter, and he stared at it, and he stared, and he thought: 212 sleeping pills?

What did they do, misread the prescription?

No.

That's not it, is it?

Cory's dead, they tell me I'm crazy, they take my ship and take my license and tell me I won't fly again, and they give me 60 uppers and 212 sleeping pills?

They really don't want me to screw up my exit.

He hadn't known where he was going or what he was doing until he'd stared at that heap of pills a while.

He thought: First they kill Cory. Then they want me dead—

The hell with that.

He raked the pills into the appropriate bottles, wondering if there was a way to get into the corporation level—

No, that *was* crazy: really crazy people went into places and killed people who didn't have anything to do with their problems. Some innocent little keypusher or some smooth corp-rat bastard—neither one was going to get to the people responsible—

Somebody was outside; somebody knocked on his door and cold panic shot through him.

"Dekker?"

"Yeah?" he said.

"Dekker?" A woman's voice—one of Bird's friends: he didn't know why his hands were shaking, he didn't know what he'd just been doing or thinking that deserved it, but his heart went double-time and reason had nothing to do with it. "It's Meg Kady. You want to open the door?"

He raked the pill bottles into the plastic bag, the bag into the drawer. Not all of it fit. He made it.

"Dekker?"

Severe spook, Sal had called him, and face to face with him, Meg was very much afraid Sal might be right. He opened the door a crack, listened with a dead cold expression while she explained she and Sal wanted to buy him a drink. "Thought you might be tired of the walls. Come on. Get some air. Have a drink or two."

He looked as if at any second he was going to slam that door and lock it in her face—maybe with reason, Meg thought: the man must know Ben didn't like him, and he might have real suspicion about the rest of Bird's friends.

"Hey," she said, and gave him her friendliest grin. "You're not afraid of *us?*"

If that and the sweater she was wearing didn't get a man out of his room she hadn't got a backup.

Dekker muttered under his breath, looked rattled, and felt over his pockets. "This place safe to leave stuff?"

"Yeah. Anybody boosts stuff from The Hole, he's Mike's breakfast sausage. —How're you feeling?"

"All right."

Dead tone: All right. Dekker came out, let his door lock, walked with her down the hall to the bar like he was primed and ready to jump.

Severe spook. Yeah. Or suspicious of them and their motives.

Sal was waiting. Easy to capture a table with space around it—traffic at this hour was real light, most people being about their business. They went through the social dance, Hello there, good looking, how're you feeling? Sal pulled a chair out, got up, he sat down, she sat down, Meg sat. Mike, thank God, got right over for the orders.

"Spiced rum?" Dekker asked.

"Premium price," Mike said.

Dekker hesitated, reached for his card. Meg put a hand in the way. "Let us buy."

Upset him. He slowly put his card on the table. "Put it on mine. All of it. Rum and whatever they're having."

Meg shot a look at Sal, and gave Mike a shrug. "What the man wants," she said, thinking: Pricey tastes he's got.

Mike took the card. Dekker started to lean back, arm over the chair back—like it was a fortified corner he wasn't going to be pried out of; but the hand was shaking. He put it on the tabletop.

Sal said, "What do you go by?"

"Dek—to friends."

"Dek." Sal reached out across the table. "Sal. Aboujib, if you got to find me."

He hesitated, then made a snatch forward and solemnly shook Sal's hand.

Meg reached hers out. "Magritte Kady." Cold fingers. Scared spitless. "Meg'll page me anywhere. There's only one on R2. —You been out of that room today?"

"Lunch," he said.

"Any good?"

He shrugged.

Mike got the drinks over, fast, thank God, a merciful few beats without conversation. Dekker picked up his drink. Meg lifted her glass with a flourish.

"Welcome to R2, Dek."

"Thanks," he said faintly.

"Thanks for the drinks. —You remember us at all?"

He nodded.

Sal said, "We'd better say, before anything else, we're the ones that have *Way Out* leased."

He didn't react at all to that, just kept looking at Sal.

"I'm the pilot," Meg said. "Sal's my numbers man. You were the primary license on your team, right?"

Dekker nodded glumly, watching them, every move. He held the rum in one hand, the other arm over the chair back. "Yeah. I was."

"Excuse." She leaned her elbows on the table and cut down the distance. "Let's be frank here. They busted your license. Bird and Ben claimed your ship—but they haven't cut you off cold, either. They risked their financial asses saving your life. Understand? Lot of expenses."

"Yeah."

"So we got a lease on what used to be your ship, and probably you aren't real happy with us."

Dekker said tonelessly: "Yeah, well. Not your fault. No hard feelings."

"But," Sal butted in, "we got to thinking how we could do you and us both some good."

Meg said, quickly: "We figure you want your license reinstated. Which you got to have board time for. Which could be expensive, if you had to get it from the company— and you still might need some help to get past the bureaucrats."

Dekker gave her a quick, plain, a what-in-hell-are-you-up-to stare.

"Chelovek," she said quietly, because even in the bar, even with the music going, you had to worry about bugs lately, since the cops had searched the place, "you ran into real trouble—got ground up in the gears entirely, you *and* your partner. —Where are you from? Sol Station?"

Dekker nodded.

"Neo out here?"

"Two years." His jaw was set, not going to say a syllable more than he had to. Improvement on yesterday, she thought.

"Brut put, Dek, you got yourself in one helluva mess,

and there's beaucou' guys on R2 who'd pick your pocket the rest of the way. But as happens we're not them, and Bird's a blue-skyer, so he knows where you come from. —Not that we owe you, mind. But Bird doesn't like to take advantage. There's some things we can't fix. But suppose we could— what's prime business on your mind right now? What can we do most for you?"

He shook his head, staring elsewhere.

"Mad, I don't blame you, jeune fils. But are you going to spite yourself? What can we do to even things up? Anything you need?"

Another shake of the head.

"Yeah, well. You know what the corp-rats want, don't you?"

That got a look, a nasty one.

"They want you all theirs, jeune fils. They really don't like the independents. Their charter makes 'em have to accept us, but they got you right down to signing with the company."

"They won't sign me with the company. I haven't got a license."

"Oh, they'll give it *back* to you, jeune fils. When you're theirs. ASTEX regulations screwing you over and ASBANK ready to lend you money. What are you running on now? Mind my asking?"

"Yeah, I mind."

"Good. Do mind. But do you want to get that license without them?"

A little reaction there. Not a word.

"We got a deal for you. You get time at our boards, you take our help, you, me, Sal, Bird and Ben, we all make our own little arrangement that gets you working again, gets you fed, boarded, and eventually reinstated. How's that?"

Interest, at last. Hostility. "Why? Goodness of your heart, rab?"

"You pay us cash for our time if you can pay us, or you pay us a share plus lease after that—that's Bird's word on it, *if* you pass muster by Sal and me."

He looked somewhere else. She let the silence hang there a moment, then said: "We're not hard to get along with, Dek. We're fair good company."

"My partner's dead, do you bloody mind?"

Sal said, "She fond of you starving? Cold *bitch* jeune rab."

Dekker looked bloody death at her but Sal sailed right on:

"But I'll guess she wasn't a cold bitch at that, and she wouldn't like what you're doing to yourself, if she was here, which she isn't, nor will be hereafter. She's signed *off*, man, we all do. Death's life, you know, and it keeps on."

"Shove off." Dekker pushed his chair back and got up. Meg did, laid a hand on his arm: he slung it off. Mike, over at the bar, was probably reaching for the length of pipe he kept.

She said, quietly, lifting both hands, "Easy. Easy. No cops here. No offense. Help, here. That's all."

"You're an antique, you know it? You're a friggin' antique. Rab's gone. You're not *in* it anymore."

She actually felt a painful spark of interest—the jeune fils more lately from Sol and more in the current. "True?" She tilted her head, took a damn-you stance and said, "You got better, little plastic?"

He was twenty, maybe—you wouldn't tell it by the eyes; but the body, the way he let himself be jerked off course, scared as he was, that was all young fool. Maybe he didn't really even want to care about what she thought now: he'd only attack blind, young-fool-like, and for just a single unquiet moment—knew she'd just attacked him back.

"Come out of it. It's the twenties."

"So? What's the twenties got to offer us the '15 didn't? Corp-rats in fancy suits? Here at R2's still the teens. Maybe I don't like your tomorrow, little corp-rat."

"It's 2323 on Sol and they're building warships to blow the human race to hell. Lot you changed, whole fuckin' lot you changed!"

"So what's the word, little plastic?"

"The word's business suits, the word's grab it before it goes. That's Sol. That's all the good you did."

Bitter news, no better than she already knew. But she balanced on the balls of her feet, hands in belt, shrugged and said, "It goes *on*, young rab. Didn't we tell you, back in the '15, wake up! You're going to fly for them?"

"I'm not flying for anybody."

"You'll be living off the corp-rat sandwich lines the rest of your life if you do the fool now. They'll own you—and you'll be flying some damn refinery pusher til you're older than Bird." She added quietly, gently: "Or you can sit down, jeune fils, listen to me, and use your brains for more than ballast."

He stood there without saying anything. Meg thought, with Sal in the tail of her eye, God's sake, don't move, Aboujib, keep your friggin' mouth shut, kid's going to blow if you draw breath.

Dekker looked away from her, then, hooked a leg around his chair front and melted down into it.

Meg heaved a sigh, sank into the chair next to him, where he had to look her in the eyes. "Let us make up, jeune rab. Let's not do deal right now. Let's just take you out on the 'deck and show you the cheapshops."

"I don't feel like it."

"Not far. Relax. We're severely reprehensible, but we don't take advantage. Won't push you. Just a little walk."

Kid was scared white. And he managed not to look her in the eyes.

"Come on," she said. "You've seen too much of hospitals. Sal and I'd like to spend a little, see you get fixed up with a bit more'n a friggin' plastic bag for a kit—like to stand you a few Personals, you copy? Even if you decide not to take the rest of our offer."

She figured Sal was having a stomach attack right now, knowing Sal. Meg, Sal'd say, you want to pass out tracts too?

Dekker's breathing grew calmer after a moment. He said, "Shove off."

"You telling us you want to go with the company. We should leave you alone, just stay out of your life?"

A few more breaths. He picked up the glass with a shaking hand, drained it and set it down empty, except the ice. Then he nodded, and seemed to fall in on himself a little. "Yeah, all right, whatever."

Like they could chop him up in pieces if they wanted to, he didn't care.

She put her hand on the back of his chair, stood up, and

he stood up. She showed him toward the door with: "Mike? Tell Bird we're shopping."

And Sal, damn her, with the nerve of a dock-monkey, locked on to Dekker's arm as they headed him out the door, saying, "I know this place. Absolute first-rate. You got to see. All right?"

"Medium," he told the dealer, embarrassed by his company, exhausted by the walk, not sure he wasn't going to be had in various ways, some possibly dangerous—but he couldn't prove it. He'd broken what Cory called Rule One, going off with Belters he didn't at all know, into shops they did know, taking their word about who to deal with and who to trust—he didn't know whether they were on Bird's side of things or not. Ben's, for all he knew, but they were having a good time and he was out of the funk he'd tried to sink into—

Drifting, a little, maybe. But they'd gotten him moving, they'd made him mad, but they'd done more for his nerves than all of Visconti's pills. He was alive. He was thinking about something besides Cory, overwhelmed with music, with colors and textures and excited, cheerful voices—

He was halfway happy for a moment.

"Now, no shiz, Pat, you give him our deal, now," Sal told the guy, whatever that meant, and Meg called after him, "No corp-rad, now! Something serious!"

The dealer brought back pants and a bulky sweater. The pants said medium. They were gray stretch and they didn't half look medium. The price said 49.99, middling high for a cheapshop.

"That's too much," he objected. The dealer whisked out another pair of pants with diagonal stripes, black and red, that looked like a rab's nightmare. Laid that out with a blue sweater.

"God," Meg said, "not blue. Red. Can you match?"

"Let's try for coveralls," he said. "Blue or gray. Something that fits."

"Oh, work stuff," Meg said. "Dull, dull. No fun. —Try the gray pants, come on, Dek. You got the figure."

"Starvation," he muttered. He told himself he should

stop this, just get the coveralls traded for something that fit. But they were both set on him trying the gray, they shoved sweaters at him, and in their enthusiasm it was just easier to do it, make a fool of himself and prove once for all it wasn't going to work.

But the mirror showed him a walking rack of bones that actually didn't look bad in the pants, and that could use a sweater twice its useful size to hide his thin shoulders.

He wasn't sure, though, about the big slash stripes on the sweater. He stepped out of the changing booth to get the dark blue one, self-conscious as hell, and the women made appreciative sounds. "*Rab* sweater," Meg said. "Oh, I do like that."

He suffered a crisis of judgment, then, looking in the mirror outside the dressing-booth, and before he could reorganize, Sal said, "Suppose he'd fit those metal-gray boots? He's got small feet."

He didn't really want a wide striped sweater. He hadn't set out to get metal-gray boots that belonged on a prostitute. He damned sure didn't need the bracelet Sal shoved on him, but: "This is my treat," Sal said. "Man, you got to. Push the sleeves up."

"I need work clothes worse. Blue. On *my* card—"

"He's trading in the coveralls," Meg said to the dealer. "Can you just size him down?"

"Yeah," the dealer said, and hauled out a pair that said small. "If these don't fit you can exchange. You're a real small medium."

That wasn't what a man wanted to hear, who'd worked hard enough getting the size in the first place. But he decided he might be, after the hospital. He got the bracelet. He bought some cheap underwear and a pair of thermals, a plain gray stimsuit, his old one having been washed to a rag—that was expensive; and he ended up with the blue sweater too, along with a pair of black pants (stretch, like the gray) and black docker's boots, used. He was tired now, dizzy, and shaking in the knees; he was ready to go back to his room and collapse, the man was toting up the charge and he felt a moment of cold panic as those numbers rolled up.

He wasn't sure now what he'd just done, wasn't even sure he dared wear what they'd talked him into: he'd had his turn with rab when he was thirteen—but not here, where rab was a statement he didn't know how to deal with—where it was corporate or where it was a badge of things he didn't understand . . .

I'm a fool, he thought. He thought how Bird and Ben were going to look at him when he got back—and the rest of the boarders at The Hole, some of whom might take serious exception to a show-off with no license: he'd forgotten his troubles, they'd made him forget for a few dazed moments and damned well set him up.

"I think we'd better go back," he said, wanting time to think. His head was going around. But Meg said, "Neg, neg, you can't go shaggy. Let's get that hair trimmed."

"Cut off that pretty hair?" Sal said, the way he'd protested once himself—when he was thirteen. "No!"

"Not all of it," Meg said. "Come on, Dek. Let's go get you fixed up. It's on the way. Won't take fifteen minutes."

"No," he said.

Which ended him up in a barber's chair dizzy and remembering he'd missed at least one batch of pills, with two women telling a helldeck barber how he wasn't to take too much off, "—except the sides," Meg said.

He'd given up. It was like the hospital. He was just too tired to fight on his own behalf, and they were right, the shoulder-length hair and the shadows under his eyes made him look like a mental case. If the cut was too extreme he could trim the top himself, with a packing-knife or something, God, he didn't care right now, it was a place to sit down.

Cory and he had cut each other's hair, to save money, conservative, Martian trim—just practical. He watched what was happening in the mirror in front of him and kept thinking, in the strobe of the barbershop neon, Cory wouldn't like this. Cory would get that disgusted, high-class look on her face and say, *Really* not your style, Dek.

Cory's first letters had told him she didn't like the rab. When she'd sent her picture and he'd realized he had to send his back—with the long hair and wild colors and, God, the gold earring, he'd forgotten that—

But he'd been thirteen. He'd seen a serious, soft-eyed girl as sober and as kind as the letters. So in another crisis of judgment he'd gone to a barber and borrowed a plain blue pullover—gotten a serious job, he'd forgotten that too—tried to hide it from his friends, but they found out and thought it was damned funny.

He hadn't had those friends after that. Hadn't had many friends at all after that—except Cory; and he'd never met her face to face.

Stupid way to be. He hadn't planned it. He hadn't been happy with his school, his work, with anything but flying. Worked the small pushers for the shipyard—he was *supposed* to be loading them: the health and safety regs didn't let kids outside the dock there. But he'd got his class 3. And the super let him sub in until he was subbing in for a guy that ran a pusher into a load of plate steel . . .

". . . up the sides," Meg said. "Yeah. Yeah!"

Sal, with her metal-clipped braids, leaned to get a direct look at him, flashed a white grin and said, "That's optimal!"

It didn't hurt a guy's feelings to have a couple of women saying he looked good, but what was developing in the mirror in front of him was someone he'd never met before: it was 2315 again—but he wasn't 11, he was 20—It was the way the deep-spacer had said, the one they'd gotten in to talk to the class back then: You live on wave-fronts. You live on a station, you ride the local wave—the time you know. You go somewhere else, it's a different wave. Maybe a whole set of waves, coming from different places, different times. There's an information wave. There's fads. There's goods. There's ideas. They propagate at different rates.

Some dumb kid had made a joke about propagation.

The merchanter had said, dead-sober, So do stationers. Some shouldn't. And there'd been this scary two beats of hostile quiet and an upset teacher, because that was what deep-spacers were notorious for, on station-call, and what stationers were fools to do—especially with deep-spacers,

who moved on and didn't care. Cory's mother had—and look
what came of it.... a girl who'd made up her mind that
Mars was irrelevant. Who said that rab was irrelevant. Cory
had used to say: The rab can't really change anything. They
can't build. They're saying reform Earth's politics—but it
won't work. Worlds are sinks, they're pits where people
learn little narrow ideas—Luna Base was a mistake. Mars
Base was. Once we'd got off Earth we shouldn't ever have
sunk another penny in a gravity well—

Cory had said more than once, I'd rather a miner ship
for the rest of my life than be stuck on a planet—

He focused on the mirror where it wasn't *Way Out*'s
cabin, it wasn't Cory's face he was seeing, and the thin,
shadow-eyed stranger who got out of the chair looked like
someone who might have a knife in his boot. He wasn't sure
Cory would recognize him. He wasn't sure Cory would ever
have liked him if she'd met him like this.

"Serious rab," Meg said, with a hand on his shoulder.
She looked past his shoulder into the mirror, red hair, glitter
and all. Sal was at his other side.

He stared at the reflection, thinking, I'm lost. I don't
know where I am.

This is who survived the wreck. It's somebody Cory
wouldn't even want to know.

But it's who is, now. And he doesn't think the way he
used to—he's not going your direction anymore, Cory. He
can't.

I've seen crazy people. Faces like statues. They just
stare like that. People leave them alone.

He doesn't look scared, does he? But he is, Cory.
God, he is.

HE'D spent money he didn't want to spend, that sliced deep into all he had to live on for the next sixty days; he had Meg on one arm and Sal on the other both telling him he looked fine, and maybe he did, but he wasn't sure his legs would hold him—wasn't sure he wasn't going to fall in a faint—the white noise of the 'deck, the echoes, the crashes, rang around his skull and left him navigating blind.

Sal kept a tight grip on his left arm, Meg on the right, Sal saying in the general echoing racket that he looked severely done; and Meg, that they shouldn't have pushed him so hard.

"We can stop in and get a bite," Meg said.

"I just want to get home," he said. They had his packages, they kept him on his feet—he had no idea where he was, and he looked at a company cop, just standing by a storefront, remembering the cop that had stopped him outside the hospital, the fact he was weaving—a fall now and they'd have him back in hospital, with Pranh shooting him full of trank and telling him he was crazy.

God, he wanted his room and his bed. He wanted not

to have been the fool he'd been going with these people—he wanted not to have spent any money, and when he finally saw familiar territory and saw The Hole's flashing sign, he could only think of getting through the door and through the bar and through the back door, that was all he asked.

It was dimmer inside, light was fuzzing and unfuzzing as he walked, only trying to remember what pocket he'd put his key in, and praying God he hadn't left it in the coveralls back at that shop—

But Bird and Ben were sitting at the table they'd had at breakfast, right by the back door. Meg and Sal steered him around to their inspection and Ben looked him up and down as if he'd seen something oozing across the floor.

"*Well.*"

Bird said: "Sit down, Dek."

"I'm just going back to my room."

"*His* room, it is, now," Ben said; and Meg, with a deathgrip on his arm:

"Ease off. Man's severely worn down. He's been shopping."

"Yeah." Ben pulled a chair back. "It looks as if. —Sit down, Dekker."

His knees were going. But Ben suddenly took as civil a tone as Ben had ever used with him, walking out on him didn't seem a good idea, and he was afraid to turn down their overtures, for whatever they were worth—there damned sure weren't any others. He sank into the offered chair, Meg and Sal pulled up a couple of others, and he gave up defending himself—if they wanted something, all right, anything. Ben would only beat hell out of him, that was all, and Ben didn't look as if he was going to do that immediately, for whatever reasons. The owner—Mike—came over to get his drink order—Bird and Ben were eating supper, and Bird suggested through the general ringing in his ears that he should do the same, but it was already too late: he couldn't get up and stand in the line over there and he wasn't sure his stomach could handle the grease and heavy spices right now. He remembered the chips. He said, "Beer and chips."

"Out of chips. Pretzels."

"Yeah," he said, "thanks. Pretzels is fine." Maybe pretzels were a little more like food, he had no idea; and beer was more like food than rum was. Anything at this point. God.

"That all you're going to eat?" Bird asked.

Ben nudged him in the ribs and said, "Must be flush today. Who's buying the pretzels, Dekker?"

Meg said, "Ease off, Ben. He's seriously zee'd."

"That's nothing new," Ben said, and Bird:

"Ben."

"I just asked who's buying the pretzels."

"I am," Dekker said. "If you want any, speak up and say please."

Ben whistled, raised a mock defense. "Oh, well, now, yeah, don't mind if I do. God, you're touchy."

He'd have come off the chair and gone for Ben, under better circumstances. He didn't have it. It wasn't smart. But something took over then and made him say, with a set of his jaw: "I didn't hear please."

"Oh. Please." An airy wave of Ben's hand. "Passing charity around, are we, now? Paying off our debts? Did finance come in?"

"Not yet. But it will. You want my card?" He pulled it out of his pocket, tossed it onto the table. "Go check it out, Pollard. Take whatever you think I owe you."

Ben looked at him, and Bird turned his head and called out, "Mike, get those beers right over here, Ben's had his foot in his mouth. —Excuse him, son. You want to get the pretzels, we'll get the drinks."

"I'll pay my own tab," he said. Too harshly. He was dizzy. He wished the drinks would hurry. He wished he was safe in his room and he wished he knew how to get there before he got into it with Ben. Mistake, he told himself, serious mistake.

"We mentioned to him about the board-time," Meg said. "He says he wants to think about it."

"What 'think'?" Ben said. "He's got no bloody choice."

"Ben," Sal said, sounding exasperated, "shut up."

"Well, there isn't." Ben was quieter, scowling. "Try to help a guy—"

"Ben," Bird said.

"We're buying his effin' drink!"

"Ben," Meg said, and slammed her palm on the table, bang, a hand with massive rings on each finger. "We talked about the lease, and the jeune fils is thinking it over, that's his privilege. Meanwhile he's *offered* to pay his own tab, all right? So don't carp. —Don't pay him any mind, Dek. Sometimes you seriously got to translate Ben. He means to say Trez bon you're on your legs again and mercy ever-so for the pretzels."

The beer and the pretzels came. Dek picked his card off the table and shoved it at Mike, said, "Put it all on mine," and tried not to think what his account must look like now.

Bird said: "You don't have to do that, son."

"It's fine," he said. He picked up his beer and felt Ben's hand land heavily on his shoulder, the way Ben had done on the ship when Ben was threatening to kill him. Ben squeezed his shoulder, leaned close to touch glasses with him.

"No hard feelings," Ben said.

He didn't trust Ben any further than he could see both his hands. His stomach was upset, he was all but shaking as was, and the glass Ben had touched the rim of suddenly seemed like poison to him, but he sat still and took the requisite polite sip of his beer.

Ben said, "So do you want the board time?"

He looked at Bird, asking without saying anything whether this was Bird's idea too. Bird didn't deny it.

"Yeah," he said.

"So there's strings to be pulled," Ben said. "Short as the time is, we have to expedite, as is, or you won't get the ops test before we're out of here—and if you don't do those forms right, they're not going through. Now, as happens, I know the people you need. You do the work in the shop—"

"What work?"

"Thought you'd talked to him," Bird said.

"I said we'd mentioned it," Meg said. "We didn't exactly get down to that point."

"Well, now we have," Ben said. "There's no other way to do it, Dek-boy. Only deal going. So you've agreed. We're waiting to hear how you're going to pay for it. Time? Or money? Or the pleasure of your company?"

They were coming at him from all sides. He wasn't sure there wasn't a moment missing there—his ears were ringing, they were all looking at him, Ben with his hand on his chair back—he lost things, the meds said he did; and he sat here surrounded by these people who as good as had a gun to his head. If they helped him he might have a chance—but if they figured out he did forget things, the word would get around and it was all over, he'd never get reinstated, he'd end up doing refinery work . . .

"You any good as a mechanic?" Bird asked.

"I kept *Way Out* working."

"As a pilot?"

"I was good." He didn't expect Bird would believe him. He added, self-consciously, "We weren't broke." Bird had seemed the best of them, Bird had kept him alive and argued for him with these people. He was desperate for Bird to take his side now. And if they robbed him, there were worse alternatives. "Cory and I had 47 k in the bank. Not counting the ship free and clear. R1 bank's sending it, but I can't draw on it for another fifty, sixty days."

"47 k," Ben jeered. "Come on, Dekker."

He didn't look at Ben. He looked at Bird and Sal, clasped his hands around the wet chill of the beer glass. "Cory's mom was pretty well set. Cory had her own account—trust funds. The hour she turned 18, she took it and she called me and bought my ticket and hers. She came out from Mars, I came from Sol—we met out here and we bought the ship. Paid a hundred fifty-eight k for her. Another 40 in parts. We made a few mistakes. We hadn't made many runs—only been out here two years. But Cory knew what she was doing. She nearly had her degree in Belt Dynamics. 28 of that 47 k we didn't have when we came out here. We were doing pretty well."

"Damned well." Bird said.

"College girl," Ben said, "come on, the company'd have snapped her up."

"She didn't admit to it. She didn't want a company slot."

"With that kind of money? She was a fool."

"Ben," Bird said.

"Well, she was."

He set his jaw, *made* himself patient. "She just didn't want it. The fact is, she wanted a share in a starship."

"Oh, for God's sake!" Ben said.

"She wanted into the merchanters. You have to buy in. Her trust fund wasn't enough—wasn't enough for both of us. And she had this idea, it was all she'd listen to."

"Why?" Sal leaned forward, chin on clasped, many-ringed hands, neon sparking fire on her metal-beaded braids. "Why, if she was rich?"

"Because," was all the answer he could manage. There was a knot in his throat and he thought if Ben opened his mouth he'd lose it. Cory had been so damned private. Cory didn't tell people her reasons. But they went on listening, waiting for him, so he shrugged and said, "Because she hated planets. Because her father was a deep-spacer—her mother wanted a kid, she didn't want a husband and she didn't want anybody in Mars Base to have that kind of claim on Cory. Cory was a solo project. Cory was her mother's doing, start to—"

—finish. That word wouldn't come out. He said, watching condensation trickle on the beer glass: "Didn't even know his name. Cory sort of built on her own ideas. Stars were all she talked about. Wanted to do tech training. Her mother wouldn't have it. So she studied astrophysics. She had the whole thing planned—getting the money, coming out here—getting us both out."

Ben said, quietly, "Hell, if she could buy a ship, she could have gotten it faster working for the company. What's the rate? Eighty, ninety thou to get your tax debt bought?"

And her mother there, he thought, her mother on MarsCorp board to pull strings, get her broke and get her back. But he didn't say that. He said: "They'd have drafted me if I'd stayed at Sol. That was part of her reason. We were going together. That was the plan."

"That crazy about you, was she?"

"Ben," Meg said, "shut up. . . ."

"I don't know why everybody's telling me to shut up. It *wasn't* the damn brightest thing she could have done. She could have gotten to Sol Station, probably bought straight into a ship with what she had—she expected to make it rich here freerunning?"

"Her mother," he said, "wanted Cory back in college. Wanted—God only." His stomach hurt. He had a sip of the beer to make his throat work. "She was under age. Couldn't get an exit visa over her mother's objection. This was as far as she could get. Til she was twenty-one."

"The ship and 47 k in the bank," Ben began. "What *do* those sons of bitches want for a buy-in, anyway?"

"Maybe a couple hundred k apiece. With the ship, we had it for one of us, tax debt to get the visa, you've got to pay that off to the government before you ever get down to paying the ship share—and Cory's was high: she had a degree. Another 70 k each to get back to Sol. I told her get out—I saw on our first run it was no good. We didn't know how hard it was out here. We *wouldn't* have done it this way—but by then we'd sunk so much into the ship . . . and just buying passage to Sol would eat up everything she had . . ."

He'd yelled at her the night before their last run, he'd said, The war's getting crazier. They've got these damn exit charges, God knows when they're going to jack them higher—if you don't go now, there's no telling what they'll do next, there's no guarantee you can *get* out . . .

He'd begged: Just leave me what's left over. I'll buy in on some other ship, work a few years—whatever ship you're on will come back here. I'll join you then—

He'd been lying about the last. She'd known he was, she'd known he didn't want to go. And she'd known he was right, that both of them weren't going to make it. She'd known she was going alone, sooner or later, or they were going to do what every freerunner ultimately did do—go into debt. That was why the shouting. That was why she'd burst into tears. . . .

"—And she said?" Meg asked.

He'd lost the thread. He blinked at Meg, confused. He honestly couldn't remember what he'd been telling them. He picked a pretzel out of the bowl, ate it without looking at them. Or answering.

Bird said, "The lad's tired."

"Yeah," he said, remembered that he was behind on his medicine, remembered that the company management were all sons of bitches and *they* were the ones that handed out the licenses. Even that was in their hands.

Bird reached out, thumped a grease-edged fingernail against his mug. "Want another round? A beer? On us? To sleep on?"

"You're right," he said. "I'm pretty tired." He thought about his room. He thought about the bed and the medicine he was supposed to take.

All those sleeping pills . . .

Meg hung a hand on his right shoulder, leaned close and said, "We better get you to bed."

He couldn't answer. He shoved her hand off and got up and left.

"Man's in severe pain," Meg said under her breath, looking over her shoulder.

"Looked all right to me," Ben said. "Looked perfectly fine, out spending money like there was no tomorrow."

She muttered, "Yeah, add it up, Ben." Across the table Bird looked mad. She figured Bird had somewhat to say and she shut up for several sips of beer.

Bird didn't say anything. Ben set his elbows on the table in an attitude that said he knew he was on Bird's bad side, but he looked mad too.

Things were going to hell fast, they were.

"Excuse us," she said, and got up and took a pinch of Sal's sleeve. Sal read a full scale alert and came with her over to the end of the bar where the guys couldn't lip-read. "Aboujib, we got a severe problem."

"Yeah. Men!"

"Easy, easy. We got a partner/partner problem developing here."

"You know Ben's a good lay. But he's being a lizard."

"I sincerely wasn't going to say that."

"I don't mind saying it. I'll bust his ass if Bird doesn't. I *told* Ben what I'd carve off him if he got too forward with me. And Bird *damn* sure won't take it."

"Bird can handle him."

"Yeah," Sal said and got a breath. "With a wrench. I tell you, I'm not putting up with this act. And I'm not standing in the fire zone either. I vote we go out to a show, leave the boys to one room."

Sometimes Sal made real good sense. "Yeah," Meg said. "Sounds good."

"I got a serious concern," Bird said.

"Yeah, well," Ben said, looking at the table. "Sorry about that, Bird."

"Why'd you push on him?"

"Hell if I know," Ben said, and didn't know, actually. Meg and Sal came back to say they were leaving: "You guys work it out," Sal said. And that made him madder. He watched them walk out. He had no notion where they were going, but he felt the ice on all sides of him.

"I don't know what the hell it is," he said without really looking at Bird. "I don't know what it is that the guy's got, but it seems to get in the way of people's good sense." He hadn't liked this partners idea from the time Sal had showed up at the 3 deck shop telling him how dealing with Dekker was going to set them all up rich, how it was such a good idea, Dekker getting his license back and all—and he'd liked it less than that when pretty-boy came sauntering in here all manicured and looking like trouble.

Bird didn't say anything for a while after that. Finally: "Maybe some people can't figure out why you got it in for him."

"Because he's crazy!" Ben said. "Because we're going to

take this loony out there where he can get his ship back—cut the girls' throats and run that ship back over the line . . ."

"You've been seeing those lurid vids again. What in hell's he going to say about two more missing persons over at R1? 'Excuse me, they took a walk together'?"

"He doesn't have to have a good excuse! He's crazy! Crazy people don't have reasons for what they do, that's why they're crazy!"

"They still have to explain it to Belt Management."

"It doesn't do Meg and Sal any fuckin' good!"

"My money'd be on Meg and Sal."

"Don't be funny, Bird, it's not funny."

"I think it's damned funny. We got a 95 k mortgage on *Way Out* with the bank, we got nothing but dock charges on *Trinidad* for the last several months, we still aren't past inspection on the refit and we still got a filing to go before we can think about getting out of here. In case you haven't noticed, Ben-me-lad, we could seriously use another pair of hands here. We're bleeding money, with two ships sitting at dock."

"Meg and Sal do just fine. We *don't* know about this guy. And we'd have had *two* pair of hands today if Meg and Sal weren't out spending money on this guy. He's *trouble*, Bird, he's been trouble from the first we laid eyes on him."

"We can always say no, if he turns out to be trouble. We got time yet at least to find it out. Let's just put him to work, see how he gets along."

"You *can't* say no, Bird, you got this severe problem with saying no. You crawl ass-backwards into what's going to cost you money. If I didn't—"

"I can say no real good, Ben, if you recall. I said no to Meg and I said no to quite a few would-be's before I took you on. Now, you and me being partners, I give you a lot I wouldn't give just anybody—but being partners goes both ways. And right now I'm asking you to just give me a little more line."

"To do what? Wait until his money comes through? Then he'll pay for his own bills? That's real convenient, Bird, that's real damned convenient. He doesn't get to pay anything, he doesn't do anything, and we're buying his meals!"

"Ben, —"

"I don't know why you believe him over me, that's all!"

"Ben, —I dunno whether the gals are right about this deal: they could be. Here I am trying to figure whether I trust Dekker, and you're acting so damn crazy I end up defending him. I can't hardly take *your* side, without having him off down the 'deck in a fit now, can I?"

"It'd be good riddance!"

"Yeah, and what if the gals are right and this guy's a good steady prospect?"

"Steady, hell! Bird, *who* are we going to get to go out with Dekker? 'What time is it? What time is it?' Who's going to put up with that?"

"The guy really got to you out there, didn't he?"

He *hated* being patronized. "He didn't *get* to me."

"Good," Bird said. "Good."

"Dammit, don't—"

"—don't what?"

Cut me off like that, Ben thought blackly. But what he said was, "All right, all right. We'll see how he does the next week or so." He took a pretzel out of the bowl. "Guy didn't take 'em." Wasteful habit. It was like somebody who had money, who was used to having it. And on the thought of the 47 k Dekker claimed to have: "If he's got the funds he claims, he's a damned walking bank. Where'd he get it, except this rich college girl? He had a lot to gain by her dying, you know."

"Yeah, looked like he was having a real good time out there, didn't it?"

He hated it when Bird got surly with him. It made him figure maybe he wasn't being reasonable.

Bird said: "The Nouri thing, you know, changed a lot. Cops with warrants to do anything they wanted, the news full of friends informing on friends . . . I don't think there was half the under the table stuff going on that the company claimed—like we were some major leak in the company accounts. We weren't. We were making it. You understand? People used to help each other, that's what was going on, then. If you got in trouble and you needed a part, you didn't go to the bank, you went to a friend. You could borrow under bank rates, if you kept your promises, if you ran a good operation and paid your debts—and damn sure people knew if you did. We were making it, and the company wasn't. Now you tell me who's the better businessmen." Bird lifted a shoulder and took a sip of a dying beer. "Now we've got a generation coming off Earth with the Attitudes. We got a generation coming out of the Institute that never heard of Shakespeare—"

"God, so give me a tape, Bird! I swear I'll listen to the sumbitch."

Bird looked at him oddly, then reached across the table, took hold of his hand, man/woman-like, which was odder still, scarily odd, coming from Bird, from the guy he shared a ship with. Bird said, "Ben, you're a good guy. You really are. *Stay* that way."

Ben rescued his hand, shaken. "What's that mean?"

Bird only said, in that same peculiar way, "Ben-me-lad, I'll look you up that tape."

Dekker stared at the ceiling and thought about a sleeping pill, thought about the whole damned bottle—but hell if he'd give the company the satisfaction.

Ben wasn't going to let him alone. That was the way it was, that was the way it was going to be. Ben didn't like him, and with Belters, that well could be the final word on it. Ben had taken his ship and now Ben had him down as trouble—that was the way it was going to be, too.

He didn't know why Ben set him off like that. He didn't know why he'd said what he had, he didn't know why he'd talked about Cory's business, or whether he had a chance left with them, under any terms now he'd walked out—and he didn't know what Bird might be thinking.

If nothing else—that he and Ben together were a problem: he had no question which way Bird would go if Ben wanted him out.

And Ben talked about getting his license back, with no dollar figure on it. Everything he had, he was sure—*if* they still took him after the blow-up out there. Ben thought he was crazy, Ben thought he'd crack if he got out there again, and, honestly speaking, he wasn't sure of himself. The deep Belt was no place to discover you'd grown scared of the dark; and handling a ship making a tag was no time to have a memory lapse, to find the next move wasn't there—or not to remember where you were in a sequence or what you'd already done. You didn't get other chances. The Belt didn't give them.

He didn't know himself what would happen when the hatch shut behind him, whether he'd panic, whether he'd be all right—whether he'd think he was all right and, the longer he was out in that ship, slowly unravel between past and present, the way he had in the shower—*that* shower, the same surroundings, nothing but his current partners' presence to anchor him in time.

Everybody seemed to be asking him to collect himself, get on with his life as if nothing had happened. It seemed to be the way everybody got by—they numbed themselves to feeling, made themselves deaf and blind to what the company got away with, just kept their mouths shut, chased what money they could get, and got used to seeing a lying sonuvabitch in the mirror every morning, because that was the only kind that had a chance in this place.

He didn't know whether he could do that. He didn't even know whether he could keep out of that pill drawer and stay alive tonight, or whether the gain was even worth it anymore.

Cory, he'd said that time they'd had the argument, maybe I don't want to go. What in hell am I going to do on a starship? I failed math. I failed physics. I don't have your brains, Cory, it was your idea all along. They won't have work for me, I'll be dead mass, the rest of my life, Cory. What kind of life is that?

She'd set him down, told him plain as plain he hadn't any chance in staying, she'd told him the company was crooked, the company was screwing the freerunners, screwing the pilots, screwing everybody that worked for them. Cory had handled big money, she knew how banks worked with the big operations. She'd told him what ASTEX was doing with their electronic datacards and their policies on finds. She'd tried to explain to him exactly what that direct-deduct stuff on LOSes did to accounts and interest, and how they were skimming on the freerunners in ways that had nothing to do with rocks.

She'd said, Dek, don't be a fool, you've no future here. They're killing the freerunners, they'll get the Shepherds in not too many years—there's no hope here.

She'd said, Don't ever think I'll leave you behind...

Sal sipped her drink in the blue neon of Scorpio's—the vid had been not-too-bad, chop and slash, the way Meg said, but not a long one, and as she had put it, it was way too early to chance walking in on the boys, besides which she had a word to drop on some friends next door. It was her favorite lounge—Shepherd territory, right next to the Association club—pricey, spif: you got the usual traffic of office types who went anywhere au courant on the edge of helldeck, but the Shepherd relationship with Scorpio's was longstanding: Shepherds got the tables in the nook past the glass pillars, and Shepherd glasses came filled to the brim, no shorting and no extra water, either.

Not a place they could afford as a steady habit, damn sure, not unless they picked up some guys with Shepherd-level finance, and they weren't shopping to do that this time.

No danger of walk-up offers this side of those pillars either, thank God: the women to men ratio on helldeck meant Shepherds were used to being courted, not the other way around, and two women who weren't signaling didn't get the pests that made sane conversation impossible in a lot of the cheaper bars, God, you got 'em in restaurants, in vid show doorways—this shift some R&R bunch was in from the shipyard, and the soldier-boys on leave down at the vid were the damn-all worst. They'd had a glut of male fools for the last few hours and Scorpio's was a refuge worth the tab, in her own considered opinion.

"I tell you," she said over an absolutely genuine margarit, "my instinct would be to take this Dek a tour before we go out, you know, personal, just friendly. Rattle him and see what shakes. I think that's a serious safety question. But we got Ben in the gears, damn 'im."

"You want my opinion, Aboujib?"

"Po-sess-ive?"

"Vir-gin, Aboujib. You're probably the first that ever asked him."

"Hell, he's that way with Bird!"

"Yeah."

She saw what Meg was saying, then. "That way about a lot of things, isn't he?"

Meg stirred her drink with the little plastic straw. "Man's got a serious problem. Hasn't cost us yet. But it's to worry about. Ni-kulturny, what he pulled on Bird tonight."

"Ochin," Sal agreed with an uncomfortable twitch of her shoulders, sipping her margarit, thinking how they weren't doing as ordinaire with Ben, how if it was anybody else but the best numbers man on R2, she'd have handed him off to Meg—switch and dump, the old disconnection technique. But, dammit, Ben was special, the absolute best, and Meg with Ben didn't do them any good. Meg didn't know the right questions and she didn't do the calc as well.

Besides which it wasn't Meg who made Ben crazy enough to show her things the Institute hadn't, that *he'd* figured, that he wouldn't hand out to anybody. She'd never met a case like Ben—you felt simpatico with him one minute and the next you wanted to break his neck. She'd never met anybody she *trusted* the way she did Ben—except Meg and Bird; Ben was the only one but Meg and Bird she'd feel safe going EV with—and, counting his crazy behavior, she couldn't figure that out.

At least he wasn't like the greasy sumbitch who'd threatened not to let her back in the ship unless she did him special favors. Numbers men were always at a disadvantage, always got the problems until you were as good as Ben, that *no*body wanted to lose. Meg had never been through that particular trouble—a numbers man didn't dare antagonize his pilot, if he had any sense; and he didn't send his pilot walkabout either—but a numbers man definitely could get out with some severely strange people in this business; and if you had some few partners you were sure of, you didn't let them go—didn't try to run their lives for them, not if you wanted all your fingers back, but hell if you wouldn't go to any length to hold on to them, to keep things the way they were.

Kill somebody? If it came to it, if you ever would—then you would. And trying to keep two tallish young guys from killing each other out there . . .

"What are we going to do, Kady?"

Meg pursed her lips. "Just what we're doing. Let Bird handle it."

Someone brushed by their table. Touched her shoulder. "Aboujib?"

God. A walk-up? Meg's frown was instant. Sal looked around and up an expensive jacket at a Shepherd—one of Sunderland's crew, friend of Mitch's—she didn't know the name. He said, very quickly, slipping something into her pocket, "That question you left?"

"Yeah," she said—different problem. *Same* problem. She held her breath. Felt something flat and round and plastic in her pocket, her heart going doubletime.

"This is Kady?"

"Yeah," she said. "You can say."

"Word is, problem's gone major. You're tagged with it. Go with it the way you said. Time's welcome. But when you get your launch date . . . you let us know. Very seriously."

The guy walked off then.

God.

"What the hell?" Meg asked.

"I dunno," she said, thinking about a shadowy 'driver sitting out there spitting chunks at the Well. And MamBitch, who prepared the charts *and* their courses, and shoved them up to $v$ and braked them. "I dunno." Her stomach felt, of a sudden, as if she'd swallowed something very cold.

"Is that what I think I heard?" Meg asked. "They think we could be in some kind of danger?"

"I don't know."

"Oh, God, great!"

"Let's not panic."

"Of course let's not panic. I don't effin' like the stakes all of a sudden."

She leaned forward on the table, pitched her voice as low as would still carry. "Meg. They're not going to let us run into trouble."

"Yeah," Meg whispered back. "Let's not hear 'run into.' I don't like the words I'm hearing. I don't like this 'Go with it.' Maybe I want a little more information than we're getting into."

"They're saying we're doing the right thing—"

"Yeah, doing the right thing. We can be fuckin' martyrs out there, is that what they want?"

She reached across the table and grabbed Meg's hand, scared Meg would bolt on her. "We got a real chance here—"

"What real chance? Chance your high and mighty friends are going to hold us a nice funeral? Chance we can collect the karma and they stay clean?"

"Meg, I can get you *in*."

"Screw that." Meg jerked her hand back. "I don't take their charity."

"Meg. For God's sake don't blow it."

Meg set her jaw. Took several slow breaths, the way she would when she was mad. "What's their guarantee? Shit, we could be bugged here—"

Sal took the flat plastic out of her coat pocket, which had a little green light showing. Palmed it, fast.

"God," Meg groaned.

"They're ahead of the game. They're not going to let us walk into it."

"Oh, you've got a lot of faith in them. That's contraband, dammit!"

"Meg, they're not fools."

"They must think we are."

"We made them an offer, Meg, they're *saying* they're agreeing. They're warning us."

"Yeah, 'tagged with him.' I like that. I really like that."

"Meg." She couldn't lay it out better than Meg already knew it. Meg looked like murder.

But Meg said finally: "So we're tagged with him. —Are we talking about giving up that lease?"

The answer was yes. Meg knew it. Meg knew it upside and down.

"Shit," Meg said.

"We've got what they want. They *want* him. They paid their debts. That's what they're saying. They're asking us take a risk, and we're in, Meg, they're making us an offer. If we screw 'em on this—or if we back out now—"

She was down to begging. There were pulls in too many directions if Meg skitted out on this one. God, everything she wanted, *everything*. "A Shepherd berth, Meg. One last run. We get Dek out in the big quiet for a few months and that's it. Ben and Bird set up with those ships. Karma paid. We're getting *out* of here, Meg. A chance at a *real* ship. Both of us."

*That* scored with Meg. Only thing that could. Meg's face got madder. Finally Meg said: "Hell if. Wake up, Aboujib."

"Hell if not. This is *big*, Meg, dammit, this is *it*."

Meg shook her head. But it meant yes. All right. We're going to be fools.

"You better be right, Aboujib. —And that jeune fils damn well better get his bearings. Fast. If they're going to make a case on him—he sincerely better not be crazy."

# CHAPTER

# 14

SPENDING his sleeptime with Bird wasn't exactly what Ben had planned. Breakfast with Dekker wasn't his idea of a good time either, but Bird insisted.

So here they were, himself and Bird at the table and Dekker in line—Meg and Sal were sleep-ins: they'd gotten in *late* last shift, up to what Ben didn't try to imagine. Dekker hadn't seemed enthusiastic about their company from his side either: Dekker had answered his door, said Yeah, he'd be there, and arrived late—clipped up the sides and all.

"All he needs is a couple of earrings," Ben muttered.

"Be nice," Bird chided him, over the sausage and unidentifiable eggs.

Ben looked at him, lifted a chilled shoulder. "Hey, did I do anything?" But he reminded himself he had better bite his tongue and keep criticisms of Bird's previous pretty-boy to himself, the way he'd made up his mind yesterday that since the insanity had gotten to Meg and Sal he had as well go along with it.

Bird shot him a look that said he didn't trust him not to

knife Dekker in his bed. That was the level things had gotten to. That was the primary reason he figured he had better go along with it.

Until Dekker slipped up. Then he was even going to be charitable about "I told you so," he sincerely was—so long as Bird saw it clear when it happened and came to his senses.

So Dekker walked up with his cup of coffee and his eggs, not quite looking at either of them, kicked back a chair and sat down.

"I have to apologize," Dekker said first off, still without looking at them.

Ben manfully kept his mouth shut.

"I sort of wandered off yesterday," Dekker said.

Bird shrugged, but Dekker wasn't going to see that gesture, looking at his plate like the zee-out he was. Bird said, "Pills will do that."

"I'm going off them," Dekker said. His hand with the fork was shaking. Badly. —A real mess, Ben thought. Wonderful. We're supposed to go out with this guy. This is going to be at the controls out there.

Dekker did look up then, shadow-eyed as if he hadn't slept much. "I cut you off yesterday. If the offer's still open—I'd like to talk about it."

"Offer's open," Bird said. Ben thought: Hell.

Dekker didn't say anything for a moment, just stirred his eggs around on his plate. Then a second look at Bird. "So I want my license back. What's the time worth?"

"Depends on your work," Bird said.

Ben did a fast calc, what Dekker had, what gave them a solid return on putting up with him. "10 k flat. With a guarantee you *get* the license."

Dekker looked bewildered—maybe a little overcome at the price and *not* understanding the quality of what he'd just thrown in. *He* wasn't exactly sure why he'd thrown it in— except he'd had this nanosecond of thinking he'd asked high and Bird was already on his tail. So it just fell out of his mouth: There you are, fancy-boy, *I* can fix it, *I* can, so you damned sure better mind your manners with me.

Bird didn't say anything, Dekker didn't, so Ben added, with a certain satisfaction, "Fair, isn't it? Guaranteed, class 1."

Bird looked a little worried. But he still didn't say anything.

"Whose guarantee?" Dekker asked.

Ben gave him a cold stare. "Mine. On the other hand, if you ask anybody the time, Dekker, if you pull *any* shit on us out there, you'll take a walk bare-assed."

"Ben," Bird said.

"I'm serious," he said, and Dekker looked worried.

"Ben's all right," Bird said. "He really is."

Dekker said, finally, "I haven't got any other offers."

"Small wonder," Ben said, and realized that he'd broken his resolution a tick before Bird glared at him.

Dekker glared at him too. Dekker said, "I'll pull my weight."

Ben said, "Damn right you will. You'll do whatever you're told to do. And you'll put up with whatever shit you're handed, whatever you think of it—with no gripes."

Bird said, "Ben, —"

Dekker glumly reached across the table. It took a moment before Ben realized he wanted his hand, that Dekker was truly calling his bluff and taking the deal.

Damn, Ben thought. He had as soon stick his hand in a grinder, but things with Bird were precarious. So he made a grimace of a smile, gave Dekker his hand and they made a limp, cheerless handshake across the plates.

No one looked convinced, not Dekker, not Bird. *He* certainly wasn't. But he said, "All right, if we're going to do this, let's get that re-cert application in right now. I take it you haven't done that."

"No craters," Meg said as they walked out into the bar. They'd come in late last shift, they'd slept late, gotten up and come out on the absolute tail end of breakfast. No Dekker, no Bird, no Ben. Meg shoved her hands into her pockets and looked at Mike over at the bar. Sal looked too, with a lift of the eyebrows.

"They kill each other?" she wondered.

Mike said, dishing up the last of the rubbery eggs, "Left like old friends, all three. Said tell you they were going up to the dock. They're leaving you a pile of scrub-up and sanding in the shop."

"Fun," Sal sourly.

"Ben with Dekker?" Meg said, with a gathering worry. "Not damn likely. We got a problem here."

Sal poured her own coffee and took the plate Mike handed her. "Kady, I think we got to use strategy."

"What strategy? I vote we shoot Ben."

"Na, na, he's playing along with Bird." Sal took the plate and the coffee back to the table and hooked a chair out, as Meg did the same. "We got, what, three weeks if we push it. If Dek's able to pitch in. The guys are going to be trouble. Trez macho."

"Trez pain in the ass. If *Bird* takes a position you need a pry-bar."

"We can't have Ben and Dekker in the same ship. That's prime."

"So Bird takes Dekker—and *we* take Ben." That, come to think of it, wasn't at all a bad idea. They'd been after Ben's numbers for two years. *That* was solid and Shepherd promises were come-ons and maybes.

Besides which, if there was anybody who could keep Dekker in line—

Sal ducked her head, checked in her pocket a beat— God, *smooth* move, there, Meg thought, with a knot in her stomach; and Sal looked up with the devil's own ideas in her eyes. "*I'll* tell you what we do, Kady, we apply to go out tandem. *All* of us. I'll tell you why." A jab of Sal's finger on the tabletop. "Because Bird doesn't want Dekker sliced and stacked. Because Bird's had one trip with Ben and Dekker already and if we give him the out to break that up—we ask for even split on the board time, just to make him believe it, we set it up with the Bitch, and we get Ben and his numbers *and* access to Dekker."

"Hell, we have got a ship coming out of refit. Shake-down run."

"That's the grounds. Only reason they'll do it."

"A skosh noisy. Do we need MamBitch's special attention on us? I *don't* think a special app is a good idea."

"Kady, we *got* the Bitch's attention. I'll ask my friends, but I don't know what worse we can do. And *if* they say do it, and if She'll let us—hell, if we can get out there tandem, we can just do our job, just ride it out while the shit flies, as may, and figure things are getting taken care of—they're *not* going to arrange anything on the way out, not unless they're pushed, and if the Association brings it up as an issue, damn *sure* the Bitch isn't going to run us into a rock on the way back. There's coincidences and there's coincidences. They're just a little from having the EC down their throats."

You had to wonder whether more understandings might have passed in that little encounter at Scorpio's than Sal had even yet admitted: and MamBitch beaming them up to $v$ on a heading MamBitch picked—on charts that might have a little technical drop-out right in their path—hadn't helped her sleep at all. MamBitch was finally admitting in the news how she might go grievance procedures with the Shepherds to settle the outstanding complaints and patch up the sore spots—MamBitch having this severely important production schedule to meet, because the Fleet High Command was breathing down her neck.

That was the public posture. Behind the doors in management there were careers on the line.

There was the Shepherds' whole existence on the line.

"I tell you," she said to Sal over the eggs, "I'd sincerely like to know if you know anything additional—now or in future."

"If I know you'll know." A solemn look. "I swear."

"Thanks," she said. She did try to believe it.

A berth with the Shepherds, Sal said. It was already an endangered species. And they themselves were fools to think otherwise: you got out of the habit of longterm thinking—when the only out you had was a break in a business that was already taking the deep dive to hell. Freerunners weren't going to last forever. Go with the lease deal or go for broke Sal's way—*see* if the Shepherds kept their bargains, or if there was a bargain—or if the Shepherds were still independents when the shakeout came.

Sal had wanted this break, God, she'd chased it for years—blew it once, by what she knew, and those sons of bitches relatives of hers had kept Sal on a string for near six years, sure, let the kid be eyes and ears on helldeck, let Aboujib run their errands and risk arrest, let Aboujib sweat long enough to be sure she took orders—

Aboujib had gotten a severe warn-off from the Shepherd Association when she'd taken up with her—and being Aboujib, she'd locked on to her mistake and damned the consequences. Her high and mighty friends had said, Drop Kady, and Sal had gone to talk to some officer or other—God only what she'd said in that meeting, or what they'd said or threatened, but Sal had stormed out of their exclusive club and not talked about a berth with the Shepherds for the better part of a month.

They'd survived the ups and down since, gotten hell and away better than they'd started—things had looked so clear and so possible, til yesterday, til the Association dangled Sal's dream in front of her, the bastards—

She'd said yes to Sal last night. She had the sinking feeling this morning she'd been a chronic fool, and committed herself to something she wouldn't have, except for those two margarits. But she hadn't exactly come up with an effective No this morning, either, both of them sitting here betting their necks on that little green light—Sal was dead set.

She still couldn't open her mouth and say, Sal, no deal. We're going with the lease.

Didn't know if you'd call it friendship. Didn't know what was wrong with her head—but the way things were getting to be on R2, the freerunners didn't have that many more years. She could worry about Bird—you couldn't call it romance, what she had with Bird. Mutual good time. And a guy she'd no desire to see run up against a rock, dammit: if Dekker was the problem, . . . they were all tagged, as the Shepherd had put it: Bird, Ben, *all* of them. The Association might be using them—but the Association might be the only protection a handful of miners had—the *Shepherds* were the only independents with any kind of leverage.

That—was enough to advise keeping one's mouth shut. And not to say No.

Couldn't tell Bird. Bird wasn't good at secrets. Damn sure not Ben.

What had the Shepherd said? The problem's major? The problem's *gone* major?

Something had shifted. Ben's charts? Something the company had done?

The dumbasses in the fire zone didn't get that kind of information.

Turn in the re-cert application, Ben had said. Move on it. *Way Out* was headed for soon-as-possible launch, dock time cost, Ben swore he had friends who could get the test scheduled within the week, and Dekker decided, in Bird's lack of comment, that Ben might be telling the truth.

So it was a good idea to do that, Dekker supposed: and found himself sitting in a Trans car between Bird and Ben, nervous as a kid headed for the dentist—only beginning to calm down and accept the idea of taking an ops test before he'd gotten the shakes out of his knees. Ten days was soon enough, Bird said. Give him a little time. Ten days to get his nerves together, ten days til he had to prove to BM that he still had it—that was still time enough to get the class 3 license pushed through, Ben said, which he had to have before he could count any time at *Way Out*'s boards.

God, he couldn't blow this.

Bird said: "After we get this done, we thought we'd take you up to the docks, show you the ship, all right?"

"All right," he said, in the same numb panic, asking himself what they were up to—*show you the ship . . .*

Maybe they wanted to see if he could take it. Maybe they were pushing him to find out if he would go off the edge—

Sudden memory of that fouled, cold interior, the suit drifting against the counter—the arm moving. He'd waked in the near-dark and imagined it was Cory beckoning to him.

Bird talked into his ear, talked about some of the damage on the ship, talked about what they'd done—

But the ship in his mind was the one he remembered. The stink, and the cold, and the fear—

"Admin," Ben said as the Trans pulled into a stop. "Here we are."

He got up, he got off with them into an office zone, all beige and gray, with the musty cold electronics smell offices had. They went into the one that said ECSAA Certifications, and Ben and Bird walked up to the counter with him.

"I want to apply for a license," he said.

"Recertification," Ben said, leaning his elbows on the desk beside him.

"Just let me do it." He couldn't think with Ben putting words in his mouth; he felt shivers coming on—he'd caught a chill in the Trans—and he didn't want to be filling in applications with his hands shaking. *Fine* impression that was in this office.

The clerk went away, came back with a datacard, directed him to a side table and a reader.

He went over to it and his entourage came with him, one on either side as he put the card in the slot and made three mistakes entering his name.

"Look, you're making me nervous."

"That's all right," Ben said. And when he tried to answer the next question, about reason for revocation: "Uh-uh," Ben said. "Neg. Say, 'Hospitalization.'"

"Look, the reason is a damned stupid doctor—"

"They don't *want* the detail." Ben reached over and moved the cursor back. "Don't explain. The only answer any department wants in its blanks is the wording in its rule books. Don't volunteer anything, don't get helpful, and if you don't know, N/A the bastard or shade it in your favor. Remember it's clerks you're talking to, not pilots. Say: 'Hospitalization.'"

That made clear sense to him. He only wished it hadn't come from Ben.

"'Reason for application'?" Ben read off the form, and pointed: "Say: 'Change in medical status.'"

He hadn't thought of having to pass the physical again. The idea of doctors upset his stomach. But he typed what Ben said.

"Sign it," Ben said. "Put your card in. That's all there is to it."

It left a lot of blank lines. "What about 'Are there any other circumstances . . . ?'"

"This is a 839-RC," Ben said, and tapped the top of the display, where it had that number. "An 839-RC *applies*, that's all it does. It doesn't explain. It's not a part of the exam. Just send it."

"Have you ever filled out one of these?"

"Doesn't matter. I worked in Assay. Answer by catch-phrases. *Don't* pose the clerks a problem or it'll go right to the bottom to the Do Pile. Don't be a problem. Send the bastard."

"Do it," Bird said.

He keyed Send. In a moment the screen blinked, notified him his account had been debited 250.00 for the application and told him he had to pass the basic operationals within sixty days, after which he had to log 200 hours in the sims or at the main boards of a working ship, by sworn affidavit of a class 1 pilot—

And take a written exam.

Someone had as well have hit him in the gut. He stood there staring at the message til Bird laid a hand on his shoulder and said they'd go on to the core now.

He was down to 95 dollars in his account, he hadn't yet paid his bill at The Hole, and he'd never *taken* the writtens, he'd come up from the cargo pushers to the short-hop beam haulers to a miner-craft; but he'd never had to take the written exams.

Ben elbowed him in the back. "Come on, moonbeam. Don't forget your card."

He took it out of the slate, he walked out of the offices with them, in a complete haze. They got to the Transstation as the Trans pulled in and the doors opened.

"Come *on*," Ben said, and Ben taking his arm was the last straw. He snarled, "Let go of me," and shook free, wanting just to go on around the helldeck, wanting to go back to his room, lock the door, take a pill and not give a damn for the rest of the day; or maybe three or four days.

"Come on." Bird got his arm and pulled at him. The Trans doors were about to close in their faces, the robot voice was advising them to get clear. "Oh, hell," he said; and let them pull him aboard, because otherwise they were going to miss their ride and stand there til the next Trans came, asking him why he was a damed fool.

They fell into seats as the doors shut and the Trans started moving. "What in hell's the matter with you?" Ben asked. "Are you being a spook again, Dekker?"

"No," he said, and slouched down into the seat, staring at a point between them.

"You have some trouble about going onto the ship?" Bird asked him.

"No." He set his jaw and got mad, lifelong habit when people who ran his life crowded him.

Ben said: "You're being a spook, Dekker."

Probably he was, he thought. And a kid might keep his mouth shut, but a grown man in debt up to his ears and about to end up on a heavyside job had finally to realize who he owed, and how much. He swallowed against the knot in his throat and muttered, "I can't pass tests."

Bird tilted an ear and said, louder: "What?"

So he had to repeat it: "I can't take tests."

"What do you mean you can't take tests?" Ben objected, loudly enough for people around them to hear. "You had a license, didn't you?"

Screw you, he wanted to yell at Ben. Let me alone! But he said quietly: "I had a license."

"Without an exam?"

"You can do that," Bird said to Ben. "Construction work lets you do that. You can jump from class to class that way, just the operationals and a few questions. Same as I did. Not everybody comes through the Institute."

"Well, then," Ben said, "—you've been a class 1. You claim you were good. You know the answers. What's a test?"

Ben made him mad. Ben could make him mad by breathing. He tried to be calm. "Because I can't pass written questions!"

"God," Ben said, sliding down in his seat. "One of those. Can you read?"

He didn't want to know what "those" Ben was talking about. He didn't want to talk about it right now. He wanted to break Ben's neck. He stared off at the corner, past Ben's shoulder. He'd go to the ship, all right, he'd restrain himself from acting like a crazy man; he'd pass the operationals and put in his hours in Bird's ship and he'd come back and fail the damned test.

But meanwhile he'd have gotten fed. He'd have gotten in with Bird. Maybe he could get a limited license to push freight, work up through ops again, on the ship construction out there: he didn't know, he didn't even know if it was possible out in the Belt. He didn't want to worry about it right now, just take it as far as he could, and not think about the mess he was in.

Bird and Ben talked in low voices and he was the topic: he could catch snatches of it over the noise. It was two more stops til the core lift. He wanted this ride over with— *wanted* to get up to the dock, the ship, anywhere, to get them on to some other subject.

"Look," Ben said, leaning forward, "on this test business, it's easy done. It's a *system*, there's a technique—"

"Easy for you!"

"You a halfway good pilot?"

"I'm damned good!"

"Then listen to me: it's the same as filling in the forms back there. Don't give real answers to deskpilots. The whole key to forms *or* tests is never give an answer smarter than the person who checks the questions."

He took in a breath, expecting Ben to have insulted him. He couldn't figure how Ben had.

"We can get you through that shit," Ben said, with a flip

of his hand. "But first let's see if you're worth anything in ops."

He didn't *want* to owe Ben anything. He told himself that Ben had probably figured out a new way to screw him—and if there was any hope at all, it was that Ben's way of screwing him happened to involve his getting his license restored.

Slave labor for him and Bird, maybe: that was all right, from where he was. Do anything they wanted—as long as it got him that permit and got him licensed again.

He thought about that til the Trans came to their stop, at the lift. They got out together, punched up for the core, and waited for the car. He tucked his hands into his pockets and tried not to think ahead, not to tests, not to the docks, not to what the ship was going to look like—

Everything was going to be all right, he wasn't going to panic, wasn't going to heave up his guts when he went null-g, it was just going to be damned cold up there, bitter cold: that was why he was shivering when he walked into the lift.

He propped himself against the wall and took a deathgrip on the safety bar while the lift made the core transit: increased g at the first and none at the end—enough to do for a stomach in itself. The car stopped, let them out in the mast Security Zone, and they shoved their cards in the slot.

The null-g here at least didn't bother him—it only felt—

—felt as if he was back in a familiar place, and wasn't, as if he were timetripping again: in his head he knew R2's mast wasn't anywhere he'd been before when he was cognizant— he kept Bird in sight to keep himself anchored, hooked on and rode the hand-line between Ben and Bird—

The booming racket, the activity, the smell of oil and cold and machinery—all of it could have been R1. Here and now, he kept telling himself, and by the time he reached *Way Out*'s berth in Refit, his stomach might have been upset, but he could reason his way toward a kind of numbness.

Even entering the ship wasn't the jolt he'd thought it would be, following Bird and Ben through the lock. Bird turned the lights up and the ship seemed—ordinary again. It smelled of disinfectant, fresh glue, and oil. He touched *Way Out*'s panels with cold-numbed fingers and looked around him. Everything around him was the way it had been, as if the wreck had never happened. Same name as she'd had—Cory's joke, actually—but they'd given her a new number, and she wasn't his and Cory's anymore.

Most of all there was no sense of Cory's existence here. That had been wiped out too. And maybe it was that presence he'd been most afraid to deal with.

"We've got the tanks replaced," Bird was saying, reorienting toward him. "We're stalled on one lousy part we're trying to organize on the exchange market—but we're closing in on finished."

"How does she look?" Ben asked, point blank, and he could say, calmly, without his teeth chattering, "You've done a lot of work with her."

"Want to get the feel of the boards?" Bird asked. "Main system's hooked in. Want to run a check?"

He knew then what they were up to, bringing him up here: they were running their own ops test. They wanted to see on their own whether he was missing pieces of his mind—just a simple thing, bring the boards up. Run a check. . . .

He took a breath of the bitter cold, he hauled down and fastened in at the main boards, uncapped switches and pushed buttons—didn't have to think about them, *didn't* think about them, until he realized he'd just keyed beyond the simple board circuit tests: memory flooded up, fingers had keyed the standard config-queries and he could breathe again, didn't damn well know where he was going, didn't know exactly at what point he was going to make himself terminate or whether they wanted him to run real checkouts that fed data onto the log—

—Number 4 trim jet wasn't firing—he caught the board anomaly in the numbers streaming past, the rapid scroll of portside drift; he compensated with a quick fade on 2 and kicked the bow brakes to fend off before the yaw could carry him further—*not* by the book—he knew it a heartbeat after he'd done it.

The screen went black. The examiner said: "Been a cargo pusher, haven't you?"

He said, trying not to let the shakes get started, "Yeah. Once." The examiner understood, then, what he'd done. And why.

The examiner—he was a man, and old—punched a button. Numbers came up, two columns. Graphs followed.

"You're a re-cert," the examiner said.

"Trying to be," he said. He kept his breath even, watched as the examiner punched another set of buttons.

"You can take your card out."

"Did I pass?"

"D-class vessel, class 3 permit with licensed observer." The examiner keyed out. "Valid for a year. —You in the Institute?"

"Private," he said, and the examiner gave him a second look.

"Who with?"

"Morrie Bird. *Trinidad*."

"Mmmn."

He wished he dared ask what that meant. But examiners in his experience didn't say what your score was, they didn't discuss the test, they rarely asked questions. This one made him nervous, but he thanked God the man *was* more than a button-pusher, he must be.

He left the simulator room with his card in hand, took the B-spoke core-lift down to the ECSAA office, feeling the shakes finally hit him while he was at the Certifications desk getting the license, shakes so bad he had to put his hands in his pockets for fear the office staff might see it.

Damn warning light had failed in the sim—or he'd flat failed to see it til it showed in the numbers. You never knew which. An alarm might have been blinking, he might have missed it, he might have just timed out—it felt like that, that time wasn't moving right when those numbers started going off, when he'd had to do a fast and dirty calc and just thought . . . *thought* it was a tight-in situation, he had no idea why, his brain just told him it was and he'd imagined impact where there wasn't any such thing in the simulation—

No, dammit, the sim had increased g sharply and for one sick moment he'd hallucinated that the engines were firing.

Maybe it was just his nerves. He wasn't sure anymore. Maybe that was the problem.

"Uh-oh," Meg said, seeing Dekker come out and down the Admin strip. They'd taken time out of the shop to shepherd Dek back . . . in case it's bad news, she'd said, and Sal had agreed.

So knowing he was already nervous they hadn't told him they were close by, hadn't come down with him—just called and asked a Certification office secretary how long a D3 permit exam might take, and they'd come down from the 3-deck shop to be here—in case.

"Doesn't look good," Sal said; and Meg had a moment of misgivings, whether they shouldn't just duck back and try to blend with the Transstop traffic—not easy in her case and not easy in Sal's. So there was no chance for cowardice. She waved.

Or maybe on second thought they might make it away unseen. Dekker was walking along looking at his feet, off in some different universe.

She said, as he came close, "Dek? How'd it go?"

He looked up, looked dazed, as if he couldn't figure them being there, or he hadn't really heard the question.

"How'd it go?" Sal asked.

"All right," he said.

"So did you get the permit?"

"Yeah."

"So, bravo, jeune rab!" Sal clapped an arm around him and gave him a squeeze. "We said, didn't we?"

He was dead white. He looked scared—and a little zee-d. "I said I'd call up to the ship—tell Bird how it came out. I need a phone."

Deep-spaced, Meg thought uneasily. Got himself through the test in one piece and just gone out. God hope they hadn't spotted it in the office. She linked her arm through his, protective custody. "Come on. Phone and lunch. In that order."

He went with them. They found a public phone near the Transstation, and she punched through to Bird. Bird said, "Good," when he heard, and Ben said, in the background, "So what's the fuss?"

Break that man's neck someday, Meg thought. With my own bare hands.

Another damned breakdown in D-28, and a pump-connection had blown out in the mast at dockside—spraying 800 liters of hydraulic fluid into free-fall toward the rotating core surface. The super swore it was worker sabotage and Salvatore, with three more cases on his desk, had a headache.

He put a tech specialist on the investigation, poured himself a cup of coffee and told himself he had to clear his desk: the stacks of datacards in the bin had reached critical mass, Admin was having a fit over the quarterly reports being a week late, it had a Fleet Lieutenant on its lap bitching about a schedule shortfall, and he couldn't find the cards the current flags referenced.

Flag on Walker. The guy had card use near an office break-in, had no business there—no apparent relation to the crime, merely a presence that didn't make sense. Flag on Kermidge: every sign of resuming bad associations. Flags on Dekker: blew hell out of the sims.

He keyed up the subfile.

Wills' voice said, out of the comp, "*Dekker passed his D3 ops. Score shot straight to the Chief Examiner. Word is the sims jumped out of D class and ran clear up in C before the examiner terminated the test—standard if there's an overrun: the Certifications office suspects a suspension at a higher grade—started searching court records, potential inquiries to Sol—*"

Oh, shit!

"*I intercepted it, told them let the license stand at a D3, pending inquiry with this office: I hope that was all right.*"

Thank God.

*"I did check the examiner's record in the files: retired pilot, ECI training, Sol based, good record, three years in his present position, et cetera. He's clean.*

*"But here's another interesting development: Bird and Pollard, the ones who brought him in, that got his ship on salvage, that're staying in the same sleepery? They've filed to run pairs, refit shakedown run with Dekker's former ship leased to one Kady and Aboujib. Dekker's on that application as a D3 wanting board time.*

*"Here's the catch. Aboujib and Kady have records— Kady's, as long as your arm. Smuggling, rab agitator— SolCorp background, opted here on an EC transfer. Aboujib's an AIP dishonorable discharge, reckless endangerment with a spacecraft, Shepherd background, small-time morals charges, one assault, bashed some guy with a bottle. Allocations hasn't ruled yet. Deny or let-pass?"*

Salvatore hit Pause, sat there with his elbows on the desk, reached for his inhaler, thinking: Son of a bitch. . . .

Not about Wills. Wills had done a good job—so far as it went. The business with the examiner jangled little alarms, no less than the immaculate Bird's shadowy associations.

Report that finding to Payne's office? Payne had said: We don't need to drag this out. The report to the ECSAA said mechanical failure, no fault of the pilot. . . .

Payne wanted the case closed; but, dammit, it kept resurfacing in the flags, and now with Wills' information came the niggling worry that where there were anomalies in official records there might also be management secrets. Salazar's threatened lawsuit, contractor disputes, the rash of incidents on the dock and in the plants—the military making demands to install Security personnel on R2—some kind of "readiness survey" involving their contracts, which was, one could suspect, strongly tied to schedule slowdowns, and, dammit, an implication of blame for *his* department—it was the whisper in the company washrooms that the Fleet was putting heavy pressure on ASTEX management, the Earth Company was worried about sabotage and slowdowns, possibly sympathizer activity—the labor agitators were looking for the right moment to embarrass the company; and damned right the radical fringes of all sorts were looking for a way to get control of the labor movement—radical fringe elements ASTEX had more than its share of, thanks to the EC's policy of letting malcontents and malefactors transfer out here— sans trial, sans publicity that might catch media attention in the motherwell, where strikes and welfare riots and lunatic religions fed on the airwaves. This Kady was probably a prime example, but monetary rather than political. *That* was no problem. Shepherd connections? Shepherds had more kids than they could find slots for. Reckless endangerment? An ECSAA violation. Not this office's province and any shift on helldeck could provide three and four assaults and a few cases for the medics.

ASTEX Security had a damn sight more on its mind than a couple of small-time malcontents and a disputed miner craft. Dekker was a watch-it, but Dekker had so far done nothing worse than show up an anomaly on a simulation— better than average. Meanwhile management had a ship over at that classified facility way behind schedule and sabotage in a plastics plant that had no damned reason except a fool of a manager.

Hell, no, it wasn't the ASTEX board that was going to take the damage: boards were never to blame—ASTEX management wasn't to blame: dump it on Security, dump it on Salvatore's desk—

So what had he got, but a missing kid with a mother on MarsCorp board, whose lawyers were threatening a negligence suit against the mechanic at R1 and trying to get those records opened. Dekker had had one incident, making wild charges against the company—but he had been quiet since then, had spent money on clothes, on food—his only current sin was applying for a re-cert in D class when he might—he read through Wills' report—have rated higher.

You did have to wonder about some ringer thrown in at higher levels, somebody working for some investigatory office, even—in these nervous days—something that should come to the attention of MI.

Blow the Dekker case wide and he could kiss his career goodbye; but if he failed to report a problem, and let something slip, his competence was at issue. Hell of a crack to be in. In his most paranoid moments he was moved to ask had there ever been a Cory Salazar—

But there was no doubt about Dekker on any level he could assess; the various departments over at R1 had his background from two years back; and no clandestine operator would be so stupid as to ring bells on a test: it didn't in any wise smell like an EC probe *or* a security problem.

Hell, Dekker had had his D1 from back in '20, he'd had working experience since, and very possibly he'd been dogging it back in '20, lying low from the military recruiters: that behavior was an epidemic among draft-age males. With that medical against him, he'd put out everything he had—and very nearly brought himself back to Ms. Salazar's attention: thank God Wills had put the stop on that.

So Dekker wanted to go back to space. It didn't seem a bad place to have him right now. You couldn't be quieter than out in the deep Belt, with no communication with anybody but BM. Alyce Salazar's lawyers couldn't serve him a summons there without a damned long arm.

Memo the doctor on Dekker's case to sign the medical release and satisfy the meddling clerk with the ECSAA rule book, get Dekker out and off the daily flags, and if Dekker went psycho out there and slash-murdered Bird and Pollard, they should have known what they were getting into. Only hope he got Kady and Aboujib with them. They didn't need the tag end of the rab acting up.

So with the push of a few keys, that was *one* problem off his desk for three months—a fix good the minute that ship cleared dock. Flag its return, flag—God!—Bird and Pollard, Aboujib and Kady, have Wills' office run down all the datatrails they might have left, at leisure. In a situation that could blow up again, on any whim of Salazar's lawyers, upper echelons could come down demanding complete files.

Pity, Salvatore thought, he couldn't sign up a few other problems for a three-month cruise in the belt . . .

Like the manager of D-28, with his dress codes and his inspections and his damned constant memos about sexual conduct off the job and his rules about mustaches, God, he'd

*like* to memo Payne that Department Manager Collin R.
Sabich had a private problem with kink vids, but owning the
vids wasn't illegal and the fact wasn't relevant to anything
but the fact Sabich was a slime. Admin knew that. Admin
had already promoted him sideways three times and evidently couldn't find anywhere less critical to put him. What
else could you do with a sonuvabitch with a kink and an
Institute degree in Plant Management?

God knew, maybe they'd give him an administrative
office to run.

# CHAPTER

# 15

ONE thing had started going right, Dekker thought,
God, and another thing followed: a message turned
up in the bar's mail-file at breakfast, addressed to
Mr. M. Bird, from Belt Management: special permit granted
for 2 ship operations in the same sector—launch permit
and all, usual permits for loading and charging, et cetera,
et cetera. They had a sector assignment, they'd get that
and the charts when they boarded, they had a launch
date, September 18th, four days from now—Bird had
shaken his head over that, one of those damned do-it-now
decisions from BM, no different at R2 than at R1. You
expected a delay, you applied early, and you got a
go-yesterday.

First the offer from Bird, then a piece of his license
back, and Ben turning downright civil: now BM approved a
joint run—and still nothing fell apart: Dekker sat holding his
coffee cup, listening to the regulars in the bar congratulate
Bird on BM's good behavior with the recollection that the
last time in his life things were going this right—

But he didn't let himself think about that. He just

stared at where he was and told himself that the letter had to be a sign his luck had turned, or maybe a signal from BM that management had decided to dog somebody else for a while. Who knew? Maybe somebody had slipped up and nobody had noticed he was on the crew. Maybe BM was signaling it would drop its feud with him and let him pick up his life if he just kept his mouth shut.

Don't worry about might-be's, was the way Meg put it. Just keep your head, don't make noise. MamBitch has a real shortterm crisis sense. There'll be some new sod on her grief list next week, and she'll forget all about you.

He truly wanted to believe the wreck might be a closed case, but experience told him no desk-sitter ever bothered to track and erase what some other desk-sitter had sent into files: that medical report and everything else in the files was going to surface time after time for the rest of his life, he was sure of it, a file uncatchable in its course through the company computers . . . probably every time he applied for a sector assignment. Damned sure if he tried to certify into C3.

And BM was putting him back to work, officially—still with no real resolution of what had happened, no answer, no justice. It was a cover-up Cory's mother evidently couldn't breach. He was sure she had to know by now—at least the official version. So what was *he* supposed to do that a mother on the MarsCorp board couldn't?

He thought about writing Alyce Salazar directly, send her his own account of what had happened, never mind Ms. Salazar hated him with a passion. But mail went through a lot of hands before it went out of R2. If anyone's mail found its way to special attention—his was a hundred percent certainty: he'd gotten that canny by now.

So it looked as if they were really going, and all he had to do was hold on to his nerves and stay out of trouble til launch, hope if the permit was a mistake nobody caught it in time—and try, meanwhile, to believe that Ben had really meant it just now when Ben had slapped him on the shoulder and said, in his subtle way, that in spite of him being an ass, he might actually work out.

Bird pocketed his datacard and remarked that since BM had a hurry-up on, they had a last few things to do in the shop, and they'd better get at it . . .

Sal said, "All right, all right, Bird. God, we put in fifty hours this week!" and Bird said: "Yeah, plenty all right if the shower doesn't work. Won't get any sympathy from me."

So it was a last-minute rush of things that had waited—no really vital jobs: they hadn't applied for their run without the big items latched down and *Way Out* past the mandatory ECSAA inspection: but Bird wanted some cleanup and the shop offered a refuge where a body could sit, put screws in holes and test circuits without a thought in his head except the job he was on, and he personally had no objections—anything that kept his hands busy.

Ben came and went, handling the legwork. Meg and Sal worked in the shop, raked over old lovers, the quality of hair dye, a vid they couldn't agree on—chatter, just chatter . . . human noise. They looked strained. Tired, yes. But he kept having the feeling it was more than that.

He didn't think. He didn't want to think.

Day before launch. He was holding on. Sal was frazzled. Bird grew short. "Launch nerves," Meg said under her breath. "Bird, dammit, just take it easy, we got it covered."

"It's a far walk after supplies," Bird snapped, and went off for another all-day stint on dockside, despite them arguing with him that old bones had as well get all the heavy time they could.

"Can't argue with him," Meg sighed. And Bird sent Ben down with a basket full of odd bits of *Trinidad's* works he wanted serviced—36 hours before launch.

"Why in hell," Sal moaned, "didn't he see about this eight weeks ago?"

Ben just shook his head. "Does it every damned time. Everything's a will-pass until he gets to packing the supplies in. *Then* this latch has got too much give and he's remembered we had a condensation problem last run."

It kept their hands busy. It took their minds off the passing hours. Dekker understood Bird's state of nerves.

Eventually, please God, they'd board and start launch routines and, Dekker thought, he might make it off R2 still sane.

"What kind of vids do you like?" Meg asked him, while he was testing a pressure switch.

He shrugged, figuring Meg meant they were going to rent a few for the trip, for all the spare time they weren't going to have, and he'd used to like the action stuff, but now that he thought about it, that wasn't what he wanted right now. Cory had made fun of his taste for his bloody-awfuls, that was what she had called them—but now he feared he'd never see an explosion in a vid without feeling that awful slam in the gut. He filed that away, in the odd total of silly, simple things he'd been robbed of in the wreck. Maybe he could handle it someday. But not now. Right now he just wanted to keep all that at arm's length. One step at a time, Mr. Dekker. . . .

"Dek?"

"Huh?"

"You want to go out tonight?"

He shook his head. "No," he said sharply—he didn't mean to be rude, but it was the truth—he didn't want to go watch things blow up: he didn't want any dark theater, God knew he didn't want any suspense—didn't know what he did want to do 24 hours before launch—but that wasn't it.

"Oh, come on," Sal said. "What about dinner? We can talk Bird into spending money. Something trez genteel. Candles and tablecloths. Give ourselves plenty of time to get through, get in and clean up. What d' you say? Dinner at 1900, cruise the bars, say our au'voirs along the 'deck."

"Yeah," he said, finally. Being with people tonight was probably a good idea. Meg and Sal were trying to include him in their festivities, trying to draw him into their conversation, but now that he'd committed himself he felt a kind of panic—as if by joining in he'd somehow stepped over an edge he'd really rather reconsider. He had no friends but these people, no future but what they'd arranged for him. They made their jokes, they talked to him, he answered what they asked, one side and the other of a trip for soft drinks and a package of chips.

But this Attitude kept coming over him—a blow-it-away kind of Attitude, resentment—outright rage at their trying to get at him: they had everything he owned and now they wanted his consent to it; now they wanted the resentment that had kept him alive—stupid way to feel, he thought, but their friendliness and Ben's made him mad, and he tried to figure out why, and not to be, as Ben called him, an ass.

But, dammit, everything hit nerves. Even their before-launch dinner. He'd done the same with Cory—Cory didn't make off-color jokes about the men she'd slept with—

Sore spot there. His mind was full of pits he didn't want to look into, this afternoon, pre-launch jitters triggering memories, God only knew what was going on with him—and that the tumbling, out of control feeling he'd had after the wreck was still there, making it impossible to take his life for granted—all the pieces were out of order. Everything felt new, dislocated.

Rab said do. Act. Move. Be.

But move where? Be what? Meg and Sal had their heads together, talking in low voices, protecting some secrecy they wouldn't admit him to—but they wanted him to take their lead. They'd dressed him like some damn doll—not a joke at his expense: far too serious for that. They had designs for him he didn't think had as much to do with sex as with way-of-life . . . making bitter jokes, flaunting their difference, trying to drag him away from Cory's way of doing things and back into all the blind outrage he'd used to feel—wake up, kid, join us, kid, be like us, be with, *think* like us and survive.

Maybe it *was* friendship. Be grateful, he told himself. Go out with them, mind your manners—today's enough. There's worse. There's hell and away worse to have fallen in with.

There's the people that run this place.

He was back on the ship for a moment. And back again sitting in the shop with a small valve switching assembly in his hand and no memory of whether he'd just started or just finished with it.

Panic shot a chill through him. He sat there staring at the piece and trying to figure out what he was doing with it.

"That's the last." Sal snatched it from his hand and tossed it into the basket. "God, Dek, come on, give it up. We're done!"

It wasn't anything he couldn't fix with a screwdriver if it stuck later. Nothing vital. Potential malfunction wasn't what scared him. It was the gap he'd slid into.

Damn nervous wreck, Sal thought, wiping sweat, kicking the null-g cart's wheels out. This one's wheels stuck. The rental office swore they didn't have another. —Get us *all* out of here—

Bang. You lifted one end and rammed it at the floor. Two times freed it up.

"Aboujib," someone said.

She turned about with an intake of breath.

Mitch's friend.

"You're still launching on the 18th?"

"Yeah."

"Don't depend on it."

"Shit! —What's going on?"

"That's the word. Keep a line on your problem. A tight line."

*"Why?"*

The Shepherd said, "You got that thing I gave you?"

"Not on me, I don't go to the core with it . . ."

"I want you to bring it to the club tomorrow. No advance word to Kady, no word to anybody. Just bring that, your friend, and your problem."

"We got a—"—launch tomorrow, she started to object. The universe turned around that point. Everything in their minds did, with manic concentration.

"Tomorrow," the Shepherd repeated.

She felt her heart sink. She thought, My God, Bird and Ben have everything they own tied up in this run . . .

They *can't* not launch tomorrow . . . Meg and me be

damned, they can't not go tomorrow. "You don't back out this close, MamBitch won't change a launch date!"

"That's not in our control," the Shepherd said, and walked away.

"Why don't you come with me?" Meg asked him. "Sal's going to run that last batch up to Bird, and if he tries to give us another lot, we'll say sorry, the shop's closed. You and I can get cleared out of here and turn the keys in. I'm going to pick up a few things at Ward's, maybe stop for coffee..."

He shook his head. "I've got gym time to do." It was the only escape he could think of. He couldn't take Meg's company right now, couldn't risk timing out with her if that was what he had just done. He left: he didn't even realize how stupid the excuse had been until in the lift down he remembered he'd left Meg with a heavy tool case to carry to the rental office.

By then it was too late to go back and catch her, and he had no idea what to do with himself but go to the gym. Nothing seemed solid of a sudden, nothing of his life was in order—*time* worried him—he was freefalling, too scared to admit just now he'd been on autopilot and didn't know it—scared that a hatch shutting behind him was going to start him unraveling—

The blip was still moving. No question.

Cory argued with him: "It's the biggest chance we'll ever have—"

A piece of memory clicked in, quietly, just there of a sudden with that sense of frightened foolishness—he'd realized the danger in the 'driver—and he'd folded the argument, folded the way he'd folded with Sal up there. He'd had the ship completely in his hands—but he'd been afraid to be afraid, he'd let Cory's college education convince him she was right when his gut was telling him a silent, advancing 'driver the company charts didn't show wasn't playing by the rules she understood—

Cory, who knew MarsCorp inside and out, had said, We're going to call their bluff; they're in contact with BM every damn minute... and he'd frozen. He couldn't say,

Cory, this scares hell out of me. He'd been too scared of Cory's education to say, Cory, this is just damned stupid—

She'd say, now, if she were here to say it, Well, I really blew that one, didn't I?

And he wouldn't. He couldn't—couldn't talk, couldn't get his words straight when he thought he could sound like a fool—

So he'd protected his damned soft spot. And Cory had died.

He bumped into someone. He mumbled an apology and kept walking, playing that moment over and over in his mind.

They'd been invulnerable—then. Nothing was going to turn out wrong. She'd made a bad choice, but rocks were her department, the ship was his. The company was crooked as hell, but he could call their bluff. He could make that ship listen—

He'd backed a wrong call. He'd known it and he'd done it. That was what he had to look at and look at til it burned its way into his brain.

# CHAPTER
# 16

THEY waited and they waited in the bar—they'd talked Bird, practically manhandled Bird, out of *Trinidad* and into the idea of a fancy dinner, best clothes, rezzes at the Europa, a bit of bar-hopping afterward—and now Dekker went missing. Ben was mad, Sal was a nervous wreck—Dekker had been acting strange all day, Meg reminded herself glumly, and spent her own money calling the gym he reasonably should have gone to hours ago.

Of course he hadn't.

Damn.

"So, look," Bird said when she reported that fact back to the table, "we just leave word with Mike. Mike can give him directions when he shows up. He'll find us."

"Leave that guy loose on the 'deck?" Ben groaned—not the way she'd have put it, but it was another worrisome side of it. "Let's just give it a little while."

"He's a big boy," Bird said. "He's found his way around the Belt, for God's sake, he's not lost. He may not have understood it was a date."

"He understood," Meg said, and was about to say she

agreed with Ben, they should give it another little while, when Mike at the bar signaled they had a call.

She stood up to take it, but Mike indicated Sal specifically, to her acute disappointment. She slid back into her chair while Sal went to take the call—probably some friend come onto R2, she decided: Dekker might call *her* if he was in a funk and he might call Bird, but Dekker asking for Sal was hardly likely.

"Probably in some bar," Ben said. "Probably drinking his way to tomorrow. Or zee'd on pills. —Dammit, Meg, think of another place."

"Pacific," Bird said.

"So let's call there," Ben said, and something else, but Meg lost it. Sal hung up on her call and flashed her a come-here signal, looking seriously worried.

"Excuse me," she murmured and got up and met Sal by the phone. Sal said, head ducked and voice low, "That was Mitch. He said meet him out front. Now."

She felt a little chill. And puzzlement. "Seriously nonreg. He say anything?"

"No. Just that." Sal looked truly scared. Terrified. "Cover me with Bird. I don't know how long this may take."

"God," Meg said. "Yeah. All right."

Sal went for the door and she went back to the table.

"What was that?" Ben asked.

"Friend with a problem."

"Dekker?"

"No."

"God, this isn't getting any more organized. We're all over the damn 'deck!"

"I think we ought to make that call to The Pacific."

"Do that," Bird said, so she pulled out her card and went for the phone again.

"No," The Pacific said. ". . . Yeah, I know him. No, he hasn't been here."

Another try gone nowhere. Sal was off. Dekker was

missing. Bird was as apt to go off next. Ben was right. She said to Mike, "Another round."

"Sal coming back?"

"I wish I knew," she said. "Skosh nervous day, Mike."

Mike gave a little shake of his head. "A lot wouldn't have the patience."

"Yeah," she said and went back to the table.

"Well?" Ben asked.

She shook her head.

"God, I don't know why we're putting up with this!"

"The lad's probably sorting out a few things," Bird said. "I'm not real surprised."

"Yeah, sorting out a few things . . . For all we know, the cops have got him."

"Look," Bird said. "Let's just put in a few phone calls. There's eight more gyms."

Sal came back, not looking like good news. She came up to the table and leaned against it with her hands. "Trouble," she said, very low. "They just found Dek's partner."

"Alive?" Meg asked.

"Neg. Shepherd found her drifting. At the Well."

Some things you heard and they just didn't make any kind of sense. A fool kid got killed in the far interface of the refinery zones, back sometime in March, and turned up a couple of hundred million k away in September, in a Shepherd recovery path?

"No way," Ben said.

"We have any word yet," Sal asked, "where Dek is?"

"No," Meg said, and leaned back as Mike brought the drinks.

"On my tab," Bird said to Mike, all business, and Mike cleverly made himself absent.

Ben hissed, "What do you mean, drifting at the Well? What in *hell's* going on?"

Sal shook her head, glitter and rattle of metal-tipped braids. "They don't know. Word's out on their net—codecom, to every Shepherd out there . . . you didn't hear that. They don't know if MamBitch can crack it, she gets mad as hell when they do it—but we got a seriously deviated 'driver out there."

"Fired a body at the Well?" Ben said. "God, somebody's stark crazy!"

"Worry what else they might do," Meg said. "If a general message is going out on the Shepherd net, that 'driver's going to hear the transmission, going to know the time and the PO, going to have an idea *what* that message was, even if they can't crack the code."

"*They're* not going to tell MamBitch anything," Sal said. Her voice was shaking. "But the question is how long the Shepherds can hold this quiet. This is a seriously bad time for Dek to go missing."

"If the cops haven't got him," Bird said. "Question is—does Mama know what's in that transmission? They'll pick him up."

Sal pulled two datacards from her pocket and laid them on the table. "That's from a couple of friends. We're them. They're real high Access. The word is Find Dek. Get him to the club next to Scorpio's, and don't use our cards or his."

Ben whispered, "Dammit, we got a launch tomorrow!"

"He may not make it."

*We* may not make it, Meg thought. The cards lay there—seriously illegal, what the Shepherds were doing and what they were risking. One kid was dead. Good chance there could be another.

She picked up one card.

Bird picked up the other.

The message stack was jammed by the time William Payne reached the office—halfway through an important dinner and three glasses of wine under his belt when the phone had rung, and he wished to hell he'd had at least one fewer. He turned on the light, slid into his chair and keyed on line, watching the flash of prioritied incomings—

His immediate superior, Crayton, with a cryptic memo: *An unexplained ship to ship message is proceeding from the Shepherds. Be alert for sabotage.*

A statement from the president of the board: *The company stands by its policy on abuse of communications.*

From Cooley, in News & Entertainment: *Continuing regular programming pending further instructions.*

From Salvatore, in Security: *Stage 1 alert in progress. Code team is assembling.*

Payne keyed on, waiting for Crayton's instructions to flow down, waiting for information to flow up from Salvatore. He was shivering. The temperature in the office was still coming up. Or it was nerves.

The Shepherd negotiations were in trouble, and *this* happened—they were clearly making a move and the company now had to break off the contract talks or lose credibility—

With agitators stirring up the dockworkers and the refinery workers spoiling for a chance to press their agendas—*real* problems in those groups. The EC insisted on dumping its touchy cases out here, and those problems didn't go away, they just recruited other problems and made demands. They opened valves in the mast. They slashed hoses. They vandalized plastics vats. Now the Shepherds committed a deliberate, massive defiance of company rules—outright challenging the company to take action, possibly even signaling the long-threatened work stoppage.

The right action, it had to be, and incoming information and outgoing instructions intersected at his desk in Public Information.

Continue the media blackout? That might keep the lid on for an hour, but it also made rumor the main source for the workers. Better to start dribbling out information as soon as he could get a policy direction out of Crayton: keep the workers glued to the vid reports and off the open decks. Some offices in the mast had equipment to hear that illicit transmission, and rumors were as quick as two workers hitting the 8-deck vending machines on coffee break. There were war jitters—and coded-com like that could set off alarms over in the shipyard, in the military base, God, clear to Earth's security zone.

He keyed up, composed a query from PI to Crayton in

General Admin. *Request clearance for news release to fore-stall rumor and speculation.*

There were going to be hard questions for every administrator in the information chain. Every decision over the next few hours was going under a magnifying glass. The EC, the UN, UI—God only knew how far and how many careers were going down with this as it was; the Shepherds, damn them, were calling the company's bluff.

He wasn't in The Pacific, wasn't in the Tycho or the Europa or the Apollo, and so far as they could find out, he wasn't in any gym they'd ever used. They fanned out, gave up communication with each other—couldn't phone when you didn't know where to phone, and you never knew when the company was listening. *I'll check 3,* Meg told Ben, last time their paths crossed on the 'deck, and she caught the Trans to 3, to check the gyms there.

"Seen a dark-haired guy, rab cut, about 20, thin?"

No, no, and no. She had a stitch in her side, she had a bash on her elbow from a fast stop in .8 g, and she was running out of places that didn't involve the cops or the hospital. She imagined odd looks at her back, imagined the rumor starting to run the corridors: *What's to do with the dark-haired rab?* On helldeck she'd gotten *Will I do's?* from guys she asked, and the last try in the gym she hadn't—out of breath and looking like no joke at all. That wasn't good. That invited questions from the cops—especially with the Shepherds sending illegal transmissions. She took the stretch back toward the Transstation at a slow walk, catching her breath and racking her brain for where next to look, when the thought hit her that she was already on 3—and Dekker obviously hadn't done anything logical, or they'd have found him.

The cops might be tracking card use by now, and using a Shepherd card was about as nervous a proposition as using her own. But there were more Shepherds than there were Meg Kadys on R2, and a cop looking for a guy might just look past her. She about-faced and went for the core lift, used the card and rode it up with a couple of obnoxious tender-jocks who wanted to get friendly. She stared obdurately at the door, arms folded, sweating, panicked, thinking, God, no trouble, I *don't* want cops... *not* carrying an illegal card...

Up through lighter and lighter decks, where you had to take hold: the tender-jocks tried to talk her into getting off at 8 and going to a sleepery with them. She said no, very patiently, and swore she was going to hunt these guys down and kill them if she got out of this.

8. The jocks got off. Thank *God*... The car made the jolting transit to the core and stopped—the Access light went on and she shoved the card in, hoping to God customs wasn't on duty right now.

The door opened. She caught the grip on the line, and rode it through the numbing cold—no jacket, obviously not dressed for the core; but she'd done it before, and customs off in their warm little office had seen her come and go like this a dozen times.

Hope to God nobody's put a watch on the ships.

She was half-frozen by the time she'd braked off the line and caught *Trinidad*'s rigging-cord—hadn't even a hand-jet: she monkeyed over to the hatch, her breath coming in ragged, teeth-chattering hisses as she opened up and hauled herself through.

The damn fool was there, just doing a little wipe-down on a cabinet. He made a slow turn to look at her, all calm—like, What's the rush, Meg? What could possibly be the matter?

She brought up against a console, hauled herself steady against the recoil, out of breath, not knowing what that look meant—that he'd lost his mind and gone totally eetee, or that he was holding it together, up here testing the limits of his sanity.

"You kind of missed a dinner date," she said.

He blinked as if he were dropping into another track of thought. "God," he said, "I'm sorry."

Blank and innocent. She wasn't entirely sure he was sane right now, or that she was even safe with him in this lonely, noise-insulated place. She said, with her teeth chattering, "Dek, we got to get down and find Bird—right now. Something's come up."

"Something wrong?"

She wasn't about to explain to him here, alone. She grabbed his arm. "We just got a problem." Her teeth rattling made it hard to talk. "Come on, Dek, for God's sake, I'm freezing."

"What's going on?"

"Tell you on the way." She made a little finger-sign that meant *bug.* "Bird wants you. Now."

He disposed of the cloth he was holding. He wiped his fingers on his sweater, looking scared now.

But he dimmed the lights and followed her out of the hatch.

Message from Salvatore: *We've got some kind of stir among the military personnel on the 'deck—MP's and officers going from bar to bar, spreading out. Looks as if they're pulling their people off leave. . . .*

Payne passed the message on to Crayton's office and grabbed the phone. "FleetCom," he told it, and got one ring after another, then a robot.

*"Input your priority please."*

"This is Payne, ASTEX Public Information Office."

*"Your call is entered in queue. Your call will be answered . . ."*

Priority beeped him off. Red lights spread like plague across the phone console.

*"Sir!"* Salvatore said into his ear, but another priority beeped Salvatore down to autorecord.

The phone said, simultaneously with the computer, on voice: *". . . This is President Towney's office. We are in receipt of an uncoded message echoed from Shepherd craft at the Well, quote: . . . At 1540 hours on September 2nd, the Shepherd Athens picked up an anomalous object in the recovery zone. It proved to be human remains, carrying the identification of Corazon Salazar, a miner registered to R1, and reported lost earlier this year during a reported bumping incident between the 'driver Industry and the miner ship*

*1-89-Z. Our calculations indicate an origin consistent with other loads fired by the aforenamed 'driver. We are in possession of charts which indicate falsification of records. We are advising the company of these facts and we are demanding that charges immediately be filed of willful murder and attempted murder, with arrest warrants issued for the chief officers of the 'driver ship—²"*

Sweating, heart thumping, Payne keyed to Salvatore: Whereabouts of Paul Dekker. Priority One.

# CHAPTER

# 17

DEKKER kept his jaw clamped on questions Meg clearly wasn't going to answer—"I don't *know* what the situation is right now," was the last information thing she'd yet said, when she'd insisted on stopping on 4-deck and walking breakneck to a lift that only took cards like the one she was using—which wasn't hers. Gold. The only card like that he'd ever seen was Shepherd Access.

He'd never seen this end of helldeck, either—where the lift let out. She led the way across the 'deck immediately to a door next to a fancy restaurant. A card-sized gold plaque was the only sign of business: the Shepherd emblem, Jupiter and the recovery track, right above the card-lock.

"What is this?" he asked.

Meg put the card in, shoved the door as the electronic lock clicked.

He ducked inside after her, into a carpeted reception room where he knew they didn't belong—by no right ought they to be here, except that card.

A blond man looked up from the reception desk.

Meg said, "This is Dek; Dek, Mitch. —Have we heard anything from the rest of us?"

"Neg," Mitch said, before Dekker could say anything, and pointed to the first door down the hall. "Wait in there. Both of you."

"I've got friends out there," Meg objected, "looking for him."

"We're *doing* something about it, Kady. We'll do it faster if you take care of him."

"Maybe you'd better tell me what's going on," Dekker said, but Meg grabbed him by the arm, said, "Dek, come on," and steered him down the hall.

"Dammit, Meg, —"

"Shit, I don't know, I don't know, come on, just awhile— sonuvabitch! I'm up to here with sons of bitches..." Meg took him back into an elegant deserted bar, left him standing while she turned on the lights and set up on her own, poured two fast, shaky drinks, one whiskey, one rum.

He came and leaned his elbows on the bar, said carefully: "We're not getting out of here tomorrow, are we?"

She took a sip of the whiskey and shoved the rum at him. "Drink up."

"Meg. What's happened? What are we doing here?"

She leaned on the bar, nudged his hand with her glass. "You seriously better have a little of that, jeune rab. —They found your partner."

*That* was it. —But the Shepherd Access, Meg's breathless rush—coming here... He stood bewildered. Meg came around the end of the bar and snagged him by the sleeve, pulled him to a table and set him down opposite her.

She said, "Dek, they found her at the Well. That sonuvabitch put her in a bucket and sent her a long tour of Jupiter. A Shepherd picked her up on the recovery path."

Meg sneaked up all gentle. Then she shot for the gut. His mind went blank and black—

That huge dark machine...

"Why in hell—" Breath dammed up in his throat. He couldn't get it out. He reached for the glass, slopped it left and right getting a drink.

Meg reached across the table, reached for his free hand as he set the glass down, squeezed his fingers til they hurt.

"Cher. Death is. Pain's life. And there's, above all, sons of bitches. Get your breath. You're not the only one who knows now. You're not alone out there. It's the independents . . . the freerunners . . . the Shepherds they were aiming at. The old, old business."

"But what in hell do they think they're doing?" His voice came out higher than he intended, hardly recognizable. "What kind of a game is this? How could they ever think they could get away with it?"

"There's crazy people. They shot us down at the company doors. News cameras everywhere. Everybody in the world saw it. How'd they get away with that, can you tell me, jeune rab? —Have your rum. The word's out on the Shepherds' com. They'll be hearing it at Sol about now. The company won't want you to talk, you understand—seriously won't want you to talk to anybody. That's what's going on. But if MamBitch pushes now, the Shepherds are going to shut MamBitch down. Let the corp-rats fly the ships with their cut-rate crews. Let the company execs fly the Well."

"I want that guy, Meg."

"Close as we can come. You got the guys that launched him. *Somebody's* job's gone. Best you can do with these sumbitches."

*He's reported in the core,* the last report from Salvatore's office had said. They were still searching; and Payne, with Towney's office requesting the Dekker file, searched screen after screen of records generated by Salvatore's investigation.

Record score on re-certification. Cleared to retrain, shipping with the two miners who'd picked him up, plus a Kady and Aboujib, both female—

Ships both due to launch on the 18th, the sleepery owner swearing he had no idea in hell where Dekker was—Dekker has missed a supper appointment: his partners had been phoning around trying to find him. Dekker could have come and gone, the owner had no idea, he'd been watching the vid. Everybody in the bar had been watching the vid . . .

Aboujib and Pollard both had Shepherd parentage. Kady was a cashiered shuttle pilot. Bird had been a suspect in the Nouri affair, close friend of Pratt and Marks—

The file had gone to Towney's desk.

And the monkey was climbing up PI's back.

Nobody had told *his* office that Dekker was anything but, at absolute worst, a skimmer who'd gotten caught and bumped. Nobody had told him that a 'driver captain was going to make a gesture like this at the Shepherds.

He keyed up *Industry*'s record. Windowed in the second chart.

*No* record of asteroid 98879 prior to the incident. *Industry*'s transmission logged the discovery to the company. March 7th.

God.

Dekker had flat spooked out about the launch—that was Ben's opinion on the matter. They'd tried restaurants, game parlors, tried the bars again in the idea he could be skipping from one to the other, but the cops and the military were getting more and more visible on the 'deck.

To *hell* with that guy! Ben thought, trying to look inconspicuous while a group of military police came past the frontage. Inside, the vid was saying something about shifts held over due to "military exercises" and "a test of security procedures. . . ."

A hand landed on his shoulder. His heart nearly stopped. He spun around nose to nose with Bird.

"Don't *do* that!"

"Now *we* got a problem. We got wall to wall cops at The Hole."

He felt of his pocket, cold of a sudden. "Card's with me. We're all right."

"'All right,'" Bird echoed him. "You got a hell of an idea of 'all right.' Have you seen Sal or Meg?"

"Not since an hour ago."

The PA blared out: "*Shifts will be held another hour.*"

*There is a Civil Defense Command exercise in progress. If you have an assigned CDC post on 3-shift, go to it immediately. If you have no assigned duty, clear the 'decks, repeat, all off-shift personnel get off the 'decks and return to quarters."*

"The hell," Bird muttered. "I've seen *this* before."

"What are they doing?"

"Cops," Bird said. "Martial law. Shit with finding the kid. They're going to shut him up, shut it down—it's Nouri all over again." Bird's hand closed on his arm. "And *we're* in it up to our ears, understand me?"

He did understand. He saw company cops moving through the crowds—saw blue-uniformed MP's too, with heavy sidearms.

Bird said, "This time we put the word out, just find some friends, spill the beans, tell them pass it on."

"Why risk *our* necks? We got enough troubles."

"That's what we said the last time."

"Bird, —those are guns out there!"

"Do you know the word 'railroad,' Ben-me-lad? Pratt and Marks were innocent. No way those boys were with Nouri's lot. Good, dumb kids. But now nobody's sure. —You do what you like."

"Where are you going?"

"Doing a little discreet talking around in various ears. The company's not hushing this one up. This time we know numbers. And dates."

His mind went scattering in panic—the launch tomorrow. . . but that wasn't going to happen. The urge to kill Dekker for involving them in this . . . but Dekker was probably the first one under arrest.

He took a fistful of Bird's coat, hauled him back. "Bird, —"

"I knew Pratt and Marks were being screwed," Bird said. "*I* had the evidence, you understand me. It could have tied *me* to Nouri—in certain eyes. Everybody was scared. Everybody was saving his own ass. And everybody lost. —Not this time."

"Bird, for God's sake—"

"This time it's *us* in the fire-path, you understand me?

And we're not dumb kids. You've got that datacard. Give it to me."

Ben felt after the flat shape in his inside pocket, desperately trying to think what old classmates he knew that could fix *this* one—but there wasn't anyone. Not a damn soul who wouldn't be, the way Bird said, saving his own ass.

"*Give* it to me."

"What are you going to do?"

"Put it on the bulletin board. And pass the word."

"Shit!"

Bird leaned close and put a hand on his shoulder. "Find yourself a hole, hear me? Get down to the club. Don't know if Sal's friends'll let you in, but, hell, you've got ties there. Use 'em. It's the only hole might cover you."

Bird trying anything under the table—Bird didn't know shit about the safeguards on the computer systems, Bird didn't know shit what he was doing, dammit, those charts were their living—

They also were the only evidence that existed about where they'd been and what they'd done, and if the company arrested them and erased it—

"Hell," he said, "you've got that Shepherd card. Thing's got 1-deck Access."

"Do what with it? Hell, Ben, that thing's probably more dangerous—"

"Just leave the computer stuff to me and stay out of it, Bird, you don't know shit how to get past the lockouts. I can get into all the boards, hell, I can get it into general systems, Bird, I know the modem codes . . ."

"Where in *hell* did you get those?"

He said, "Just give me the fuckin' card, Bird, and tell 'em the filename's *Dekker*."

"*Mr. Crayton is in conference,*" the secretary said, and Payne shot the memo through in desperation. "Give *that* to him. We've got to have a policy decision. Thirty minutes ago!"

"*I believe that's the subject of the con—*"

Payne hung up in frustration, and stared at the stalled

press release on his screen. Then he shot it unapproved to News & Entertainment, for release.

*The nature of a coded Shepherd transmission has been revealed as a query to Shepherd senior administration regarding the discovery of human remains in a Shepherd recovery zone. Company records have tentatively identified the body as likely that of Corazon Salazar, lost earlier this year in an accident near the R2/R1 boundary. Ms. Salazar, daughter of Alyce Salazar, a MarsCorp board member and prominent member of the Defense Advisory Council, was two years resident on R1. She was apparently struck and killed while EVA when a tank explosion sent her ship out of control. The ship then traveled helplessly at high velocity into R2 zone. Dr. Ronald Michaels, of the Institute, has offered the theory that the body, traveling in the firepath of the 'driver ship Industry, was struck by one of the loads and carried along with it at a velocity sufficient to delivery it to the recovery site.*

*The Shepherd discovery adds another chapter to the already tragic story of the ill-fated miner craft* Way Out. *The surviving partner, Mr. Paul Dekker, was rescued earlier this year by an R2 ship dispatched to his rescue. Mr. Dekker, surviving isolation, cold and failing lifesupport after an amazing 71 days adrift, was released from James R. Reynolds Hospital after extensive treatment for physiological and psychological trauma. A spokesman for the hospital this shift expressed concern that Mr. Dekker has not responded to urgent attempts to notify him in advance of public release of this news. Mr. Dekker currently remains unlocatable on R2. Dr. Emil Visconti, Mr. Dekker's physician, authorized release of the news in the fear that Mr. Dekker has heard the report via other sources and appealed for Mr. Dekker or anyone knowing his whereabouts to call Security or the information desk at Reynolds Hospital immediately. Mr. Dekker is on medication and may have suffered disorientation or mental confusion due to the stress of this tragic report, and may be despondent. A spokesman for ASTEX Administration assures Mr. Dekker that he has been cleared of all fault in the accident, which occurred as the result of a catastrophic equipment failure, and urges Mr. Dekker to contact the hospital immediately. . . .*

Damn him. Damn Crayton—dumping a case like this on him with no indication at all that it had hidden problems.

Now Crayton couldn't even clear a press release. He had to put his neck on the line, *try* to keep the lid on—knowing that win or lose, this was something the company would want black-holed. Lost. Forgotten. Along with anybody in any way tainted with it.

The comp took the message. Another one windowed up, for Salvatore:

*A Shepherd came and went at the core between 2041 and 2108h. Customs didn't see him. They were in the office listening to the outlaw transmission. The card belonged to a tech named Nate Chaney, who isn't answering to calls at his listed numbers . . .*

No way to get to the rental comp at The Hole—but any phone would do, that had a keypad, and Io's fancy establishment had that amenity. Neon flashed, dyed the beer green and red while it shook in the glass. Couldn't hear a core blowout in this place, Ben thought, and it was crawling with low-level corporates—but he was wearing his best 'deck casuals and the corner of the bar afforded a dark area. Shepherd card first: then his:

Boot file: PROCESS. Invoke: CALL13; README5; ADD2; ADD1; ADD3

Boot memory resident file: PROCESS2. Enter.

Student pranks. The datawindow showed dots, the Egg assembling its parts and pieces.

The datawindow said: CALLME: INS TXT

INPUT: $/CHART.CUR; CHART.14; CHART.15

OUTPUT: DEKKER

The datawindow said: ENTER SYSACC

His hands trembled over the keys. He didn't think about cops. Or the corporate behind him, waiting to use the phone. He thought about data. He typed, rapid-fire:*2;20;W489\209;INSTAL:C\$/$y;*BOOT3;*3.l/$;{rs/#}/p*280:#[TAG/*1]

He switched datacards—inserted the Shepherd's before the pause ran out.

Phone charge went to the Shepherd card. The Run trigger waited the first phone user after him. Nasty trick on the guy fidgeting behind him. *He'd* be out of the bar.

He sipped the beer, punched charge, extracted the card and palmed it for his, held that one up, right color for a miner, if it mattered in the blue strobe, indication to the bar he'd paid: "Thanks," he called out, drowned in the general thunder of the bass line, left his beer on the bar and went out the door.

He had the general shakes by then—but, damn, he'd really *done* it, he'd actually *run* the thing—his own tinkered-up finesse on an old Institute prank—with Assay Office bank and com direct line access numbers and a Shepherd's 1-deck phone system authorizations. The question was now whether he was ahead of the current game with the trap programs—

—and whether he could get Bird off the 'deck—whether he could *find* Bird, before the cops did.

The cops were out in force, clearing the 'deck. It was the old game, the cops said Move along, you said, Yes, sir, and you went somewhere else you didn't live—helldeck played that game, the cops knew it was a game—didn't push it too hard, helldeck crowd being what they were. They were going to have to make the sleeperies close their bars to everybody but residents, if they were serious and not just Making the Presence Felt: and *that* move would lock legitimate residents out on the 'deck and have angry confrontations left and right—not what they were after, Ben told himself; but if it was your face they might be looking for, it seemed a good idea to hang to the back of crowds, keep behind taller people and drift on when they did.

God, he thought, no knowing what Bird's puttering around into. I got to get him to cover somewhere—and if they pick us up, we just go along with it, take it easy, wait for the upper echelons to sort it out.

No way they're going to screw us for this one—too many people know the truth, too many people on corp-deck are going to be covering their asses, and to do that, they have to cover *ours*, axe that sumbitch captain out there—and any clerk they can pin it on: those are the ones who need to worry.

Maybe we can even parlay this into a company buyoff, get us that helldeck office—

Justice, hell, Bird, —it's the names you know that matter. It's where they are and what you can do to them in court.

Wipe down this card is all—

Slip it right into the trashbin.

"Screwed the kid good," Bird said, leaning close to Abe Persky, whispering over the music in the Europa. "But what they did to the girl, that wasn't any company order. That was a 'driver/Shepherd piece of business—damn sight more than letting a rock drift from a sling, this time. Shepherds are broadcasting it, outside code now—they'll hear it clear to Earth, plain as plain. *That's* what the alert is about."

"Damn," Persky said with a shake of his head.

"Listen. I dumped my charts to the helldeck board— might check it before they catch it. Filename's *Dekker. D-e-k-k-e-r.*" He nudged Persky's arm. "Pass it on, everyone you know."

"Got you," Persky said, and reached for his datacard. Nudged him back as he was leaving. "*Careful,* Bird."

Collins' table next. Collins was a company pilot now, but he didn't like being that. He came to helldeck to keep up old acquaintances. He was sitting with Robley—Robley was doing factory work now: the kidneys had gone.

He sat down with Collins and Robley, and saw Persky pay out and leave.

Just one and two at a time. But the 'deck telegraph moved like lightning.

Another call from Payne's office. Salvatore said, "Yes, sir," and, "We're trying, sir, we've thought of that, sir, we're trying that too . . ."

Payne said: "Don't tell me 'trying.' I want all the records, I want the whole file on this guy. On *all* of them.

Don't give me another dead kid with relatives in MarsCorp, dammit, Administration's had enough surprises in this case! I want to know who this Dekker is, I want to know if he's got a record, I don't care if it's a misdemeanor, I want a total profile on him! You hear me? All the files, no ten-year cutoff, I want them as far back as they go, and I want them yesterday!"

Payne hung up. The comp flashed up a new message: *Workers in Textiles 2B are demanding to be let go. There's been some breakage, some pushing and shoving, manager's scared and wants some help.*

And another from Crayton's office: *Fleet Operations is recalling its personnel from liberty, stationing armed guards at two shuttle docks and at essential lifesupport and manufacturing accesses. We need immediate operations coordination. . . .*

God, Salvatore thought, and a report from Wills came in:

*Morris Bird had dinner reservations at the Europa, for five. It was a no-show.*

He *wanted* the inhaler. He didn't dare. "Call my wife at home," he told his secretary. "Tell her to check on my daughter. Make sure she's in the dorm." He sipped cold coffee, trying to think who he could spare to liaison with the MP's.

More messages crawled across the screen. *A man is having chest pains in Textiles 2B. Paramedics have been called. . . .*

Wills again: *Brown's turned up a witness in customs who thinks Meg Kady was in the core at about 2040h. He's not sure on that, says he saw all of them come and go the last few days taking parts back and forth—they had a permit for that, a ship in refit. We do have a confirmation on a card access for Dekker up there at 1723h. No exit. No card use at all from Kady since a phone call at 1846, from The Black Hole to The Pacific. The owner at The Black Hole claims they all left about 1900. He thinks.*

Two people slipping a security gate on a borrowed card. Happened once or twice a week, usually for assignations.

The mast was a hell of a job to search, even under optimum conditions.

*Textiles 2B reports a riot in progress. Manager requests additional security and paramedics...*

Priority came through, bumped that: *Virus Alert: Technical level shutdown.*

Priority override: *A virus is copying an unauthorized file through the Belt Management System. Contents are illicit sector charts. Virus variation on COPYIT. Request computer crimes division to trace and erase proliferation through BM system.*

"... *cleared of all fault in the accident, which occurred as the result of a catastrophic equipment failure, and urges Mr. Dekker to contact the hospital immediately....*"

Bird gave the vid a look over his shoulder, shook his head and looked at Tim Egel. "You're a good numbers man. You believe that line?"

"No," Egel said. "Not the tooth fairy either. Shoved to the Well by a load. I'd like to see the math on that one."

"They don't teach physics in Business Ad."

"Don't teach math either, do they?" That was a tender-jock, in on it, beer in hand. "What kind of stuff is that they're giving out?"

"They want Dekker back in hospital. They worked him over with drugs. But he remembered the numbers anyway. That's what they can't cover up. 79, 709, 12. There was a bloody great rock there. That's what it was about. That 'driver came down on them while they were tagging it. Now the 'driver's sitting out there stripping that rock to loads. I'd like to match those loads with the sample Dekker had in his sling."

"Can anybody do that?"

"I got the sample. It's on record in Assay."

"This here's Morrie Bird," Egel said. "The guy that brought Dekker in."

"No shit! I heard of you! You're the *old* guy!"

Being famous got you drinks. Being famous could also get you arrested. He took a couple of swigs from the beer the guy insisted to buy him, and set it down, said, "If you're curious, check the boards for a file named Dekker. With two k's."

"Dekker," the jock said.

Egel said, in Bird's diminishing hearing, "*I'll* tell you what they're up to, friend. They weren't going to pay that rock out to any freerunner. Pretty soon they won't pay it to a company miner either. Or the tenders. When the freerunners go, there go the perks *anybody* gets on the company ticket. When they don't have to compete with independents like us..."

"They can't do that," somebody else said.

Time to leave, Bird thought. Getting a little warm in here. He set his drink down and slid backward in the crowd, faced about for an escape and saw cops coming into the place.

The cops waded in through the middle of the crowd yelling something about a closing order and residents only; and he stuck to the shadows until there was a clear doorway.

Outside, then. In the clear. But that was it—cops were getting just a little active.

"Where *are* they?" Meg asked the only live human being she could find in the place—no Mitch, now, just this pasty-faced guy at the desk with the phone, with no calls coming in that she'd heard. Nothing was coming in, that she could tell, not even the vid, for what good it might be.

"No word yet," the Shepherd said—guy in his thirties, serious longnose, busy with the com-plug in his ear—*not* liking real rab on his clean club carpet. He focused for a moment, lifted a manicured hand to delay her. "Ms. Kady—go a little easy on the whiskey."

She'd started away. She came back, leaned her hands on the desk. "I'm all right on the whiskey, mister. Where's Mitch? Where's my partner?"

"We have other problems."

"What?"

A wave-off. A frown on the Shepherd's face. He was listening to something. Then not.

"Look. I hate like hell to inconvenience you guys, but I have a seriously upset guy in there who's damned tired of runarounds. So am I. Suppose you tell me what's going on."

"A great many police is what's going on. They're still holding 2-shift."

"Shit."

"Don't be an ass, Kady. —That door's locked."

"Then open it!"

"Kady, get the hell back to the bar—get that kid back in there."

"Meg?"

She turned around, saw Dekker in the foyer. "Dek, just be patient, I'm trying to get some answers."

"There aren't any answers, Kady, just keep the kid entertained."

She saw a flash of total red. Bang, with her hand on the counter. "Listen, you son of a bitch—where the fuck is my partner?"

"I don't know where your partner is. If she followed orders she'd be here."

"She doesn't know we've got him! She's not on your network!"

"I don't know where a lot of people are, right now, Kady—we've got a lot more problems than your—" The Shepherd pressed his earpiece closer, held up a hand for silence.

"What?"

"They're bringing that warship's engines up, over at the 'yard. They want us out of here."

"They. Who, 'they'?"

"The *Hamilton*. There's a shuttle on the mast. But we aren't getting com with it. *Hamilton*'s saying it can't raise it. That's our contingency sitting up there."

"Shit! This is going to hell, mister!"

"Shut *up*, Kady!"

Message from CCrimes: *Ordering immediate shutdown of the banking system. The virus has entered 2-deck bulletin boards, spreading on infected cards with each use . . .*

The man in Textiles 2B had died. There was a broken leg in a fall off a catwalk, there was damage to the machinery, a woman had gone into labor—Salvatore had a view from an Optex and it was a mess. They had the phones stopped on 2, but the damn chart had proliferated from the bulletin boards to the card charge system, sent itself into every trade establishment on R2, and they didn't know if it was into the bank databank itself.

He washed an antacid down with stale coffee, and tried to placate Payne. Payne said he had to go to a meeting. Payne said his aide LeBrun was handling the office.

Damned right there was a meeting. There had better be a meeting real soon now. With some faster policy decisions. Salvatore's hands were shaking, and he didn't know who he could trust to handle emergencies long enough for him to get to the restroom and back.

"Sir," the intercom said, "sir, a Lt. Porey to see you."

He didn't have any Lt. Porey on his list. He started to protest he wasn't seeing anybody, but the door opened without further warning, and a Fleet officer walked in on him, *with* his aide. "Mr. Salvatore," the man said. African features. An accent he couldn't place. And a deep-spacer prig Attitude, he'd lay money on it, expecting stations to run on *his* schedule.

He got up. A second aide showed up, blocked his secretary out of the doorway. And shut the door.

"Mr. Porey." He offered a grudging hand to a crisp, perfunctory grip, all the while thinking: We're going to discuss this one with Crayton. Damned if not.

"*Mr.* Salvatore, we have a developing situation on 2-deck. Rumor is loose, and some *ass* in your office is referring FleetCom to PI—"

God, a *pissed-off* Fleet prig. "That's the chain of command."

"Not in *our* operations. I want the files on this Dekker and I want the files on the entire Shepherd leadership."

"I'm afraid all that's under our jurisdiction, Mr. Porey: you'll have to get an administrative clearance for that access. I can refer you to Mr. Crayton, in General Admin—"

Porey reached inside his coat, pulled a card from his pocket and tossed it down on his desk. "Put *that* authorization in your reader."

Salvatore picked up the card with the least dawning apprehension they were in deep, EC-level trouble, and put it in the reader slot.

It said, *Earth Company Executive Order, Office of the President, Sol Station, Earth Administration Zone.*

*To all officers and agents of Security and Communications, ASTEX Administrative Territories:*

*By the authority of the Executive Board and a unanimous vote of the Directors, a state of emergency is deemed to exist in ASTEX operations which place military priority contracts in jeopardy. ASTEX Security and Communications agencies and employees are hereby notified of the transfer of all affected assets and operations to the authority of EcoCorp, under ASTEX Charter provision 28 hereafter appended, and subject to the orders of EcoCorp Directors . . . I hereby and herewith order ASTEX company police and life services officers to place themselves directly under the order of UDC Security Office in safeguarding records and personnel during this transfer of operational authority.*

Salvatore sat down and read it again.

"Effectively," Porey said, "your paycheck comes directly from the EC now. You're a civilian law enforcement officer in a strategically sensitive operation, subject to the rules and decisions of the UDC, the UN and the EC officers and board. I'm directing you to turn over those files."

"You can't have gotten an order from the EC—you haven't had the time to get a reply."

"Good, Mr. Salvatore. You are a critical thinker. There were triggering mechanisms. The transfer document has lain on my commanding officer's desk for some few days. But I'd think again about destroying files, or advising your former administrators of your change of loyalties. You have a long career with the EC in front of you if you use your head. I can't say that about all your managers." A second card hit the desk. "That goes in a Security terminal. It will make its own accesses. Can you trust your secretary?"

"I—" He saw the guns—automatics. Explosive shells. Not riot control gear. And not ASTEX any longer. "I think I'd better explain it to him," he said, and thought about his wife, about his daughter. He took the card, slid it into the computer and pressed ENTER.

The screen went to Access, and came up again with a series of dots. Porey folded his arms and watched it a moment, looked his way then with the tilt of a brow.

"The *Industry* file. Purge it, among first things."

"*Purge* it? *Erase* it?"

"It's become irrelevant. Personnel have already been transferred. Certain questions won't be asked beyond this office. That's official, Mr. Salvatore. Your career could rise or fall on that simple point. Take great care how you dispose of it. —Mr. Paget."

"Sir!"

"*Find* Paul Dekker and escort him to the dock."


"So what's the new plan?" Meg asked, she thought with great restraint, standing between Dekker's temper and some fill-in Shepherd data-jock with a rulebook up his ass who persisted in trying to get contact with a shuttle that was probably—

The Shepherd said, "They're still not getting through to Mitch—they're jamming us."

"So what do you expect? It's not just the company anymore, it's the soldiers, for God's sake, and you can't *hide* on a station—"

"You can't hide a ship, either, Kady. I'm not sure how long my ship can hold position out there—"

"Then let's get up to the dock. Play it by ear for God's sake!"

"This isn't a game, woman, we don't know if the lifts are working—"

"Sit on your ass a little longer and we won't know what *else* won't be working when we need it."

"I'm the only contact our people *have* on this station—I have my orders—Mitch is—"

"*Mitch* isn't answering, you're not contacting anybody out there, the phones are down, the soldiers are all up and down the 'deck, for God's sake—let's get the *hell* up to the dock, if that's our option!"

"It does us no good to get to the shuttle, our pilot's out there on the 'deck!"

"Is *that* your problem? Well, you're in luck, mister! You're up to your ass in pilots."

"C-class, Kady, not a miner craft—"

"Earth to orbit, ship to station, *B1*, anything you can dock at this hellhole. Let's just get the hell up there."

"Kady, there's police out there. There's armed police in front of our door. D' you have a way we're going to get past them?"

*Good* question.

A whole squad of soldiers passed, going somewhere in a hurry. Ben found sudden interest in a bar window, in a crowd of exiting patrons. They *were* shutting the bars, dammit. At least closing the doors.

Serious time to get somewhere. Bird might have headed back to The Hole, Bird might have been arrested by now, God only where he was.

A touch brushed his arm. His heart turned over. He looked in that direction and saw a coffee-dark face under a docker's knit cap.

Dock monkey's coveralls, too. When women were damn scarce on the docks. "What are *you* doing?"

"Getting to the club unobviously as I can, which I think the both of us urgently better. Any word on Dekker?"

"No, damn him, I'm looking for Bird right now."

"We better get him. They got soldier-boys with rifles now. They pulled those lads off liberty and they're putting some of them down by the offices."

"Damn, I don't like that."

"No argument, cher. Some of those guys are still flying a little."

"Bright. Corporate bright, there."

"Ain't corp-rat, cher, that's the so'jers—which we got gathering right down there. Don't look. Just let's stroll along and find Bird."

He hadn't been entirely scared until now. He started to walk, hearing distant shouting. People were coming out of the bar behind their backs.

A beer mug hit the deck and broke.

"Just keep walking," Sal said.

"Don't hold my arm. You're a guy, dammit!"

"Yeah," Sal said, and dropped it.

*Try* to find a match on a refinery station—

"There's candles in Scorpio's," the Shepherd said, rummaging the repair-kit.

"Not excessively helpful, mister. Never mind the screwdriver. Screw. Have you got a brass screw? Wire?"

Dekker objected, "Meg, what are you doing?"

She pulled the cover off the door-switch. "Wait-see, cher rab. God, the man has wire. What are we coming to?"

"A short's only going to start the—"

Dekker got this look then.

"Yeah," she said, winding wire about bare contacts. "Remember the '15, cher? Want you to take a few napkins, and the vodka bottles. . . . Won't take me a minute here."

"That door's going to seal," the Shepherd said, "the second the fire-sensor goes off. We'll suffocate."

"Uh-uh. Door's going to stay open. Make me happy. Say we got fire-masks in here."

# CHAPTER

# 18

THE emergency speakers said, from every other store front: *This is a full security alert. Go to your residences immediately. Go to your residences immediately. Clear the walkways for emergency vehicles.*

Sal said: "So what are we supposed to do, go home or clear the walkways? Stupid shits!"

"I don't like this," Ben said.

"Seriously time to get down to the club."

The wires sparked and melted, the door opened, Meg whipped a chair into the doorway and ducked back. Shots spattered. Dekker kept his hands steady: the toilet paper caught, the cloth fibers caught, the cloth caught, blue fire in the folds; Dekker lit the next and Meg snatched the bottle and threw it into the hall.

It shattered. Dekker lit a third vodka bottle, passed it, and Meg lobbed the second out the door and ducked back as somebody screamed in pain.

The Shepherd was on a chair with another bit of burning cloth. The smoke alarm went off inside. The fire-system started spraying, the door tried to shut as shots spattered off the edge and blew hell out of the chair-back. They were down to gin bottles.

Fire-spray started outside, white chemical clouds billowing up.

"That's got it," Meg said, pulled her mask up, trod on the chair and cleared it into the smoke outside as shots went past the door.

No notion whether she'd made it, no knowledge how to dodge or duck—he just deafened himself to the shots, cleared the chair and hugged the wall in the neon-lit smoke—running shadows rushed out of Scorpio's, screaming in panic.

Shots slammed into the crowd. Bodies flew; voices shrieked above the wailing siren. He sprinted past the restaurant's blue glare, dodged runners in the mist, not caring right now if the Shepherd was behind them or not—Meg was ahead of him trying for the Emergency Shaft, Meg had the Shepherds' key, and people who'd been taking cover in the restaurant were running every which way through the mist and into the gunfire.

He saw Meg stop, saw her trying to get the key in a slot.

A shot blasted a gouge in the wall beyond her—he flinched, pressed himself as flat to the wall as he could.

"Take the lift on the next level," the Shepherd gasped, clutching at his shoulder, beside them. "They're bound to have our cards blocked— Use your own. Berth 18 if we get separated—"

People were bunching up around them in panic—somebody in a waiter's uniform had a key, shoved Meg aside. The door opened. Meg slid in with the crowd and he pushed after her, he didn't care who he knocked out of the way—there were more and more pushing at their backs, the rush shoving them past the second door and up the steps. He pulled his mask down for air, grabbed the rail to keep from being shoved down and pushed all the way into the clear, with the Shepherd close behind, around the turn and up.

"3-deck damn door isn't going to work!" the Shepherd

yelled out of the clangor behind them in the stairwell. "Door's still open down there! Go for 4-deck, get a door shut behind us!"

Dekker turned his shoulders, grabbed a handhold, forced his way past panicked, flagging clerks and restaurant help—the Shepherd yelling "Go!" and shoving him from behind.

A hundred feet each deck level. No way clerks and waiters could outclimb spacer legs—on the end of four months' gym time. Meg was out of sight above them.

A siren had started in the distance—around the curvature of the 'deck. Ben couldn't see where—but, God, it was the direction of the club—where they were going.

"Come *on*," Sal cried, trying to hurry him—grabbed his hand and pulled him through the crowd coming out of the Amalthea, but steps raced behind them. "Hold it!" a shout came from close at their backs: a hand grabbed Ben's shoulder and spun him around and back, bang up against the plex front of the bar. He found himself nose to nose with a cop, with a stick jammed up under his chin.

"Pollard, is it?"

Shit, he thought, struggling for air.

Out of nowhere, Bird's voice said, "Hey! Hey, what do you think you're dealing with?" Bird came up and caught the cop's shoulder, another cop grabbed Bird and somebody in the crowd spun the cop around face-on with a beer mug.

"Hold it," Ben tried to say, "wait, dammit, —*Bird!*"

Something banged, the plex window shook to an impact, and there was blood all over—he slipped, and the cop's riot stick came away as he hit on his knees, Bird was lying there with a bloody great hole in his sleeve and a look of shock on his face. All else he could see was legs and all else he could hear was people cursing and screaming. He scrambled over, grabbed Bird's coat and dragged him up close against the frontage, Bird fainting on him, people trampling them until he had a moment of clear space and Sal grabbed his arm to pull him to his feet.

"Ben! Come *on!*"

He scrambled for his feet, pulling at Bird. Sal hauled,

Bird tried to get his legs under him, and they threw arms around him and ran with the crowd, battered and staggered by people passing them, Bird doing the best he could, Sal shoving him up from the other side—gunfire and shouts echoed at their backs.

Screaming broke out ahead of them, and the crowd ebbed back at them without warning, shoved them the other way. The PA said, echoing over the shouting and the distant siren, *This is not a test. This is a real emergency*—

"Stairs," Bird gasped, and Ben thought, God, where are they? You passed them time and again, the utility accesses—between the frontages, back in the bars—

—used to use them in the Institute, up and down the dorms, you used to duck under the security cameras—

One was right next to The Hole, that was where.

His lungs were burning, Bird was losing his footing, stumbling with every step as they reached the alcove and Sal shoved at the door.

"Mike's got a key," Bird gasped.

"Hell with that," Ben said, and hit #, /, and 9 simultaneously, 8, 0, and /. Management Emergency Access.

They weren't the only ones that wanted the stairs—"Get out of my way!" Ben snapped at Sal, feeling the panic in the crowd as they pushed for the opening door—God, they couldn't climb and carry Bird between them: he got a shoulder under him and carried him solo, with Sal running the stairs ahead of him. Hysterical people shoved him from behind, shoved past, nearly knocked him down, and then somebody with sense, thank God, pulled him square again and shoved him forward when his balance faltered.

"Lock *through*, dammit!" Sal yelled—downside door shut was the only way the door up on 3-deck would open; and the guys ahead of her got out. Ben saw it through a black-rimmed blur, heard it through the ringing of the steps and the pounding in his chest, one thin feminine voice, "E-drill, *ten at a time*, you dumbass bastards!"

They had a human wave behind them. Sal was holding the door open. Sal screamed at them to get in, and the guys behind—thank God, must have had the sense to turn around in the lock and shove the tide back. The doors shut, the hallway door opened, and they had the clear cold air of 3-deck.

"Core-lift!" Sal yelled, grabbing him. He didn't know how he could do it, but Bird wasn't in any shape to carry himself. His knees and his ankles were giving and wobbling with every step, his vision was nearly gone—people were scattering past them in every direction, piling into the Trans, any way in hell they could get away. He couldn't get enough wind, he knew his knees were going, but it was close . . . he knew it was close.

He couldn't see anything but blurs—didn't even know where they were, except Sal kept him straight, and Sal hit the button when they got there and propped him on his feet—he kept blinking sweat out of his eyes, couldn't hear anything but his heartbeat and distant screams, was scared mindless the core-lift was shut off at 3 with the alarms down on helldeck, but the door opened, welcomed them with white light and cold air.

She got the door shut. He stooped, eased Bird down from his shoulder, held on to him til he could lean him against the wall—Bird's face was white even after the head-down carry, Bird's blood was soaking him, but Bird breathed something coherent about the door.

Sal was trying to card it to move. He staggered to the panel to try the E-code, but abruptly the power cut in without his touching it and the car rose—

"What did you do?" he gasped—but then the car slowed down again, on 4, and the door opened, on an out-of-breath Meg, Dekker, and a Shepherd with a key—

"God," Meg said. And: "Bird?"

The Shepherd shoved them in ahead of him and keyed them from the core as fast as Ben could get his next breath—bent double with the pain in his gut, while Meg and Sal were kneeling and trying to take care of Bird.

"We waited," Dekker panted. "Long as we could—"

Ben nodded. He didn't have the breath to tell Dekker he was an ass and it was his damned fault, he wasn't sure he could get his next gasp. He waved a helpless gesture at Bird, meaning take care of him, fool, do something for him: he couldn't straighten—while the car shot for the core and the Shepherd said, "We don't know what's going to be waiting for us up there. The minute the door's open, out and hit the handlines. If he can't hold the line—" A breathless wave of the hand in Bird's direction. "There's no way to take him."

"Screw you!" Dekker said. "We're taking him."

"There's guards on the dock up there!"

"Then screw them too!" Dekker yelled.

"Listen, kid, —"

"Shut *up!*" Meg yelled, and Ben saw the way Meg was holding Bird—how of a sudden Bird had become weight in her arms and his eyes and his mouth were still open. No, Ben thought; he couldn't move, just stood there, waiting for Bird to move, bent over with the ache in his gut, until Sal got up and took hold of him and a handhold, because they were approaching the null-zone.

Meg said, between breaths, Bird still locked in her arms, "We got a shuttle at 18, clear down the far end of the mast, dumb shits couldn't park it closer—going to take us out to a Shepherd ship. They got that carrier coming this way from the shipyard, don't know if it's got guns mounted."

"It's fast," the Shepherd said. "Too damn fast."

Their talk went past Ben's ears. It ran through his brain, as a set of facts explaining where they were going and that their chances weren't good. He thought he ought to come up with a better idea, but his brain wasn't working right—he just felt the lift reach that queasy spot and felt his gut knot up.

Bird wasn't dead, Bird couldn't be gone—it didn't make sense to him. He'd done everything he could and somehow Bird just—went out on them and he didn't know what to do with him. It wasn't damned fair, what had happened—he'd *carried* him, dammit, til his gut was full of knives, and Bird wasn't friggin' dead, he couldn't go like that—

Dekker reached in slow-motion after his arm as the car clanked into the interface. Dekker held on to him until the car stopped and the doors opened. The Shepherd made the first swing from the lift's safety grip to the mounting bar and hand-over-handed himself toward the line. Meg had let Bird go, and Meg went next—

Nothing else to do, Ben thought, with an anguished glance at Bird drifting there so white and different, among beads of blood, and grabbed the mounting bar and went, fast as he could. Without Bird.

Eerie quiet in the core. The chute was silent. You could hear the line moving in the slot, you could hear the low static hum of the rotation interface. Couldn't see anything for a moment but the line's motor housing slipping past them.

He looked back, to be sure it was all real. But Sal and Dekker were reaching for the line, blocking his view of the inside of the car.

Meg was on the line behind the Shepherd, he was three spaces back. They passed the housing out into the open, out where the core spun to a dizzy vanishing point and tricked the eye and an already aching stomach. He held on—just held on, while muscles cramped in the cold.

Past the customs zone. He kept thinking—what if someone had a gun—what if they know where we are? Nothing they could do up here. Nothing but go at the pace of the line. Cold chilled his blood-soaked clothing and turned it stiff. Fingers lost all feeling, eyes teared from the cold, more bitter than he'd ever felt it, and the line moved at the same steady pace, clank, clank, clank—with his teeth chattering and the only thought in his head now just keeping his fingers closed on the hand-grip. Meg had said berth 18. 18 was hell and gone at the end of the mast. Shuttle out to a ship that was going to take Dekker and the rest of them out of here, he guessed, but the only thought that kept replaying, over and over again, was that gun going off, Bird getting hit—

He hadn't had time to stop the bleeding, dammit. Hadn't had time—Sal had known where she was going, Sal had known about the shuttle—hadn't told them, God, he should have told her to go to hell, taken Bird to the Trans, taken him to the hospital—Bird shouldn't be dead. . . .

It was *Trinidad* they were passing, now, *Way Out* mated

to her for the trip they weren't going to take. They'd been so damn close—

Movement caught his eye, against the steady spin of the core, big supply can drifting free—hell! he thought, shocked by the sight, damned dangerous, a thing the size of a skimmer floating along like that with no pusher attached—

He thought—as clearly as he was thinking at all—that's wrong.

That's *wrong*, that is—

The line jolted and stopped.

"Shit!" Sal gasped, loud in that sudden silence, and Dekker thought—we're not going to get there, it's not going to work—we're hanging up here and we can't reach the shuttle—can't reach the dismount lines. . . .

"Hand off the line!" Meg yelled of a sudden, juvie lessons, old safety drill. He reached for Sal, caught her hand—saw, all of a sudden, the whole line bucking, a wave coming toward them.

Dekker yelled, "Let *go!*" and threw everything he had into the chain they made, hand to hand—he threw his whole body into that snap-the-whip twist, aimed as best he could and let *go*—

A moment of floating free, then, nothing they could do if that line hit them, if they missed the dismount-line—

The wave sang overhead and passed. The Shepherd snagged a dismount line with his foot and hauled them all toward it.

Meg called out, "Center-mast! We can't make the shuttle, we got our *own* ship there. Her tanks are charged!"

"Won't dock!" the Shepherd yelled back. "Won't *mate*, dammit!"

"Take what we can fuckin' *get*," Sal yelled. "They've turned the line loose, there's no way we can get there, Sammy, move your butt!"

Fire popped, somewhere, Dekker had learned that sound. "They're shooting at something," he called out, following Sal and Ben down the line that connected along the dockage.

Something sang past him. He thought, God, they're *fools*, there's seals where we are and they're shooting bullets—

Another ricochet—he saw Meg kicked sideways, blood spraying—thought she was going off the line, but her left hand held the line, and Sal caught up and grabbed her jacket. He made a fast catch-up to help both of them, but Meg had caught Sal's coat with her left hand, blood floating in great dark beads near her other arm. Sal screamed at Ben to get out of her way, get the hatch open.

Ben scrambled along the line and overtook the Shepherd at *Trinidad*'s entry. Sal took a swing and floated free toward them and Dekker hurled himself after, caught Meg's arm and got his hand over the bleeding as Ben and the Shepherd grabbed their clothes and hauled them into the open hatch.

"Get it closed!" he gasped, stopping with a shove of his foot on a touch-pad. "Meg, —"

Meg's own hand shoved his aside, clamped down on the arm. "I got it, I got it," Meg said between her teeth. "God, just get me a patch—get us the hell out of here! Get us to the shuttle, 18, this guy'll tell you—"

"We can't mate with a shuttle-dock!" the Shepherd cried. "We've lost it, dammit, all we are is under cover. Aboujib, get com, get contact with the *Hamilton*, tell them our situation, see if they can talk us out of this—"

"Severely small chance, Sammy."

Severely small, Meg told herself, couldn't move her arm for Ben to get a wrap on it, sleeve and all—spurting blood everywhere, real close to going out.

Like Bird.

No fuss, not overmuch pain, just—going out.

"Hang on," Ben said, and hurt her with the bandage. "Damn it, Meg, pay attention! Hold on to it!"

Grapples banged loose. She thought, Good boy, Dek, . . .

. . . Bills every damn where on the table, Bird excused himself up to the bar, talked to Mike a minute, Bird about as upset as she'd ever seen him during the days when they were trying to fix that ship. Bird was working himself up to a heart attack. Meanwhile she sat there looking at her finger-nails, telling herself she was a fool for staying with this whole crazy idea.

Old anger, she told herself. So the company won another round. So another kid died. A lot of them had died—

She kept hearing the gunfire behind the rattle of glass-ware. Watching the rab go down. Kids, with shocked looks on their faces. The company cops with no faces, just silver visors that reflected back the smoke and the frightened faces of their victims.

Lawless rab.

Property rights. Company rules.

"We got to fix this," Bird said the day Dekker came to them. "What they've done isn't fair." And she thought, sick at her stomach, Dammit, Bird, they'll kill you. . . .

Trim jets kept firing. She felt the bursts.

The shuttle's mains kicked in, in the high lonely cold above Earth's atmosphere, the transition she loved. You knew you were going home, then, the motherwell couldn't hold you—

Up, not down—

Black for a while. She felt the push of braking, had Sal's arm around her, the aux boards in front of her, Sal trying to get her belted in. She reached with the arm that didn't hurt, took the belt and snapped the clip in, solid click. Tested it for a rough ride. She told Sal: "Get yourself belted, Aboujib, I got it, all right. . . ."

Another burst of trim jets. Dek was maneuvering, Ben was fastening his belt for him while the Shepherd—Sammy, Sal called him—was filling in at the com, saying, urgently, "They're warning us to pull back in. That carrier's moving in fast. The Hamilton's powering up now—we can't make it, there's no time for them to pick us up—"

Trim jets fired constantly at the rate of one and two a second, this side and that—she had the camera view, a row of docked skimmers blurring in the number two monitor as they skimmed along the mast surface—damn close, there, kid—

Static burst from the general com: the Shepherd had

cut B channel in. "*AMC Twenty-nine Hamilton,* this is FleetCom. You're in violation of UDC directives. Stand down—"

"Cut that damn thing off!" Ben snarled. "We got enough on our minds."

"We can't *dock,*" the Shepherd yelled. Sal was belting in. Ben was. Acceleration was increasing in hammer blows from the main engines. The mast whipped past faster and faster—

Then nothing. Sudden long shove from the bow stabilizers and the mast swung back in view, retreating now—going for decel—another burst of *Trinidad's* mains. . . .

No, she thought—*Way Out's* mains . . . we're coupled. Double mass. —Are we giving up? Going back? Shuttle's on the mast, Dek, did we miss it. Don't get rattled, kid, . . .

Ben said something. Dek said something, and the trim jets fired another long burst, taking the ship—God, felt like a right angle to the station.

God, he's going after the *Hamilton*—

Mains again, *hard* push—pain, from the arm, real pain—

This is interesting, she thought, feeling the accel, figuring vectors. Hell of a ride, Dek, —you tell 'em we're coming?

Big shove. Dark again. She could hear the beeps from the distance indicators, the higher ready-beeps from systems on standby—she thought: that's nice, *nice* sound, that, everything's optimum config, that sumbitch interface back there worked, didn't it?

Loud argument, and the whine of the forward bay hydraulics.

"What the fuck are you doing?" a man's voice shouted. "They're ready to move, dammit, we're in their blast pattern—they got a carrier on intercept—"

Sal's voice, clear and sane: "Shut up, Sammy!"

Thank God, Meg thought, listening for the beeps and tones, easier that than keeping her eyes open. Plenty of information there: bay was open, manipulator arm was working—Sammy was saying, "God, you fool, you damned fool . . ."

Worth a look. She blinked the blurry monitors clear, saw an irregular surface, slotted with dust-deflectors and bolted-onto with tether stanchions—the arm extending out in front of them, white in the spots, shadowed onto the irregular plating—

"Go for it, go for it!" Sal said, "you got it, Ben!"

Neat touch. Hardly felt it.

Attached. To a tether stanchion. The manipulator grip closed and locked.

"*Nice* job," she said. She wasn't sure anybody heard.

The Shepherd yelled, "*Go!*"

Acceleration started, built and built.

Better dump those tanks, Dek, better just uncouple *Way Out*, let her go, and just hope to hell the arm mount holds—no way we can decel off what a Shepherd can put on us, anyway . . .

Ought to tell the kid. But just hard to get organized—hard to get the mouth to work.

Unstable load. Lot of push on. Pressure built in her arm and deserted her brain.

Going *up*, guys, going *up*, long and hard as we can. . . .

Quiet. Couldn't even hear the fans. But no more g.

Taste of blood.

Explosion—

But they weren't tumbling. Wasn't the way it had been. He opened his eyes, got the board in focus in this peaceful drifting—neck was stiff, muscles sprained. He turned his head and saw Ben out cold—the Shepherd beside him, headset drifting loose. If there was sound he couldn't hear it, except the fans.

Then he remembered shutting down. Remembered Meg—tried to move. There wasn't a muscle that didn't hurt. But he unclipped, pushed off and turned, getting to Meg's position.

Blood made a fine mist. She was white as a ghost and cold when he touched her face. She looked dead.

But tension came back, dead one moment, then unconscious, but *there*, by some subtle change that wasn't even movement until the eyelids showed stress. Ben was moving—number 2 boards and the best place, his and Ben's, to ride out the push.

"She make it?" Ben asked fuzzily.

"Yeah," Meg mumbled, speaking for herself. At least that was what it sounded like.

"Are we still grappled?"

"I don't know," Dekker said. "We seem stable."

Ben freed himself and drifted over to see to Sal—Sal was coming to. The Shepherd was still out. Dekker reached for the headset, heard faint static and a thin voice before he held it to his ear. ". . . alive in there?" he heard, and: "I'm hearing voices. Their com is open. . . ."

"Yeah," he said, pulling the mike into line. "This is miner ship *Trinidad*. Is this the *Hamilton*?"

# 19

"H E wasn't doing a damn thing," Ben said—there was blood all over him and Sal, blood dried on his own hands, Dekker saw, Bird's, Meg's, he had no idea. There was too much of it.

"Nothing?" the officer asked.

"Cops had *me*, dammit, he didn't need to be there, he wasn't doing a damn thing, just objected to them grabbing me, and some fool—just—pulled a trigger."

Dekker stared at the backs of his hands, seeing what he hadn't been there to see. Seeing Meg in the lift, holding on to Bird.

Sal said, "*I* saw it. They were arming guys straight off leave, some of them still higher than company corruption: green kids, didn't know shit what they were doing."

"It was a soldier."

"Damn right it was a soldier. Marine. Couldn't have been twenty."

The *Hamilton*'s purser clicked off the recorder. "We've got that. We'll send it before we make our burn."

Dekker said: "How *is* the fuel situation?"

"Not optimum," the purser said.

"Shit." Sal shook her head. The purser left. Ben didn't say anything, just got a long breath and clasped his hands between his knees.

It was as much information as they'd gotten. The same information as they'd gotten since they'd come aboard. Hadn't seen Sammy—Sammy had gone offshift, probably in his own bunk asleep or tranked out if he hadn't gotten the news yet. Sammy—Ford was his last name—had been fairly well shaken up, hadn't asked for the position he'd been handed—the situation at the dock had gone to hell, the shuttle crew hadn't answered, the 8-deck group hadn't answered, they'd suspected their com was being monitored: Mitch had gone next door to use the restaurant's phone to get contact with his crew and hadn't come back, arrested or worse, they still hadn't found out. Sammy wasn't flight ops, he was the legal affairs liaison, a Shepherd negotiator, for God's sake, who'd come aboard R2 to deal with management, if the plan had gone right, if the soldiers hadn't come in . . .

Sammy'd done all right, Dekker decided. All right, for a guy who'd probably never gotten his hands dirty. Had to tell Meg when she came to. She'd get a laugh out of it.

Another officer, this one straight past them, where they waited in the tight confines of the medstation. Right into the surgery.

Angry voice beyond the door, an answer of some kind.

"Think they've got a hurry-up," Sal muttered.

More voices. Something about paralysis and another thirty minutes. Voice saying, quite clearly, ". . . doesn't do her any good if she's dead, Hank, we haven't got your thirty minutes. Get your patient prepped, we're moving."

Man came back through the door then, looked at them, said, more quietly, "We've got your ship free, we've got a positional problem and we're doing a correction burn, about as fast as the EV-team can get in and I can get up to the bridge. Best we can do. You've got belts there. Use them. Staff's got take-holds."

Bad, then. Dekker clamped his jaw and reached for the

belt housed in the side of the seat as Sal and Ben did the same. The officer was out the door and gone.

"Shit-all," Ben muttered. His hands were shaking. Sal's were clenched in her lap.

They were in trouble. No question. Headed into the Well, nobody had to say it. "Positional problem" on a Jupiter-bound vector meant only one thing, and a hurry-up like that meant they were on their own, no beam, just the fuel they had left—which wasn't a big argument against the Well's gravity slope.

*Way Out*'s whole mass had had to go—that had been his decision: save *Hamilton* the fuel hauling it, keep *Trinidad*'s manipulator arm from shearing off at the bolts, or maybe taking the bulkhead with it: but that fuel in *Trinidad*'s tanks had been a big load—*big* load, on those bolts. He'd made a split-second judgment call, last move he'd made before he'd gone out. Maybe opening that valve had saved their lives. If that bulkhead had gone they'd have decompressed; but an uncalc'ed mass attached to *Hamilton*, three-quarters of it dumped without warning a few seconds into the burn...hadn't helped their situation. Computers had recomped. But their center of mass had changed twice in that accel; and when the arm gearing had fractured—they'd had to lase through the tether ring—they must have swung flat against *Hamilton*'s frame and that would have changed it again. He'd gone out by the time that had happened. Didn't know how long they'd pushed, but with a warship moving on them, they'd had to give it a clear choice between chasing them or dealing with R2.

*Hamilton* crew couldn't be real damn happy with their passengers right now.

The lock hydraulics cycled and stopped. A siren shrieked. A recorded voice said: Take Hold Immediately.

"*All hands prepare for course correction burn. Mark. Repeat—*"

"The Bitch won't give 'em a beam," Sal muttered, teeth chattering as she checked her belt. "The Bitch is damn well hoping we'll all take the deep one. Won't lift a finger."

"We're going to be all right," he said.

"'Going to be all right,'" Ben said. "'Going to be all

right.' You know if you weren't a damn spook Bird'd be alive. Meg wouldn't be in there. We wouldn't be where we are. This whole damn mess is your fault."

"Yeah," he said, on a deep breath. "I know that."

"His damn fault, too," Ben muttered. "They weren't after him, they didn't know who the hell he was. He was clear, damn him, he was clear. I don't know what he did it for."

Engines fired. *Hamilton* threw everything she had into her try at skimming the Well.

He thought, I could just have pulled us off and out. Didn't *have* to go to the *Hamilton*. Wasn't thinking of anything else.

They'd have picked us up. But the shooting would have stopped by then. And we wouldn't be in this mess. Ben's right.

"Didn't make sense," Ben said. "Damn him, he never *did* make sense..."

*Somebody* had started shooting. The police swore they were military rounds, and Crayton's office wanted that information released immediately.

The statement from Crayton's office said: ...*greatly regrets the loss of life*...

Morris Bird was a name Payne fervently wished he'd never heard. Thirty-year veteran, oldest miner in the Belt, involved with Pratt and Marks, and popular on the 'deck—a damn martyr was what they had. Somebody had sprayed BIRD in red paint all along a stretch of 3-deck. BIRD was turning up scratched in paint on 8, and they didn't need any other word. The hospital was bedding down wounded in the halls, a file named DEKKER was proliferating into places they still hadn't found and the Shepherd net was broadcasting its own news releases, calling for EC intervention and demanding the resignation of the board and the suspension of martial law.

Now it was vid transmission—a Shepherd captain explaining how the miner ship *Trinidad* had made a run for the *Hamilton*—more names he'd heard all too much about. A pilot who'd had his license pulled as impaired. A crew who'd been with Bird when the shooting happened. The story was growing by the minute—acquiring stranger and stranger angles, and N & E couldn't get ahead of them by any small measures.

*... A spokesman for the company has expressed relief at the safe recovery of the* Trinidad *and all aboard. The same source has strongly condemned the use of deadly force against unarmed demonstrators and promises a thorough ...*

The door opened. He blinked, looking at rifles, at two blue-uniformed marines. At a third, who followed them in, and said,

"William Payne? This office is under UDC authority, under emergency provisions of the Defense Act, Section 18, Article 2."

He looked at the rifles, looked at the officer. Tried to think of right procedures. "I need to contact the head office."

"Go right ahead, Mr. Payne."

He doubted his safety to do that. He hesitated at picking up the phone, hesitated at pushing the button. "This *is* Administration I'm calling. Do you want to be sure of that?"

"Check it out wherever you like, Mr. Payne. Your computer will give you an explanation. Go ahead. Access Administration."

He took a breath, touched keys, windowed up Executive Access.

It said, *Earth Company Executive Order...*

It said Charter Provision 28, and Defense Act, Section 18, Article 2.

"We have a press release for you, Mr. Payne."

"Yes, *sir,*" he said. No questions. No hesitations. He reached for the datacard the officer put on his desk and put it into the comp.

It said: *The UDC has assumed control of ASTEX operations. All workers, independent operators and contractors, and all ASTEX employees below management levels will be retained. President Towney is under arrest by civil warrant, charged with misappropriation of funds and tax evasion. Various members of the board are likewise under investigation by the EC. Residents who have information on such cases are directed to deliver that information to the military police, Access 14, on the system.*

*All residents who report to the UDC office on their decks will have their cards revalidated and will be passed without question or exception under a general amnesty for all non-executive personnel of R2.*

*The UDC will meet with delegations from the independents, the contractors, and civilian employees to discuss grievances . . .*

"Hell of a mess," Meg said, propped on pillows in the peculiar kind of g you got in small installations—still light-headed, but the fingers could move in the cast, she'd tested that.

"Couldn't tell you from the sheets when they brought you in." Sal sat down carefully on the edge of the bed, reached out a dark hand and squeezed her good one. Skins brut sure didn't match right now, Meg thought, seeing that combination, and then thought about Bird, left adrift in that lift-car. Hell of a thing to do. Bird had deserved better than that. But he'd always been a practical sumbitch, where it counted.

Water trickled from the corner of her left eye. Sal wiped it with her thumb.

"Hell," she said, and tried to put her arm over her eyes, but every joint she owned was sprained. She blinked and drew a couple of breaths. "They get us out of the dive yet?"

Sal didn't answer right off. Hadn't, she thought. Welcome back, Kady. We're still going to die.

Sal said, "We still got a little vector problem. Where'd you hear it?"

"Meds said. Thought I was out. Are we going in?"

Another hesitation. "Say we're going in a lot slower. They're having a discussion with the EC right now. Idea is, deploy the sail to half, see if we can get a line-up with the R2-23, just get a little different tack going."

"That'd be nice."

"Listen, ice-for-nerves, we got word the military's taken over—got Towney under arrest—yeah. And the board. They'll bring the beams up, they damn well have to. They're talking deal with helldeck right now—they're asking for Mitch and Persky and some of the guys to come and talk grievances—"

"It's a trick."

"They going to put so'jer-boys to picking rocks? Beaucou' d' luck, Kady. First tag they try they'll be finding bits of some ship clear to Saturn."

"They'll deal. Maybe even get us our beam. Wouldn't be surprised. But it won't change, Aboujib. Won't change."

Sal didn't say anything for a moment. And she was on a dive of her own. Wasn't fair to Sal. Sal had real vivid nightmares about gravity wells.

She said to Sal, only bit of optimism she could come up with, "Won't be Towney in charge, anyhow."

"They're sending out this EC manager. Meanwhile it's the so'jers."

Not good news for the guys on R2. Long time til the new manager got here. Meanwhile *they* were trying their best not to fall into the Well. She wondered how good their options were. Beams going up again, yeah, if the soldiers hadn't some damn administrative mess-up that was going to wait on authorizations, or if it wasn't just convenient to the EC to have them gone. Beside which, if they were talking about a bad line, and they were having to use R2-23, they evidently were in one of those vectors where getting a beam was a sincere bitch. R2-23 was a geosync. Geosyncs at the Well were a neverending problem, always screwed, Shepherds futzed them into line and refueled them with robot tugs, and hauled them out of the radiation intense area and fixed them when they'd gotten screwed beyond the usual— useful position, that particular beam, what odd times its computer wasn't fried—

"Got two nice-looking guys want to see you," Sal said, looking seriously fragile right now. Doing her best to be cheerful.

"Shit. I got any makeup on?"

"Forgot to pack," Sal said, squeezed her shoulder and staggered off to the door—hadn't got her ship-legs yet.

Neither had the boys. They looked like hell. Scrubbed up, at least. But limping and not walking real well, especially Ben. Good time to be horizontal, she decided, sore as she was—*Hamilton* was fair-sized, but her *g* differential still wanted to drop you on your ass, besides which your feet swelled til your body adapted. Went through it all again when you went stationside.

If they ever saw stationside again.

She patted the bedside. "Sit," she said. They sat down very carefully, one on a side of the footboard.

"Hurt much?" Ben asked. Stupid question.

"I've had nicer times in bed. You all right?"

"Fine," Dekker said. "We're fine."

"Yeah," she said, surveying the bruises. "We're a set, all right."

*Course correction put them in reach of R2-23*, the message from Ops said. *That's their last serious option. Calculations extremely marginal even at this point. Situation with beam goes zero chance at 0828h. We checked out that cap and their fill, and the miner-crafts' registered mass. Unless they got something from the remaining miner's tanks, they have nothing left. Cap on Athens indicates zero chance intercept. Dumping the tugs didn't do it. Athens would put itself in danger. We estimate their continuing on course is only for the negotiators. Our data appended.*

Porey tapped the stylus on the desk, called up the figures, considered it, considered a communication from the meeting in the corporate HQ, typed a brief message. *Tell their negotiators we've calc'ed Athens and the chances on the beam go neg at 0828. Tell them we'd be glad to provide them the figures and we're standing by our offer.*

No time for another cause with the miners. Or the Shepherds.

Good PR. Magnanimity. General amnesty, revalidate the cards, put Towney's arrest on vid, get the beams up again and get the *Hamilton* out of its situation.

The minute the Shepherds came to terms.

Breakfast.

Marmalade. Dekker hadn't tasted it since he was a kid—Ben and Sal never had. Meg said it brought back memories of her smuggling days.

"I used to run this stuff," Meg said. "Course we'd lose a jar or two now and again."

Sal made the sign for eavesdroppers, and Dekker felt it in his gut. But Meg said, "Hell, if they got time to worry about us—"

"Kind of sour," Ben said. "Bitter. Not bad, though."

"Ben, cher," Sal said. "Learn to appreciate. Life's ever-so prettier that way."

"I appreciate it. It's bitter. And sour. Isn't it? What's the matter with that?"

Meg rolled her eyes.

The door opened. Dekker turned his head.

Officer.

Breakfast stopped.

"Sorry to interrupt you," the Shepherd said, leaning against the doorframe, arms folded. Afro, one-sided shave job, Shepherd tech insignia and a gold collar-clip on that expensive jacket that meant he was senior-tech-something. "Though you'd appreciate a briefing. We've got a rescue coming."

Dekker replayed that a second. Maybe they all did.

*Good* news?

"Who?" Meg asked.

"That carrier. Moving like a bat."

"Shee—" Meg held it.

Dekker thought, God, why? But he didn't ask. He left that to Meg and Sal, who had the credit here—who *weren't* the ones who'd put them in the mess they were in.

"Looks as if we're getting out of this," Meg said.

"God," Ben said after a moment. No yelling and celebrating. You held it that long, doing business as usual as much as possible, and when you got good news you just didn't know how to take it.

"Where's the catch?" Sal asked. "They can just overtake and haul us out?"

"Thing was .75 our current $v$ two minutes away from R2. They're not wasting any time."

Dekker did rough math in his head, thought—God. And us well onto the slope, as we have to be now—

"They're talking deal," the Shepherd said. "Seems the Fleet's figured out they need us. Seems the Association's said there's no deal without the freerunners, they're hanging on to that point—they've axed Towney, that's certain now. Thought you'd want to know. —Mr. Dekker?"

"Sir."

"The captain wants to see you."

Another why? But maybe if they were out of their emergency stand-by. . . the captain wanted to make a serious point with the resident fool. He shrugged, looked back at Meg and Sal and Ben, with: "I'll *see* you—" Meaning that they could think about later, and being alive day after tomorrow.

God, the shakes had gotten him, too—he didn't figure what he was scared of now—a dressing-down by a Shepherd captain, good enough, he had it coming: or maybe it was suddenly *having* a future, in which he didn't know what he was going to be doing hereafter. The Shepherd might take Meg and might take Sal—even Ben turned out to have a claim.

But him?

Credit with the *Hamilton* might be real scant about now. *Trinidad* was gone, likewise *Way Out*—nothing like *Trinidad*'s velocity when they'd dumped her, but not in R2's near neighborhood by now, either, and on the same track. If she was catchable at all, the law made her somebody else's salvage. He had the bank account—but God knew what shape that was in, or what kind of lawsuits might shape up against him—corp-rats were corp-rats, Meg would say, and he had no faith the EC was going to forget him and let him be. Not with people dead and the property damage.

It wasn't a far walk to Sunderland's office. The tech-chief showed him in—announced him to a gray-haired, frail-looking man, who offered his hand—not crew-type courtesies, Dekker thought. That in a strange way seemed ominous; Sunderland didn't look angry, rather worn and worried and, by some strange impression, regretful.

That disturbed him too.

"Mr. Dekker. Coffee?"

"No, sir, thank you. I just had breakfast."

"Good you have an appetite—have a seat, there. —I confess mine hasn't been much the last while."

He made the chair, sank into it. "I know 'sorry' doesn't cover it. I shouldn't have dumped the tanks."

"We wouldn't have you if you hadn't; bulkhead wouldn't have stood it. Tried to tell you to do it. Don't know if you heard."

He shook his head. "No, sir." And thought, Just not enough hands. Not enough time.

"Things were going pretty fast, weren't they?"

"Yes, sir."

"Things have been going pretty hot and hard here, too. You know about the ship coming."

"Yessir." He felt light-headed—g difference. Sitting down and standing up could do that.

"Took some talking. But I didn't seriously figure they were going to let us go down. The EC wouldn't. R2-23 was an option—best we had without the EC's help, I'm sure you were following that, and a couple of exotic, chancy possibilities that we really didn't want to get down to, but when they called us this morning and told us the R2-23 computer was down, . . . I had a good idea that ship was going to move. I had a good idea they had it calc'ed down to the fine figures and they were going to carry it live on vid. Clear to Sol. The EC doesn't want us in the Well. *Bad* media, Mr. Dekker. Bad media with the miners. They've resorbed ASTEX, you've heard that, Towney's dismissed, . . . a lot of changes, a lot of them for the better. We can work with the contractors. We can work with the EC. We can work with the UDC. They know that. They just wanted the best deal they could get."

The captain called him in to talk politics?

Hell. What's he getting to.

"We've got the numbers on the accident," Sunderland said. "I don't know how much you've been told . . ."

"I'm told you'd found her weeks before you reported it." He'd found that out this morning, from Ben, and it was on its way to making him mad. "You didn't tell us, you let us go clear into prep, didn't warn us—"

"Didn't have any idea how you'd react—*whether* you

could keep it together and do business as usual. Didn't know, frankly, whether Aboujib was going to jump our way or not. We thought so. But she's a hair trigger in a situation like this. And we were pushing for all the time we could, to get at records we needed. We knew about the bumping. We knew there was a miner missing. We were already comparing charts and finding discrepancies when *Athens* found your partner. We knew you were going out—quite frankly, we waited because we were still doing the legal prep. Sam Ford—you met Ford—was down there making sure the t's were crossed and the i's were dotted: when you go up against the company in a lawsuit, you'd better not have a loophole. We advised Aboujib, we set everything up for a quiet transfer hours before the thing went out over the com, we were going to get you quietly up to the dock, shuttle you aboard where they couldn't get at you and get some essential changes out of the company—I'm being altogether honest with you now—while we were helping you pursue your case against the company. Unfortunately—"

"I took a walk."

"Not that it mattered, I'm afraid, at least in the majority of what happened. We factored in the company's stupidity— we expected the military to involve themselves, but not— not that an EC order to resorb the company was already lying on FleetCommander's desk, waiting for any legal excuse it could, frankly, arrange. *They* were preparing a general audit of the company, to do it under one provision, but there was an emergency clause in the charter, that had to do with the threat to operations; and there is the Defense Act, that would let the military outright seize control if things were falling apart. And they were ready—ready because of the labor situation, ready because they thought the managers might try to destroy records—"

"They did."

"They tried. We had one piece. There were others. FleetCommander had that carrier fueled. We'd gotten that rumor. We didn't like what we were hearing. We knew when we did move we'd be dealing with the Fleet on a legal level—we even expected a confrontation at the dock. But not that they'd be as fast as they were and not that they had the legal documents to take control of the company without a time-lagged information exchange with Earth. That was eight to ten hours we turned out not to have. They had their people on R2, they had weapons on their transport, they turned out and they took the dock and our shuttle crew, and when that happened we were in deep trouble. But it *has* shaken out: we didn't anticipate dealing with the UDC this fast—but we've gotten what we were trying to force: we're dealing directly with the parent corporation, now, and very anxious defense contractors *and* the Fleet, all of whom have a budget and absolutely no personnel who can do what we do—efficiently. We can meet their quotas. We. The miners *and* the Shepherds. And the 'drivers, who *have* to come into line. Ultimately they have to. That's where it stands."

"Morrie Bird's dead. A lot of people are dead."

"We regret that. We regret that very sincerely. But we're not defense experts. We fought with what we had, the best way we knew. People *were* being killed. The way your partner was killed. You understand? ASTEX was killing miners, killing us—ultimately something would have happened. Something possibly with worse loss of life. With one of the refineries going."

He believed that, at least. He thought about it. Thought about the system the way it was and didn't believe the military was going to be better. "Bastards could have pulled us back ten hours ago," he said. "Are they better than Towney?"

"No. But they're saner."

"They let us fall for ten hours—"

"Part of the game, Mr. Dekker. We fall toward the Well at a given acceleration . . . their negotiation team meanwhile meets with ours, they won't get the beam tracking system working, the EC is hours time-lagged and not talking to us, and everybody pretends they're not going to reach a compromise. I've been through too many years of this to believe it would go any differently than, ultimately, it did. Hair's gone gray a long time ago—between the Well and the shit from ASTEX. Last few went this morning til we knew that ship was moving. But we were fairly sure. All along, all of us were fairly sure."

"Yessir," he said, in Sunderland's wait for a reaction. Adrenaline was running high, there was no place to send it. He'd gotten the rules by now. They included not expressing opinions to Shepherd captains. He looked somewhere past Sunderland's shoulder, seeing Meg and that dockside, and the blood floating there. Seeing Bird, in the lift-car. Ben covered with blood.

"I'd like, for the record, Mr. Dekker, to have your version of what happened out there, with *Industry*."

"God, I've told it. Doesn't *anybody* have the record?"

"Just in brief. For a record ASTEX hasn't touched."

That was understandable, at least. He drew a wider breath, leaned back in the chair, recited it all again. "We found a rock, we went for it, the 'driver went too, and we figured he was going to try to beat us to it. And maybe muscle us off if he didn't. So we wanted a sample on our ship before BM told us to get out. But they didn't do that. They ran us down."

"Bumped you."

"No damn bump. Sir."

"I know that. I know other details, if you want them."

"All right. Then what the hell were they doing?"

"Trying to stop an independent from the biggest find in years. Trying to keep the company from a major pay-out— that could have made the difference between profit and loss that quarter—"

"God."

"What you may not know, or may not have thought about—'drivers keep track of miners—they have *all* the charts. They are a Base. And you moved, I'm guessing—on your own engines. Maybe you made quite a bit of *v*, on quite a long run."

Another piece of memory clicked.

"True?"

He nodded, seeing in his mind all the instruments of a tracking station, a long, long move for a miner, with no request for a beam. Anomaly. Cory'd suspected BM. They hadn't thought about a 'driver monitoring what they were doing. BM did. But you could move in a sector without saying... if you could do it on your own engines.

Stupid, he thought, the other side of experience. Fatally stupid. But...

"They could have ordered us off. They could have claimed it on optics."

"Why didn't you?"

"Because—because Cory said they might not log it. They might just claim the 'driver had it first."

"Politics. Politics. They *did* log it. They gave it a number."

"Then why didn't they call us and tell us? We saw them moving. But BM didn't tell us a damned thing—not 'They've got it,' not 'Pull back,' not—"

"They *wanted* that 'driver to beat you there. Crayton's office had stepped in and said they shouldn't have logged it that way, they should undo it because they hadn't made a policy decision yet. They'd called Legal Affairs and asked for advice. We can't reconstruct all of it: the military's sitting on those records—but what I guess is there was a 'driver damned determined to get there; BM was waffling—trying to figure out how to solve it, finally figuring they were in a situation—*nobody* believes BM. Nobody'd believe you weren't screwed. It'd be all over the 'deck at R1, one opinion in management was afraid it would touch off trouble, another said otherwise—they went ass-backwards into 'letting the local base handle it'... that's BM code for the shit's on the captain. 'Use your discretion,' is the way they word it. That means do something illegal."

He heard the tone of voice, he looked into neutral pale eyes in a lean, aged face and thought: This is a man who's been put in that position...

"They just hushed it all," Sunderland said. "They left it to the 'driver. They didn't *make* a policy decision. And *he* was under communication blackout, because that's the way things go when you're 'handling it' for the company. The consensus was you'd spook and run."

"They didn't know my partner."

"Extraordinary young woman, by what I know. Extraordinarily determined. Did you call it on optics? Did you try that?"

(—we just use the fuel, Cory had said. Trusting BM to get them home.)

"We were close enough we could get an assay sample before they got there. They weren't talking to us. We figured they'd pull something with the records, so it just didn't damn well matter. We thought they'd brake, that'd give us the time. And if we had the sample aboard—and our log against theirs of when we moved—we could make a case. We knew—we were sure BM knew what was going on. We didn't except they'd run right over us."

"You understand bumpings? You know the game?"

The man thought he was a fool. There was "poor, stupid kids" in his voice. He set his jaw and said, "I've heard. I'd heard then."

"Usual is a low-$v$ nudge, usually near the Refineries. Like a bad dock. Usually it's their tenders, just give you a scrape, make you spend time checking damage. But this time you'd beat him. You'd outdone his best speed even with a beam-assist. And his ass was on the line with the company. No time for nudges from his tenders. They didn't want a sample in your hands. If you had it, they wanted it dumped. Radio silence—from his side. Nothing to get on record. So he kept on course—had it all figured, closest pass he dared, bearing in mind you don't brake those sumbitches by the seat of your pants. Scare hell out of you. Get you so scared you'd do anything he said. But you moved *toward* his path, didn't you? And his Helm hadn't calc'ed that eventuality."

"What was I *supposed* to do?"

"Most would get out of the way."

"My partner was out there!"

"Some might. Some might run all the way to elsewhere. Maybe just tell BM there'd been an accident. Maybe have a 'driver tender claim a rescue."

"Hell!" But he'd known—known it wasn't quite a collision course. He'd known they were trying to shake him, he'd called their bluff—

They'd called his.

"Damn single correction," he muttered. "All they had to do. Fire the directionals and brake. Hell, he'd already braked off the beam, he was coming in well inside his maneuvering limits. He was as able to stop as I was."

"Their Helm was Belter. And that's a class A ship. Automated to the hilt. You understand me? Didn't even remotely occur to an Institute cut-rate a move like that was a choice—*he* wouldn't, so he didn't have it laid into his computer in advance. Not the directionals. Without it, running on auto—the jets won't fire if you don't take the autopilot off. He hit the jets, all right. With the autopilot on. Nothing. Some projection on the ship hit you.'"

"God."

"*I'd* have fired him. Damn sure. But there the 'driver was, he'd hit you. Your ship had blown a tank, you'd shot off into R2, his tenders couldn't catch you without getting a beam, you'd hit the rock as well as taken the scrape that blew the tank—they were in shit up to their necks—and Ms. Salazar was dead in the explosion. We're sure of that. —Do you want this part? You don't have to hear it. Your choice."

"I want to hear anything you know. I'm very used to the idea she's dead." But it wasn't that easy. His hands were shaking. He folded them under his arms and went on listening, thinking: The ship hit her. *I* did.

Sunderland said: "Captain Manning—that's the senior captain on the 'driver, was the one who made the decisions at this point. He had one dead. He figured your chances were zero. He had no doubt whatsoever the company was going to black-hole the whole business. And they wouldn't clear him to chase a ship that wasn't supposed to be there in the first place. BM wouldn't want that in the log. He knew he had to get rid of the body himself. So they reported they'd acquired the rock, BM didn't ask what had happened—*Registry* wasn't in the information flow. Your emergency beeper was working. BCOM upper management *knew* what was going on with the 'driver, so it wasn't asking questions. Nobody in management was going to ask, and maybe—here, I'm attributing thoughts to Manning that may not have been—but maybe he was worried you *could* be alive. At any rate he never filed a report that he'd actually hit the ship. There'd been a flash the military could well have picked up—but flashes near 'drivers are ordinary. Your radio was out, just gone—you were traveling near a 'driver fire-path, so you weren't going to be found for a long time. If any tech reported that signal of yours, I'm betting it just got a real fast silence from upper echelons for the next couple of months. You never called in for a beam, and somebody erased *Way Out* off the missed-report list. Just—erased it. You were in R2 zone, you weren't on R2's list, and nobody was going to put you there, and nobody in R2 was calc'ing your course, except that eventually the 'driver and maybe management knew you'd go into the Well, and that would be that."

"But why did he send Cory there? What the hell was he doing? What was he trying to prove?"

"My guess? His tenders had gone after Ms. Salazar's body. . . he couldn't call them back from a rescue mission. They *knew* it had been a bumping; they knew it had all gone very wrong, and Manning wanted them too scared to talk. So he made accomplices of the 'driver crew, the techs, everybody aboard—to scare them into silence; to prove, maybe, if they had any doubt—that the company was going to hush it up."

He was numb. "So they could've fired *at* the Well. They didn't have to leave a trace."

"I'm not saying Manning isn't crazy. But there's no love lost between us and the company crews. He was pissed, if you want my opinion, about the job he was sent on, he was pissed at BM, pissed at management, he was upset as hell about the accident and he had no doubt whatsoever the company'd back him against us when we did find the body—just like the bumpings, just like that, bad blood, a way of shedding some of the fallout on us—because we couldn't prove a damned thing. Even with a body—because there'd be no record. There'd be some story about a 'driver accident. Nothing would get done. It's been that way since they put company crews on those ships. And the company keeps them out there years at a run. They're bitter. They're mad. They're jealous as hell of our deal with the company. They blame us for the company losses that mean they'd been told they were staying out additional weeks. But they're not totally crazy. They had absolutely no idea you could possibly survive. It was clerks that handled the distress signal, they'd already said too much to Bird and Pollard before they'd had any higher-ups involved, and my guess is they just decided they might as well bring the ship in, get it off the books—they just didn't want Bird and Pollard telling how there was some ghost signal out there that BM didn't know about. War jitters. Nervous Fleet establishment. They decided to go on it, they panicked when they found out you were alive—but do them credit, they didn't even think of having you killed. In their own eyes they weren't killers; it really *was* an accident, and they weren't going to have you die in hospital or on the 'deck. Too bad for them. Good for us. A lot of people are very grateful to you, Mr. Dekker. —Let me tell you, no matter Cory's mother's influence, no matter anything we could do—without you staying alive, without you holding out against the company, there'd have been nothing but a body at the Well. Nothing we could prove. Ever. So you did do something. You did win. You're a hero. You and Morris Bird. People *liked* him. People truly liked him . . ."

Hard even to organize his thoughts. Or to talk about Bird. He couldn't.

"You're the ultimate survivor, Mr. Dekker. That's something near magical to Belters—and the rest of us who know what you were up against. But there's a time—maybe now—to quit while you're still winning."

"What do you mean?"

"You have an enemy, one very bad enemy."

"Manning?"

Sunderland shook his head, hands joined in front of his lips. "Alyce Salazar. She's not being reasonable. Her daughter's death—the manner in which she was found—hasn't helped her state of mind. You're not behind a corporate barrier any longer. The EC's already tried to reason with her. She pulled strings to get the UDC to investigate

ASTEX, she wanted ASTEX resorbed—simply so she could get at its records, and so she could get at you. In effect, that order was under consideration, stalled in the EC's top levels, but it was lying on FleetCommand's desk principally because Alyce Salazar called in every senatorial favor she owned—favors enough to tip the balance, corporately and governmentally. And she wants you on trial, Mr. Dekker. The military's sitting on the records. It doesn't want this ASTEX situation blown up again, it doesn't want a trial, the EC doesn't want it, but the civil system can't be stopped that easily. Financial misconduct is the likeliest charge she'll try for; but she's trying for criminal negligence."

It hurt. For some reason it truly hurt, that Cory's mother was that bitter toward him.

"She doesn't have to be right, of course. She doesn't even have to win. The damage will be done. She has the money for the lawyers and she has the influence to get past the EC. They honestly don't want you in court—for various reasons. They don't want you arrested, or tried, or talking to senatorial committees—and they don't want the fallout with the miners and the factory workers and us, at a *very* strategic facility. But most certainly they don't want you on a ship headed into the Well—when R2 knows about it. They might come after us. But they *damn* sure won't let you take the ride."

It was going somewhere that didn't sound good. Same song, his mother had used to say—different verse. He asked, in Sunderland's momentary silence, "So what are they going to do?"

"Our rescue? That ship that's coming after us? —They'll pull us out. Save our collective hides. But you aren't going back to R2. They want you: the Fleet wants you. That was the sticking point the last ten hours. We tried. We've stalled, but they're moving now. We've no other options but them. God knows we can't run. And if we don't turn you over, they'll board—I have that very clear impression. In which case anything we do is a gesture, we've risked the ship, and various people can get hurt."

He had trouble getting his breath. He couldn't feel his own fingers. "Am I under arrest?"

"They tell me no. The fact is, you've been drafted."

The bottom dropped out of his stomach. "Shit!" he said before he thought who he said it to—and told himself he was a fool, they were pulling him out of the Well, they were rescuing a hundred plus people, he had damn-all reason to object to the service—

—to getting thrown into the belly of a warship and getting blown to hell that way.

"May not be altogether bad. They tell me they're interested in you for reasons that have nothing to do with the EC. They want you in pilot training."

"They want me where I won't talk. They think that'll get me aboard. I'll be lucky if they don't arrange a training accident. A lot of people get killed that way."

"You're a suspicious young man, Mr. Dekker."

"Well, God, I've learned to be."

"And I'm one more smiling bastard. Yes. I am. —And I'm sorry. I *don't* like the role I've been cast in. I hate like hell what they're doing. But we don't have any choice. I risked my crew and my ship getting you away in the first place, because you were that important, I hung on in negotiations as long as I could, and, bluntly put, we've gotten as much as we can get, we can't help you, and it's time to make a final deal. In some measure I suspect certain offices would rather see all of us dead than you in court: in some negotiations the compromises get *too* half and half, and sanity can go out the chute. People can get shot trying to protect you. Two ships can go to hell. Literally. You understand what I'm saying?"

He did understand. He thought about the kid who'd helped Meg with the vodka bottles. The fool who'd habitually lost his temper over things he couldn't even remember the importance of, this side of things. Damned fool, he thought. Damned, dumb fool. I can't even get mad now. The mess is too complicated, too wide, it just rolls on and over people. Like Bird. Like Meg.

Sunderland said, more gently, "If they're not on the

level, I think you can *put* them that way, you understand?
What they tell me, your reflexes are in the top two percentile—
you don't train that. That's hardwired. They tell me ... the
speeds these FTLs operate at ... even with computers doing
the hands-on ops, the human reaction time has to be there.
Mentally *and* physically. Whole new game, Mr. Dekker. And
I'll tell you another reason they don't want to antagonize us.
The Fleet's looking at the Shepherd pilots, the Shepherd
techs—as a very valuable resource. I'm not eager for it. I'll
do what I'm doing the rest of my life, and it's what I want to
do. But the young ones, a good many of the young ones—
may do something different before they're done."

He was in flow-through. Sunderland spoke and he
believed it because he wanted to believe it. Sunderland
stopped speaking, the spell broke, and he told himself
Sunderland was a fool or a liar: there were a lot of reasons
for the military to want Sunderland to believe that—a very
clear reason for Sunderland to want *him* to believe it.

He said, in the remote chance this man was naive: "I'll
be wherever it is before you. I hope it's all right." Hear me,
man. Watch me. Watch what happens. It'll be important to
you—

I don't trust anyone's assurances. Maybe Meg's. But
you have to know her angles.

Meg knew a whole lot more than she told Bird. And Sal
knew more than she ever told any of us. And Ben's figured
that. That's why it's gone cold between them ... that's why,
in the shakeout, it's only partners that count.

Mine's paid out, now. Done everything I could, Cory, ...

The interview was over. He got up, Sunderland got up.
Sunderland offered his hand. He found the good grace to
take it.

Hard adjustment—they hadn't *had* problems except the
fact they were out of fuel and falling closer and closer to
Jupiter, and in consequence of that, the morbid question
whether they'd fry in his envelope before they got there or
live long enough to hear the ship start compressing around
them. Intellectual question, and one Meg had mulled over

in the dark corners of her mind—speculation right now hell and away more entertaining that wondering what the soldier-boys were going to do with the company, and what it was going to be like in this future they now had, living on Shepherd charity.

Sal and Ben might be all right—Ben was still subdued, just real quiet—missing Bird and probably asking himself the same question—how to live now that they had a good chance they weren't going to die.

Point one: something could still go wrong. When you knew you were diving for the big one, hell, you focused on *trying* things, and you lined up your chances and you took them in order of likeliest to work and fastest to set up. But when you knew you were going to be rescued by somebody else's decisions and that it was somebody else's competency or lack of it that was going to pull you out or screw everything up, *then* you sweated, then you imagined all the ways some fool could lose that chance you had.

Point two: Sal was just real spooky right now—scared, jumpy: Sal had held out against her fancy friends once before when the Shepherds were trying to drive a wedge between them, and Sal had all the feel of it right now, wanting them so hard it was embarrassing to watch it—and Sal was hearing those sons of bitches, she was damn sure of it, saying, Yeah, that's all real fine, Aboujib, but Kady's an albatross—Kady's got problems with the EC, that we're trying to deal with in future—

—Only thing Kady can do is fly, they'd be saying; and meaning shit-all chance there was of that, with their own pilots having a god complex *and* seniority out the ass. Might be better to split from Sal, get out of her life, quit screwing up her chances with her distant relatives, and go do mining again—maybe with Ben, who knew?

But, God, it's going to be interesting times. So'jer rules, more and more. They'll make sweettalk with the miners til they got a brut solid hold on the situation, then they'll just chip away at everything they agreed to.

Dek—Dek could come out of this all right; but, God, Dek maybe hadn't figured what she was hearing from the meds, how he'd gotten notorious, how *he* was so damn hot an item it was keeping the pressure on the EC to get them out of this—couldn't drop *Dekker* into the Well, not like some dumb shit Shepherd crew that got themselves in trouble. Dekker was system-wide famous, in Bird's way of saying. And that was both a good thing and a bad one, as she could figure—majorly bad, for a kid who'd just got his pieces picked up and didn't get on well with asses.

Lot of asses wanted to use you if you were famous. Piss one off and he'd knife you in the back. She'd got *that* lesson down pat.

Good, in that consideration, if the Shepherds kept him on the *Hamilton.* But she didn't think they would—kid with no seniority, a lot of rep, and a knife-edge mental balance . . . coming in on senior pilots with a god-habit. Critical load in a week. And if they put him back on R2, God help him, same thing with the new management.

That left Sol and the EC. And that meant public. And all the shit that went with it.

She was severely worried about Dek. She kept asking herself—while from time to time they were telling each other how wonderful it was they weren't going to die and all, and Ben and Sal looked more scared right now than they'd been in all this mess—

—asking herself, too, what they were telling Dekker, somewhere on the ship.

Giving him an official briefing on his partner, maybe. Everybody'd been somewhat busy til now; and the heat being off (literally) the senior staff was probably going down its list of next-to-do's.

Or maybe they were telling him something else altogether.

The door opened. Dek came back quiet and looking upset.

"What was it?" Ben asked, on his feet. (God, she'd strangle him the day she got the cast off.)

But Dekker looked up at Ben the way he'd looked at her when she'd found him on the ship: no anger. Just a lost, confused look.

Maybe for once in his life Ben understood he should urgently shut up now.

But Dekker paid more attention to walking from the door to the end of the bed—getting his legs fairly well, she thought, better than she was, the little they let her up.

He said, "Got an explanation, at least. Pretty much what we guessed, about Cory. And it's solid, about the ship on its way. We're all right."

"*You* all right?" she asked.

He didn't answer right away. He looked down at the blanket. There was too much quiet in the room, too long. Sal finally edged over and put her hand on his shoulder.

He said, "I'm real tired."

Meg moved her legs over. "There's room. Why don't you just go horizontal awhile? Don't think. It's all right, Dek."

He let out a long slow sigh, leaned over and put his hand on her knee. Just kept it there a while and she didn't know what to say to him. Sal came and massaged his shoulders. Ben lowered himself into the chair by the bed and said, "So is this ship going to grapple and tow us or just pick us off?"

"Tow," Dekker said. "As I gather. Thing's probably not doing all it can, even the way it's moving."

"Starship," Meg said, thinking of a certain flight. "I've seen 'em glow when they come in."

"Freighters," Sal said. "This thing's something else."

An old rab had a chill, thinking about that "something else" next that one pretty memory. Thought—Earth's blind. Earth's severely blind.

Feathers on the wind. Colonies won't come back.

Kids don't come home again. Not the same, they don't.

Lot of noise. Dekker had no idea how big the carrier was, but it had a solid grip on them, and they could move around now, get what they needed before they sounded the take-hold and shut the rotation down for the push back to R2.

But before that, they had a personnel line rigged, lock to lock, and he had an escort coming over to pick him up.

The Fleet wasn't taking any chances of a standoff—while they were falling closer and closer to the mag-sphere.

Hadn't told Meg and Sal. Hadn't told Ben either. He intended to, on his way to the lock. Meanwhile he wanted just to get his belongings together. The *Hamilton* had had their personals out of *Trinidad* before they freed her, Bird's too: they'd been packed and ready to go, all the food and last-to-go-aboards stowed in *Trinidad,* that being where they'd enter and where they'd ride out the initial burn. It was all jumbled together now—*Hamilton* had had no idea who'd owned what—and he found an old paper photo—a group of people, two boys in front, arms around each other, mountains in the background.

Blue-sky. He didn't know what these people had been to Bird. He thought one of the boys looked a little *like* Bird. He didn't know what mountains they were—he knew the Moon better than he knew Earth and its geography—another class he'd cut more than he'd attended.

But he looked at it a long time. He didn't think it was right to take what was Bird's—he hadn't had any claim on him. Ben did. But you could put away a picture in your mind and remember it, years after.

If there were years after.

He took what was his. Put on the bracelet Sal had bought him—he thought that would make her happy. He didn't know, point of fact, whether they'd let him keep anything. Worth asking, he thought.

"Dek?" Sal asked.

About finished, anyway. He stuffed a shirt into the bag, wiped his hair out of his eyes and caught his balance against the lockers as he stood up.

All of them—including Meg. Sal was holding her on her feet. Ben, behind them.

"Meg, God, I wasn't going to skip out—the meds'll have a seizure."

Meg said, "Thought we'd walk down to the lift with you." In that tone of voice Meg had that didn't admit there were other choices. "Hell of a thing, Dek."

"Yeah, well, I wasn't going to worry you. —Walk you back to your cabin."

"Doing just fine, thanks. Going to check these so'jer-boys out. See if we approve the company they're putting you into."

He picked up his duffel, put a hand on the wall and came closer. Familiar faces. Faces he'd gotten used to seeing— even Ben. And Meg. Especially Meg.

He leaned over, very carefully kissed her on the cheek. Meg said, "Oh, hell, Dek," and it wasn't his cheek she kissed, for as long as gave him time to know Meg wasn't joking, and that close as he'd been with Cory, it wasn't what he felt right now.

Sal kissed him too, same way. But not the same. He couldn't talk.

Ben said, holding up a hand, "If you think I'm going to, you're wrong."

You never knew about Ben. Ben saved him losing it. He got a breath, halfway laughed, and picked up the bag again, hearing the lock operating.

"Sounds like my appointment," he said. "Better move, so they can get us all under way. Risky neighborhood."

"Yeah, well," Meg said, following him, on Sal's arm. Hard breath. "They better take care of you. *Letters* are a good thing."

"May be a while," he said, glancing back as he walked. Not good for the balance. "But I will. Soon as I can. Soon as I have a paycheck. Don't know whether I'll be at the shipyard or where. Sol, maybe. I just can't say."

Trying to pack every thought he had into a handful of minutes. Thinking about the Fleet's tight security, and the tighter security around him.

"Maybe if you ask the Shepherds they can find out where I'm stationed. Maybe the captain can get a letter to me, even if I can't get one out. My mother's Ingrid Dekker, she's on maintenance at Sol—write to her, if that doesn't work. She may know where I am."

Or maybe not, he thought, as they came into the ops area, where the lift was, to take him up to the lock. Fleet uniform on the blond and two marine MP's, with pistols. Standing with Sunderland. He hoped they didn't take him off in handcuffs. Not in front of Meg, please God. . . .

"Mr. Dekker?" the crew-type said—young, insignia he couldn't read. Outheld hand. He took the offer. Didn't read any threat. "Name's Graff. Going to take you across and see you signed in."

Didn't sound like a threat. It wasn't handcuffs at least. Graff said, "This your crew?"

"Meg Kady, Sal Aboujib, Ben Pollard." He spotted Sam Ford over to the right, Ford with his arm in a sling. "Sam Ford. Ran the com for us." He wasn't sure Ford liked the notoriety. Maybe he shouldn't have opened his mouth. But damn-all the Fleet was going to do about the rest. They were getting the one they'd bargained for, and Graff didn't look like a note-taker. He shook hands with the captain, waved a small goodbye at his shipmates, took Graff's signal they were going.

Lift took him and Graff and one guard. That was all that would fit. Graff said, on the way up, "Ops training's real glad to get its hands on you. Move of yours gave the lieutenant an attack. You didn't hear that."

He looked Graff in the face. Saw amusement. Saw the MP biting his lip.

Lift let out at the dock. Cold up here. He stood and shivered, thought then to ask, "They going to let me keep my personals? Or should I leave them?"

"Put them in stowage. Few months, you can get them back."

The lift was coming up again. It opened.

Ben came out with the other MP.

"Thought we *said* goodbye," Dekker said.

"Yeah, well," Ben said, and said to Graff, "Got room for another one?"

*Different* kind of ship. ECS5 was her designation—didn't have a name yet, and wouldn't, til she was commissioned. Gray and claustrophobic, huge flexing sections on the bridge. Instruments he didn't understand. Most of it was dark. The crew was minimal, evidently, or the boards weren't live yet. The personnel ring wasn't operational—it was acceleration that let them walk the deck, g-plus at that, with the *Hamilton*'s mass. Graff had said he'd do a walk-around with them.

Real quiet walk-around. It was a working ship. They didn't belong here. They weren't under arrest. Graff, Dekker got the idea, was doing a sell-job. "Good program," Graff said, about flight training. "They don't *want* you to come in with a lot of experience—new tech. Whole new kind of ship. Can't talk about it. Can't talk about it covers a lot we deal with."

He didn't know what he thought. The machine around him wasn't anything he'd even seen photos of.

Wasn't the only thing that puzzled him. He said to Ben, while Graff was talking to one of the techs, "Are you sure what you're doing?"

Ben gave one of his shrugs. Ben looked pale in the dark, in the light off the monitors. Sweating a little and it wasn't warm in here. "No way to get ahead. You lost the ship, Dek-boy. Debt up to our necks... but a man with my background—there's a real *chance* in this stuff. Military's where the edge is, the way R2's going now. Fleet's the way up, you remember I said it. There's an After to this war."

"You're out of your mind."

"Officer before I'm done. Brass pin and all. Damn right, Dek-boy. You remember you know me. You fly 'em and I'll be sitting in some safe office in Sol HQ telling 'em how to do it. Odds on it?"

"Out of your mind," Dekker repeated under his breath; and looked around him at things he wanted to understand, thinking, he couldn't help it: God, Cory should have seen this. . . .